TARNISHED SILVER

by

Myra H. Wolfson

PUBLISHING CO
EST. 1920
PITTSBURGH, PENNSYLVANIA 15238

Dear Joanne,
Glad to share this book
with a friend of Rita's.
You will meet Lorraine who
will be with Ian. Then it
will be Rosey & Tammy, then
Rainey & Jake, then who ???
Do you believe in the world of
spirit? You will !!!
Surprises all along. At the
end will be a great "Surprise".
Don't peak! Fondly
Myra H Wolfson

ACKNOWLEDGEMENTS

I would like to thank and acknowledge my dearest friend of almost thirty years, Susan Steinberg. She has always been my cheerleader. When I had writers block, she urged me to forge ahead. She knew I could make my dreams come true as a published author. I'm now writing this second book during the Coronavirus Pandemic. Since I don't have access to the Internet, Susan has conducted all of my research. There were a lot of text messages back and forth as she obtained information I needed. Additionally, she researched printed documents and sent them to me through the mail. I would also like to thank her husband, Dennis Steinberg, for his participation in allowing me to borrow so much of Susan's time. Most of all, I would like to thank both of them for all their long distance telephone technical support. They have helped me through many difficult days while writing this, my second book.

Thanks to another very old and valuable friend from over 40 years ago. Her name is Dena Britton. There was a time when she was in a very comfortable place in life. She realized I was not. I was divorced with three children, and not receiving any child support payments. The only income I had was working sporadically for a temporary agency. Dena owned a market research firm. She took a chance and hired me as a writer. As I went forward, we both discovered that I had hidden talents. The type of writing I did for her then has brought me to the present. I learned about writing as one with multiple personalities. I have now used that talent in writing this book.

Thanks goes out to my cousin Wendy Goldstein (Marcus) Penner for all of her support. Every time I had a new curve for my story, she was the one I would call. Wendy is the only extension of the Marcus family with any memories of the family in Sag Harbor, Patchogue and Montauk.

I would like to give thanks to many women who live in my apartment complex on Jamison Avenue. They bought my first book, and then shared it with others. Several who bought them asked me to sign the front page with a personal note. They felt that if I ever became famous, they could say, "I knew her when, and knew her well."

MEMORIAL PAGE

Leonard Robert Marcus

Edith Rebecca Marcus (Bubba Becky)

William Marcus (Papa Bill)

Tanta Sara Marcus

Tanta Minnie Marcus Diamond

Esther Marcus Goldstein

Fran Marcus Chacker

Sandy Marcus Abramson

Dena Britton
Expired February 18, 2022

INTRODUCTION

I'd like to tell you about the Silver family. My father was Ian Silver, M.D. He had a medical practice in dermatology. He chose that specialty because he was never on call. He could just schedule his own office hours. Mother was Lorraine (Rainey) Silver, R.N. She worked in father's office until she gave birth to me and my brother. By choice, she stayed home with us until we went to school a full day. Before returning to work, she attended a class to become certified as an ICU/Trauma nurse. She then worked in our area hospital. Steven Silver, M.D. is my brother. He practices family medicine. His wife, Hannah, is his receptionist and office manager. They have a son, Samuel Silver. I'm Stephanie (Steffy) Silver, R.N. I also became certified as an ICU/Trauma nurse like Mother. I'm still single.

Every decade my parents had a formal dinner party at the country club for their wedding anniversary. Our family was very small. Therefore, most of the guests were friends and synagogue congregants. The last party was for their fortieth anniversary. Mother always hired a professional photographer for formal pictures of the family. My father was always dressed in a tuxedo and Mother in a gown. Steven and I were also in formal wear.

After the party, Steven and his family left for the parking lot. My father had to park a great distance away. He left by himself to get the car. Mother and I waited for him at the door. While waiting, a woman who was unfamiliar approached us. She said, "My name is Gwen, and I was not on your guest list. I'm here with a friend from your congregation. I have heard so much about the Silver family, all incredibly wonderful. It's so special to see a couple who are still married after forty years. I've been watching all of you, and the love and closeness is so beautiful. I will pray that the Silver family always shines, and are never tarnished."

As a family, we did appear to be shiny. Nobody except my aunts Abby and Helen knew the secrets in the marriage of my parents. There aren't enough jars of silver polish to clean off all the tarnish. This book will begin slowly, but will eventually take you whirling and twirling. You may possibly reach a point where you won't know who is who. It will teach you to never believe anything or anyone from what you see and hear.

IT MAY ALL BE A MISCONCEPTION OR AN ILLUSION. We all wear a shiny silver cover on our book of life. Underneath there is always some tarnish, which eventually comes to the surface.

PROLOGUE

My name is Stephanie (Steffy) Ruth Silver, a forty-four-year-old murderess. I'm also labeled as one who committed "matricide". One who murders her own mother. Nobody will ever understand that I did it out of the love I had for Mother. She had no memory of Tommy, but she needed to go be with Jake. I had to do it so she could be with him again. Or was it Tommy who she needed to be with? Yes, I think it was Tommy. Oddly enough, the family never knew Jake, or did we? To whom did I send Mother?

This is so humiliating! I'm not ashamed to tell you that I murdered Mother, but almost ashamed to tell you what they just did to me. This is a prison just for women. I think I might be in a section for the crazies. I was fingerprinted and photographed. Then I was brought into a bath shower room by a female guard. She made me strip down to naked, and threw my clothes into a bag. While being processed, they already took my jewelry and gave it to my brother Steven. Then the worst! She did a full body search. First she looked into my mouth, throat, nose, and ears. Next she pushed me into a bent over position. She stuck her fingers up my ass and deep into my vagina. Had she been a man, I might have gotten sexually aroused, but not.

I then had to step into an old metal shower stall. She told me to wash from head to toe. At first I just stood in the stall, but didn't turn on the water. I just stared at the guard. She looked sternly at me. "Hey, turn that water on and wash your body and your hair. When we're done here, you'll get a haircut." I turned on the water and reached for the washcloth. It was really a rag in a sealed bag. I guess they were kind enough to not give me one already used. At home, I used soft, cushy sponges. Then, the bar of soap! It was in a small sealed box. It smelled like crap. Nothing like the rose petal bath soap I loved and used at home. The shampoo was in a small bottle, also sealed. It smelled like tar. I'm not sure, but I think it's something that was used to kill head lice. Maybe they had to be sure I didn't have any. My hair! My hair is so beautiful and blond, bleached of course. How short will they cut it, and do they have a good hair salon? Well, first I had to dry my body and my hair. I stepped out of the stall. The guard handed me two towels, hard and crisp like toast.

She was holding another sealed bag and explained these were my clothes. I think she meant to say, my temporary clothes. She asked me to open the bag and put on the contents. Her voice was strong and harsh, yet her words semi-polite.

I was having a lot of trouble grasping that I was not home and never would be again. But Steven could bring me my cushy sponges, rose petal bath soap, and rose smelling shampoo. I would also ask him to bring me a supply of giant fluffy towels for my body, and some smaller ones for my hair. Surely after a few days, they'll realize adjustments will have to be made to accommodate my needs. Steven will fill them in on everything.

I opened the bag of clothes. On the top was a bra and a pair of panties. Both were wrapped, clean but disgusting. They were made of plain, rough, white cotton. Later, they would also have to make that adjustment. Perhaps Steven will bring me some silky underwear from my apartment. There were still two small wrapped bags. One was a pair of white cotton socks, and one a pair of slip on sneakers. More adjustments for them to make! Then the ultimate! Oh My God! Green, not green! I look like a swamp frog in green. The guard handed me a thick, almost wrinkled, swamp frog green jumpsuit! I saw her carrying it, but didn't know it was for me. I guess I was taking my time and suddenly the semi-polite guard yelled, "Move it, lady, I don't have all day." I slipped into my new temporary clothes, and decided to make the best of it for a few days. Fortunately, they were able to judge my size. Everything was a good fit. I would go to the hair salon later in the day for my haircut.

The guard then took me to a small cell, which would also be temporary. They would never keep me permanently in such a cell for the length of my sentence. It had an open toilet and sink, and such a small wall mirror. Steven and my attorney would take care of everything for me. Therefore, I will just relax and roll with this for a few days.

"My sister Steffy was not put into a cell with bars. She was placed in a small locked room with no access to the outside world. As she was taken to her new home, first she was singing. Then she spoke to me."

Tommy and Rosey sitting on a swing KISSING.
Tommy and Rosey laying in a bed FUCKING.
Steffy Silver have a heart, please don't keep us apart.

"Steven, I did the right thing. Their spirits just appeared to me as sparkling red hearts. They were thanking me for not keeping them apart."

PART ONE

CHAPTER I-I

Jill Cohen was born in 1916 in Wilmington, Delaware. She was an only child and grew up with her parents, Joshua and Wilma. They lived in a small row house in the somewhat poor section of the city. Her parents were both American born. Joshua was an electrician and Wilma a homemaker. Jill was a bright little girl and spent a lot of time reading. She loved to sit outside on the two cold, white marbleized steps used to enter the house. There was a small fuzzy pillow always in the hallway. Her mom kept it there for when Jill went outside to read. She also kept a small lawn table outside. It was used for snacks and a beverage for Jill. Her interests grew through reading. She wanted to spread knowledge to all who hungered to learn from books. Therefore, Jill became a teacher. She graduated from Wilmington City College with a degree in Elementary Education in 1938. Her parents perished in a car accident shortly thereafter. Jill continued living in the house. They were of the Jewish faith. Many of the congregants from the synagogue where they attended kept an eye on her.

David (Dave) Stone was born in 1916, the youngest of three children. His family and life were totally different. His parents, Papa Bill and Mama Becky Stone, were born in Russia. They came to America and settled in Sag Harbor, on Long Island, New York (NY). A family member, who was their sponsor, provided the financial assistance needed to make the move. An apartment was given to them upstairs from an antique shop. Papa Bill worked there to pay the rent. While in Sag Harbor, they had three children. Esther was born in 1912, Minya in 1914, and Dave in 1916. Both of Dave's sisters went to school, but had a lot of responsibilities at home. Mama Becky had medical problems and was always quite ill and weak. Esther did most of the housework. Minya loved to cook and bake. She was rather good at it, and they became her jobs at home. As people came to the antique shop, Mama Becky and Minya baked and sold cakes and bread. Even as a young boy, Dave worked with Papa Bill in the shop after school and on Sundays. Esther didn't do well in school, but Minya and Dave were excellent students. Mama Becky passed away in 1930 from colon cancer. She was buried in a very old Orthodox Jewish cemetery there in Sag Harbor. One couldn't even drive up to the gravesite. There was no road for cars. Everyone had to park and walk from the main road. Esther was 18, Minya was 16, and Dave was only 14 years old.

Papa Bill decided to take his children and move to another town. He heard from some of his customers about a town called Patchogue. It was also on Long Island. Papa Bill and Mama Becky had friends named Izzy and Jenny Potowicz. They were a bit well to do and had a car. One Sunday morning, they took Papa Bill for a ride to Patchogue. They showed him around all of the different areas. He found and rented a two-bedroom apartment right on Main Street. It was on the second floor of a large, fancy white house. The owner's name was Anna Nowen, and she was a masseuse. There was a shingle hanging from a post on the front lawn. Her massage room, office, and living quarters were all on the first floor. Papa Bill had money from running the antique shop. He was able to pay off all of his debts before leaving Sag Harbor. He bought a used truck and, with his children, moved to Patchogue in late 1930.

Minya and Dave were registered in the area school. Esther found a job on a factory assembly line. She also continued being the housekeeper. Minya was old enough to get government papers, which would allow her to work part-time. She found a job in a pharmacy, also on Main Street. It was within walking distance of their apartment. The area was called the Village of Patchogue. It was similar to the areas of today like New Hope and Peddler's Village in Pennsylvania. There were quaint little shops where one could buy almost anything. Minya went to school and worked two evenings a week and the day shift on Sundays. Papa Bill had no training of any kind. In time, he too found a factory job. His working days were cut short, as he had a very weak heart. He was then able to collect disability payments from the state. The family was Orthodox. Nobody worked on Shabbat, which was from Friday at sundown until Saturday at sundown. Also, they never worked on any Jewish holidays. Esther, being the oldest woman in the house, lit the Shabbat candles every Friday night. She and Minya prepared the Shabbat evening meal.

Esther graduated from high school before leaving Sag Harbor. Minya graduated in 1932. She continued working in the pharmacy, now full time. In those days, she was just called a pill counter. She was the smarter of the two sisters and always moved to advance. Her dream was to become a pharmacist. It just wasn't in the plan. She eventually learned all there was to know about pharmaceutical drugs. Her title in the store then became "pharmaceutical technician".

In 1934, Dave graduated from Patchogue High School. He had incredible grades in all subjects, but had a great interest in numbers and taxes. His desire was to become an accountant, and then a Certified Public Accountant. While there were wonderful colleges in New York, Dave's research led him towards Wilmington City College. Dave really loved his father and sisters, but felt he was ready to leave home.

Through a Jewish Foundation, Dave found Nathan and Sara Brownstein. They rented rooms in their house to male students. They were Jewish, but not kosher or observant. That took a lot of adjustments for Dave. He attended services whenever possible. Nathan had a car and was very kind. He would drive him to synagogue and then pick him up. Unfortunately, they never had any biological children. Through the years, as the young men moved in and out of their house, they had many sons.

They charged rent, which covered the room, a shared bathroom, and meals. Dave had two sisters so he knew about sharing a bathroom. All the great meals were cooked by Sara. There was one other young college student who lived there. His name was Jerry Dworkin, and he attended the same college. He was from Georgia, where Jews were not always welcome in some areas. His parents decided he would be more educationally productive living in a Jewish area. He could just concentrate on his studies. Dave and Jerry bonded instantly. Their classes were at the same time, and they took the bus together. Nathan wasn't much of a morning person like Sara. They saved him for errands later in the day. Dave was in the accounting program, and Jerry was in pre-law. They both got their degree in 1938. Through many years they stayed in touch.

Dave went home to Patchogue periodically, mostly for Jewish holidays. During break times from semesters, he sometimes spent a few weeks with Papa Bill, Esther, and Minya. His arrival was always treated like a holiday. He traveled back and forth on the train. They were happy with his living arrangements except he was not living the total Jewish life. Hopefully, one day he would meet a nice Jewish girl.

CHAPTER 1-2

Dave and Jill were married in Wilmington, Delaware in February, 1940 at the age of twenty-four. Jill was still living in the home of her late parents. It made sense for Dave to move in there after the wedding. Dave was an accountant and preparing to take the test to become a Certified Public Accountant. Jill was an elementary school teacher. Their first daughter, Abigail Beth (Abby), was born on May 1st, 1941. Slightly more than a year later came Lorraine Rose (Rainey) who was born on August 31st, 1942. Dave and Jill worked, and the girls stayed in a daycare home until they went to school.

When Daddy moved into the house, money was very tight. He was working in an accounting office, and Mommy was working in a school on weekdays. To make extra money, she tutored at home on weekends. The house had three bedrooms, one bathroom, and a lovely backyard. They had given it all of their personal touches and decorations, and loved living there.

We very rarely went to Shabbat services on Friday evenings or Saturday mornings. Of course, we always went on Rosh Hashanah and Yom Kippur, the Jewish High Holidays. Daddy reserved and paid for family seats. We dressed up and went to synagogue. Mommy was an excellent cook, and always made traditional holiday dinners. The Stone family dinners were just for the small family of four. Mommy was an only child. Daddy had his Papa Bill and two sisters, but they couldn't travel. Frequently, Abby and I were taken to Patchogue.

Abby was a very healthy young girl, but I wasn't. By the age of ten, I was a very poor eater, very thin and pale. There were times when I would throw up in school, and I began having occasional petit mal seizures. Additionally, I would also throw up on the rare mornings that the family went to synagogue. Some mornings I was so sleepy that it was almost like being in a stupor. It became quite apparent that something was seriously wrong, almost every morning. Daddy and Mommy had no idea, but it was time to search for a diagnosis. There had to be a reason for these ailments. Also, there seemed to be a pattern. Maybe being too close, they made no association of anything.

It was determined that I needed the best of care. Therefore, they took me to a major teaching hospital in Baltimore, Maryland. Daddy made an early morning appointment. Abby went to school, and Daddy and Mommy took me for a check-up. They were asked to bring all of my medical records from our primary care physician. Also, I had to come on an empty stomach to have a fasting blood test. That would be the only one totally accurate. Blood and urine were taken, and a CT scan of my stomach was performed. I was very upset and cried through the entire ordeal. While waiting for results, we went to the hospital cafeteria. I was then permitted to eat, but only had a banana. A diagnosis came quickly. The doctor believed I was having episodes of throwing up, seizures and lethargy due to an endocrine disorder. He was speaking of something similar to diabetes. He called it "hypoglycemia", the opposite of diabetes. During a question and answer period, I began to throw up. That confirmed the diagnosis. My blood sugar level was very low. They immediately gave me a can of soda with sugar and a muffin. They waited an hour and drew blood again. My sugar was still low, but not as it had been before I had nourishment. The diagnosis was definitely "hypoglycemia".

As Daddy and the doctor spoke, it came to light that I ate very little breakfast most mornings before going to school. I also ate very little on the rare mornings we went to synagogue. When the family went to services, we always went to a restaurant later for lunch. Daddy told the doctor of how awful it was for me when I threw up in the middle of class. I couldn't move fast enough to run to the bathroom. More times than not, it all went onto my lap. One morning, I leaned over and threw up in the lap of a boy sitting next to me. There was a combination of yelps, screams, and laughter in the classroom. It led to total embarrassment for me, along with my parents when they were called to school. An explanation certainly had to be given to the boy and his parents. Before leaving, the doctor gave us a list of foods, amounts and times of day I would have to eat. Back in 1952, hypoglycemia was not known or accepted as an actual disease as it is today. My parents made sure that I had perfect dietary habits and I did very well.

Daddy tried to keep us closely tied to his family. It was a long four-hour ride to Patchogue. Mommy and Abby didn't like to go. They said Papa Bill's kisses were too wet.

Daddy was very artistic. There was a room on the lower level of the house where he kept his art supplies. He had an easel, oil and water color paints, pastels, and charcoal. He completed two full paintings at the house. One was a very large picture of Mama Becky. It was beautiful and so lifelike. We took it to Patchogue on one of our trips, and it was hung on the wall in the living room.

Another was a picture of a tailor sitting in a chair doing hand sewing. Abby and I have no talent, but can see when it's there. The tailor has his legs crossed at the knee. The details of the pants are incredible. You can see the definition of each crease in the pants. Daddy signed and dated it as being painted in 1942. That was the year I was born. It now hangs in my home.

In one corner on the floor, there was a large painting of a sailboat. Again, such talent! The lines in the sails actually look like they are blowing in the wind. Daddy told the story of how he sat on the beach in Montauk with his art supplies. He painted this ship as many were passing. When he was about 16 years old, Papa Bill occasionally let him take his truck to Montauk. He said the scenery for painting there was the best. In later years, some of his other paintings from Montauk were found. They had been kept in the attic of what later became the family house on Munsell Road. They were rotted and had to be discarded. We had the sailboat.

Daddy had other talents. He liked to sing and dance. He did a great impersonation of Al Jolsen singing "The Anniversary Waltz". He taught it to me. He sounded like Al Jolsen, and I sounded like a howling wolf. The words were:

"Oh how we danced on the night we were wed. We vowed our true love though a word wasn't said. The world was in bloom, there were stars in the skies, except for the few that were there in your eyes. Dear as I held you so close in my arms, angels were singing a hymn to your charms. Two hearts gently beating were murmuring low, my darling, I love you so!

The night seemed to fade into blossoming dawn. The sun shone anew but the dance lingered on. Could we but recall that sweet moment sublime, we'd find that our love is unaltered by time. Dear as I held you so close in my arms, angels were singing a hymn to your charms. Two hearts gently beating were murmuring low, my darling, I love you so!"

I promised Daddy when I got married, I would have him sing it at my wedding, and he did. He asked me to join him, but I declined. Daddy also played the violin. When I was about 11 years old, I decided to take lessons. Daddy hired a private teacher for me. I was pretty good. There were a few summers when Daddy took me to Patchogue. I sometimes stayed with the family for a week or two. I took the violin and played for them. They loved it!

CHAPTER 1-3

Daddy and Mommy took me and Abby to Patchogue as often as possible. In 1956, when Abby was 15 and I was 14, Papa Bill passed away. We all drove to the funeral. He too was buried in the very old Orthodox Jewish cemetery in Sag Harbor, along side of Mama Becky. Immediately after his passing, it was discovered he had been making payments on a very large life insurance policy. It was mostly a surprise because Papa Bill had a heart condition and wasn't working. He was still collecting disability payments from the state. Apparently, he was paying a very high monthly payment on that policy. The Tantas were the beneficiaries. They were Orthodox and insisted that their titles be "Tanta", the Yiddish word for aunt. Daddy asked that we honor their request. There was more than enough money to pay for his funeral and burial. Papa Bill had a will apologizing to Daddy for not leaving him anything. He felt that since his daughters took care of him, he had to take care of them. Daddy was not upset about it at all. Papa Bill did the right thing.

One day Daddy got a call from Tanta Minya. "You must bring Jill and the girls to Patchogue. We decided not to waste any of the money Papa Bill left for us. We bought a house here in Patchogue. Friends from the synagogue helped us, and we're already living in our gorgeous new house. The new address is 455 Munsell Road. We have two bedrooms and a cot for visitors. Please sleep over with us one night." Daddy was so happy and excited. He put them on hold while he told us the story of the house. It was decided that we would leave for Patchogue on Saturday morning. The Tantas were Orthodox and wouldn't ride on Shabbat, but we would. Daddy was no longer totally observant.

Early Saturday morning, we packed up the car and left for Patchogue. It was a long ride. We made several bathroom and food stops. Finally, we drove into Patchogue. Daddy had the address and a map, which he followed and found Munsell Road. The houses were amazing! They were like small mansions. Daddy drove along checking the address numbers on the mailboxes. There was one at the end of each property. "Jill, how the hell do you think my sisters can afford one of these houses?" Before she could respond, they saw a mailbox with number "455". There was a driveway, but no house.

Daddy drove up the pebbled driveway, and there was a small wood frame house. In the front we could see an enclosed porch with lacy curtains hanging on the windows. He kept on going towards the back of the house. Daddy and Mommy could hear Abby and me making fun of our Tantas and the house. Daddy yelled. "Shut up! Do you hear me? I said shut up! You will never make fun of my sisters again. They are two of the most loving, incredible women. They took care of Mama, Papa, and they helped raise me. You will walk into that house, give them hugs and kisses as always, and congratulate them on the house. Do you understand?" We both jumped as we never heard Daddy raise his voice like that. We apologized. Daddy blew the horn and the Tantas came outside.

We went into the house by the back door. The kitchen was located there and it was huge. There was a wonderful familiar smell of apples and cinnamon. Tanta Minya always baked for visitors. There were freshly baked cakes all along the counter tops. We were given a tour of the house. It was really lovely. They were so proud, as they should be.

Tanta Minya was preparing lunch and told us there would be other guests. "One of the synagogue members is coming with her single son. Everyone just calls her Mom Diamond. She is well into her seventies and lives on a farm here in Patchogue. Her son's name is Barry. Like me, he is 42 years old and has never been married. I met him a few times in the pharmacy where I work. He discovered I was paying a driver for transportation to the village on my work days. I was no longer living on Main Street. He also learned I'm Orthodox and work on Sundays, never Saturdays. I really like him and know he likes me. He's now my driver, and maybe my boyfriend. He works in a factory and is a volunteer fireman. The fire house company is having a dinner dance next week. He's taking me as his date. I hope you'll like him."

Mom Diamond and Barry arrived. They lived on a farm, a real farm. They had all kinds of animals. At a later time, we went to visit. Tall geese chased us down the driveway. It was frightening, but so funny. On a separate visit, my parents, Abby, and I joined the two families in the farm kitchen for lunch. We suddenly heard this loud shrilling voice. "Beryl, you son of a bitch. You better get back in this house." It was Laura, their parrot. When Barry was a young boy, he used to climb out of his bedroom window in the middle of the night. He was always fascinated with the firehouse, and tried to sneak out to go there. He always got caught. Laura always told the story.

Barry and Tanta Minya looked at each other with a glow in their eyes. We stayed until the next day. Before we left, Tanta Minya said there might be a wedding soon. If there is, Barry will move into the house with her and Tanta Esther. They will both work and Tanta Esther would continue taking care of the household chores. In late 1956, we went to their synagogue in Patchogue for the wedding of Minya Stone and Barry Diamond.

Every time Daddy and Mommy took us to Patchogue, there were always side trips. Once they drove to Sag Harbor to the graves of our grandparents. That time we stayed behind at the house. There were other trips to Sag Harbor, and Daddy was like a tour guide. Uncle Barry loved taking us to the firehouse. Pictures of us sitting on the fire engines were always taken. Sleeping at night was difficult at their house. Uncle Barry had a special two-way radio in the kitchen. It made announcements regarding fires and accidents taking place during the night. A few times we were taken to the Hamptons. Daddy said that was where the rich people live. There were beautiful beaches, but we never went on them. We just did a lot of walking around, looked at the huge houses, and always stopped some place for lunch.

Many times we went to Montauk. That was where Daddy painted the sailboat. It had been his favorite place to visit and paint. Montauk was beautiful and quite different. It's a village at the east end of the Long Island Peninsula. We were also told it's an island and all the surrounding water is part of the Atlantic Ocean. It was known for its beaches with a strong Atlantic surf. They ranked among the top in the country. We never went on their beaches. Visits to Montauk were only short day trips. The Montauk Lighthouse is a national historic landmark. My Daddy also painted the lighthouse. It was one of the pictures later found in the attic. The Tantas always packed a lunch for everybody. We ate sitting in the grass around the lighthouse. We would always take a walk and stop in one of their shops for ice cream. We did see a ferry, but never asked where it was going.

As the years passed, we still continued going to Patchogue. In 1962, Tanta Esther turned 50 years old. We went there for a large house party. Shortly thereafter, she developed dementia, and had to be placed in a nursing home. She quickly passed away in 1963. Daddy and Mommy went alone for the funeral.

Uncle Barry and Tanta Minya were doing fairly well. They both continued working for a while, but had major health issues. Uncle Barry passed away in 1994 at the age of 80. Tanta

Minya eventually sold the house and was placed in a nursing home. She passed away there in 2004 at the age of 90. Abby and I did all we could to keep Daddy connected to Tanta Minya before his passing. A few times a year, even when he was sick and disoriented, we drove him to Patchogue to see her. Daddy passed away in 2000 at the age of 84, and Mommy in 2002 at the age of 86. Tanta Minya was heartbroken that Daddy passed away before her.

PART TWO

CHAPTER 2-1

Abby was a good student. She graduated from high school with honors in 1959. She went onto college and became a teacher like our mother. At the school where she began teaching in 1963, she met Scott Rubin. He was also a teacher. Abby matured beautifully. She had a great body and nice breasts. The boys always ran after her. She and Scott were married in 1965. They had one child, Emily Jane (Emmy), as Abby had fertility problems.

I graduated from high school in 1960. In June of 1964, I graduated from a major university's nursing program. Now I was a registered nurse, an R.N. I was very careful with my diet and eventually gained weight. My food problem prompted me to become a registered nurse with a possible specialty in nutrition. I never developed a womanly figure. My legs were very thin, my hips narrow, my butt flat, and my breasts were quite small. I always described my legs as spindly.

I had been living in the college dorm, and traveled a lot between Wilmington and Philadelphia (Philly). Since I didn't have a car, I spent a lot of time on the train or a bus. My first position was going to be at a major hospital in Philly. Before beginning my new career, I had to find an apartment near the hospital. I preferred walking to work or using public transportation. Mommy and I drove to Philly and first met with a realtor. Later we joined a group of new employees for an orientation and tour of the facility. Additionally, we were told if someone had an apartment to rent or share, it would be posted on a bulletin board in the main lobby. All the apartments suggested by the realtor that day were too expensive. Mommy and I went directly to the bulletin board. I wanted to live alone. There was one that sounded interesting. It was a one-bedroom apartment in a small building on Broad Street, just blocks from the hospital. There was a telephone number and I called. It was a privately owned building. The manager was Mr. Barnes. He invited us to come there immediately. We met with him, and got all of the details of cost and house rules. The rent was $300 a month plus gas and electric.

It was a three-story building. Mr. Barnes told us all of the renters were hospital employees. The vacant apartment was on the second floor. It was unfurnished and we were anxious to see it. Mr. Barnes got the keys and together we walked up the steps. The apartment was clean and very nicely painted. All of the walls were off white. It had a small living room, galley kitchen, bedroom, and a very nicely sized bathroom. The building was quite old. It had woodwork that was carved around each doorway and window. There was one window in the living room and one in the bedroom. It was a front apartment. I could look out right onto Broad Street. There were two very small closets. Mommy said she and Daddy would buy a portable closet to put in the bedroom. Mr. Barnes left us alone in the apartment. He knew we would need to have a private discussion.

I was so excited, and told Mommy I really wanted this as my home. We went downstairs to speak with Mr. Barnes. I told him my starting date was in two weeks. Of course, there was something major that nobody as yet mentioned. Could I afford the rent of $300 a month, plus pay the bills for gas and electric? Mommy told Mr. Barnes not to be concerned. If I needed financial help, it would be there for me. Perfect! I gave him a letter of reference and a check for the security deposit and first month's rent. We told Mr. Barnes one of us would call and let him know my moving in date. Mommy suggested that they buy a new bed and dresser for me. She preferred my bedroom set be left at the house. Of course, I would go home for visits. It was still my home and my room. At that point, it was agreed that only my clothes and personal belongings would be brought from the house. Mommy said she and Daddy would take me shopping in Philly. We would buy the portable closet and bedroom furniture, and have it delivered directly to the apartment. They would also buy a love seat and new large television. That would get me started with living room furniture.

In late June of 1964, my parents drove up on Broad Street with all I would need for my new home. They had everything for the bedroom, bathroom, and little kitchen. I had a small television and clock radio from the house, which would go into the bedroom. Daddy and Mommy got everything moved in. I arranged things to where I needed them to be. I was so excited but actually very hungry. I had to eat! Daddy knocked on the office door and introduced himself to Mr. Barnes. We went out for lunch, then grocery shopping and stocked up the kitchen.

While living in the dorm, I was sharing a room. It was always crowded and noisy. This was now going to be the first time I would live alone. There were mixed emotions. My parents were very proud. They reminded me they only lived about 90 minutes away. If needed, all I had to do was call. Abby would also be available for me. She was a great big sister!

We have always been so close. As little girls, we danced up and down the street holding hands. Our favorite game was Ring Around the Rosie. We got to dance in a circle holding hands. Neighbors always spoke of how cute we were. As teenagers, we danced to the music on the radio, television, or our records. Always holding hands. Abby and I are still very close. We are best friends, and always dance together. We hold hands at family celebrations, or in a time of crisis.

CHAPTER 2-2

On my first day, I stood in the cafeteria line at lunch time and was approached. A nice looking young man glanced at my tray and asked if I was on a diet. I was embarrassed because he apparently noticed my thinness. Yes, I was very thin, but knew how to put myself together. I was really quite pretty! I knew exactly what color make-up to wear, as I was still rather pale. I always wore bright colored scrub uniforms and matching sneakers. My hair was dark brown, long and silky. At the hospital, I wore it in a pony tail. There was always a circle of flowers over the rubber band holding my hair in place. I never wore heavy perfume, only very light, pleasant smelling creams and lotions.

He was also wearing scrubs. That meant he could be a doctor, a nurse, or maybe someone who performed maintenance duties. Maybe he cleaned the operating rooms.

What an opening line asking me if I was on a diet. Was he inexperienced at meeting a young woman? We both looked at each other and smiled. I moved forward in line to pay for my lunch at the cash register. The room was crowded, but I found a seat. I motioned for him to join me. He held up his index finger as if to say, "I'll be there in a minute." He went to the large urns, poured himself a cup of coffee, and then came to my table. "May I sit down?"

"Please do." I told him my name was Rainey Stone; it was my first day on the staff, and that I was a registered nurse.

"My name is Ian Silver. I'm a rotating resident in the surgical department. I know I want to be a surgeon, but still don't know in which specialty." I couldn't show it, but every part of my insides was jumping from excitement. A doctor, he's a doctor! I calmed down and slowly ate my sparse lunch. I always had peanut butter crackers and hard candy in my pockets. I knew when to go into a hallway and chomp down on something to keep my sugar regulated.

I told Ian my father is an accountant, my mother a teacher, and they live in Wilmington, Delaware. He exclaimed to be a Philly boy and his family were city people. They lived at Broad and Olney Streets, where he grew up. He added that both of his parents are pharmacists. We both checked watches and had to run. In the next days and weeks, we passed each other in the hallway. Both always in a hurry.

One day, Ian walked over to me and gently took my arm. "I walk past you and look at your gorgeous blue eyes. I want to see more of them. How about if we check schedules and have dinner some night outside of the hospital? There are some nice restaurants in this area. May I have your telephone number?" I took a pen and paper out of my pocket, wrote down the number, and handed it to him. We both smiled and parted.

A short time later he called. He was on duty but told me which evenings he would be available. One of those evenings was also good for me. Neither one of us had a car. Ian suggested a steak house restaurant a few blocks away from the hospital. We agreed to meet there at 7:00. Oh my God! I'm going on my first date in Philly, and with a doctor! I called my parents and Abby with such excitement. I could hardly speak. They told me to calm down. They spoke at great length and concentrated on discussing my diet, health, and job.

The night came. I put giant rollers in my hair so when it dried it would be fluffy. There would not be a pony tail. I chose a skirt outfit and a pair of low heeled shoes. It was August, and I didn't need a coat. For sure, I would look different and much nicer than I did in scrubs and sneakers. When I arrived at the restaurant, he was already inside. He was such a gentleman. He pulled my chair out and I sat down. We were both hungry and decided to check the menu and order our dinner first. There would be plenty of time to talk later over some wine and dessert.

First we told of our families. I had already told him my father is an accountant, and my mother a teacher. I then added that I have an older sister, Abby, who is also a teacher. Ian said he is an only child, so his parents doted on him. He told of their large house. His maternal grandparents shared the house with them part of the year. They were both retired and spent winters in Florida to get out of the cold. Ian followed with telling that his parents owned a pharmacy called The Apothecary. It was located on the bottom level of their house. They only filled prescriptions and sold over-the-counter medications. There was no candy, soda, or any types of food.

Everything seemed to be perfect. Then Ian hit me with a loaded question. My religion! I told him I'm Jewish. I leaned forward and pulled a silver chain out of my blouse. Attached to it was a marcasite Star of David. Ian then bent forward and pulled a silver chain out of his shirt. He too was wearing a Star of David. Ian laughed and said, "I see we both like silver." He was never permitted to date a girl not of the Jewish faith. We dropped the subject, completed the evening, and he walked me home. I had to go back to taking care of my diet, health, and job.

I continued going to work each day and tried not to think about Ian. He was the first man I met at the hospital, and there would be more. I would not even consider that my social life was over after just one date with him. Our schedules at the hospital were so different. I was on the 7:00 to 3:00 shift. Ian's schedule constantly changed. He was summoned to go in and out of operating rooms. Some of the surgeries were lengthy. He needed time to eat and sleep. The surgical residents were also on call for critical patients who came in through the Emergency Room. I had steady hours like my parents, but Ian had crazy hours. I just continued to hope for him to call again. Of course, in a hospital that size, there were so many men, but nobody else approached me.

One evening I called Abby. She brought it to my attention that more than a boyfriend, I needed to find lady friends. Sitting alone in my apartment, when not working, was not the way to live my life. Abby suggested checking around the neighborhood for a synagogue or Jewish Community Center. She remembered that our family synagogue had listings of social functions for different age groups. I began feeling guilty. Since moving to Philly, I had never given it a thought about synagogue.

I came to Philly in June. Now it was coming close to the High Holidays. After speaking to my parents, it was decided I would try to schedule days off and go home. I might work the second day of Rosh Hashanah, but never on Yom Kippur. There is a ten-day span between the two holidays. I couldn't go home for that length of time. I would have to schedule two separate days. Daddy said he would provide me with transportation.

CHAPTER 2-3

Every day at the hospital, I still scanned the hallways and cafeteria looking for Ian. Little did I know, he too was looking for me. Again, we met in the cafeteria line. Was it a coincidence that he happened to end up in line directly behind me? Probably not! Ian asked if we could sit together as he wanted to talk to me. "Of course!" We found a table. I sat quietly waiting for him to speak. At first, he was stuttering a bit and just asked general questions. "I'm sorry I walked away after only one date. I should have at least followed up with a telephone call. My work hours are so crazy, and sometimes I meet with friends. My parents are always upset with me. I don't get to see them very often. I really like you, and want to have another dinner date with you outside of the hospital. As soon as I get the schedule for my next rotating shift, may I call you?" "Of course!" We both agreed that our work hours kept us busy, along with seeing friends and family. Ian didn't realize I grew up in Wilmington, and had no friends or family in Philly.

Rainey tells me everything! She and Ian were now seeing each other for about six months. They are together very often but not alone. Love was really blooming. She was ready to commit to a sexual relationship, and went on the pill. The problem had been when and where. She can't have a man come to her apartment. His parents are always home. They both feel a hotel room would make it seem cheap. They were waiting for the right time and place. For the first time in her life, she knew what it felt like to be hot and bothered. She told me her crotch was always wet. They see each other in the hospital, and now Ian had a plan for their first time. He told Rainey it's an awful plan, but they can't wait. Ian had the keys to a storage room in a part of the hospital very rarely used. He went in, cleaned the room, and put clean sheets on a gurney. Rainey told him this was crazy. He said it may be crazy, but he would finally get to fuck her. He was crazed with wanting her. She was a virgin and aware the first time could be uncomfortable or even painful. She didn't care. My sister wanted to have an orgasm! A few nights later, she called again and bragged that she was no longer a virgin. She could almost feel her eyes roll back into her head. I said, "Mazel Tov, and you thought a hotel room would make it seem cheap."

Everything rolled around beautifully. Ian and Rainey were married in 1966. I called it a "Silver Wedding" for sure. Our parents didn't have a lot of money to make a big wedding. Additionally, our family was very small. I don't think Ian's parents liked Rainey or our family. They always put out a lot of money, as they did for the wedding, but never anything of themselves. We hardly ever saw his family. They always stayed away almost as if we were strangers. Ian changed his mind about what type of medicine he would practice. After spending several years as a surgeon, he knew it was not how he wanted to spend his life. He chose dermatology, and would never have to be on call. Once he had his own office, he could make his own hours. Additionally, he could perform surgery in the office. It would be very rare for him to see a patient in the hospital. Ian's parents and grandparents were quite wealthy, and bought him a practice. It was located in a small medical building in Northeast Philly. Rainey left her job at the hospital and worked with Ian in his office. At first they rented an apartment. Ian's family stepped in again, and gave them a very generous amount of money. It was to be used for a down payment on a house. They bought a very large, four-bedroom, and three-bathroom single house in Huntingdon Valley.

Ian and Rainey really wanted children. She didn't become pregnant for a few years after they married. Ian had a crazy thing about the name "Silver". Their son was born in 1970 and named Steven Sterling Silver. They found a reliable caregiver for him at the house. In 1973, Stephanie (Steffy) Ruth was born. It was decided that Rainey would no longer work in the office. She was going to be an at-home mom until both children went to school. She loved being with them. Before returning to work, she attended a class to become certified as an ICU/Trauma nurse. There was an opening on the ICU/Trauma floor of our area hospital. She applied and was accepted. After working three months, she became pregnant. On September 30, 1979, she had a miscarriage and stopped working for three months.

Steven and Steffy were two great kids. They loved playing with my daughter, Emmy. Vacations were always wonderful. We took them together mostly because of the children. Scott and I didn't have as much money as Ian and Rainey, but they always covered us. We went to every Disney Park in the country, cruises, islands, amusement and water parks. All geared for the children. Eventually, Emmy made more friends and wanted to spend more time with them. Our vacations were then mostly taken separately. Very often, we took our parents with us. They were still healthy and strong enough to travel. Additionally, Ian and Rainey made many trips to Patchogue. They took Steven, Steffy, and our parents to visit with Uncle Barry and Tanta Minya.

In the spring of 1984, Steven was 14 and Steffy was 11 years old. They didn't want to continue going to the same vacation places. I went on the Internet and began a search. Ian and I decided we should find a vacation resort in the USA. Coincidentally, I discovered a great place to go was Montauk, in Long Island, NY. My daddy was born and grew up in Long Island. As a child and young girl, my parents took me there. It was always a short side trip when we went to Patchogue to see my daddy's family. The only thing we did there was have lunch around the lighthouse and take walks. I never knew all of the great things about Montauk until after doing this search. I was absolutely in awe of what I discovered.

I printed out six pages and asked Ian and the children to read them. Most of what I gave them was about the history of the island. At first, Steven and Steffy snubbed at it. Both said they didn't want to vacation at a place which would include a history lesson. They wanted a place for summer fun.

The literature said, "Montauk is about nature, the beaches, water sports, fishing, trail walking." It listed playgrounds; skate, county and state parks; baseball fields; miniature golf; boating; tennis courts, and walking, hiking, and biking trails through Montauk. Of course, there was that famous national historic landmark, the Montauk Lighthouse.

CHAPTER 2-4

Ian and I decided to make a trip to see the family in Patchogue. We would stay overnight in a hotel, and go to Montauk the following morning. My daddy and mommy asked to join us. I believed, from what I read, a lot of the island businesses don't open up until after Memorial Day. Therefore, June would be a good time to go. We visited the family and took off to Montauk. We had a van so there was plenty of room for six of us. The first place we noticed when coming off the Montauk Highway was a diner. We were hungry and stopped for lunch. Ian and I didn't work in the month of August, and decided to spend it there.

The owner of the diner recommended a realtor. We went to see her and discussed renting a house big enough for eight people. The family stayed at her office, and she took me and Ian to see a house. It was exactly what we wanted, including a small swimming pool. We signed a contract for the month of August and up until right after Labor Day. My parents, Abby and Scott, and my crew would all be there for my August 31st birthday. We packed up and left for Montauk on the first of August.

A month is a long time to spend in any one place for a vacation. The first thing we did was buy a tremendous amount of groceries, cleaning and laundry items. I knew Ian would get restless and go home occasionally. Abby and Scott felt the same way. My parents pulled up chairs at the pool and said they were just fine. They never liked the ocean and sand.

Wouldn't you know it, but a week after we arrived, Steffy said, "I need a haircut." I inquired and found a hair dressing/barber shop. We went there and met Helen and Leon Walsh. Helen gave Steffy a beautiful haircut. Then Steven wanted one so he sat down in Leon's chair. Helen suggested that I allow her to treat me to a curly hair perm. I wouldn't have to fuss when I went swimming or got windblown. I did get the perm and loved it. Helen and I bonded instantly. We were so different. I was a 42-year-old Jewish woman from Philly. Around my neck I was wearing a silver chain with a marcasite Star of David attached. Helen was a 41-year-old devout Irish Catholic woman with a slight brogue. Around her neck, she was wearing a large silver crucifix. Helen was born in Ireland and came to Montauk with her mother and brother when she was a teenager. Leon was a local, born in Montauk. Helen and Leon had the shop open from Wednesday to Saturday. They went to Mass every Sunday morning, and then out to brunch. That first Sunday, my parents sat at the pool. Abby, Scott, Ian, and my children went to one of the beaches. I went to brunch with Helen and Leon. They told me there was a ferry that went from Montauk to Block Island. They said it was another world in itself. It also had its own history. My family planned on dinner out that evening. I invited Helen and Leon to join us. They did, and Leon began telling stories about the ghosts on Block Island. Steven and Steffy listened intensely. Perhaps we will get there before we leave in September.

In all the times I went to Patchogue, and briefly to Montauk, I never heard of Block Island. In my tote bag, I had the copies of the six pages I originally printed from the Internet. Again, Steven and Steffy said they didn't want a history lesson. One morning Helen called and asked to stop by the house. Steven and Steffy were really the two people they wanted to see. They invited them to go out on the ferry the following day to Block Island. My children were promised a great day that they would love.

Leon briefly told them some of the places where there were shipwrecks going back to 1738. He told of Captain Kidd's frequent trips to Block Island. Many speculated that he hid at least some of his buried treasure there. While Montauk and Block Island are a part of history, it's a great experience to actually go there. He got their attention. The following day Steven and Steffy spent the day with Helen and Leon. They were out all day and came back with more stories. He told them of pirates, smuggling, and ghosts. Additionally, there might be some Captain Kidd treasure hidden in Montauk. None has ever been found. With every story, Leon took them to the site of where everything supposedly took place.

The following evening, we all had dinner together again. Leon really caught more of their attention. He told of Captain Kidd supposedly leaving two chests of his loot in Money Pond. However, in more recent years, loot was in the form of liquor. It could possibly be found on Montauk's beaches. The thirteen years of prohibition went from 1920 to 1933. Rum Runners, as they were called locally, used Montauk as a drop off place for liquor. Some remember signals from the ships moored out past the legal limit rousing the men to sea. They came in small boats to bring the cargo in the dark. The cargo, which was liquor, was brought to the sand dunes. It was dug into the dunes and later picked up and transported to New York City in armed trucks.

Leon, being a local, knew everything there was to know about Montauk. He loved it there and loved telling the stories. He really had Steven and Steffy listening to him. They both almost went into a trance as he spoke. It was discussed that one day we would all go to the Montauk Lighthouse. Leon said it's a national historical landmark and something not to be missed. Leon now had two great buddies. My children spent a lot of time with him enjoying Montauk. Helen and Leon didn't have any children of their own. Mine became theirs that summer. It was instant love with the four of them. We were staying for a month, and needed beach and pool time too.

Helen and Leon had a small house right in Montauk. Their living quarters were upstairs and the shop downstairs. There was an inner flight of steps to get from one floor to another. Helen apologized for not being able to have all of us there for dinner, but had a possible alternate plan. She had a married brother who lived in a very large house on the beach. It was on the outskirts of town. She wanted all of us to meet him, and would see what could be arranged. All eight of us were extended an invitation, along with Helen and Leon, to a beach bar-b-que. Her brother and sister-in-law were Tommy and Cindy Monahan. He teaches English in Montauk High School, and Cindy is an attorney. In the summer months when school is closed, Tommy operates the ferry to Block Island. That was where they met. Cindy practices law in New York City and commutes every day on the Long Island train. They too have no children.

I'm not sure why, but Cindy wanted to know everyone's ages. Of course she knew Helen was 41 and Leon 44. I told her I was 42 and Ian 45. She then approached Abby and Scott who told her they were both 43. I could see my parents were offended and just laughed. She said Tommy was 37 and she was 34. Then she asked about our jobs. She was told that Abby and Scott were teachers like Tommy. She was impressed to hear that Ian was a medical doctor and I'm an ICU/Trauma registered nurse. Again, my parents refused to answer her. Tommy was so nice, but she was bitchy. We really disliked her, and when we returned to the house, we expressed it to each other. I did wonder why Helen and Tommy's mom wasn't there to meet us. They never spoke of her.

After almost three weeks, Ian, Abby, Scott, and my parents went home. Mommy gave us the old saying, "It's a nice place to visit, but I wouldn't want to live here." They came back again for my birthday, and to pack up our things to go home. We all had to go back to work and school. Things were always so hectic that we never got to Block Island or the Montauk Lighthouse. Abby and I bonded very closely with Helen. We vowed to keep in touch on a regular basis, and we did. We became almost like three sisters. We communicated by telephone, texting, and emails. We also vowed to return to Montauk the following summer.

CHAPTER 2-5

Christmas came and we were all invited to Montauk for the holiday. Steven and Steffy had their winter vacation from school. Abby and Scott also had their winter vacation. Our parents decided to remain at home. Ian and I took off a few days. We rented a hotel suite for the four days we were there. It was large enough for the six of us.

Since Tommy and Cindy had the big house, we were invited there for a Christmas Eve dinner. Helen and Tommy did the cooking for all of us. This was the second time at the house. It was briefly mentioned that Tommy's mom lived with him and Cindy. We never met her and never asked where she was, especially on Christmas Eve. Gifts were given and received. In the morning, everything in Montauk was closed. Everyone but Abby and me stayed at the hotel. We went to Christmas Mass with Helen, Leon, and Tommy. It was beautiful! We were told Cindy was also Catholic, but she never went to church with them. I knew I didn't like her. Abby and I aren't Catholic, but there are occasions to share with loved ones. In just a short time, Abby and I made Helen and Leon our loved ones. Helen and Tommy's mom was also not seen at church on Christmas morning. We still didn't ask. There must be a story, just not one to be told.

Of course, I knew Tommy and I were both married. I caught him staring at me a few times. I too was staring at him. He is about five years younger than me. My guess is he's about 6 feet tall, and his body is broad, rugged, and muscular. His hair is salt and pepper, tussled, and he has a mustache. When at his house, I noticed he wears reading glasses. His big blue eyes actually dance when he laughs. He has a great tan on his arms and legs. His face is dark, tan, and ruddy. He has more grey hair and more lines on his face than a man should have at his age. I guess that's normal. He does live on the beach, and rides back and forth on the ferry all summer. Perhaps it was the sound and tone of his voice that I liked. It was low, almost gruff, raspy and sexy. He also had a slight brogue like Helen.

I don't know why he was staring at me. Not for my looks. Cindy has a beautiful body with large boobs. She looked great in a two-piece bathing suit. I have no ass, tiny boobs, and spindly legs. That past summer when we met, I wasn't wearing any make-up and blush. Now in winter, I still don't look great while wearing the make-up and blush. I'm just lucky that I have enough money to shop at some of the more expensive stores. I buy top cosmetic brands.

Ian and I took Steven and Steffy back to Montauk for the next three summers. It was always in the month of August. We just rented a small motel apartment with a pool. Abby and Scott just joined us for one week. They rented a room at the same motel. Every summer, Leon added more stories for Steven and Steffy. They were always about Montauk and the history of its surrounding areas. He also spent a lot of quality time taking them to the places in his stories. The only one who kept a distance was Ian. My husband wasn't the warmest person, so I wasn't surprised.

Abby and I took many a short trip to see Helen and Leon through those years. We three sisters always spent our birthdays together. Because of weather, we didn't go back for Christmas. Several times, Helen and Leon came to Philly. Ian and I had such a big house that there was plenty of room for them to stay with us. Abby and I took them sight-seeing in historical Philly. Montauk has no boardwalks, so we took them to Atlantic City. One summer we went to Hershey Park. Helen loves Hershey bars. Longwood Gardens is truly an exciting experience during the Christmas season. They loved that too.

It was now the fall of 1988. Steven is 18 and going into college. He's going to have a long rough road ahead. He plans on becoming a medical doctor like his father. Steffy is now 15 and in high school. Nothing is definite yet, but I believe she plans on going to nursing school. I'm thrilled that my children are healthy and happy. Ian is bursting that the "Silver" children are going into the medical field. He loves to brag, mostly with parties, big parties! After meeting Helen and Leon, we included them in everything!

The Stone and Silver families had what all other families experience. Ian's parents moved to Florida, and we never saw them again. They passed away there and were cremated. Ian didn't arrange any type of service, but he sat Shiva here for each one. We had that giant house. He had giant crowds coming to see him. Going way back, there was a briss when Steven was eight days old. I always thought it should be a family event. Ian rented the country club. He made a party following the Jewish traditional circumcision of his son. He must have invited over one hundred people. Many brought gifts. I got stuck with about fifty onesies. Three years later when Steffy was born, there was another country club party. He and my daddy went to synagogue and she was given a Hebrew name. This is indicated in our faith for a new born baby girl. When Steven was 13, there was a Bar Mitzvah. It followed that when Steffy was 13, she had a Bat Mitzvah. Parties? You don't know what a party is unless you attended one of these Silver celebrations. Ian had a crazy thing with the name Silver. He once said he would like his children, boy or girl, to be named Silver Silver Silver. I think he had the country club, caterers, florists, and live music performers on speed dial. Decorations? Always silver! My family came from and lived in a different world.

All of us are getting older and not able to do what we did years ago. Life always changes. In my days of nurses training, I had to attend a seminar on "Suicide Prevention". One of the biggest things I remember is that for everyone, life never stays the same. If one feels hopeless one day, the following day will be different. It might be better, and if not that day, perhaps the next. If you end life, the best to come might be days away, and you will have missed it. There is no turning back. It's the same with age. There is no turning back.

It's been four years of going to Montauk. We were totally connected to Helen and Leon like family. After the first year, we never saw Tommy and Cindy again. Still no mention of Helen and Tommy's mom!

PART THREE

CHAPTER 3-I

It's now year 2006. I'm 64, and Ian is 67 years old. We're married forty years. Every decade, Ian insists on a formal party at the country club. It's always like a wedding with all the trimmings, including silver decorations. His need to be showy has never diminished. Helen and Leon were invited, but Leon was recovering from surgery on his knee.

Steven is now 36 years old and an M.D., a medical doctor. He practices family medicine and is listed as a primary care physician. He's married to the most wonderful young woman. Her name is Hannah. She has a degree in business management, and works with Steven in his office. He's a great doctor, man, husband, father, and son. Steven is over six feet tall, and carrying a bit too much weight. I call him a big lug. I'm 5'8" but very thin. He sometimes teases that he could lift me and carry me around under his arm. Their son, my grandson, is now 11 years old. His name is Samuel Sterling Silver. Steven followed through the craziness of Ian with the name. I'm semi-retired, and we have a special bedroom in the house for him. I call him Sammala and he calls me Baba. He stays with us quite often. Sometimes Steven and Hannah have long hours in the office. Sometimes they need an alone vacation. His regular babysitter isn't always available.

Steffy is now 33 years old. She went to one of the most prestigious nursing colleges and earned her degree as an R.N. Steffy followed in my footsteps and became certified as an

ICU/Trauma nurse. She is still single. My daughter is an absolutely gorgeous young woman. Her face, hair, body are all flawless. She is warm, compassionate, loving, and all that a good woman should be. Sadly, she has not found just the right man to complete her life. I really shouldn't say that. A woman can be complete without a man. I hope in time she will find someone to love her as she deserves to be loved. I would also like her to know the feeling of loving a man, as I have loved her father. She dates and has had several relationships. Some last for months and one was for a few years. She tells me when they end, but not why. I never probe.

I believed when Ian and I reached the forty year mark, life would be in such a good place.

Remember, **IT MAY ALL BE A MISCONCEPTION OR AN ILLUSION.** What was to follow turned my life into almost a horror story!

During the following two years, Ian seemed to disappear when he should have been in the office. Many times I called, and his receptionist gave me excuses as to why he wasn't available. He was always at lunch, with a patient, or had an errand. I tried texting him, but he very rarely responded. I began questioning him. He would either walk away with no response or yell at me. Of course, what would I think? He must be having an affair. He had become unresponsive to me in bed, and always said he was tired. It had to be an affair! Well it wasn't! One evening my husband came home with a bombshell. He told me to sit down and just listen.

"I'm in a predicament with only one solution. We have to immediately sell the house, and some of the valuable contents. I have been gambling, big time. When I'm not in the office or tell you I'm at a medical convention for a few days, I'm somewhere gambling. I have been playing high stakes poker, going to Las Vegas, casinos in the area, and the racetracks in the tri-state area. I tried to stop, but couldn't. One of my colleagues knew what I was doing, and threatened to tell you. I strongly discouraged him. I didn't want him, you, or the family involved. The worst is now I'm in deep shit with loan sharks. I owe a total of $700,000. I sold my life insurance policy and fired our financial advisor. All of our investments have been dissolved. I'm now in the process of selling my practice. Now, do you know why we must sell the house?"

I couldn't speak even if I wanted to respond. There was nothing to say. He made one other statement that will ring in my brain forever. "I'm warning you! Nobody, especially our children, can ever know what I've done. We will create matching stories to present to them."

Within days, the house went up for sale. We told Steven and Steffy that the house was too big for just the two of us. Ian was supposedly still working and I was working part-time. ICU/Trauma nurses usually work twelve-hour shifts on their feet. I was getting too old for that. The house quickly sold for a bit over one million dollars. The buyer bought a lot of our artwork and sculptures. We almost gave them away. Ian found another house and bought it for us. He never took me to see it until after the sale was final. He bought it in his name. There was enough cash left to pay for the house, have it all painted, modernized with new carpets and appliances, and have the cement repaired outside. Again, I was warned. The children were not to be told of the sale price of the house, and what happened to all the money. I wasn't even allowed to tell them where we were moving until Ian gave the order. We waited a few days until we were unpacked and settled. When using cell phones and texting, one never knows the location of another person.

It was a very small, three-bedroom, one-bathroom, twin ranch house on Krewsberry Road in Northeast Philly. There was a family room three steps down from the hallway. That was where a powder room and laundry room were located. I knew the children would think we were suddenly cheap or economical. There were no new purchases. Everything in the new house was from the old house. We moved everything from three of the bedrooms. I wanted everything from our bedroom. The second and third bedrooms were set up as they were in the old house. One had been Steffy's, and the other had a combination of things belonging to Steven and Sam. We brought our favorite pieces for the living room, dining room, and kitchen. Outside there was a nice two-car garage.

Steven, Hannah, Sam and Steffy came to see our new home. They were in total shock! There was the assumption that we were now rolling in money. They knew we liked the suburbs. A luxury apartment building, perhaps in Wyncote, was where they expected us to move. Somebody, please nominate me for an Academy Award for my performance that day. I had a nice lunch tray for them. They ate and talked, while I choked. There was no choice. They accepted that their parents were now living on Krewsberry Road. Steven said since this move worked for us, it worked for them. They were now just visitors.

My ugly story hasn't even begun!

CHAPTER 3-2

Our life in the house seemed to be peaceful, laid back, and quiet. The children still questioned why everything changed so drastically. I always let Ian answer their questions.

It was now 2008. Abby and I were still in close contact with Helen and Leon. That loving friendship never ended. Abby and I periodically spent a spring or summer weekend in Montauk. They in turn came to Philly and now stayed with Abby and Scott. They are the only four people who know my secret about the house. If I didn't have them, I would go insane. They want to be made aware of any new problems with Ian as they unfold.

Steven, Hannah, and Sam also go to Montauk and spend time with Helen and Leon. They are family! No different than the Stone family in Patchogue. Eventually, it became Sam's time on the ferry with Leon. He took him to Block Island and told all of his incredible stories. Steffy also went to Montauk to visit with them as she would to family. Occasionally, she took a suitor with her. She loved Helen as an aunt as she loved Abby. Steffy sometimes imitated Helen's words, brogue, and actions. She did it in front of Helen who knew Steffy was never making fun of her. Steffy would say, "Jesus, Mary, and Joseph!" and cross herself. Steffy had fun teaching Helen Yiddish words like putts, schmuck, knish, and korva. She taught her that the word shiksa is not a derogatory word, but a descriptive word. It only means that she is a Gentile woman. The differences in our religions, cultures, and environment enhanced our relationships with Helen and Leon. There was pure family love between all of us. Except for Ian.

Now I'm sure Ian is having an affair. Everything about him and between us is totally different. Additionally, he has become verbally abusive. Once I heard him on the telephone and caught a name. I think he was speaking to someone named Gwen. Where did I hear that name? Yes, I remember. It was the day of our fortieth wedding anniversary party. She introduced herself to me and Steffy. Gwen was a fairly tall, very heavily made up woman with humungous breasts. She complimented our family. Perhaps, she would like to be one of us, minus me.

Ian suddenly began insulting my flat ass, tiny boobs, and skinny legs. He started calling me Plainey Rainey. Every time he hurt me, I had the need to come back at him with something. Then I gave up. My words meant nothing to him. Eventually, in 2009 I learned about Gwen. My husband of over forty years didn't even have enough respect for me to try to hide anything. Ian Silver became a man who I no longer knew. He had to tell me the truth about everything. Telling me was the only way to hurt me. Why? He was the one who destroyed our life and marriage!

He didn't like being broke and wanted a rich woman. Gwen was extremely rich, and could give him that life again. She looked him up at his office after our fortieth wedding anniversary party. Her apartment was on the sixth floor of an expensive high rise building in Wyncote. That's where our children believed Ian and I would be living. He was disappearing for days at a time, and sleeping with her at the apartment. She paid for them to go on short trips. He became so ugly. Sometimes he physically forced me to sit in a chair while he described his sex life with her. This confession time, at my mental expense, took place about once a week. He made me listen to how he loved to be naked in bed with her. Fucking her was great because she was a woman, not a pile of bones like me.

He would wear her tits like ear muffs, and suck on her giant nipples. One of them was bigger than my whole chest. I somehow learned to turn off my mind, sing quietly, and rock back and forth. That's something I've been doing since I'm a child. I guess it's my way of temporarily coping with a crisis. It was very rare, but sometimes he came home and forced himself on me. It was like he needed a receptacle. Ian always said, "I'm warning you! Nobody, especially our children, can ever know what I've done and what I'm doing now!" He truly frightened me!

I asked Abby to invite Helen and Leon to come for a secretive visit. They knew something was wrong. I went to Abby's house and met with her, Scott, Helen and Leon. I knew I was going to crack. There was more to tell than just about the house! I told the entire story going back to 2006, after the fortieth wedding anniversary party. They were mortified! They asked why I tolerated such behavior. I told them I was too frightened to disobey Ian. I couldn't be sure if he was gambling and in debt again. He was involved with some dangerous people. "You must promise me that you will never let him know I've shared this with you. I'm afraid for myself and my family." They all agreed not to confront him, as long as he didn't hurt me physically.

Abby believed this was the time to tell Helen and Leon about my rocking. "Since Rainey is a little girl, she sits and slowly rocks back and forth in her seat when in an emotional crisis. It's almost like somebody would just take a deep breath. Our parents discovered it when she was about five years old. Somehow it's almost like her mind takes a brief break from reality. It doesn't last very long and isn't any form of mental illness. I think it's her way of temporarily protecting herself emotionally. I'm telling you because if you ever observe her doing it, you will know why. Her life now certainly is in crisis."

Poor Helen was already helping to carry the emotional baggage for her brother Tommy. We had only seen Tommy with his wife back in 1984. Helen really never spoke of him. She began telling me the story. "Tommy met Cindy when she was a tourist in Montauk. They quickly fell in love, but the problem was where they would live. He wouldn't leave Montauk, and she was from New York City. He taught high school and she was an attorney. Cindy made three times more money than Tommy. She wanted to use some of it to build a house to her specifications. He made a nice living between teaching and operating the ferry during the summer. Being single until he was in his thirties also gave him time to save and make investments. He's not a poor man. Cindy commuted on the train each work day and never complained. The last two years they were married, she stayed in New York City for extra days and sometimes weeks. Tommy was told she was working on a large lawsuit. She was working on a man wearing a large law suit. She left him after being married 25 years. He's now 62 years old. Not an easy age to deal with this. Tommy didn't handle it well and preferred that I not tell you.

Tommy suspected that she was having affairs, but refused to totally accept that it could be true. Divorcing her was not something he would consider. He was a stick it out kind of man. He spent all those lonely years praying one day she would come home to him and stay. She could have opened a practice in Montauk. He couldn't comprehend that she would leave him after all those years. She asked him to be away from the house for an entire day. That would give her time to remove her personal belongings. He spent the day with me. When he returned, there was a large manila envelope. In it was a set of divorce papers for him to sign. Additionally, there was an agreement statement. It gave Tommy full ownership of the house and all of its contents. The note asked him to sign the two sets of papers, make copies for himself, and have the originals sent back to her by FedEx. He did as she asked and put the house totally in my name. His logic is that if something happens to me or Leon on our property, surviving spouse takes all. In his case, if he leaves me the house in a will, there will be a lot of paperwork. Also, I would have to pay inheritance taxes. Tommy was too good and possibly too naïve. He didn't deserve this. He told Leon the house was too girlie for him. Leon, who had been a carpenter, helped him make some changes. They made it look more like the house of just a man. He got rid of all the formal frilly furniture in the living room. If someone wanted a drink of water, Cindy would take them to the kitchen. He turned it into a warm room where everybody could feel comfortable and welcome. He also bought a great recliner for himself. My brother is devastated! I believe it will take an incredibly saintly woman to come along for him to ever trust and love again.

Abby and Helen reminded me that if Ian ever hurt me physically, I must go to the children. I agreed, but it was too late. He was pushing me out of bed when I was sleeping. I always ended up with bruises somewhere on my body. Since he was a dermatologist, he always brought home make-up to cover the bruises. He knew which ones I should use. Once when he pushed me, I hurt my right leg and was limping. I told everybody it was a bit of arthritis.

Things became crazy and cruel. Ian asked me to make plans for us to visit Helen and Leon. They were hoping he was going to tell them what he had been doing. Perhaps he wanted help to make amends. Not so! "Possibly Rainey has told you that I have a wealthy lady friend. She wants to take me on European trips for two or three weeks at a time. It would only be two or three times a year for now. There's only one way I can do it without Steven and Steffy knowing. Rainey and I will tell them we're going to Europe, and what country my lady friend chooses. Rainey and I will pack for such a trip. We'll leave the house together, but not stay together. I'd like to bring her here to stay for those few weeks without anyone knowing. I'll then meet my friend at the Newark airport. On my return, I'll come back to pick her up. Then she and I will go home. Again, Steven and Steffy will never know we were not together. There will be no questions. Well, is it a deal? I know you love her and she'll be in good hands with you."

Helen and I were crying. This was as much a shock to me as it was to her and Leon. As she cried, her lips were moving. I knew she was praying as she continuously crossed herself. Leon stood up and screamed. "This is something people do when they want to go on vacation and need to take their dog to a boarding kennel! How can you do this to your wife? You are as fucking a sick man as I have ever known! I can speak for Helen as well as myself when I say, yes, we will keep her safe with us."

In 2010, I was left there three times. The first time was in the spring when we were supposedly in Rome for two weeks. What got us through were international calls, and texting can be made on the deluxe phones Ian and I had. The second time that year, we were spending two weeks in Paris. The third time we were supposedly skiing in the Swiss Alps for one week. We never took cameras. Therefore, nobody asked for pictures. Please keep in mind that the children never knew where the money went from the sale of the house. They had no reason to wonder how we could afford to take these trips. Now Abby, Scott, Helen, and Leon knew everything! They were just relieved to know while Ian was happy, I was safe with Helen and Leon.

My brother Tommy was now divorced since 2008 and doing fairly well. Several times he had dinner with us when Rainey was here. I know he goes out some evenings. I just don't know where or with whom. I don't want to know. He's a grown man and has a right to his own life and privacy. The first time he had dinner here with Rainey, he said something quite interesting.

It was about her name. Rainy days were sometimes bad, gloomy, or sad times for many. He asked if she had a middle name. "My birth name is Lorraine Rose."

"To me your name will now be Rosey." In Montauk, Rainey is now Rosey. I immediately called Abby and told her. I knew she would want to know her sister was doing well. She asked to speak with Tommy to thank him for caring. She knew his life was also in crisis. He said it was his pleasure. He had been told why Rosey was here periodically for weeks at a time. He also told Abby he would do everything to make her stays with us as easy as possible.

CHAPTER 3-3

It was now the beginning of 2011, and the second year I'm left in Montauk. This time Ian went to Germany with Gwen, and I'm back with Helen and Leon. He was going to be away again for two weeks. Helen and Leon still had to open their shop and work. They couldn't babysit for me full time. Tommy also worked all week. Since I was alone so much with each season, I tried to make myself a local. One of them always let me borrow a car, and I drove around the island. I got lost many times. Tommy and I began spending some time together. We were only alone when he took me driving in his car. He wanted to help me become more familiar with the area.

As I spent so much time with Helen, she invited me to work with her to make jewelry. She did it mostly in the winter time, and believed it would be therapeutic for me. There was a hall closet full of big bags of chains, beads, jewels, stones, paint, glue, and everything one would need to make jewelry. Several sample pieces were already made. Leon was good with wood and made small jewelry boxes. Helen painted and bejeweled them. In the nice weather, they sold the jewelry and boxes at outdoor flea markets. There were also indoor flea and farmer markets in the winter. Helen told me that many of the vendors were low income and needed the extra money they made.

I'm now a jewelry maker. I love it! I sit at the kitchen table with Helen. She showed me how to design on the table before gluing a piece together. We always have some wine or a bit of brandy. Leon complains that he can't hear the television because we laugh so loud. During these times, I completely forget why I'm there. One afternoon we made about forty pieces. The next day we went to the flea market and sold almost all of them. Everybody there knows Helen. She introduced me as her friend Rosey from Philly.

Helen and Leon had tickets to take the train to New York City to see a Broadway matinee show. They were going to have dinner afterwards and take the 8:00 train back home. It was a Wednesday and they closed the shop for the day. I was alone in their house. The door opened. It was Tommy. He assumed I was with them, apologized, and turned around to leave. He had just come from school and it was 3:30. I asked him to stay, keep me company, and tell me about his life. He already knew everything about mine. "Where do you want me to begin?"

"How about when you came from Ireland with your mom?"

Tommy was an English teacher and was used to storytelling, but mostly from books. "We had a cousin Catherine here in Montauk, and she paid for our trip. Helen was 14 and I was 10 years old when we came in 1957. I'm not sure, but I believe our Mom was about 32 years old. We both went to school, and Mom worked cleaning people's houses. There are a lot of wealthy people who are locals, and those who have summer homes. We lived with Catherine until Mom made enough money for a small apartment for the three of us. Helen graduated from high school in 1961. She worked part-time in a beauty shop and had the skills to be a professional. The shop owner helped Mom pay Helen's tuition at a beauty academy. That was where she met Leon. He was becoming a barber. Within a year, they were married and bought a small house. They made their home upstairs and the shop downstairs. I think you know that. Mom and I were still living in the apartment. She worked a lot of extra time because she wanted to be sure I could go to college. When I graduated from high school, I had top grades. I was awarded a scholarship to Montauk County College. My degree is in English Literature. I immediately got the teaching job at Montauk High School. Every summer, I also work operating the ferry to Block Island. I met Cindy when I was 36 years old. We fell in love and married within a few weeks. She moved into the apartment with me and Mom. I had a lot of savings and investments, but Cindy was quite wealthy. She insisted on having a house built immediately. It was to be only to her specifications not mine. She and Mom got along beautifully. Mom was invited to continue living with us.

"Cindy and I spoke about having children. Of course we never used protection, but nothing happened. I wanted to see a fertility specialist, but she refused. She said if it didn't happen, then that's the way it would be. I didn't know she came to hate living in Montauk and came to resent me. When she left me, she admitted to having several affairs in New York City. I was also told of her being on the birth control pill from the time we were married. She really didn't want children. The most hurtful was when she said if the pill failed, it would never be known who fathered her baby. She wasn't using protection with any of the men. My God, I don't even know for sure how many men fucked my wife in New York City all of those years. She went back and forth as if I was her seasonal home and lover. Not her husband. I just don't understand why she stayed with me for 25 years. That will always be a mystery I'll not be able to solve.

"Mom passed away in 2000 at the age of 75. She loved Cindy and I'm glad wasn't here to witness this catastrophe. Perhaps you are wondering why you never met my Mom. At a later time, I will tell you the story. Just never mention Mom to Helen."

"May I ask how you have been living your life these last three years? I know you teach and then operate the ferry in the summer. Have you dated? Please talk to me. I need to forget all about myself."

"The first thing I did was have Leon help me make the house look more like a man's house. I decided I wanted company. I went to the dog pound to adopt a big manly type dog. I came home with two toy poodles. What can I say? I fell in love. Both were about two years old and from different litters. They had been mistreated and not fed very well. They were extremely thin. One is white and I named her Sugar. She reminds me of a sugar cookie. The other one is brown and I named her Coco. Not like the chocolate. I named her after Coco Chanel. I call them my girls. During the school year, I wake up at 5:30. I have a small fenced-in area. At that time, I just let them out. My routine is then I make coffee and pack food to take with me. I also get their food ready for when they come back in. My first two classes run from 7:30 to 9:00. Then I get my first break from 9:00 until 10:00. My next two classes go from 10:15 to 11:45. Afterwards, I eat lunch and then go back to class again until 2:30. It's a tough day because of it being broken up into so many segments.

"I get home about 3:30. My girls hear the car and run to the door. They know it's time for hugs, kisses, treats, and a long walk on the beach outside my house. As little as they are, they need to run. Since I eat small portions of food all day, I eat a good dinner. I make a great lasagna, and Helen cooks for me. Early every evening, weather permitting, I go bike riding on one of the designated area bike trails. Now, Rosey darlin', here's a great story for you. I have a wire basket on the bike. I had it padded in pink. The girls ride in the basket. If you're a dog lover, you would enjoy seeing their ears fly in the breeze. Nobody wants to be alone. I certainly don't. The girls do fill up some space in my life. I'm pretty much a creature of habit. All week, I do the same thing, at the same time every day.

"Now, I'll back track. After Cindy left, I began some heavy drinking, mostly scotch. It became obvious at school. I was called to see the district superintendent. He told me they would pay my full salary for a month if I would go into a 30-day rehab. If not, they would have to fire me. That would leave me with never being able to get a reference to teach again. Of course, I went in and Helen took care of the girls for me. I'm now a recovering alcoholic for two and a half years.

"No, I haven't dated. Living in a small town has people always wanting to do a fix-up. I know almost all the women in town, and I don't want another tourist. In order to stay sober, I must live a peaceful life. I love the kids at school. They knew why I was away, and welcomed me back with open arms. I was asked to stay one day after school. The principal invited me into the conference room. Many of my students and the staff had a large cake for me. I was then given the greatest gift. My students and staff know I love poetry. In general conversation, I had mentioned a specific book of poetry I would buy one day. It was a first edition and expensive. The staff and many of the students put their money together, and presented me with that book. It did bring tears to my eyes.

"Now you know pretty much how I live my life as a bachelor."

"Now I have another question. I'm sure you won't give me an answer. Please just don't punch me. How do you deal with sex, or lack of it?"

"Okay, Rosey darlin', I will give you an answer, and would never hit a woman or a poodle. I've heard Helen say when a woman has a bonded, trusted friendship with her hairdresser, she becomes her therapist. She tells her everything. My therapists are bartenders. No, I don't masturbate. Please excuse my dirty mouth, but I love to fuck. That's what I do. I go to three different bars. When I was still drinking, I went to one of the bars and had a few glasses of scotch. There was always a lady of the night waiting for me. It was arranged in advance by the bartender. The bars are in small motels outside of Montauk. I need a fix, one to three times a week. If I had enough money, I would go seven times a week. I don't have to answer to anybody on how I spend my time after work. I call late afternoon, ask them to line up somebody for me, and word gets out. There are a few regulars who request to know when I'm asking for someone. Not to brag, but I'm big. Oh well, why not brag. I'm also known for good presentation and productivity. Since I no longer drink, it's arranged to meet right in one of the motel rooms.

"They don't know my complete name, where I live, work, or what kind of work I do. Believe it or not, they know me as 'Tom Cat'. I also have rules. There is to be no kissing, no mouth on me and mine not on them. I supply the condom. They can't drink before meeting with me. I don't want the smell of alcohol on them or in the room. I only want the smell of sex in the room. There is such a thing. I prefer eyes closed. The next time I fuck a woman with eyes open, it has to be with looking at each other with love. I ask a lot, give a lot, and pay a lot. All I want and need is some hand foreplay and a pure, good, hot fuck. I'm 64 years old and can still go a second time in about four hours. There is one woman who really likes me. She hangs out in the room with me until I can go again. With her, for the same money, I get a second fuck. I make them leave first. Then I take a shower alone before I go home. I can see you trying not to smile. You asked a question and I gave you an honest answer."

"At one time, Helen briefly told me about what happened between you and Cindy. She just didn't tell me about this part of your life. Chances are pretty good she doesn't know about Tom Cat. Consider me to be like Sugar and Coco. We'll never tell."

CHAPTER 3-4

"You are correct. I did ask a question and you did give me an honest answer. I have respect for you because of what you do and how you do it. I don't mean how you fuck. I too use that word. You are keeping it at a business level arrangement and not playing with the feelings of any vulnerable women.

"Another question I have has two parts. Why do you call me darlin'? You are an English teacher. The word actually ends with a 'g'. Why don't you complete the word?"

"I call you darlin' because you are. I don't add the 'g' because without, it's the Irish way. It's almost 5:00 and an hour past walking my girls and having dinner. Helen has her reasons, but she doesn't want us spending time alone. I know why, but I'm not at liberty to share it with you. She and Leon won't be home for about four more hours. I hate to just leave you here. Would you like to come home with me, meet my girls, and have dinner with us? I have some leftover lasagna and can make a quick salad. If you come with me, I'll get you back before Helen gets home. I'll then let it be your decision whether or not you tell her we were alone together."

"Yes, I'll go home with you. I'll decide about telling Helen after I see how it goes. At least I know your girls won't tell Helen I was there.

"In two more days, Ian will be back to take me home and play the game. You have told me about your life. You always know what to expect. I don't. When I'm sleeping, he pushes me out of bed. I fall to the floor and always have bruises. I have to cover them with special make-up. I limp when my leg hurts. I have to lie to my children. I'm always nervous and scared. Some nights I'm afraid to fall asleep. I might wake up with a jolt as I'm pushed to the floor. I feel like I live in a dark hole with no way to get out. The only way is if Ian dies or I die.

"I'm not sure, but I think he plans on another trip for this summer. Then I'll be back again for a few weeks. Additionally, Abby and I will be here off and on for a few days. She loves to come here and spend a few days with Helen."

We both did tell Helen. She blamed Tommy. Apparently, she told him her reasons, but neither one would share them with me.

Abby and I had been back and forth to Montauk in the spring to see Helen. We drive to 30th Street train station, and leave the car in their secured parking lot. We take the train to New York City, then the Long Island train. It's about a four hour trip, but we love the ride. We usually go early Sunday morning and stay until Tuesday. Helen opens her shop on Wednesday. Upon our last return home, Ian told me Gwen was planning their next trip. He would give me enough notice. Of course, we had to tell Steven and Steffy of our plans. I also had to let Helen and Leon know when I would be there.

The plan was for about the middle of June.

In early June, I was thrown out of bed again at about 3:00 a.m. It had been a while so I thought it was over. I fell and landed on my right wrist. Ian always left the house immediately after he pushed me. I guess he wasn't interested in seeing the damage he had done. My wrist swelled, and I had a lot of pain. I used ice packs, but it didn't help. Abby was so disgusted with me protecting Ian. At about 9:00, I took a cab to an Emergency Room. I didn't go to the hospital where I used to work. I told the doctor I stepped on the wet kitchen floor, slipped, and fell.

I was casted from about just below my wrist to about six inches above the wrist. I did call Abby from the hospital. She came and took me home. All she did was shake her head at me. She helped me get undressed, made me eat some breakfast, and gave me a pain pill. She followed up with calling Steffy, who wasn't scheduled to work that day. Ian came home when Steffy was there. He asked what happened. Would you believe he had the fucking audacity to suggest that I might need a CT scan of my head? His reasoning was that I was having too many accidents.

It was now the middle of June. Not even two weeks after my wrist was broken. As Ian was loading the luggage into the car, Steffy was there screaming at her father. This time we were supposed to be going to Los Angeles for two weeks. Steffy told him I should be at home. "I'm a doctor, and she's my wife. I certainly can take care of her." We then left for Montauk.

There was hardly any traffic, and we got there earlier than expected. It was a Monday and the shop was closed. Helen, Leon, and Tommy were sitting on their patio when we arrived. When Tommy saw the cast, I saw the look on his face. He knew what happened to me. He began talking, but Helen grabbed his arm and pulled him back. Ian left quickly. I spent the next two days in their apartment. It was raining. On Wednesday they had to open the shop. Helen helped me get dressed and gave me breakfast. She sat down and said, "Girl, this can't go on." I told her I knew how she felt and agreed. I swore that when I got home, and the cast came off, I would finally tell Steven and Steffy. I would have Abby with me when I told them.

The problem now was who would help me throughout the day. Helen said she hated to do it but would ask Tommy to get me out of her apartment a bit. I heard her talk to him. "Tommy, I'm trusting you to do the right thing. Don't take her to your house again. I know how much you have come to care for her, but you will have to deal with it. She is emotionally fragile and married. You can't complicate her life with any more than she already has on her plate."

Tommy arranged to take a few days off from the ferry company. Of course, Helen would help me shower at night and get me undressed, then help dress me again in the morning. I was still having a lot of pain and not sleeping. At one time, I told Helen that I always fall asleep in the car on a long ride. It was decided that Tommy would take me for a ride, and I could just sit in the car. It would be a sight-seeing tour. He could show me some areas where I had never been. It had rained for a few days and finally stopped. He could now get us out riding. Hopefully, I would fall asleep. I took a pain pill before we left. It was a certainty that Tommy knew why Helen didn't want us to be alone. I'm not dumb. I didn't need it spelled out for me. She noticed how we look at each other. Turning to each other for the wrong reasons would be bad for both of us. Especially me! I'm married!

Tommy didn't drive too far when I started to fall asleep, but I was still aware. He parked the car near a small body of water. I could see sections of high, skinny green grass. The blades of grass were bent down partly onto the road. I thought the dirt was so wet that the roots lifted. It was a very quiet and secluded area. It was almost like Tommy drove me into a green tunnel. He got out of the car, came over to my side, put the seat in a reclining position, and took my seat belt off. I'm not sure, but I think he kissed me on my lips. Maybe I was already in a sound sleep and dreaming. I think I felt his muzzy on my lip. That's what my mommy called a mustache.

I don't know how long I slept. At first I was alarmed. It was almost like part of the car was wrapped in a green octopus. Then I remembered the leaning grass. I woke up and looked over at Tommy. I once heard him say he hates it when someone describes a grown man as cute and adorable. Well, at that moment in time, Tommy looked cute and adorable. His seat was also in a reclining position. He had a book open across his chest. His reading glasses were hanging off his nose almost in his mouth. He was sound asleep. His shorts were of a thin fabric. I could see the outline of his penis. I wanted to touch him so badly. I did. My right arm was in the cast and my left one was free. I reached over and put my hand on his upper thigh. He began to awaken. I thought he would push my hand away and I would be embarrassed.

Tommy put his one hand on top of mine, and moved it into his groin. Then he moved it to his crotch. I could see and feel him rising. He was so big, hard, and standing erect in his shorts. I already knew his voice was low, almost gruff, and raspy. He began to speak. "Please let me slide totally out of my shorts. I want to feel the bare skin of your hand on the bare skin on my penis." My one hand was still on him, and I helped him. Once out of his shorts, he looked like he had a large flag pole coming out of his body. He moved my hand onto his naked penis. Then in a rotating rhythmic motion, he moved my hand up and down, and then onto the tip. He knew what would give him the greatest orgasm. Then he took his hand off. I believed he was giving me permission to continue on my own. His mouth was open a bit. He was softly panting. His pelvis area was slightly gyrating. He spoke again. "Can we both watch me come?" As I massaged his penis, it began to pulsate. His panting became heavier. He sounded like he was gasping for breath. As we watched, I knew exactly when his orgasm peaked, and he began to come. I could see and feel his hot, wet ejaculation fall onto him and my hand. Slowly I moved away back into my seat. Not a word was said. Tommy had a box of baby wipes on the back seat. He gave me a few for my hand. I asked why he had baby wipes. He said they were good when he took the girls out in the car. He wiped himself, and pulled his shorts back up. I couldn't even look at him. What had I done?

Tommy was a man of words. "Rosey darlin', I'm sorry I couldn't do the same for you. I owe you one. My fantasy was our first time would be in my bed and we would come together. On a serious note, Helen must never know what just happened! This must never happen again! We must never mention it even to each other!" I agreed. Tommy drove to his house and asked me to wait in the car.

As I sat there, I wondered about him needing to be totally naked on the bottom. My guess was a man would just let his penis hang out the front of his pants. I guess with him naked, he could really see everything. He wanted both of us to watch me massage him, and then watch him come. Was it unusual for a man to want that? I'm sure all men have sexual proclivities, but how would I know? I have only been with one man my entire life. All I can do is guess.

Tommy had to clean himself and change his pants before taking me back to Helen's house. He brought out a few wet wipes for my hands. On the way, he stopped at a drive-up window for ice cream. He said eating ice cream is a neutralizer when you need all things to appear normal. That was how he had to present us when he took me back to Helen.

I stayed at Helen's house most days. Tommy took me out for lunch a few times. I love a good cheeseburger, but couldn't hold it with one hand. He cut it up for me into many pieces, and I ate it with a fork. I did manage to eat my own ice cream with a spoon. Tommy never took me back to his house, and we never spoke of what I initiated in the car. Several times, he held my hand and walked me down to one of the pier areas. He always seemed to find a reason to reach out and hold my hand. Of course, I liked it. Helen was always very annoyed. We were always surrounded by a lot of people, never alone.

Were Helen's fears correct? Were we becoming too emotionally involved with each other? Was it now the beginning

66

of becoming intimately involved? It didn't matter. The two weeks passed by quickly, and Ian came to take me home.

I held back on telling Steven and Steffy about their father. The fall came and went. Ian wasn't planning the next trip until after the New Year of 2012. In the meantime, things were peaceful. Ian and I played the husband and wife game with our children and Sam on Hanukkah. There were always holiday parties at the country club. Ian insisted that we attend. To the world, we appeared normal.

Tommy said eating ice cream is a neutralizer when you need all things to appear normal. But we had no ice cream!

Again, I repeat:

IT MAY ALL BE A MISCONCEPTION OR AN ILLUSION.

CHAPTER 3-5

January and February 2012 came and went. Ian was still staying away for days at a time. Of course, I knew he was with Gwen. My feeling was when he pushed me out of bed he was frustrated. Perhaps things were not going well with her. Maybe now they were. I reached a point when I was no longer afraid to go to sleep. If he was in a good place with Gwen, I was safe. Not so!

In April, I was pushed out of bed again. This time I fell in such a way that my head tilted. The corner of my right eye hit the point of the night table. Of course, he always did "hit and run". The pain was so bad and there was so much blood. I called 911. They in turn called Abby.

There was a cut at the outer edge of my eye, and I needed a few stitches. My entire eye socket swelled. I very quickly had a beautiful shiner. I told the doctor I lost my balance and fell into the night table. Abby took me home and I begged her not to call Helen. I promised her that I would tell Steven and Steffy after the last incident, but I didn't. Steven and Steffy were given the same story as the doctor. Steven sat down on the end of my bed. "Mother, maybe Daddy is right. You have had so many accidents and falls in the last two years. Maybe it's time to check and see if there is a physical reason. After your eye heals, we can talk about it and together make a decision."

On the morning of Wednesday, May 2, 2012, my door bell rang at 6:00 a.m. I looked out and saw a police car. I became frantic.

I thought something happened to one of my children or Sam. I opened my door and the police officer stepped in. He asked if I'm Mrs. Ian Silver. I nodded. Without hesitation, he coldly responded, "Ma'am, I have two pieces of bad news for you. Your husband has passed away, but the cause of death has not yet been determined. He was in the home of a woman by the first name of Gwen. When someone passes away in what might be a suspicious manner, specific laws must be followed. Your husband has been taken to the medical examiner for an autopsy. The authorities must be sure there was no foul play. I'm sorry, but I must ask you to sign this form giving your permission for the autopsy. It will also give you the rights to claim his body after there is results. Ma'am, I'm sorry for your loss, but you don't seem to be too upset. Would you like me to call someone for you?"

"That won't be necessary. Just in case you're wondering, she was his sugar mama. I've known about her for a long time. I'm actually relieved and I'll show you why." I showed him the fairly new scar next to my eye. He nodded, turned around, and left.

I called Steven, Steffy, and Abby. I told them to come to the house immediately. Abby was the first to arrive. She then became the first to know Ian died and where. I hate the word died. I prefer saying someone has passed away. This is different. Ian *died*! God forgive us, but we held hands and danced around the living room. I had to be prepared to talk to the rest of my family. While I waited for them, I sent text messages to Helen, Leon, and Tommy. I gave as many details as I could, and told them we would talk later. I ended my message saying, "Now I can come out of my dark hole into the light. I'm no longer married. My days of being an emotionally, mentally, and physically abused woman are over. I LOVE YOU."

I got an almost immediate response from Helen. She said they would put a sign on the shop saying, "CLOSED FOR FAMILY EMERGENCY". Tommy could take their appointment books and call their customers to reschedule. They knew I would need them. Tommy also wanted to come. Helen knew it was a very bad idea. When he and I look at each other, it's very obvious there are feelings that shouldn't be there. Now it was vital that Steven and Steffy don't see those looks. We can't allow them to even suspect there was anything going on in Montauk between Tommy and me. Remember, now they will know I was never traveling with their father. They will know how much time I was in Montauk.

Steven and Steffy arrived. I sat them down and first had to tell them their father died. I took half a Xanax so I could do this. With Abby holding my hand, I told them where he died, and with whom. Then I backtracked to their father's gambling, the house, loss of all the money, his relationship with Gwen, his travels with her, my so-called accidents, and me being taken to Montauk. Abby told them she was aware of everything, along with Helen, Leon, and Tommy. While their father was living the high life with Gwen, they were my caregivers.

My children were devastated! They asked why I never told them anything. They questioned why I endured all of this alone. "I wasn't alone. Abby was always there for me. She begged me to tell you, but I was too frightened. At the beginning, your father told me he was involved with some dangerous people. We sold the house in order for him to repay his debt to them. I kept everything secretive to protect you, Hannah and Sam. I never knew if he was involved with them again. I wasn't protecting him; I was protecting my family. I also had Helen and Leon. When I had the broken wrist, I spent those weeks with them. They took care of me. Tommy also stepped in and helped when they had to be in their shop. There were times when he would cut up my food so I could eat. Helen and Leon are on their way. They know you since childhood. They love all of us like we are their own. They'll stay with me.

"The bottom line is there was never any money from the sale of the house. The small amount left was spent on buying

71

this house. Your father bought it alone and put it only in his name. I'm now going to have fucking holy hell to deal with everything. The only income I have is my social security and a small pension from the hospital. I think I'm going to need a lawyer." Steven said he would step in, work with me and pay for a lawyer.

Ian's body was ready for release. There was no foul play. He died of a coronary occlusion, a heart attack. A decision had to be made about where to take him, and what kind of funeral to plan. Steven spoke, "You know it will eventually come down to questions about where Daddy was when he died. We can't just invent stories. He always had a thing about the name Silver. He said it should never be tarnished. Well, he did a fucking good job on that one. His life these last years, and now his death, have tarnished the Silver name. We are beyond needing any amount of polish. I know you already have prepaid burial plots, if he didn't sell them too. I'd like to have his body taken to the crematorium in Huntingdon Valley. One of the graves can be opened and the ashes placed inside. Only one death announcement should be made. It should only say, 'ALL FUNERAL, BURIAL AND SHIVA WILL BE PRIVATE.' I can't attend a phony traditional Jewish funeral and burial for him. Also, I will not sit Shiva. He lived a disgraceful life, and died in the bed of his whore. Mother, you as his legal heir have the right to make these decisions. Please don't allow this to become a circus." Steffy chimed in and agreed with Steven. I too agreed.

I read a book, possibly sci-fi when I was in my early teens. It told of the possibility that one who was in the process of dying could hear all of their surroundings. They knew who was in the room, and what was being said by loved ones. There was one story about a man in his last moments. His wife was crying and screaming. He could hear her but couldn't comfort her. In the book, it was written as we always say, one should rest in

72

peace. I believe everyone should also pass in peace. They should not hear and know a loved one is in such horrible pain. There should be nothing but sweet words and thoughts going into the mind of the dying. There were many times I had a patient in the final stage of life. If nobody was there, I always held a hand and whispered sweet words into their mind. That also gave me peace when I lost someone. Ian knew how I felt about that. Again, may God forgive me, but I hope he died hearing Gwen screaming. **May he not rest in peace!**

Helen, Leon, and Sam helped me empty the house of all Ian's belongings. Steven and Steffy had to return to work. Abby and Scott were always there. I was contacted by Steven's attorney. He told me the house would be put in my name. I was married to Ian for more than ten years. Therefore, I could change from the amount of my social security payments to his, which was greater. There were other legal things I had to take care of with the attorney. I sold the burial plot next to the one where the ashes of the shiny Dr. Ian Silver were buried.

Everyone questioned the disappearance of Ian. We had to keep it private except for a trusted rabbi. I was not a black widow, but a merry widow. I had to play a game for the public. In Judaism, there are several rules a woman should follow after the death of her husband. I wore a cut black mourning ribbon for thirty days, but only in public. There are different writings, and I decided which one I would follow. It says a woman should mourn her husband for thirty days, and can marry on day thirty-one. I certainly was not in mourning, but had no plans to marry.

Helen and Leon returned to Montauk. A few weeks later I joined them, but refused to see Tommy. I still needed more time and space to search inside myself. I had to examine my feelings for him, and the reasons behind them. I had to be sure before going to him.

CHAPTER 3-6

I observed the thirty days of the phony mourning period. On Saturday, June 2, 2012, day thirty-one, I went to Tommy's house unannounced. Helen and Leon were in the shop. I knew I was madly, wildly, and passionately in love with Thomas Patrick Monahan. I was ready to tell him. I nervously rang the bell. He opened the door and grabbed me into his arms. I knew that was the answer to the question I came to ask. Was he also madly, wildly, and passionately in love with me? When did we actually fall in love? We both declared that it happened on an unknown day and time. Perhaps it was the day I seduced him in the car with my left hand. Could it possibly have happened back in 1984 when we couldn't stop looking at each other? Now it was the time to make our mutual fantasy come true. We undressed each other, and Tommy took me to his bed. He was big and did look like he had a large flag pole coming out of his body. There was no time for foreplay.

I could feel exactly where he was every step of the way. It went from the time he entered me until nature caused him to fall out of me. I was so hot and wet that it allowed him to have an easy entry. Then he picked up pushing and thrusting movements. They became harder and harder. His tip was deep in as far as he could go. He put one hand under me and pulled my body even closer to his, if that was possible. We were a perfect fit. While I was enjoying my own passion, I was partially feeling his from the sounds. His mouth was slightly open like it was in the car. I could again hear him panting. His breathing became heavier, and his entire body was almost spastic. I knew the exact moment when he began coming and when he ended. I could feel the heat of his total experience when he shot inside of me. I could hear the sounds, and feel those final pushes as he released the last drops. This time I got to really feel him pulsate and come inside of me. Our fantasy now became reality. We did come together.

We rolled over onto our backs. Tommy reached over and took my hand. That became a habit he developed. "We didn't have time for foreplay, but did you ever do after play?" No, I hadn't. I told Tommy that Ian was a fuck, come, and go man. When it was over, it was over. Tommy said it was the same with Cindy. He explained what it entailed. One at a time, one to the other has to create and perform a seduction. In Tommy's words, "The greatest of fucks need follow-up. There is a man and woman still aroused and wanting more." We both did want more. Tommy was to lie on his back in the bed, and I could do anything I wanted to him. Then he would do the same to me. In general conversation, we had already established that the back end was forbidden. Also, there was the option to say "STOP".

It was decided that I would first begin on Tommy. I told him since I'm a lightweight, I would like to climb up on his muscular chest to begin. I would then refer to his chest as my mountain. He agreed. I had loved him for so long and wanted him for so long. Now was my chance to act upon my total fantasy. The seduction in the car was only a partial. I climbed on top of my mountain. I began tasting his mouth, then his neck. With my hands, mouth, and open legs began moving slowly down. His body was so sweet smelling and tasting. He couldn't rise or come because not enough time had passed. He was hot, opened his mouth and began panting and breathing heavy again. I thought he would put his head back, close his eyes, and enjoy. Suddenly, I remembered he liked to watch. His head was propped up on a few pillows. I stopped at his belly. Then I changed positions and went down to his legs. I massaged up and into his inner thighs. His body was writhing. He began a loud moan that I hadn't heard earlier. He was hot and wild! The seduction was still not completed. I moved onto his penis and the tip. It was jumping and rocking. He couldn't do a full ejaculation, but he dripped a bit. I didn't just kiss his body. I tasted it. Tommy was delicious! Then I calmed him by climbing up on my mountain again and soothing him. When I came down, I rolled on my back and didn't say a word.

Next it was Tommy's turn to seduce me. There are only so many things that one can do to a human body to create a seduction. He did it all! Hopefully, I was also delicious. The only difference was that Tommy would probably go to confession.

I called Helen and told her I was there. "Helen, about an hour ago, did you see fireworks, hear jets flying overhead, see sky writing, and hear angels singing? Did you also see hundreds of different colored balloons flying in the beautiful summer Montauk sky? They were all in celebration of the first true coming together of Tommy and Rosey."

She said, "Jesus, Mary, And Joseph!" I'm sure she crossed herself. Tommy got on the phone and invited them to his house for dinner at 7:00. Since the year 2006, this was my first day of total peace and tranquility in Montauk.

This was the first night we were going to sleep together. He asked for us to always sleep naked. He called it "skin to skin". We fell asleep with our arms and legs intertwined. If anyone peeked, they would not be able to tell where each of our bodies began and ended. There would only be one way. He's the one with the hairy legs! It would now be impossible for one of us to freely get out of bed. I was the one who needed to get to the bathroom. I had to nudge him, poke him, and pinch him on his naked adorably shaped tush. He woke up and asked if something was wrong. I got out of bed, went to the bathroom, and returned. He was now wide awake and propped up on the pillows. His legs were wide open, with about half a flag pole. I couldn't resist. My hands went up his legs and directly to his crotch. I massaged just enough to make him wild again. He grabbed me and returned the favor. We had to work out something on this bathroom deal. The only thing we could think of was a smack on the tush. Whoever had to get up would smack the other one, and gently pull out of the hold. Then smack again on return. We'd have to give it a try.

In the morning, we took a shower together, dressed, and went downstairs. Tommy made breakfast, and after we ate we moved into the den. He told me since we had now bonded, there was something personal he needed to tell me about himself.

"This is something I never planned on telling you. It was way back in my past and just didn't matter. Now that something wonderful has happened between us, I must tell you."

Yes, something wonderful has happened between Tommy and me. I now have things I will tell him later. I'll let him go first. I made a new discovery about him. It's something I couldn't have known until he fucked me. He does look like there is a large flag pole coming out of his body. But he fucks like a jack hammer. He went in so deep and hard. His pushing and thrusting was so strong. I remember once seeing a street team repairing a road. There was a tall muscular man operating the jack hammer. Until now, I never gave it a thought. Does that man fuck like a jack hammer? Well, Tommy does.

I can't believe that Cindy could have found any man in New York City to fuck her any better. She was married to him all of those years. She also had to know what a kind, gentle, loving man she married. Perhaps her power as an attorney and money she earned were more important to her. She broke his heart. While he suffered so greatly when she left him, he partially recovered. Now we have taken each other into full recovery from Cindy and Ian.

CHAPTER 3-7

"I was a virgin until I turned 22 years old. Being raised by Mom and Helen, mostly in the church, wasn't easy. My hormones, body needs, and religious taboos were driving me crazy! I needed to talk about sex so I went to Leon.

"Mothers spoke to their daughters because of menstruation and how not to become pregnant. Many fathers seemed not to be able to discuss sex with their sons. Some families sent boys in their late teens to be with a whore. They believed if he spent a few hours with one, she would teach him everything. Sometimes the woman would have intercourse with them if past the legal age. It had to be done to turn a boy into a man. They always knew where these whores were located and what her charge would be.

"Leon then told me about a woman in the Hamptons. Her name was Jerri. She was said to be a sex therapist, but was really a whore. Of course, she didn't advertise anywhere. Somehow, through the years word got around. He told me that beauty and barber shops are the best places to get such information. If I would like to go, he would inquire for me. Mom and Helen were not to know. I agreed to go.

Leon gave me her phone number. I called and spoke to her. She told me of only working with young men who were virgins. They had to be at least 21 years old, and very clean. She informed me that because of her profession, she had a hysterectomy many years ago. There would be no fear of pregnancy. She would trust my word that I was disease free. On both counts, there would be no need for protection with her. It would only be necessary at a later time when I went out into the world. She promised to show me how to properly place a condom on my penis. Her fee was $200, cash only, for a two hour session. I just graduated from college and got my teaching job. Money would not be a problem. She was by appointment only. I arranged to go that Saturday morning from 10:00 to 12:00. All but Leon were told I was going to a teaching seminar.

"I had her address and directions. Well macho Tommy wasn't feeling so macho. I pulled up at her house and almost turned around and left. I took a deep breath, went to the door, and knocked. The door opened. Standing there was a gorgeous woman. I guessed she was about middle to late forties. I told her I was Tommy, and she held her hand out for me to enter. She asked me to follow her. I was led to a room where everything was gold velvet, and was shown where to sit. She left and came back with a tray of tea and cookies. I handed her the money. I was so scared that I almost threw up. In the back of my mind, I was thinking of part of an old saying. I mean the part that any dog in the street can fuck. Why can't I? Why this?

"She sat down and began speaking. Her voice was low and sweet, very comforting. She then began her speech:

'Tommy, of course you know why you're here. In spite of anything you've heard about me, I'm always a lady. I only use one naughty word. That word is *fuck*! That's what I'm going to help you do.

"'The first thing you must learn is the proper way for a man and woman to undress each other. It really needs to be part of the foreplay. There is nothing uglier than a man and woman pulling clothes off and throwing them around. Also, both must be totally naked to properly enjoy fucking or any other sexual act. There must be total body skin to skin contact. Of course, you must master the art of control. You will become aroused and erect, but must have control. You don't want to allow yourself to prematurely ejaculate. That would mean you can't perform the act of fucking. You might also make a mess on yourself or the woman. Remember *control*. I'm going to take you through several steps in these two hours. Performing foreplay will be first. Then you can fuck me. Oh, by the way. Were you told that I'm a nymph and love to fuck with young virgins?'

"She led me into a bedroom. This room was decorated in red velvet. There were no lights, just red candles all over the room. The flickering was so exciting. She had us both standing facing each other. She was wearing a long silky robe with oriental flower designs. There was a long zipper to open it down the front. She said there would be no kissing on the mouth. She began slowly taking off the clothes on top of my body. She kept on whispering the word 'control'. She asked me to open her robe. I did and she was totally naked. It slid to the floor. I was shocked to see that she had no pubic hair. Again she said 'control'. I was so hard and erect. She took off my pants and shorts, and put herself onto the bed with legs wide open. I was glued to the floor. She held her arms out for me to go to her. I did. Gently she pulled me on top of her. Then she reached for my hand and put it onto her vagina. Next she repositioned herself and guided my penis into her vagina. I felt like yelling, 'Look everybody! Thomas Patrick Monahan is finally fucking!'

"Pumping in and out of her became natural. No lesson needed there. In my wildest imagination, I would never know how good it would feel. Then came the orgasm! I thought I must have died and was in some kind of heaven. Then I realized what I was doing is a sin. I wouldn't go to heaven. I would go to hell.

"She knew I loved it and so did she. I was a young virgin fucking for the first time. Now she was going to introduce me to after play. Again, she left the room and returned with two warm wash cloths. I was asked to wash her body and then she washed mine. We stayed in the bed propped up on pillows. She needed to tell me more before we performed after play. The subject of oral sex came into her discussion. I was told that it's not just mouth to genitals. She said passionate kissing is oral sex. When mouths and tongues meet in a wet bodily environment, that's oral sex.

"She explained after play to me as I explained it to you last night, with an exception. Jerri said men and women share mind, heart, soul and body, but not the spiritual body. The only way a man and woman can become a spirit of one comes from tasting. Kissing a body is sensual, but it doesn't join the spirits. There must be the presence of real passion. Then a man and woman must physically use their mouth and taste each other. She hoped one day a woman would come into my life who would taste me. She began to perform after play on me and asked that I perform it on her. There was that one exception. She and I would kiss bodies, but not taste. We will not become a spirit of one.

"I was so rattled! The two hours ended, and we were still naked. I thought she was going to ask me to dress and escort me to the door. I was looking at her naked body and she was staring at my crotch. She called me big boy and commented on my size. She kept her promise and showed me how to place a condom on my penis. I practiced a few times. There would not be an overtime charge, but she asked me to practice what she taught me. She asked me to fuck her again using a condom. It felt awful! I guess I'm going to make that adjustment. Like the dog in the street who can fuck, I can't have Tommy babies running around Montauk. She really was a mistress nymph, and I became a master fucker.

"That was 43 years ago. After that I began a very active sex life of only fucking. That was all I needed and wanted. No frills. It continued until I married Cindy. Then you know about Tom

Cat. Last night you didn't need lessons for after play. You seduced me. You've learned I have to watch when you play with my body. I love to watch myself come. I watched and realized you weren't just kissing my body. You were tasting me! Then I tasted you. We have now become a spirit of one. We will never be apart!"

"Tommy, how accurate is this story from 43 years ago? It's almost funny! It doesn't matter. You are still my flag pole and jack hammer." I explained.

CHAPTER 3-8

This was only the third time I went into the house. The first time was Christmas Eve of 1984. The second was when Tommy took me home for dinner, and angered Helen. I had only seen the outside and all on the lower level. Now I have seen Tommy's bedroom, private bathroom, and upstairs den. The house is located on a private drive off the main road. On the right, there is beautiful greenery and a cement path to the beach. The house is on the left. It's all white with black shutters and trim. There are three steps to the door. It's so wide that Tommy could drive his Lincoln right into the house. The front and sides around the house have beautiful flower gardens. Tommy said he has a gardener to take care of the grounds except for the flowers. He does that himself.

The house is so big! I asked for a tour since I hope to be spending a lot of time there.

When you walk in, the first thing you see is a very long center hall. It leads to the back of the house. On the right is the living room. After Cindy left, Tommy changed it from being formal to welcoming. The furniture is all traditional, cozy and comfortable. There is a 90-inch television on the wall. Behind the living room is an area with the washer, dryer, heat/AC units, and a powder room. There is a door to the outside. It leads to an enclosure with a metal shower stall and small heater. It can also be entered with a key from the outside.

Upon entering, to the left is a rounded stairway to the upper level. Then there is a formal dining room, and an open doorway leading to the kitchen. Both equal the length of the living room. Behind the kitchen wall is another area. There is no basement or garage. That's the space Tommy uses for storage. There is another door leading out. It's fenced in and can't be entered from the outside. That's where the girls go out alone and are safe. Best of all, there is a hot tub.

On the upper level there are four bedrooms, Tommy's private bathroom, and a den with a 72-inch television on the wall. This is where he watches television when home alone. That room is also his library and computer room. It's furnished with mostly navy blue leather furniture. He has a very large recliner, where he sits to do most of his reading. It has always been his private space in the house. He uses the computer to do his lesson planning for school, among other things. Tommy hates social media. He considers specific rooms in the house as the social place for visitors. Not the Internet.

There are two other bathrooms upstairs. One is what I would call a normal deluxe bathroom. The other one is a spa. It has a shower with benches and openings in the walls for steam. The bathtub is a whirlpool and big enough for a gang bang. I did notice that except for the kitchen and bathrooms, the floors are hardwood. There are area rugs in all of those rooms. A few of them are exquisite oriental rugs. I love oriental decorations.

The entire back wall on the lower level leads to the beach. Outside the door, there is a slightly raised patio the width of the house. It's decorated with potted plants, ornamental benches, and lots of comfortable outdoor furniture. There are three steps down to the beach. Sliding glass and screen doors cover floor to ceiling. What is open or closed depends on the weather. There is one very large window in the living room and one in every bedroom. Of course, there are two poodle beds in the living room, and two in Tommy's upstairs den. That's where they sleep at night.

I did ask one complex question. I asked why the door on the right leads to an enclosure with a shower, and access from the beach. The left side is enclosed with no access from the beach. I assumed the shower was for after coming off the beach before entering the house. That would make sense. Tommy explained it was used for that now, but was originally put in for a different reason.

"Mom's name was Emma. She didn't have to continue working after we moved into the house. Cindy and I had more than enough money to take care of everything. Mom needed her independence, which meant going to work and having her own money. She never wanted to be in a position to ask us to pay for anything. At the age of 65, she began collecting social security payments. Her health was still good, but she was tired of cleaning houses for the rich people.

"Mom began searching through the want ads, and went on an interview. When she came home, we were told she was just hired to work in one of the local Catholic funeral homes. The job was cleaning their embalming room following each procedure. We thought she was making a joke, but she wasn't. The funeral business is spotty. Sometimes they had three funerals in one week, and sometimes none for a week or two. She would be on-call, but the money was great. There was a tour, and she found all of the rooms very interesting. They told her she would be given a paper throw-away gown, cap, mask, and rubber gloves.

"A few days later, she got the first call. They had just completed the preparation of a body for a viewing. As she went out the door, she crossed herself and mumbled a prayer. About five hours later she came home. She cleaned the embalming room, then dusted the casket show room, the viewing room, and did all of the vacuuming. The third time, there was a terrible odor about her when she came home. She smelled like death, and the chemicals used for the embalming and preps. That's why we put in the shower. When returning from that job, she came in the door with a key. She undressed and immediately took a shower. A robe and clean clothes were always there for her. On that side of the house is the washer and dryer. She immediately washed the clothes she took off.

"Mom worked at that job for about eight years. Eventually, her legs became arthritic and she couldn't stand up to do the floor cleaning. She worked long and hard enough all of her life. Now was the time for her to be a lady of leisure. Cindy and I had a cleaning service do the work in our house. Mom just insisted on cooking. Cindy and I both worked.

"Mom always had to be doing something. She told us that many Irish families have their own traditions. As a young girl, she saw the older relatives making burial covers for younger relatives. She took one out of her closet and showed it to us. Her aunt made it for her and she brought it from Ireland. It was wrapped and looked brand new. It was white with hand sewn religious symbols on it. 'I believe now is the time to make my request. When I pass, please cover me with it on top of my clothes. The family believes that it helps keep one warm on the path to the arms of Jesus.' She made one for me, but not for Helen. Mom spent her last years going to Mass, social church functions, and times with just me and Cindy.

"Mom refused to ever speak of her age. Based on the ages of Helen and myself, she was about 75 years old when she passed away. She had lung cancer. We believed it came at least partially from the chemicals in the embalming room.

"I just told you the nice public story of Mom. Now I'll tell you the true private story of Mom. You have asked me why you never met her, especially at Christmas in 1984. I told you at a later time I would explain. I also asked that you never mention Mom to Helen. The story is ugly and painful! I'm going to tell you now because I pray one day very soon you will marry me. I know everything about you and your secrets. Now I need to tell you mine. There should be no secrets.

"You know we came from Ireland in 1957. Helen was 14 and I was 10 years old. I also told you we went to live with our cousin Catherine. She was not our cousin or a nun, but called the church lady. Our village in Ireland was very poor. The schools, orphanages, and jobs were all run by the church. We were sent here because Mom was considered to be 'loose'. She was sleeping around at a very young age. There was no pill, condom use, or abortion.

"She gave birth to Helen when she was 18 years old. Remember, Mom's actual age was always in question. Mom was living in the convent with her baby girl. In order to get food for herself and Helen, she did domestic work in the convent, rectory, and church. Again, time is iffy. About two years later, Mom was pregnant again. She gave birth to a baby boy. He was taken away from her and sent away to be adopted. On November 23, 1947 she gave birth to another baby boy. They also wanted to take him away from her. They couldn't continue feeding her children. She begged and pleaded not to take another baby boy away from her. They let her keep me. Yes, that baby boy was me!

"Mom was apparently still loose, but didn't become pregnant again in Ireland. Helen and I remembered men in and out at night. There was never one man for us to call 'Daddy'. Catherine volunteered to take us to live with her in Montauk. You know that in time Helen and I came to live in a small apartment with Mom. Helen lived with us out of need, and to watch over me. She was so lucky when she met Leon. They fell in love like us. After Helen got married in 1963, she left the apartment, but still watched over me. There was so much gossip about Mom. Helen was ashamed to be known as her daughter. Since then she never saw our Mom or spoke to her. I was never to mention her name. It was always difficult, especially on holidays. We had to do everything separately.

"As time went by and Helen and I got older, we learned more. Emma was our natural mom, but Helen and I have different fathers. Mom didn't even know who they were. She only wanted to bring me with her from Ireland and leave Helen behind. Catherine wouldn't allow that to happen. Helen learned that Mom didn't want her, only her baby boy. We also knew that Mom made me a burial cover, but never made one for Helen. As all of the truths came out, it brought Helen and me closer together. She loves Leon and I love you. If the truth be known, there is no greater love than what is between me and Helen. She could let go of Mom, but I couldn't. Now you know why you must never mention Mom to Helen. You, Abby, and Helen are three sisters. Please, let it stay that way forever.

"There is one more part of the story. Mom knew if she went out of town for a few days, Helen would take care of me. She always did at every age. I knew there were times when Mom went to New York City and stayed with Cindy. Sometimes it was for a few days, or as long as two weeks. She said Cindy was there working so hard and was always alone. Mom said she was taking care of her.

"The day Cindy left me, she also told me Mom knew she was fucking around. Sometimes she was in one bedroom, while Cindy was in the other one with men. I guess Cindy and Mom did have reasons to like each other.

"The day of the bar-b-que, Cindy and Mom were told Helen was bringing her friends from Philly to the house. I gave my approval. Mom just went out for the day. On Christmas Eve, Mom was told again that Helen was bringing her friends to the house for dinner. Again, with my approval. Mom served dinner at the church. Cindy and Mom went together to Christmas Eve Mass. You and Abby went to morning Mass with me, Helen, and Leon. Mom was at the house with Cindy. Now you know where Mom was in 1984.

"When I began drinking, I had two issues to work on in rehab. One was Cindy and my marriage. The other one was my Mom, along with her relationship with Cindy. I was hit with a triple barrel. I don't mean to cry like this! Except for Helen and now you, nobody has ever loved me so much."

"Tommy, just as it's over with Ian, it's now over with both Cindy and your Mom. You will never need to drink again. I love you so fucking much! Helen once said she believed it will take an incredibly saintly woman for you to ever trust and love again. I know she was praying that it would be me. I'm no saint, but I am so deeply in love with you. Sometimes I miss you terribly when you go to work. I take out one of the shirts you have already worn. I wear it until right before you come home. I wear it because it lets me feel and smell you when we're apart!

"Now, no more secrets. Let's stop crying and set a wedding date!"

CHAPTER 3-9

On Thursday, August 30, 2012, one day before my 70th birthday, I became Mrs. Thomas Patrick Monahan. The decision was made, but not without thought or heart. When I announced our plans to my family, I made them understand that it was not a quick decision. Tommy and I met and had a wonderful friendship for almost two years. While they thought I was traveling with their father, I was in Montauk for weeks at a time with Helen, Leon, and Tommy. I reminded them that Tommy and I never had an affair. We were never intimate. Tommy is too fine a man, and too good a Catholic to ever sleep with a married woman. In turn, I am too fine and moral a woman to ever break my marriage vows. We just knew we had fallen madly, wildly, and passionately in love with each other.

The wedding was on a Thursday because I can't marry on a Saturday and Tommy can't marry on a Sunday. It took place at 3:00 on the beach outside of what would now be our house. In attendance were only Helen, Leon, Steven, Hannah, Sam, Steffy, Abby, and Scott. Since we were going to be on the beach and patio, everyone was told to come very summer casual. The ceremony was performed by a judge.

Tommy asked my children to keep me in Philly for a few days. He wanted to be the one to decorate the patio and beach for me. He didn't want me to return until the morning of the ceremony. The windows and shades would be closed on the back of the house. Tommy was not at all a controlling man, but a very loving, caring, and sensitive man. He was a pleaser, and had to make this an incredible day for me. His ex-wife left him for other men and broke his heart. The last six years of my life had been a horror. He told Helen that my love healed his heart. His love now had to be powerful enough to mend more than a heart for me.

I stayed with Steffy in her condo until early Thursday. We got back to the house about noon time. I had already been living there so all of my clothes were in the house. Steffy and I went directly up to the bedroom I shared with Tommy. Hanging on the closet door was a gorgeous semi-sheer long white dress. On the bed was a set of lace underwear, and a pair of bejeweled white sandals. There was a note saying the clothes were from Tommy. He asked me to wear them for our wedding. The note also said the sandals were a gift from Helen. Of course, she makes jewelry and decorates jewelry boxes.

I got dressed and put on very little light make-up. I was going to be outside. Steffy presented me with a necklace and a pair of matching earrings to wear. She was instructed to bring me downstairs to the doorway of the beach at 2:45. Tommy met me at the door. He was going to take me outside. He looked so handsome! He was wearing white slacks and a white shirt. It was open in the front like Harry Belafonte. When the doors opened, I saw a chupah.

Tommy and Leon built the chupah, and set it up on the beach. As I walked out with Tommy, I could see it closer just a few feet away. It was covered with satin and red roses. There were red rose pedals scattered all over the beach. All the beach chairs were red.

The judge began with a Hebrew prayer. My grandson Sam gave it to him and asked that he read it before the ceremony. Sam is familiar with Hebrew and rewrote it phonetically. A traditional ceremony began. Sam was holding the rings and gave them to us. Tommy and I chose to wear plain gold bands, and we did the exchange of the rings. The judge then said, "Before I say the final words to complete this union of Tommy and Rosey, they have asked to speak to each other."

Tommy and I faced each other holding hands. We always hold hands.

I looked at Tommy and said, "You are an English teacher. I defy you to find a word that describes how much I love you. I don't think one exists. I was in a dark hole, and didn't believe I would ever come out. Suddenly, God made a change in my life. He brought me out of the dark hole and into the light. Thomas Patrick Monahan, you are that light. I now have a gift for you. Please open this box. Put my gift around your neck and never take it off." Tommy opened the box and cried. I gave him a gold chain with a Miraculous Medal attached. Helen also cried.

Next it was Tommy's turn. First, he spoke of his love for me. He also briefly told of how he too was living in the dark, and God showed him the light. That light was me, Lorraine Rose Stone. He then said, "I also have a gift for you." He walked to the side of the house and quickly returned with a white adult tricycle. There were red roses painted on it and a red seat. On the front handle bars was a white basket with red padding inside. Everybody was hysterical! Tommy loved speaking in front of groups and was a great orator. He then went into a bit of a long-winded speech. "Rosey told me she never learned how to ride. Her parents were always afraid she would fall and get hurt. Before she came to live with me, my only companions and housemates were Sugar Cookie and Coco Chanel. They are the two toy poodles I rescued from the dog pound. I call them my girls. Weather permitting, I go riding every evening on one of the designated area bicycle paths. My bike is black. On the front is a wire basket with pink padding inside. I take the girls with me. Since Rosey is living with me, she always stays home while we go riding. Now I don't have to teach her how to ride or worry about her falling and getting hurt. She will also be safe riding around alone during the day. Now, in the evening, we'll all go out together."

The judge was still waiting to complete the ceremony, but we kept on interrupting him. Helen and Leon asked if they could offer a small wedding gift. Leon made a large wooden trinket box, lined it with satin, painted it with oriental flowers, and finished it with lacquer. Helen put jewels on the lid to match the colors and motif of the flowers. They asked that we use it to place small mementos inside of things we will share through our lives. What a joyous surprise!

It was time for the judge to say, "I now pronounce you husband and wife. Tommy, you may kiss your bride." This time, I stopped him. I had one more thing to say. "Tommy, now that you are my husband, I want you to know I will never be able to breathe or live without you. Therefore, I will never leave you or let you go. We will always be one."

Tommy then looked at me and repeated it back to me. "Rosey, now that you are my wife, I want you to know I will never be able to breathe or live without you. Therefore, I will never leave you or let you go. We will always be one."

Finally, the ceremony ended and Tommy did kiss his bride. He leaned over and whispered in my ear, "Did he say I may now kiss my bride or fuck my bride?" That's my dirty mouth Tommy!

Helen took care of the catering, and all of the set-up on the patio. They were told there was to be no alcohol or any food cooked with wine. It was a buffet dinner with a waiter standing at each table to serve. We were only a group of ten. There were cocktail tables and chairs also set up on the patio. When it was time for cake, we did the usual and fed it to each other. It had white icing with big red rose decorations.

Steven asked for everyone's attention. He stood up and asked for everybody to lift a glass of whatever they were drinking. "I would like everybody to drink a toast to Mother and her wonderful new husband. Of course, Abby and Scott will call their new brother-in-law Tommy as always. Tommy, if it's alright with you, Steffy, Hannah, and I would like to call you Dad. Sam would like to call you Pops." I saw tears run down Tommy's face. He was now a dad and a Pops. Of course, Helen and Leon would still hold the titles of Aunt and Uncle to my children. Everyone hugged.

Tommy had speakers outside and a remote to play music. First, he played a romantic slow song and everybody watched as we had our first dance as Mr. and Mrs. Thomas Patrick Monahan. Then Tommy picked up the pace for everybody else to dance. It was hot, yet breezy on the beach from the ocean. Everybody had their shoes off and danced at the edge of the water. My new husband and I love reggae. That was where he began. He took off his shirt. I never saw him dance like he did that day. His body movements were unbelievably sultry. Then the music was on a dance disc. One song played after another in different genres.

Tommy had a special outdoor sprinkler system on one side of the patio. It was for cleaning off the sand before going into the house. By about seven o'clock, everybody was ready to leave. The catering staff did the clean-up, gathered the trash, and folded the furniture. Leon said he would put all the lawn furniture back in place and clean the beach the next day. Tommy and I insisted that there be no gifts. Their presence on our special day was the only gift we needed. We were going to spend our wedding night in the house.

Everyone left. Tommy locked up the back of the house and closed all of the window treatments. It finally got dark outside, and now was dark inside. In a matter of minutes, my husband took off my clothes and reached for me to do the same to him. His flag pole rose quickly. Somehow, he managed to get it inside of me in a standing up position. Both of us were so hot that we came in record time. We went upstairs to the bedroom, and completed our wedding night with what should have been foreplay.

I had one adjustment to make with Tommy. It is said that a woman is supposed to be a lady in the parlor and a whore in the bedroom. With my Tommy, it's totally in reverse. He is always the most proper gentleman in public, but a dirty-mouthed man privately with me. He never makes any demands of me, and never refuses any requests I make of him. Now I had to honor his one request. For all he is to me, I can't deny him this freedom of speech. After all, it is the First Amendment. He has his own words he insists be used for dirty talk. They are words he only uses with me. They are his Cock, my Pussy, and we don't make love, we fuck. He says he loves to fuck me and wants to tell me. At his age, his almost perpetual hard-on can rise about every four hours. There was a weekend when we had a Fuckathon. Imagine, every three to five hours. He had a slogan. "Up and in." If he could get it up, I had to let him in. We also laughed a lot that weekend. It was actually fun. We loved it! The dirty talk isn't just in bed. He's a sneaky kind of guy. We can be hand in hand walking through a mall or in the supermarket when he quietly whispers in my ear. Something he might say is, "Rosey darlin', my giant, hard, flag pole Cock is ready to go. My jack hammer is going to fuck the hell out of your Pussy." He whispers many things, but I think that's his favorite. If he says he's going to do it, he does. Sometimes he refers to himself as "Rosey's Riveter".

There were two others that had to make an adjustment. They were Sugar and Coco. I don't know if they were afraid of me, or just didn't like me. These two adorable poodies, as I call them, snarled at me every time I got near Tommy. He got this crazy idea that if I smelled like him, I belonged in the house with him. It took a few days of me wearing his shirt after he took it off. It wasn't such a crazy idea. There was a sudden turn around and all was well.

One might say I'm a cougar. My husband is only 65 years old. Is it true what they say about an older woman with a younger man? Yes! Yet, we are different. The cougar is supposed to be the sex teacher to the younger man. I had only been with one man in a missionary sexual marriage. I had nothing to teach. My new husband didn't marry the first time until he was 36 years old. He got around and knew it all. I was very happy to learn from him. I gladly allowed him to take the lead. Tommy once told me the story of "Tom Cat". He loved to fuck, but had rules. Tom Cat is now dead, but Tommy is alive and well. There are no rules. We fuck with eyes open seeing the love in each other's eyes. We use our hands and mouths. We passionately kiss and taste the clean, sweet bodies of each other. Tommy was right when he told me sex has a smell. Our entire house always has the smell of sex. We have fucked in almost every room of the house.

Tommy has done what I asked of him with my wedding gift. He never takes it off. He is so handsome and sexy! While it is a very religious medal, it gives him such a look of distinction. When he's not wearing a shirt, it lays against his beautiful, muscular chest. When he's wearing any type of shirt, it always hangs on top for everyone to see. He's big on his dirty words, but clams up on something sentimental.

I certainly don't need tricycle lessons. I just hope nobody makes fun of me when I ride on the bicycle paths alone during the day. I will probably become the laughing joke of Montauk. That's alright. I will now be able to ride with my husband in the evening.

CHAPTER 3-10

Thanksgiving came, and we four Montauk folks went to Steven's house for dinner. November 23rd was also Tommy's 66th birthday, and we had a cake for him. We stayed a few days in my house. I'm glad I never sold it. Keeping it means we always have a place to stay in Philly. Next was Hanukkah and Christmas. It was a combined holiday on Christmas Eve at mine and Tommy's house. This time the Philly people all came to Montauk. Everyone stayed home for New Year's 2013.

Two events took place that summer. Helen and Leon decided to retire in June, and sold their property. Helen is now 70 and Leon 73 years old. It was time they got off their feet. They bought a condominium in a 55-plus development. Helen no longer had to worry about Tommy. Perhaps they would travel a bit. Tommy and I bought tickets for a show in New York City. The four of us saw a Broadway musical and had dinner. We had fun just riding the train together. It was just a small retirement gift. They deserved much more, but asked for nothing more than seeing me and Tommy together.

Tommy was also now ready to retire. He put in more than enough years with the school district to get a full pension. Additionally, he applied for social security benefits. His love for teaching was always great. Now he said his love for me was greater. He wanted to spend more of his life with me. The school district staff, teachers, and other school staff told us there was going to be a party to honor Tommy. Some of his former and present students would also be attending. It was going to be held in the banquet room above the Montauk Fire House. My family, Helen, and Leon were all invited. Tommy and I walked in and couldn't believe what we saw. There must have been 200 people. They were all there to show love and respect to my incredible husband. Everyone knew Tommy was in rehab a few years back when his ex-wife left him. No alcohol was served. The dinner was excellent, and the speeches eventually became boring. Tommy was given a gold wall plaque for service to his students. Of course, he gave a beautiful speech of gratitude. One might not know it, but he truly is a sensitive man. He is never too tough to let anyone see him cry, and he did.

There were still several weeks left in summer. I knew Tommy loved operating the ferry to Block Island. I suggested that he continue. He no longer would be returning to school in the fall. In my opinion, he needed to hold onto that part of his life. I would never ask him to give it up. He would still be with me nine months out of the year. Also, he could just go out on the ferry a few days a week. He agreed, and thanked me.

My birthday was coming up again. I will be 71 years old. It was also going to be our first wedding anniversary. Tommy and I decided to spend it alone in the house. It would be as it was on our wedding night with one difference. We would begin in the bedroom. Before these special days, my Tommy asked me a question. "Do you trust me?"

"Of course!" He asked me to take off the Star of David I always wear around my neck and give it to him. He also asked if I would trust him to make two trips to New York City alone on the train. He would go one day, and then a second time about a week later. "I trust you, my husband. Just let me know when. I can plan to take you to the train station and then pick you up." I surely knew he wasn't going to see Cindy. Three days later, I drove him to the station. He was gone almost all day. I picked him up at 5:30 and didn't realize how much I missed him. When he got into the car, I did all but grab him. We walked into the house and undressed each other. There was a quickie right on the floor. I think he missed me too.

A week later, Tommy left alone on the morning train for the second trip. He asked me to take a later train and meet him at the station at 4:00. Since I was meeting him in New York City, I knew to dress up a bit more than at home. He was carrying a few packages and flagged down a cab. We went to one of New York's top hotels. He had a reservation for dinner in their main dining room. It was incredible. My husband then announced he also reserved a room for the night. We checked into what the hotel called "The Anniversary Suite." An apology followed saying he hoped I wouldn't be upset with him. He knew we planned on spending our anniversary at home. What moron woman would be upset with her husband for this surprise?

As always, first we undressed each other. This time it wasn't just a quick pure fuck. My husband made beautiful love to me. We always fuck, but somehow it was different. He always puts a different twist or description on our sex. Afterwards, we showered and put on a robe. The high priced hotels gave out man/woman robes for this suite. Tommy asked me to sit down. He would now show me why he needed two trips to New York City. He would also show me why he wanted my Star of David necklace.

Tommy had been meeting with a custom jewelry designer. He was recommended by one of Tommy's colleagues from the high school. First, I had to open my birthday gift. He had my Star of David placed and linked to the center of three strands of gold, and made into a bracelet. It was gorgeous! He put it on my wrist. Of course, I grabbed him and cried. I saw a second box, and was almost hysterical. It was a gold necklace. There were two hands joined together, with small diamonds forming a heart in the middle. He then placed the necklace on me. There was more. He bought me a bottle of my favorite fragrance. It was actually his favorite. He loved to nuzzle into my neck and smell and taste me. He admitted to having removed one bracelet and one necklace from my jewelry box. They were used for measurements. Strawberry shortcake for later was also in one of the packages he was carrying. We both love it! Nothing was said, but I noticed he had everything set in 14K yellow gold, no silver.

"Tommy, I didn't buy you a gift."

"Rosey darlin', I wake up every morning and your naked body is curled up against my naked body. I go to sleep every night and your naked body is again curled up against my naked body. You allow me to do my dirty talk in and out of bed. If my flag pole is up, you know I need to go in. You open your legs and welcome me. You understand that I'm a sexual man who needs and loves to fuck. Tom Cat died the morning you rang my door bell and told me how much you loved me. Since that morning, Tommy fucks only you with eyes wide open! So you see Rosey darlin', you give me a gift every day. You give me your mind, heart, soul, and delicious body. You give me life!"

It was an incredible night. We made love, fucked, and ate our strawberry shortcake. In the morning, we left very early for home. Helen knew where we were and couldn't wait to see my new jewelry. She left a text message asking the time our train would get to Montauk, and she would be at the station.

We had a few family conference calls and made a major decision. It had really become too difficult for all of us to drive back and forth between Philly and Montauk so often. The agreement was that on birthdays, anniversaries, and American holidays, like Memorial Day, we would only be together by choice, not commitment. We would plan and arrange mostly for Passover/Easter, Hanukkah/Christmas, and special numbered birthday and anniversaries. I told the family, "We know your doors and lives are open to us and ours are always open to you. Since Tommy and I live on the beach, even if we aren't here, you may still come and enjoy the house. Helen and

Leon are now retired. Tommy is retired from teaching, but will still continue operating the ferry part-time all summer. We all plan on doing some traveling, but never together. We will never take Sugar and Coco to be boarded. When Ian took me to Montauk the first time to stay with Helen and Leon, he was going on vacation with Gwen. Leon exploded. He accused him of treating me like a dog who needed to be boarded."

I'm ashamed to say I had not been to synagogue since 2011. I felt so guilty. I don't even remember what I did on the days of those holidays in 2012. When Ian was alive and things were so awful, he and I always went to synagogue on the High Holidays. The Silver family always had to put on a show.

Ian passed away in May 2012, and I got married in August 2012. I made some inquiries and discovered there is a reform synagogue in Sag Harbor. It's about thirty minutes away. I called and arranged for reserved seats. Tommy, Helen, and Leon had never been to synagogue. This would be a good first time experience. When I went to church with them, they sat together and I sat in the back row and observed. I didn't know how they wanted to arrange this. They asked to sit with me so I wouldn't be alone, and Tommy is now my husband. We all went for the first day of the New Year. Afterwards, I made a traditional Jewish dinner. One has to acquire a taste for gefilte fish and chopped liver. The rest of the meal was chicken matzo ball soup, brisket, potatoes, salad, vegetables, and dessert. Just Tommy and I went back on the Eve of Yom Kippur. They were fascinated and actually picked out a few similarities in our services. I couldn't fast because of medications and my stupid hypoglycemia.

It was now late October, and the fall weather hit pretty hard. Tommy developed what seemed to be just a bad head cold. It was 7:00 in the morning. He touched my arm to wake me up. His hand was on fire. I jumped up and his body was so hot. He was shaking. He had such a bad sore throat that he could hardly speak. We always slept naked, but with top sheets and quilts on the bed. I wrapped him up in a sheet, got the thermometer, and took his temperature. It was 103°. I gave him two Tylenol and called his doctor's answering service. A prescription for an antibiotic was called in for him. Delivery was scheduled. I couldn't let him dehydrate from the high fever. I asked them to also send six bottles of Pedialite.

Have you ever heard of a woman lifting a car when someone she loved was underneath? It would make her adrenalin run. That was me. I had to go from being Tommy's wife to an ICU/Trauma nurse. I was frantic, and had to move just as I would in a hospital ICU.

We have a king-sized bed. Tommy was sweating profusely. The bed under him was wet. I went to his side and pushed him to my side where it was dry. My training taught me how to roll a patient and change the sheets at the same time. Only this time it was harder because the bed is so wide. I was climbing up and down, off and on the bed, and pushing Tommy back and forth. I was no longer naked. I put on a sweat suit that allowed me to move freely.

I knew the next step had to be cold compresses. Tommy was coherent. Therefore, as I went along, I told him everything I was going to do. I couldn't frighten him. I put him naked on his back. I knew there was a time frame of no more than about 60 minutes to get that temperature to drop. If not, I would call the paramedics, and have him taken to the hospital. I pulled out about a dozen washcloths and dipped them in cool water. I put them on his head, neck, chest, stomach, groin on both sides, and his thighs. I kept on touching his body all over, and checking the compresses. As they became warm from his body, I ran back and forth to the bathroom to put them in cool water again. I had him drinking so much that he had to urinate. There was no way he could get up, even with my help. I had to empty a jar and use it as a urine bottle. He was so weak and sick, and didn't want to wet himself or the bed. I held the jar in one hand, and his penis in my other hand. I think he was a bit embarrassed, but we had no choice. I gave him a big kiss on his belly. He smiled at me. His temperature was now down to 101°. For the third time, I rolled him over and changed the sheets. I had a dry towel under him, gave him a sponge bath, and washed his face. I put him in a pair of boxer shorts and a T-shirt. Now he needed to sleep. I was so tired, sore, and short of breath. That was alright. Now I looked at Tommy again as my husband, not a patient. He was sleeping peacefully and out of danger. No hospital!

I called Helen and Leon and told them what was happening. I also explained why I didn't call them sooner. Helen cried. "I knew once he married you, I would not have to spend my life worrying about my brother." They asked if I needed help. I hadn't eaten and was exhausted and dizzy. They were at the house in about thirty minutes. Helen knew about my hypoglycemia. She went directly to the kitchen and prepared a full breakfast for me. Tommy was no longer naked so Leon stayed in the bedroom chair next to him. Helen put me to bed in one of the other bedrooms. They fed the girls and got them out. I asked them to call me as soon as Tommy woke up. I would have to take his temperature again. It came down to 100.6°. I gave him his next dose of medication, and some very cold iced tea. He had to drink.

CHAPTER 3-II

Helen and Leon had been there every day. Tommy was much improved and we were now alone. I had been standing him up in our private bathroom and helping him with a sponge bath. My husband was weak, but hot again. I don't mean fever! He asked me to take him into the shower and join him. Since I could push him across the bed, I knew he would be alright in the shower with me. "Rosey, my body is used to having an orgasm at least once a day. It's now almost a week. My body feels revved up with nowhere to go." He needed release. I was asked to massage him in the shower so he could come. Instead, I got us both out quickly, dried him, and wrapped him in two big towels. I put on my robe and sat him down in his recliner in the upstairs den. After all this time, he needed more than a quickie. "Tommy, put your head back, close your eyes, and relax. I'll take care of you." How could I forget so quickly? My husband has to watch. I gave his Cock, as he calls it, a massage. He had a joyful coming. Me? Normally, I'm so hot for my Tommy that I could have an orgasm just watching him walk into a room. Now, my body was still too tired.

Tommy's temperature was back to normal and so was he. The first thing he asked was, "Did my Cock rise during the time I was so sick?"

"No it didn't. Chances are I don't have the correct definition, but to me it looked like a 'Dangling Participle'. As an English language teacher, feel free to correct me."

It took him about ten days until he said, "Hey Rosey darlin', my Cock is ready to fuck your Pussy." I hate to sound like him, but I was now ready for his Cock to fuck my Pussy. My husband fucked me between one and three times almost every day. I did miss it!

Tommy was now well enough for cake on November 23rd. It was his 67th birthday.

It was spring of 2014. I didn't tell Tommy, but I was having problems with my right knee. I tried to hide it, but one day I fell on the front outside steps. Then it was true confession time. I let him know I had been to see an orthopedic doctor while in Philly. It was the knee that was badly bruised one of the times Ian pushed me out of the bed. It was strongly suggested that I get a knee replacement. Another appointment was made to see the doctor. He and Steffy went with me. Yes, it was time. Arrangements were made to have the surgery in Philly. Tommy and I knew we would be staying at my house for six to eight weeks. It would be better for me because I knew the doctor so well. Also, there were no steps in my house. I would have the surgery on a Friday, and stay in the hospital until Monday. I would then be moved to a rehab for about ten days. My medical insurance would cover everything. We met with a representative from the company. We had to discuss the after care plan for when I came home. I would definitely need a physical therapist. Steffy told her she is a nurse and would take care of the incision. Tommy told her he would take care of my personal needs. The girls stayed with Helen and Leon.

I took Mother, Abby, and Tommy to the hospital. Mother had to check in that morning at 6:00. The doctor came out to greet us. He explained that the surgery would take about three hours, and not to worry. Except for her hypoglycemia, she was in excellent health. The IVs would adjust her sugar levels. A nurse came out to get Mother. She hugged and kissed us. I thought Tommy wasn't going to let go of her. Off she went. Abby and I talked Tommy into going to the cafeteria with us for breakfast. We ate and then came back to the waiting room.

At about 9:00, the doctor came out to speak to us. He said the surgery went very well, but Mother was in ICU/Trauma. She lost a lot of blood, which lowered her blood pressure. She would now be given three units of blood. Tommy turned white and sat back down in his chair. "I'm her husband and would like to see her."

The doctor said, "Follow me." He wasn't in there too long, and was much better when he came out. He told us she was drowsy, but alert and gave him a giant smile. The nurse was so nice and let him kiss her. That evening, she was moved to a room, and we saw her for a few minutes. We took Tommy to the house, and then we went home. He was ready to go back early the next morning. I asked him not to go until later in the day. I explained about all the activities that would take place in the morning. He waited and went at 4:00. He did the same thing on Sunday. On Monday she was moved to the rehab. They both really missed each other.

I knew in rehab Mother would have to be dressed every day. She could only sleep in a nightgown or pajamas. The days are full with physical therapy and rest. I packed a bag for Mother, and Tommy took it to her. Abby, Steven, Hannah, and Sam only went twice during that time. They knew how she would need to work that knee, and rest. They also knew Mother and Tommy didn't do well without each other. He went every day in time to be there for her dinner.

I called Rosey every morning before her therapy sessions began. I let her have the day. I waited until about 4:00 to go be with her. Rosey told the staff I'm her husband. She went into the rehab on a Monday. By Thursday, I was going crazy as I did after being sick. Again, no release for a week. It was as if she could read me. Well, I think she could. That night, she told the aide her husband would take her into the bathroom. He would help her get ready for bed. She would be one less patient for her. Rosey gave me some funny looks. She told me what to bring into the bathroom. We went in and she locked the door. I helped her change. She put her finger over my mouth as if to shush me. In a minute my pants were down. She held me over the toilet so my release would go directly in. There would be no evidence of what took place. She took me in hand and began to massage. We both watched me come. My wife took care of me in the bathroom every evening. Rosey called this manual "pleasuring" and told me about this word.

"My grandmother was a great joke teller. Sometimes in her old age, she loved to use the word fuck. Her favorite joke was about an old woman. She lived on the fifth floor of a tenement apartment building in Brooklyn. The kids outside loved to annoy her. They always threw balls at her window. One day she opened the window and yelled out some Yiddish obscenities. A boy yelled back, "Fuck you lady." She yelled back again. "It would be such a mahiaya (spelling iffy)." Translation is, "It would be such a pleasure."

After being there for a week, Steffy and I took her home. She was great! The activities now began. While Rosey was in rehab, I had some changes made in the bathroom. I had a high rise toilet installed, and bars put on the walls of the stall shower for support. The physical therapist came three days a week, and worked with her for an hour. She allowed me to watch her do the exercises. Rosey had to do them twice a day, every day. I helped her and worked with her. She was determined to heal and go back to our life in Montauk. Steffy came a few days later and removed the surgical staples from her knee. She said the incision was healing well and looked good. When the physical therapist thought she was ready, I took Rosey outside with a walker. I took care of her meals, and did the laundry. Many evenings, we played 500 Rummy. It was usually 10,000 Rummy. She never let me win.

Steffy suggested that I help her mother into the shower every day, especially after doing the exercises. She said the warm water was a good healing tool. I didn't have to be told twice. I guess Steffy thought I was going to put her in and just stand by to be sure she was safe. Hell no! Steffy had no idea that we showered together every day. For the first few weeks, Rosey pleasured me in the shower. She said her body didn't require anything yet. My blessed wife was happy to just take care of me. By the fifth week, my Rosey darlin' was ready. She got into bed naked again and said, "I'm crotchless." I knew exactly what she wanted, and possibly in multiples. My wife was finally ready for her jack hammer!

Helen and Leon called us almost every evening. They were anxious to see us. Tommy and I decided it would also be good to see them. It had been several weeks, and we all missed each other. We asked them to come and stay at the house with us. They brought Sugar and Coco with them. When the girls saw Tommy, they were so excited. They jumped all over him and almost licked his face off. Me? I don't think they noticed I was there. When we got back to Montauk, Tommy took me into the whirlpool tub inside and hot tub outside. Oh boy! We fucked up a storm in those two places. Of course, both places were therapeutic for my knee.

Tommy was so sick, and then I had surgery. We decided to make a few changes in our life, but what? Tommy and I deny each other nothing. We are so into each other's mind, heart, soul, and spiritual body. Once in a while I do make a request of Tommy. It's very rare and he knows when and how it will take place.

It was winter, and we were both wearing warm sweat suits. I was still upstairs and Tommy was downstairs getting our coats ready. I called him to come up. I took him by the hand and led him to the bed. We always lead each other around by the hand. He knew it wasn't more sex. I had him lie down on his back, and I climbed up on my mountain. Then I gave him kissy-wissys and smoochie-woochies all over his face. He knew what's coming, and it's not one of us. I suggested a change of scenery about every few months. "We live here, which is great, and then my house in Philly when necessary. How about if we leave Montauk for a hotel close by? No, not the ones where Tom Cat went! Perhaps we could go to the Hamptons, Sag Harbor, or Patchogue. It was great when we stayed overnight in New York City for our anniversary. How about going on the Internet and look for a classy hotel in each town. I'm sure they all have one. A reservation for a 3:00 check-in would be perfect. We can call for room service and have dinner brought to the room at 4:00. Spending a night away from home would be fun. We don't need a change of scenery for our sex life, but we need it for our everyday life. We can do role-playing and pretend all sorts of things. I may be talking out of the top of my head, but it's just an idea. What do you think?"

"It sounds great to me! Let's do it!"

Our first reservation was made for a hotel in Sag Harbor. We checked in at 3:00. We looked at the room service menu, and ordered dinner to be brought at about 4:00. Tommy saw me carrying a bag that was not familiar. He didn't know I went on the Internet and found sex games which required costumes. One for me and one for him! I also took my small flowered satchel. I packed us each a set of fresh underwear for the next morning.

The room was elegant. It should be for $300. We managed not to get into any sexual activities. Rosey needed me prime for her later plan. We sat on the lounging sofas and talked. Dinner wasn't brought to the room until after 5:00. That's late for me. When I was teaching, I came home at 3:30 and ate dinner every day at 4:00. After Rosey moved in with me, she continued on my schedule. We rested and then Rosey handed me a bag.

She told me to go into the bathroom. I was to close the door and not dare come out until she called my name. "No cheating and no peeking!" When I came out, I was to be wearing only a special pair of briefs that were in the bag. Oh my God! It's a G-string with the front pouch made of a black see-through fabric. It was so small. I wondered if I could tuck myself into it, even when soft. Then she called me. I opened the door, walked out, and saw her standing next to the bed. I was speechless and breathless! I was experiencing every man's fantasy, and it was only for me.

Rosey was wearing large red crystal earrings. On her breasts were matching pasties. As my eyes moved down, there was a red crystal in her naval. Lower, I saw she was wearing a black lace garter belt. At the crotch, there was a red crystal emblem hanging off the belt. Attached to the belt were black fish net stockings. She was wearing red stiletto heels. She looked at me and in a very sweet, sultry voice said, "Don't you want to touch?" I didn't think I could without having a very wet orgasm all over her or inside my G-string. I had some control, but this was asking a lot. I would just have to try.

CHAPTER 3-12

I walked over to her and started removing the items. I began with the earrings, the pasties, and the crystal in her naval. Then I got to the danger point. How could I keep from just shooting out? Alright, Tommy, keep trying! I decided to stay away from her crotch area as long as possible. I sat down on the floor. One at a time, I removed her shoes and stockings. With each stocking, I massaged from her thigh down to her toes. I was still trying to keep it together, but I don't think she was. This was a crazy way to seduce me. Did she give it a thought that she might not have control? I then removed the emblem from her crotch. Another surprise! Except in magazines, I had never seen a woman wearing a garter belt. I didn't know it was crotchless. She was breathing so heavy, and her pelvis was rocking. She was fucking hot and horny for me! I pulled the belt off. Neither one of us could hold on much longer. We were standing on the floor directly next to the bed.

I once saw a couple in a movie fucking in a position new to me. Perhaps tonight I'll give it a try. The man has to be much heavier than the woman. That is a perfect description of me and Rosey. She has fucked up a few of our fucks, so maybe it's my turn. I put her on the bed in a weird position. I had her back on the bed, knees bent, and her legs dangling. I slid my body and hand between her legs. Her crotch was already wet. I entered my flag pole. It was such a great, tight fit. Now I decided to try the next part. I lifted her off the bed, and she instinctively wrapped her legs around me and held on. I gently pushed, and her back was against the wall. My flag pole was still tight inside her. I just kept on pumping in and out. It was great! Rosey always says I pant with my mouth open, and I sound like I'm gasping for breath. This time we were both so loud. I'm sure we could be heard in China. We came together and then got back on the bed. This was a great, great fuck, but not for me. I'm too old for this. We already have many different positions for people our age.

We both woke up about 6:00, had a great older folk's fuck, and then took a shower together. We got dressed and left the hotel room at 9:00. Breakfast was being served in their dining room. After eating we left for home. Rosey was carrying a small brown paper bag. I saw her throw it into a lobby trash can. She said it was all of the costume pieces from the night before. No reruns.

I just had another birthday and I'm 72 years old. It was now the fall of 2014. I'm not sure why, but I didn't plan to go to synagogue again. There was something Abby and I had to do. We had not gone to the grave of our parents for a few years. Tommy was going to drive me back to Philly for a few days. Abby and I had a ritual. Each of us typed up a long letter to them. She never knew what was in mine, and I never knew what was in hers. We told them stories of our lives, and reminded them of things we shared. The envelopes were sealed and we took them to the cemetery. We put them on top of the double gravestone. They were typed, and no names were mentioned. Daddy and Mommy knew they were from us. I sat at the computer the night before Tommy and I were leaving for Philly.

It's now November 23, 2014 and my Tommy is 68 years old, and still hot, hot, hot!

The mailman always brings our mail and puts it into a lock box. He has the combination. There was a beautiful invitation just for Tommy. The church was sponsoring a men's night out for Christmas. Tommy believed it was being done to raise funds for the church. Leon was also invited. I had never seen either one of them in a suit and tie. Tommy always wore nice slacks, shirt, and tie to school, but very rarely a jacket. At our wedding, he was dressed in beach clothes. Leon was always wearing a uniform shirt or casual clothes. First there would be a Mass at 4:00, which is my husband's dinnertime. He would have to wait because dinner was scheduled for 6:00. Tommy knew there would also be speeches. He felt terrible because we did different things alone during the day, but never in the evenings. We were always together. Tommy looked so handsome! I told him he looked so delicious that I wanted to eat him up. No time for that. I had to wait until he came home.

That was a night to remember! I got a text from Tommy close to 9:00.

"Rosey darlin', evening was nice. There was no alcohol with dinner. The time came when they were looking for donations, so I wrote a check. Then they began sitting around smoking cigars and drinking brandy. Time to go! Leon also wrote a check and left with me. I'm not accustomed to being away from you in the evening. I miss you! Hope you miss me. This is close to our evening fucking time. How about if you fill up the whirlpool bathtub and get naked. Be home in about 20 minutes. Meet you in the bathroom with my flag pole and jack hammer."

I really did miss him. Our normal is that we have sex about three times a day while we still can. It was usually at 5:30 in the morning before Tommy went to work. His flag pole was always up and stiff with the sun or clouds. Why waste a flag pole? Now that he's retired, the time varies. Midday can be any time, depending on plans. One of us usually catches up with the other. It can happen in any room of the house. Early evening or night, we always have our sex in the bedroom. That's when we call it love making. It's when we have our most active sex.

We do it all! There's always an incredible fuck, but somehow it's different at night. I think there is more emotion. We are both so happy with our marriage and our life together. It's always like a celebration of our love at the end of every day. Then we curl up into each other and go to sleep.

Tommy sometimes gets really frustrated. He can only have one big massive come, and I can have multiples. I make it up to him because he taught me about the after play. He's always ultra sensitive, and lets me massage his Dangling Participle. I begin by taking my fingers and walk up his legs into his groin. I make him wild. I tease him, and then close in to give him a little bitty come. We both know there will be a time when his flag pole will always be just a Dangling Participle.

I did what he asked. I got naked and filled the tub. I heard the door open and him set the house alarm. He flew up the steps with his flag pole already naked. He sure did take his clothes off quickly. I hope he didn't do it in the car. We got into the tub and couldn't wait for him to enter. I loved it best when he went hard and deep, and he always does. Sometimes it feels like his entire body is inside of me. This time I became verbal and panted out words. "Oh, Tommy, go deeper." I was so lost into myself that I didn't realize he was just about ready to come. I usually know by the pulsating of his Cock and his sounds. "Rosey, if I go any deeper my Cock will be in your throat." We both began to laugh. He fell out of me and ended up coming in the water. "Rosey darlin', you just fucked up such a good fuck." We got out of the tub, put in our cleansing pellet, and turned on the filter. We went into the other bathroom and showered. Then I played my game with him again to release some droplets. I don't know why, but I love playing with his body. Once when we were in the tub, I got a bit wild. We splashed so much water that we flooded the bathroom floor.

The longer Tommy and I were together, new habits developed between us. Normally, after our nighttime sex session, we roll over into each other and fall asleep. Sometimes, we just cuddle and hold hands. That's when we have quiet discussions. One night I told him he is so handsome. "Rosey, nobody has ever called me handsome. I was always average or possibly less than average looking. Through the years as I dated, I was only known as giving a good fuck because I'm so big. I think Cindy loved me, but she never called me handsome. How do you look and see me that way? I have wiry hair, wrinkled skin on my face, and a mustache covering the scar on my upper lip. You must know about my lip."

"I think you are handsome because I see you through my eyes of love. Your hair is fun to play with, and you like when I massage your scalp. I don't see wrinkles on your face. I only see and touch the face of the man I love. Of course I know about your lip. I love you so much that I devour your mouth. Whatever has happened to your lip doesn't matter to me. It's who you are. My handsome husband! You are also beautiful. I know there are words you don't like, and that's one of them. Your mind, heart, soul, and spiritual body are beautiful."

Tommy took my hand and put it on his crotch and asked, "What do you call this?"

"Cute and adorable!" That's the worst! He hates those words being used for anything about a grown man. That's why I said it. As I did, I got out of bed and ran down the hall. He ran after me, grabbed me, and carried me back to the bed. At first I thought he was angry, but I couldn't have been more wrong.

There was no flag pole, but Tommy started at my face and worked his way down. He made passionate love to me like never before. It wasn't supposed to be about sex, but I did come twice. There is only one word to describe what he did that night and how I felt. The word was "exquisite".

Tommy and I had such a good time when we went to the hotel for a night in Sag Harbor. We went about three more times to different hotels. Each time I had costumes and games.

Once I made him a cowboy. He had to wear chaps made of soft flannel with nothing underneath. I wore a mini skirt made of the same fabric with nothing underneath. Another time I was a French maid and had him wear nothing but a beret. It's a good thing I am the elder of the two. If he was five years older than me, I might cause him to have a fatal heart attack. We didn't play too many more games, but did enjoy an occasional night at a hotel. We had dinner brought to the room at 4:00. It always ended with strawberry shortcake. Each time, I took along a small flowered satchel with fresh underwear for the next day.

CHAPTER 3-13

The weeks, months, and years pass by so quickly. Everybody in my life was doing well. Helen and Leon were doing some traveling. They had never been away from Montauk except to see Broadway shows in New York City. Holidays came and went. Both families always merged when possible. We stayed home a lot, fucked a lot, and enjoyed our time together.

Tommy and I decided to plan on a few trips for the beginning of 2015. No summer resorts with a beach. We live on the beach in a summer resort. We decided on Las Vegas. We're not big on gambling, but we spent five days there. It was not my first time, but it was the first for Tommy. He had never been in a casino. We separated after Tommy got his bearings. I only play slot machines. He wanted to try his hand at blackjack and roulette. We had cell phones to stay connected. Tommy loved the food buffets, and he ate so much. There were buffets with breakfast $2.99, lunch $6.99, and then way up for dinner. It depended on what you wanted to eat. Every night we ate dinner in a fine restaurant in different casinos. Tommy also got to see the topless dancers. We always went to the very late show. I knew Tommy's flag pole would rise. I think he has his Cock and jack hammer on a battery pack. They never failed us!

Sam is now 21 years old and attending college in Marietta, Georgia. We made plans to visit with him for a few days in April. He told me he has a girlfriend. She is looking forward to meeting his grandparents.

We are not just sexual beings. There is a lot more to us and our life than sex. In all seasons, we do our errands and shopping together during the day. We love the malls, and eat lunch in the food courts. Inside walking is great in bad weather. Sometimes we stop for a gourmet coffee and rest on a bench. Helen and I are still making jewelry. We go to flea or farmers markets to sell things we make. While we sit at our tables, Tommy and Leon like to walk around. Sometimes they buy something that gets their attention. Sometimes they look at the young girls who get their attention. We very rarely go to see a movie. The theatres are always so crowded; people talk, and phones are ringing. Tommy and I have a large projector screen in the living room. That's where we watch movies. More times than not, Helen and Leon are with us. She and I cook together inside, and the men do the cooking outside. Tommy still likes a good hot meal a few nights a week at 4:00. I have introduced him to sweet and sour meatballs. He loves them! In the nice weather, he likes to grill. He always has his girls under foot begging. He does give them something, but never at the table. That's a bad habit. We also go out to some of our favorite restaurants.

When Tommy and I go in the hot tub, we're naked. Helen and Leon love it in there, but we all wear bathing suits. My Tommy is such a clown. He knows Helen is such a prude. He likes to tease her. One night he dared her to take off her bathing suit, and we would all follow. Of course, she said a little prayer for her brother and crossed herself.

Before we go upstairs to begin our sexual rituals, downstairs time is quiet. When it's hot outside, we have the air conditioner on. We both like hot tea in any kind of temperature. I make two pots. Tommy found them at a flea market. They are just big enough for two cups. Each one has different color flowery paintings. There is a small strand of pearls that wraps from the lid to the spout. I make peppermint for Tommy, and spearmint for me. Sometimes we have strawberry shortcake.

We take turns on the computer. I write love letters to Tommy, and he writes poems to me. Next to me, I think poetry is his passion. They are typed, but we always sign our name with a little heart. Afterwards, we put them into the trinket box Helen and Leon gave us on our wedding day. We read separately, but sometimes find a book we want to share. We sit together, sometimes under a throw, and read out loud to each other. I like it most when Tommy and I cuddle while he reads me literary love stories. We do like a good movie and watch some comedies. Many nights we only watch all the world news on television. Tommy sometimes falls asleep in the recliner with a book on his chest. His reading glasses are always almost in his mouth. I'll never forget the first time I saw him like that. It was the day I seduced him in the car. Of course, before we go upstairs, the girls get a snack and their last outing. They sleep in their beds in the upstairs den.

Our schedules still include what Tommy did alone before I moved into the house and we got married. There are many things we do outside, weather permitting. Tommy takes care of the flowers, and we now have a red rose garden. We walk on the beach with his girls, and go bike riding in the evening. In nice weather, we always sit on the beach or on our ocean side patio. Nights usually include ice cream. Tommy put in beautiful different color lights and they shine onto the ocean. I surprised Tommy and had delivered a new chaise lounge. It's a double so we can sit together. Cindy bought the property to build a house on the beach. I don't know why. Tommy doesn't like the ocean water except on the ferry. One day I'll go out with him. I've been to the lighthouse, but still haven't been to Block Island.

Now that he and Leon are retired, they both play cards in the community room of the church. My friends in Philly would be happy to know I have made a few friends here. I have taught them how to play canasta. We usually play at my house when the men are at the church. I'm always in touch with my Philly friends. Tommy and I have gotten together with them when we visit. We have invited them to come here, but so far nobody has.

We began making some holidays a bit different. I convinced Leon to help me do an egg hunt on Easter morning after church. It would be for us to hide an egg with a gift inside for our wives. We invited Rosey's family to have Easter dinner with us. That year it didn't interfere with the food of Passover. Sometimes they do run into each other. They're not kosher so they ate everything. We made turkey, not ham. We made them crazy. Leon and I placed plastic eggs inside and outside the house. Every one of them participated in the hunt, and had so much fun before dinner. We put gift cards in for everybody to restaurants in Philly. Helen and my Rosey got a pair of diamond stud earrings.

The next holiday was Passover. We four Montaukians, as I named us, were going to a Seder at Steven's house. Before we left home, Rosey took cereal, bread, pretzels, and a few other foods to the church. She didn't clean the entire kitchen, but she did her part and I went along with it all. I was adjusted as Rosey does it every year since we're together. Now the family decided to get even with me for having them go on an egg hunt. They made me, and only me, play "find the matzo". A board is wrapped in foil and hidden somewhere in the house. The tradition is the youngest child is supposed to do the hunt. They followed me as I went through the house. Each yelled if I was getting hot or cold. I finally gave up. It was in the bathtub. The meal Hannah made was superb. She stuffed a chicken with matzo, not bread. I like fried matzo. Rosey makes it for me and adds cheese, onions, and mushrooms. It comes out like an omelet. The Passover cookies and cakes are different and delicious. I especially like the rainbow cakes. I think they have a touch of marzipan in them and they're covered with chocolate.

Another birthday for me on August 31, 2015, and I'm really getting to be my Tommy's old lady. I am now 73 years old.

I was getting so daring with my husband. His body is so clean and delicious, but I convinced him to go for a pedicure. He fought with me all the way to the nail salon. Once he saw other men, he had it done and made an announcement on the way home. "Hey Rosey, I think I want to have the cute little girl make house calls just for me when I'm home alone." He loved it!

One night, I talked him into fucking me in his car. He drove to a dark isolated area. It was a late summer night. He was wearing Bermuda shorts. I was wearing a mini dress with just bikini panties underneath. His car is a Lincoln and very spacious. First he moved his driver's side seat back. Then he tilted the steering wheel forward, and out of the way. My hands went into his pants and pulled them down. I pulled my panties off as I lifted my dress. By that time, he had a terrific hard on. He was hot, horny, and petrified! He was scared of getting caught, but loving this crazy adventure. This was the first time I heard my Tommy whimper as he was coming. He really was scared, but I know he'll do it again.

We always like to find different things to do. Rosey bought a bread maker and pasta maker. Helen and Leon now have dinner with us every Friday evening. Rosey makes a traditional Shabbat dinner. Each week, I make the noodles for the chicken soup. I also make a challah bread. She has brought a set of candle holders from her house. She lights Shabbat candles and says a prayer. It's so interesting. She covers her head with a lace doily, closes her eyes, and waves her hands over the candles. The love and acceptance between us is so special!

Rosey's Star of David is now the bracelet I had made for her on our first wedding anniversary. I have kept my wedding promise to my wife. I never take off the Miraculous Medal she gave me. I just think I'm probably sinning big time. Rosey is my wife, but I fuck her while wearing the medal.

Another birthday for my darling husband. It is November 23, 2015, and he is now 69 years old. I can't believe how quickly time is passing. We have now completed Hanukkah and Christmas 2015, and are getting ready for the new year of 2016.

Everybody made their own plans for New Year's Eve. Helen and Leon were going away for the holiday. Tommy and I chose to attend a house party at the home of my old friends from the country club. They are Eric and Nancy Holmes. They were anxious to meet Tommy. I told them he is a recovering alcoholic. We never go any place where alcohol will be served. Nancy told me she and Eric have what is called a "dry house". A friend died in a car accident many years ago after a party where everyone was drinking. She wasn't happy to hear Tommy has a problem, but happy to know we would come to their party. They just loved my Tommy. He was a gentleman as always in public. The entire evening was clean. Nobody said one curse word. It was wonderful. We invited them to Montauk when the weather is nice. They said they had never been there and would love to visit. We spent a few days in Philly and got to see the family.

CHAPTER 3-14

Winter in Montauk isn't very pleasant. Helen and Leon called and said they needed some cold fresh air. We made arrangements to meet them on one of the piers, and just take a walk. Helen said we could go back to their condo afterwards for lunch. Tommy and I bundled up and drove to the pier area. Helen and Leon were waiting for us.

Tommy and Rosey were walking arm in arm. We were directly behind them. Suddenly, Tommy made a strange noise and fell onto the pier. Rosey fell with him. His eyes were open briefly and he looked at her. She was holding him in her arms with his head on her chest. She began screaming. We ran over and Leon called the paramedics. As a nurse, I think she knew the look. That fast, our Tommy was gone. She couldn't stop screaming. As she held him, she rocked him. When the paramedics came, she was still holding Tommy, screaming and rocking. She began kissing his face, mouth, and eyes. They asked her to let go of him and she refused. I sat down on the pier crying. "Rosey, let him go. He's now safe in the arms of Jesus." The paramedics wanted to take him. I had to physically pry her hands and body off of him.

As she was still screaming, Leon told the paramedics Rosey is his wife. He gave them information they needed, along with ours. We took her back to our condo. She was shaking so badly. I knew she was cold. I wrapped her up in a warm blanket, and

Leon called her family. Steven told Leon they would be here as quickly as possible. It's about a four hour ride from Philly. By 5:00, they were all here. She stopped screaming. She actually became very quiet, but was still rocking. Steven is a big guy. He took her on his lap and rocked with her.

She looked at Steven. "My son, you're a doctor. You have to fix this for me. Bring him back for just five minutes. He went so quickly. I didn't get the chance to say sweet things into his ear as he passed. You know how important that is to me. Steven, the last thing he heard was me screaming. I let him pass knowing he caused me pain. I need to do this over again. I need him for just five minutes for a do-over. Steven, how will I breathe or live without him? Steven, do you think I'm being punished? When Ian died, I hoped he heard Gwen screaming. I said, 'May he not rest in peace.' Is this now a payback from someone?"

"Mother, you know I can't bring Tommy back. Look around the room. See how many of us are here for you and love you. We'll help you get through this. Helen said Tommy's eyes were open briefly, and he looked directly into yours. Therefore, the last thing he saw was your love. You were holding him in your arms against your chest. I'm sure he didn't hear you scream. I believe the last thing he heard was your heart beating with love for him. You're not being punished. Ian did terrible things to you and the family. He really should not be allowed to rest in peace. God understands and knows the truth."

Steven went into a bag he was carrying. He took out a hypodermic needle, and injected her with a sedative. Leon and Steven put her in my bed. She slept for about three hours. When she woke up, she asked to be taken to the house. "Please let me go there. I have to lie down in our bed on his side. Maybe I'll feel him. I know I'll smell him. He always smelled so clean and sweet. We became spiritual before our wedding day. That means we became one, and will always be connected even after death. He'll know I'm there in our bed." Abby took her by the hand as always. They agreed that Abby, Steven, and Steffy would take her. I asked them to pack some clothes because I would keep her here with Leon and me. I also asked them to bring Tommy's girls.

When they returned, she fell asleep again wearing one of Tommy's sweatshirts. She brought it from the house. She wouldn't take it off. While she slept, I made some food and drinks. This wasn't easy for me. I lost my beloved brother. I was trying to hold myself together. Someone called from the hospital. I was told Tommy passed away from an embolism, a blood clot to his brain. It hit him quickly, and took him quickly. I told them I would call them back in a few hours.

I let it be their decision if they wanted to stay at a hotel or Rosey's house. They chose a hotel and returned very early. Rosey slept until morning and asked me to do something for her. She seemed almost like her normal self. She wanted me to get Tommy's wedding band, gold watch, and the medal she gave him as a wedding gift. She wants to wear all three. Also, she asked to have the book of poetry he was given as a gift at the school. That was his favorite. He read it over and over, sometimes out loud to her. It is sitting with a pair of his reading glasses, which she would also like to have. They are on the table next to the recliner upstairs. I would get them for her.

Rosey listened as I told her family I would have to make the funeral arrangements. She wouldn't know the proper way of making a Catholic funeral, and arranging for a funeral Mass. She interrupted, "Helen, one day Tommy and I had a general discussion of what he wanted if he passed away before me. He asked not to be taken to the funeral home where your mom washed the floors in the embalming room. Please have him taken to a different place. He also said he didn't want a viewing in any funeral home. He wanted to be viewed in the church. His burial cover your mom made for him is in the bedroom closet on the top shelf. You know he wants to have it. Please do as he asked."

"Absolutely, Rosey darlin'." Her family had questions about our mom. Rosey actually got herself together enough to tell them the story. I couldn't stay and listen.

Rosey mentioned my mom. I know Tommy told her the ugly story before they got married. Under normal circumstances, I would be furious with her. Not now. I'm sure she doesn't remember that nobody was ever to speak of her in my presence.

She loved Tommy so much! I said prayers for them to be together for a long time. Many couples live to be in their nineties. They both had lonely empty marriages. Finally, when she was 70 and Tommy 65 years old, they found the most incredible love and life with each other. I knew about their sex life. Tommy was always a gentleman. In his young days, before and after Cindy, he loved to brag about his sexual escapades. With Rosey, it was different. It was almost like that part of his life with her was sacred. Sometimes Rosey shared personal sexual stories with me. It was like girlie talk. They both actually believed to be spiritual as one.

"Family, I must tell you a story. Now is the right time. You know I was 14 and Tommy was 10 years old when we came to Montauk. We were almost like mother and child, not sister and brother. He was sometimes confused. He knew we didn't have a daddy, but I was his sister and he was my brother. He sometimes called me Sister Helen. I began calling him Brother Tommy. It continued until now. Tommy was so cute and adorable. His hair was reddish brown and his eyes so bright and blue. When he was 10, I got him ready for school. That first winter, I buttoned his coat, and put on his hat and scarf. He liked putting on his own gloves. As he left, I kissed him on his forehead. One morning he said, 'Sister Helen, I'm now 11 years old. I'm a big boy! I can button my own coat, and put on my hat and scarf. Please don't call me cute and adorable anymore. Those are words for a baby.'

"Leon and I are old hat. We are also madly in love with each other, but don't share issues with anyone. We just quietly work them through without outside discussions. It was different with Tommy and Rosey. They were two seniors, in a new and wonderful love and life. Sometimes they needed adjustments. I think more than some other couples. Rosey is as soft and easy going as silk. Tommy was too many good things to list, but still had a rough side. His voice was low, deep and raspy. Sometimes folks took his sound as tough, but not his words.

"I know Rosey sometimes told Tommy he was cute and adorable. He hated those words. He would tell her they were not words to be used for a grown man. She did it anyway just to razz him. I believe you all knew Tommy loved ice cream. He believed it was a good neutralizing tool to be eaten in a serious mood. There were times Tommy and Rosey ran into a snag. While it had already been resolved with love, they sometimes wanted to share it with us.

"One evening, they showed up at my door carrying four ice cream sundaes. They needed to share something special with me. It stemmed from Tommy's childhood. It was the first winter they were together. Tommy was getting ready to go to work at the school. He took out his warmest coat. He put it on and Rosey reached out to button it for him. She was also holding his hat and scarf. He pushed her away. 'Wife Rosey, I'm a grown man. I can button my own coat and put on my own hat and scarf.' She began crying and walked away from him. He went after her, grabbed her, and held her. It was a flash back, from the age of 10, which brought him to that moment. He explained it to her. They both cried. He then brought her close, then pulled back. 'Wife Rosey, please button my coat today and every day. I also need you to put on my hat and scarf. I can do the gloves. Just don't kiss me on my forehead. Kiss me as you always do every morning when you walk me to the door.' I was so touched that night.

"After I compose myself, I must tell you one more thing. We met on the pier today and we all hugged. Tommy said, 'Sister Helen, I still let Rosey button my coat. She does a good job. Look at her coat. I buttoned it and didn't match the buttons to the holes. It's all crooked. She refused to let me change it.' Thanks to Rosey, my Brother Tommy passed away with his coat properly buttoned. He was also wearing the hat and scarf she placed on him. He always put on his own gloves. I'm sure they shared an incredible kiss before leaving the house."

CHAPTER 3-15

An obituary was placed in the Montauk newspaper.

Thomas Patrick Monahan (Tommy)

It is with the deepest sorrow that we announce the passing of Thomas Patrick Monahan (Tommy) on Monday, January 18, 2016. Tommy was 69 years old. He was a resident of Montauk since 1957 when he arrived from Ireland with his mother, Emma Monahan, and his sister Helen Monahan Walsh.

Tommy was an English teacher at Montauk High School until his retirement in 2013. He also operated the ferry to Block Island for many summers. He was a known, respected, and very well liked gentleman.

Tommy is survived by his beloved wife Lorraine Stone Monahan (Rosey), his sister Helen Monahan Walsh, and his brother-in-law Leon Walsh.

He will be missed by his children Stephanie, Steven and Hannah Silver, his grandson Samuel Silver, and Abigail and Scott Rubin.

Funeral arrangements and Mass are pending.

We all knew it would be too much for Rosey to have the viewing one evening and the Mass the next morning. Everything would be at one time. All was arranged. Rosey's family stayed the entire time with us. The night before the funeral, Steffy, Steven, and Abby asked if they could speak to me privately. They all offered to allow me to let go and cry. They knew I was hanging by a thread. I did just that. Then they told me there had been a discussion at the hotel. They agreed that after the funeral and burial, they should take the three of us back to Philly. We could stay at Rosey's house. They believed we should leave Montauk for a while. Rosey heard us talking and walked into the room. "I want to go back to the house in Philly. I have to sleep where Tommy slept. Don't forget we are spiritual. He will find me in either bed where we slept together. I'll let you know when I can go back to the beach house. There are some personal things there that I need."

She asked something else of us. "My Tommy was Catholic, but I'm Jewish. My faith says I need to wear a cut black mourning ribbon for thirty days. Will you please find a rabbi who will come here, place a ribbon on me, cut it, and say the prayers? Also, in my tradition, Tommy's personal things in his house should not be disrupted or moved for thirty days. Will you please honor these requests?"

Again, Helen responded, "Absolutely, Rosey darlin'."

We were able to find Rabbi Daniel from Sag Harbor. He agreed to come, and arrived the following day. We all stood with her while he placed the ribbon on Tommy's sweatshirt. She was still wearing it over her clothes. He was a kind and understanding man, and did what was necessary. We asked if he would attend Tommy's funeral to help get her through. "Yes, of course."

Steven gave Rosey a lot of medication before we left for the funeral. He and Steffy weren't sure how she would react when seeing him in the casket. Steven told her she couldn't touch him. She did put her hand to her mouth, kiss her fingers, and gently place them on his mouth. She was pleased to see he had the burial cover on over his clothes. As the people began to arrive, she stood by the casket at Tommy's head. She spoke to nobody, and responded to nobody. The entire time before the Mass, she just kept leaning over and quietly talking to him.

"I'm so sorry that you heard me scream as you were passing. It just happened so fast that I was in shock. It's alright now. Steven explained everything to me. He said the last thing you saw was the love I have for you in my eyes. You were also in my arms with your head on my chest. I'm now sure the last thing you heard was my heart beating with love for you. Since we became spiritual as one, I have no doubt that we will be together very soon. You'll find me because I'll be wearing the fragrance you like. You can nuzzle into my neck to smell and taste me like you always did. Reach out your hand to me and I'll reach mine out to you. Then we'll be together and go to hotels again. We can stay overnight and have more fun sex. I'll bring my small flowered satchel with fresh underwear for both of us. You know how fussy I am about fresh underwear. There will be dinner at 4:00 every day. Perhaps in our new world together, there will be strawberry shortcake. You doubted me when I said you are handsome. Everyone here agrees. I'm so excited, my husband. Tommy I love you and can't wait for you to come and take me. I guess that's how it will happen. You know I can't breathe or live without you. I was told not to touch you. I'll just wait and then touch and taste you all over. I know how much you love it when I kiss your belly. You know it means I'm working my way down to you know where. I hope nobody can hear us. In the meantime, with your help, I will take my mind elsewhere and not dwell on missing you so much."

Steven and Steffy were both holding her. They heard what she was telling Tommy. Does she really believe he can come and take her? She never cried. When they took her away, she was smiling. Was this the drugs or just the beginning of her insanity?

When the limousine arrived at the cemetery, she refused to get out. Quietly she spoke to Sam, "Tommy and I are spiritual as one. We both still speak to each other. He has instructed me to stay in the car during his burial. It would be too much for me to see his casket put into the ground. Please just stay here with me." We watched and saw Sam sobbing as he held her. She was fine!

We went back, packed up everything, including Tommy's girls, and drove to Philly. When we arrived at the house, Steffy and Abby took Rosey into the bedroom where she fell asleep. We all worked and made food and coffee for everyone.

"Rosey darlin'. Finally you are alone!"

"Tommy, my husband, is that you? I hope you heard the last thing I said before they closed the casket. 'In the meantime, with your help, I will take my mind elsewhere and not dwell on missing you so much.' Please help me!"

"Yes, Rosey darlin'. That's why I'm here. I have a lot to tell you, but I don't know how much time they will allow. Listen closely and carefully.

"I'm so proud of how you got through my funeral as I asked. Now you will play the game of not having any memory of me. Chances are they will place you in a mental facility for a while. Be smart! Accept no medications, only therapy through talking. You need to be clear headed. When you go home, you must live your life to the fullest. Be with friends and family. Be social as you were before moving to Montauk. Play cards, Mah Jong; go to the theatre; and always have Sister Helen style your hair. Go back to having breakfast on Fridays with our grandson Sam. Have Saturday brunch with Steffy and Abby.

"I'm in the world just called 'spirit'. I've only been here five days. A few nice folks welcomed me and gave me a tour. I was then taken to a conference room. Quickly I learned there are no religious affiliations here. You have God, but I have three powers who run everything. They are Fate and Destiny, who are men. The third is Lady Karma. She seems to be the one who controls more than the others. I was given a manual and asked to study it carefully. There is so much to learn that my head

is spinning. I'm so confused! Surely, I will confuse you. They emphasized one thing I must always remember. 'When the time is right.' Eventually we will be together, but when they decide the time is right.

"There are rules of living here that are different. You may replace me with another man. Here, I'm not permitted to have another. You were my spiritual wife, and I can only have you, when the time is right.

"I never want you to feel pain from my physical loss. So now I will tell you where to take your mind. You don't need anybody to help you with a do-over. You will create it yourself.

"Go into the private confines of your mind. That space will belong to only you. Go in and out as the need presents itself. Just as Helen put us together, she will match you with a man named Jake. He will be the one to take your mind elsewhere. You will build an entire life in there with him. It will be based on memories of me. He will be there any time you need him. You will go into the confines of your mind with him, but he will be me. You will take every memory of me into a do-over with Jake. He must fit my exact physical description. You will be with Jake, but see me. Also, he must have my exact voice, except for the brogue. Taking me alone into the confines of your mind will only cause pain. Being with Jake will give you a new temporary life. It will only be your private place with him, and not to be shared. You must allow yourself to believe I have been replaced with a man who makes you happy.

"Create your life with Jake. Use memories of what we did together. Love him like you love me. Let him love you as I love you. Call it making love or fucking, but do it with him as you did with me. Let him have a big cock to fit into your beautiful pussy. It doesn't matter who is on top or who is on bottom. When his body is inside of yours, try to come together. Always with eyes open seeing love. No matter where you are or what you're doing in this fantasy, you will only see me. My wiry hair, and my dark ruddy-colored face. You will feel the imperfection on my lip when you kiss him. Taste Jake and let him taste you. Just remember, there is no Jake, only your husband Tommy. But Jake is the one who will take your mind elsewhere. We are already spirits. That's why I'm able to speak to you.

"Rosey darlin', please give me a few things in your fantasy. You know I wanted children. Jake is going to be a widower, age 77 years old. Just as I had a cold, almost sexless marriage, I want him to tell you of having the same. You are the woman who gave me love and incredible sex. You will give it to him. Of course, through me. No jealousy here. I must repeat that Jake is only a fantasy to take your mind elsewhere. I want Jake's late wife to be named Cindy. Let them have two sons. One must be gay. That's because of all the people who said I was gay. They based it on my marriage history, and riding around Montauk with poodles. The other son must be married. The family is Jewish, like you. Please name him Harvey. He will marry an Irish Catholic girl named Eleanor. They have two sons, my two grandsons. Of course, I love Sam. He was my grandson. Again, this is a fantasy. My grandsons will be named for me. They will be Thomas and Patrick. Around their necks, they will wear the same Miraculous Medal you gave me on our wedding day. Speaking of wedding day, you will only have a faux wedding with Jake.

"I've just been told I'm running out of time. You will now live with Jake and I'll be watching. I will know you are only with me. Don't hesitate to go into the confines of your mind with Jake. It will only be until we are together again. When the time is right, I will let you know when to come out without him. Then you will be with me in the world called spirit.

"The best part of a fantasy is that you can make it to your specifications. Perhaps you will sell your house in Huntingdon Valley after Ian dies. Then you can become quite wealthy. You might want to live with Jake in the fancy apartment you wanted in Wyncote.

"The world is yours in a fantasy, and time has no restrictions.

"Lady Karma will let us know 'when the time is right.'

"Hey, Rosey. You know I'm a winker. Sorry I couldn't wink at you today. I love you Rosey darlin'!"

Rosey came out and looked around the room. "Why is everybody here? You should have told me you were coming. I certainly wouldn't have gone in for a nap if I knew. Is there any reason for this little get together?"

"Rosey darlin', don't you remember?"

"Who's Rosey? My name is Rainey."

Mother had a total break with reality. She remembers all of us, but not any events of the last days. Her memory of living in Montauk as Tommy's wife is gone. She only remembers meeting him twice in 1984. At the casket, she spoke of taking her mind elsewhere. Then she wouldn't miss him so much. Is it possible that she's able to will herself to forget him?

Mother was admitted to the psychiatric unit at the hospital on the Pike in February 2016. She had no memory of all that she did from June 2012 when she bonded with Tommy, August 2012 when she married him, and when he passed away in January 2016. She believes that she just spent it with her children, grandson, and friends as always. The day of her admission, we heard her giggle. She said there was a tickling feeling at her neck.

I had the responsibility of cleaning out Tommy's house. Legally, it belonged to me. Steffy, Abby, Scott, and Sam came to help me and Leon. After he and Rosey got married, I asked my brother to sell that house and go into something smaller. The house is so big that they could lose each other. Rosey was all for it, but not Tommy. I knew he didn't feel connected to Cindy through that house. He just loved living there. He had been there for over twenty-five years.

Sam and Scott helped Leon with the large heavy pieces. Abby and Steffy went through Rosey's belongings. They packed up some clothes, personal items, and fragrance bottles. We knew she would never return. She didn't even remember Tommy. I asked if I could keep the trinket box I gave them as a wedding present. "Of course." I asked Steffy about the bracelet, necklace, and wedding band Tommy gave her mother. She said they were found on her dresser before she went into the hospital. They were put into a safe deposit box. I told them I had the things she wanted of Tommy's belongings. Perhaps one day she will remember him, and want them returned to her. They are in the trinket box.

It was decided that everything nobody else wanted would be donated to low-income families in Montauk. We all just sat for a while and cried!

I got two million dollars for the house. Leon and I are over 70 years old. What would we do with the money? We gave a generous donation to our church and the dog pound where Tommy rescued his girls. Both are in Montauk. A donation was also given to the synagogue where Rabbi Daniel presided. He helped Rosey observe proper Jewish ruling of mourning for her husband. The saddest part is that she never wore the ribbon. How could she? After the funeral, there was no memory of Tommy. Substantial donations were given to hospitals who care for children with cancer, catastrophic illness, and physical disabilities. A section of the school library was dedicated in memory of Tommy. Of course, a donation went to the school.

Tommy really loved Sam as his grandson. Because of that bitch Cindy, Tommy never had a chance to be a dad or a Pops. We're going to set up a trust fund for Sam. Leon and I will go to Philly and set it up at a bank there. Steven and Hannah will have control until Sam is 30 years old. They will get their own money along with Steffy, Abby, and Scott. Last, but not least, I will set up an account to be sure that Rosey always has the best medical care.

Mother was in the psychiatric unit at the hospital on the Pike until May 27, 2016.

PART FOUR

CHAPTER 4-1

It's now the end of May 2016 and I'm a 73-year-old widow. My late husband, Dr. Ian Silver, passed away in May of 2012. I just came home from the hospital on the Pike. My family told me I had a nervous breakdown. They said I lost all touch with reality. Of course I did. I had a stroke. They forget I'm a retired ICU/Trauma nurse. I certainly know the difference between the two. My recovery went so well. After three months, I'm now able to resume my life's activities. I just have to take a lot of medication. Sometimes I get a bit mixed up and confused, especially with time. Other than that, I'm fine!

Steffy told me there are several different Jewish versions of proper mourning for a widow. One says she should mourn her spouse for thirty days, and can marry on day thirty-one. Another says it is permitted to marry one year after the death of a spouse. I always shut her down. I told her if I ever considered dating, it would be if and when I was ready. It would not be because something written so many years ago gave me permission. I was doing a bit of dating, and also went to spousal bereavement groups. It was all a disaster. I hated every man I met during that time. Once they knew where I lived, they saw dollar signs. Many of them were disgusting old farts. Some were even greasy and unkempt looking. Most of my dates were from fix-ups. I never went on a second date with any of them. Maybe I'm a bit of a snob. I like men who are nicely and neatly dressed, with a pleasant disposition and personality. The snob part comes in where I like them to speak properly, like an English professor. I cringe at a man who says, "I ain't got." I just don't want Steven or Steffy to know anything. I prefer keeping that part of my life totally private, and I don't want to be pushed.

Why is Steffy suddenly bothering me with meeting men, and Jewish rules for a widow to follow? It's already been four years since her father passed away. I'm not new at this. Sometimes I think my family has lost touch with reality.

I really have no interest in meeting any more men and having a relationship. One reason is that I don't believe there is a man out there for me. Another is I have secrets. They are those I can never share with anyone except my sisters Abby and Helen. I will probably have to deal with them forever. Abby is a teacher, and believes that writing is therapeutic. She suggested that I begin a journal. Most of the time, when terrible things happened, she was available for me. Occasionally, when she wasn't, I could explode on paper. I began writing after being married to Ian for forty years. Several times, Abby begged me to allow her to confront him. I refused. I wanted no confrontations, and didn't want to smear Ian in the eyes of Steven and Steffy. I've noticed that since the stroke, I do sometimes get confused, especially with time. My writings were short and not dated. Time wasn't important, only the event. The entries just followed as the events took place, and I needed a temporary outlet. I hid the journal in a metal box in the bottom of my bedroom closet. It was underneath some extra blankets. I knew nobody would ever find it and read. Ian and the children never snooped into my side of the closet.

Ian and I seemed to have a good marriage on the outside. We had two incredible children, and were then blessed with a grandson. We were both very family oriented. That stemmed from the life we had with wonderful parents. I was left quite wealthy. Ian's medical practice had been lucrative. It brought in a lot of money through the years. Ian insisted that we have a financial advisor. He knew how and where to invest our money. We both worked, and didn't go into full retirement until I was 67, and he was 70 years old. We were strong and healthy, and began to travel. We went mostly to different European countries. People envied me, but make no mistake. Ian and Rainey Silver were not the couple to envy. **IT MAY ALL BE A MISCONCEPTION OR AN ILLUSION.** We had many issues in our marriage, all geared in several directions. Ian felt I should make the best of it since we were already married forty years. He warned me that there would be no divorce in the Silver family! When Ian issued a warning, I obeyed.

My son Steven is now 46 years old, and married to Hannah. He is an M.D. with a practice in family medicine. Hannah is his receptionist and office manager. Their son Sam is 21 years old and still in college. He's majoring in business, is a brilliant young man, and a go-getter. When he was graduating from high school, he said, "Baba, one day I want to be the CEO of a big corporation. I'm willing to work hard to get there."

"My Sammala, I know you will." They are in a good place in their life. My daughter Steffy is another story. She is an R.N. also certified in ICU/Trauma nursing. Steffy is restless and too picky about men. Therefore, she is 43 years old and still single. Maybe it's partly because I spoiled her. She was always my Princess Steffy. Additionally, I held her too close and sometimes made her my companion.

One of my secrets is that when Ian passed away, I was seen as the bereaved black widow. In truth, I was a merry widow. There was no more neglect, mental and emotional anguish, and occasional physical abuse. Therefore, there was no reason to continue writing in the journal. I just kept it in a metal box, in the bottom of my bedroom closet, under some extra blankets. I never took it out again. I knew nobody would ever find it to read. I sold the old house where we lived in Huntingdon Valley. I made a fortune on that sale. Ian was also very heavily insured.

I needed a new start, and rented a very expensive apartment in Wyncote. Almost everything was new. I bought furniture and fabrics with an oriental flair. Ian hated it, so I loved it and bought lots. I still lived part of my social life as closely as I had when Ian was alive. Moving into a new home opened doors for more options.

Every Monday morning, I began having breakfast in the building café with three new friends. Afterwards, we played canasta in the social room. I rejoined a theatre group with some old friends. We bought season tickets to The Arden Theatre in Center City Philadelphia. There were five shows a season that ran from September to June. We usually went to Wednesday matinees. My friend Sandy ordered the tickets, and we paid her. On Thursday mornings at 11:00, I always go to the hair salon. Thursday evening is my Mah Jong night. We take turns playing in different homes, as we all live in different areas. My grandson Sam comes to my apartment every Friday morning for breakfast. Steven and Hannah always had to spend so much time in their office. I played a big part in his care. When his regular babysitter wasn't available, I always stepped in. At about the age of 3, Sam learned the days of the week have names. He always wanted to be with me every Friday. I always did everything possible to make it happen. Saturday brunch with Steffy and Abby is a given.

CHAPTER 4-2

It's June 2016 and I continue to get my hair styled as always. I go to the salon every Thursday morning at 11:00. I also have my nails manicured, and eyebrows waxed. I met Helen Walsh, my hairdresser, when she and her husband Leon moved to Philly. They had been living in Montauk, Long Island, New York (NY). They have a beauty/barber shop. She is now 72 years old, and about to retire. Their shop is in a very uppity area on Old York Road. I have been going to Helen for about thirty-two years. I would never allow anyone else to put a scissors to my hair. I'm still slim, very attractive, and always take care of myself. My hair is still a beautiful dark brown. Of course, that's because of the coloring Helen puts on my hair. The month of June is when I always get my usual spring/summer hairstyle. Helen gives me a curly perm. I'm free to go swimming and shower, and not fuss with my hair. During that time, I only see Helen a few times professionally for maintenance haircuts and coloring. She and I, along with my sister Abby, are like three sisters. Therefore, I see her very often all through the year. I go back to the weekly routine after Labor Day when the pool closes.

One day, Helen asked me to join her in the break room for a cup of coffee. I had a feeling she was up to something, and she was. "Rainey, you are too beautiful a woman inside and outside to continue being alone. I know a really nice man, and think you and he might be a great match."

"Oh no!" There is one thing I have learned through the years about a woman and her hairdresser. If they are bonded, there is comfort and trust. She becomes her therapist, and best friend. Helen and I are already best friends and like sisters. She knows the entire personal history of my marriage. All of my secrets are with her, along with my sister Abby. I have kept them hidden from my children, and the rest of the world. The man she is referring to also has a marriage history, but different than mine.

"Please let me tell you all about him before you decide."

"Go ahead."

Helen began by telling me his name is Dr. Jacob Miller, and everyone calls him "Jake". He is a retired high school mathematics teacher with a Ph.D. in Mathematics Education. For the last fifty years, he has been living in Cheltenham. Financially, he is very comfortable. Helen knows I like a fine, educated man. His late wife, Cindy, was also a retired school teacher. She was one of her clients for many years. Jake is 77 years old, physically healthy and active, about 6 feet tall, broad and muscular, has a nice head of salt and pepper tussled hair, and a matching mustache. He wears reading glasses over his big blue eyes, and has a great disposition and personality. She added he periodically works out at his golf club. He gets a nice tan much of the year, and has great arms and legs. I asked her how she knows so much about his body. Through the years, she had seen him in short sleeve shirts and shorts when doing Cindy's hair. We laughed as she said, "No. You know Leon and I are happily married." Cindy had Alzheimer's disease. During the last four years of their marriage, she drifted in and out. She could no longer be trusted to drive. Jake brought her to the salon every week, and stayed with her. The last year, Cindy didn't recognize Jake, or their children. He chose to keep her at home, and had aides come in for her personal care. Jake knew while Cindy wasn't aware, she would still want to look nice. Therefore, Helen spent a great deal of time with Jake. First it was at the salon, and then styling her hair at the house. I guess she did have a lot of time to check out his body. She said Jake was such a kind man! Cindy passed away from the complications of the disease. After that, Helen didn't see Jake for about a year.

Helen just ran into him in the supermarket. They hugged, and she spoke to him of his dedication to Cindy. Jake reminded her that it was over a year since Cindy passed away. He admitted to being very lonely. Friends always say, "Have I got a girl for you." He had several dates in the last year with no chemistry. There wasn't even enough for a second cup of coffee with any of them. Helen said, "Rainey. I yelled, have I got a girl for you."

Helen was determined to pique an interest in both of us before meeting. She admitted to Jake and me that she shared some of each other's marital secrets with us. She knew it was wrong. Her belief was we should know a small amount of the other one's story. Hopefully, it would make for more comfort when we meet.

I agreed to allow Helen to give Jake my telephone number. The following week, she told me of her call to him. He too hesitated. It took another week until my telephone rang, and I saw his name on my caller ID. I had to think fast. Answer or not answer? I did and he asked for me. Our conversation went smoothly. Jake then said, "Helen wants us to get to know each other. If we talk too long on the telephone, we'll have nothing left to talk about when we meet. She's anxious for that to happen. How about having dinner with me on Friday?" Oh my God! It's Wednesday! I was shocked! So quick! Of course, I accepted his invitation. We agreed to meet at the seafood restaurant on Rhawn Street at 4:00. He explained that the early bird specials begin at that time. Then he continued by saying he's not cheap. That's the time he can get a table quicker. He doesn't like standing around in a crowd of people for an hour, especially on a blind date.

I arrived at the restaurant at about 3:50. I told the hostess I was meeting someone. I whispered it's a blind date. I'm not sure what he looks like. She asked if my name is Rainey. When I said yes, she waved her arm towards the back of the restaurant. A very hunky, nice-looking man came forward. My insides were spinning, and I could hardly walk. Helen did an excellent job on the description. He was even more than I expected or could hope for. He was so polite. There was a table already set up, and he asked to escort me to my seat. How formal! He took my hand, walked me to the table, and pulled out the chair for me to sit down. It was already a great date.

Two of the instant discoveries we made is that we're both Jewish, and love to gamble. He plays blackjack and I love the slots. I had been alone four years since Ian suddenly passed away. Jake was actually alone for six years. The bottom line was we admitted that time didn't matter. We were both very lonely. I didn't tell him I had a stroke! It was not the right time.

Jake suggested that we order dinner and then talk. His voice alone excited me. It was low, almost gruff, raspy, and sexy. We both knew what was coming. That's why Jake arrived early and got a private table in the back corner of the restaurant. I said, "Helen is aware of everything in my life because we have been friends for such a long time. Your marriage stories came from two sides, yours and Cindy's. She spent so much time at your house that you became comfortable talking to her. I think she deems us a good match because our present needs are the same." Jake agreed. "May I suggest that we have a nice dinner together now, and talk in a different place? If we both still want to share everything, would you like to come to my apartment after dinner? There would be privacy with no intrusions." Jake just nodded. Helen told Jake that I have a beautiful apartment.

Since we weren't going to do the serious talking during dinner, he asked me for a description. His belief is sometimes one's environment tells something about a person. "Please

Rainey, tell me about your environment." Wow, what a sexy voice! I began and noticed he was listening with such intensity.

"I live in the Lane House in Wyncote. When you enter my apartment, you're in the foyer. There's a coat closet and a sitting area with assorted furniture. It consists of two oriental carved love seats with two matching chairs. On one wall, there's a section of the dining room breakfront from my house. It's oriental in style, and finished with shiny black lacquer. In sections, there is inlaid mother of pearl. They create assorted images of beautiful woman in oriental garb. The background has muted gold paintings of scenery. It's too large for the living room, but a perfect fit on the main foyer wall. The pictures on the walls are oriental art, and there is a large vase on the floor with flowers.

"There's a combination living and dining room. I have family pictures on the walls in that area. They are pictures of my son Steven, his wife Hannah, and my grandson Sam at different ages. Also, there are many pictures of my gorgeous daughter Steffy. The only separation between those two rooms is a large oriental printed screen. It only covers a small area, and was properly placed to see from one room to another. My taste leans almost to all oriental decorations and accessories. I don't have a full-sized kitchen, just a small galley kitchen.

"My bedroom is very large with a master bathroom. The other room is supposed to be a second bedroom, but I have it set up as a den. That's where I have my computer, stereo, and an 82-inch television on the wall. I also have one wall set up as a small library. The furniture is big and cozy. In the hallway, there's a large bathroom with an attached laundry room. Except for the bathrooms and kitchen, the floors are covered with thick plush carpeting." I waited for a response.

"Your environment sounds wonderful. Apparently, you also like more than home decorations oriental style. I believe your dress has an oriental flair."

"Thanks for noticing."

CHAPTER 4-3

Dinner was so nice! I think we were both happy and having fun. We spoke on many general lighthearted subjects. What I did notice is that we were both flirting. At different times, one of us reached across the table and we touched hands.

When we left, he took my hand again and walked me to my car. "If I picked you up, I certainly would be a gentleman; take you home, and walk you to the door. I would want to be sure I got you home safely. May I follow and walk you to the door?"

Is this man for real? "Yes you may walk me to the door. If you still want to talk, you may come inside the door with me. Get in your car and follow me." We each got in our cars, and I began driving. I used turn signals for him to follow. It was a good thing he couldn't hear me being a friggin' idiot as I drove. I was laughing hysterically and squealing. I kept on asking myself, over and over again, if he was for real. We got to my building, and I guided him to where we would park. I just sat in my car and waited for him to walk over. He opened my car door and I got out. I stood still and said something really stupid. "If you were a lost little poodle and followed me home, you might want to stay, and I might want to keep you."

He responded with one word. "Perhaps." During dinner, I noticed he used that word a few times. This time, I took his hand and we walked into the main lobby. We took the elevator to the third floor, and went just down the hall to my apartment. Just me and my lost little poodle, who I might want to keep!

I gave Jake a quick tour. He could then identify what I told him with actually seeing everything. We sat down in the living room. I assumed since he chose to come home with me he felt comfortable. I asked if he wanted to open up and have me do the same. "Let's talk and see how it goes. After talking, we'll know if Helen did the right thing by putting us together." I asked him to go first. "I will, but as a man, this is going to be very difficult for me. I'm going to spill my guts out to a stranger. Why? Because a hairdresser said it might give me a new life with that stranger. So alright, stranger, here I go. I just ask that you let me go on and on and not make any comments or ask questions until I finish." I agreed.

"Cindy and I met in college, and were both taking education classes. We graduated at the same time, and got jobs in different schools. We were both about 23, became friends, but didn't start seriously dating until way after graduation. I went back to school later for my Ph.D. I believe we fell in love, but decided to hold off on marriage. We wanted to save money and buy a house together. Then if we chose to have children immediately, she could stop working for a few years. All seemed to be great except for one major problem. I wasn't thrilled, but Cindy chose to be a virgin when we married. She knew I wasn't. Please excuse my language, but I fucked my way through college. Many times, I paid $5 for quickie blowjobs. I was a normal, healthy young man with needs. I'm not ashamed or embarrassed to tell you that I love sex. I also love being naked with the right person at the right time. Cindy and I did lots of kissing, touching, and petting, but always fully clothed. Lots of times I ejaculated in my pants. I tried to convince her that to be a virgin meant no intercourse. We could still be naked together and do other things. She said my sounds told her how hot I got during those sessions. Her fear was if we were naked, I might try to encourage her to go further. We were making plans for our lives, but I still hadn't put a ring on her finger.

Therefore, I was still going elsewhere for sex, and she was fine with it. She just didn't want to know when or with whom. Can you imagine going two years like that until the wedding? Perhaps, I was lucky. I had the young woman I loved waiting for me, and was still able to fuck around when I needed a fix. She didn't ask, and I didn't tell.

"One evening I went to discuss the situation with my dad. My mom was already gone. His advice was to not marry her. In his opinion, sex in a marriage isn't just to have babies. It's also to give mutual pleasure to each other. It should be a form of love that you don't share with anybody else. Dad added, 'There's something wrong with a young woman who doesn't have a problem with your arrangement. How much does she really love you? How much do you really love her? I think even after marriage, you're not going to be sexually compatible. To me, that's a bad thing.' In closing, he strongly believed she was wrong for me. Did I listen to my dad? Of course not!

"We were both 25 years old when we were married. Our wedding was in a banquet area of a major hotel. A room was reserved there for our wedding night. We were scheduled to take an early morning flight to Orlando for a five-day honeymoon.

"Our wedding night was a disaster, and set the stage for our entire marriage. She came out of the bathroom wearing a beautiful sheer negligee. At my bachelor party, I got an appropriate gift to wear that night. It was boxer shorts with small writing at the opening. It said 'TO BE OPENED ON WEDDING NIGHT'. To me, the woman's naked body wasn't a shock, just all so different. She slowly took off her negligee. Her body was beautiful and shapely. I already knew she had large breasts. I'm a breast man. Many times she teased me by wearing very low cut tops. Her breasts and cleavage were always quite prominent. I was really hot, excited, aroused, and in full bloom. Now it was good because she was my wife. I asked if she wanted to take off my shorts, or if she preferred I do it. She wouldn't even get close enough to read the writing. I knew our wedding night might be awkward or clumsy the first time, but not like this.

"Cindy went into some sort of panic attack. She had seen pictures of men's naked bodies. Apparently, she didn't realize we also all look different. She knew I had erections, but I was always enclosed in my pants. The sight of my erection, naked, was too much for her. 'Oh my God! I heard the first time it could hurt and you are so big. I can't do this!' She grabbed her negligee off the floor and ran into the bathroom. I got back into my shorts and a pair of slacks. I knocked on the door and asked her to come out. It was getting late, and we had to be at the airport early in the morning. I told her to sleep in the bed, and I'd sleep on the sofa. She came out tearful and apologetic, got into bed, and fell asleep. Me? On my wedding night, I jerked off in the bathroom!

"In the morning, we left for the airport. All of our time there was spent out of bed, except to sleep. I guess she was afraid I might become aroused and attempt to make love to her. She wore clothing to bed. No revealing negligees. We went to Disney, and sat at the pool. Again, maybe she was afraid I might become aroused. She never wore her bathing suit. Instead she wore shorts and a T-shirt. We ate at the parks, and had quiet dinners in nice restaurants. I was even too depressed to go into the bathroom every night to do myself.

"When we came home, I demanded that we get professional help. I told her she had two choices. She would either get an immediate appointment with a marriage/sex therapist, or I would get an immediate appointment with an attorney. I would have our marriage annulled. She made an appointment with a female therapist within three days.

"Cindy said she heard the first time is painful, especially if the man is big. The therapist said she should have discussed her fear with me before the wedding. We could have made a mutual decision to get professional help. 'There are gynecologists who do a sterile procedure. They go into the vagina with a sharp tool. The hymen is then broken prior to the wedding. This hopefully eliminates the chance of a catastrophic wedding night.' She also explained that sometimes the woman has no fear, but her hymen is very thick. It can't always be penetrated with the man's first entry for intercourse. Cindy agreed to allow her to make an appointment with this doctor. She went the very next morning, and asked to go alone. She was sore, uncomfortable, and distant for about a week. Our first time was not what it should have been. There was no wedding night! We had many more appointments with the marriage/sex therapist. Sometimes alone, and sometimes together.

"The marriage then became only fairly good. As I lived with her on an everyday basis, more unexpected issues presented themselves. There was only occasional sex, which was always like a cold chore for her. She would just lie on her back, put herself into position, and allow me entry. I always tried to make it loving, romantic, and pleasurable. I still don't know if she ever had an orgasm. If she did, it was silent. When I made natural sounds, she cringed. All I really had was a physical release. I was quite capable of doing that myself. After each encounter, she went into the bathroom to douche. Sometimes she made me feel like I was raping her. She complained that she didn't like the texture of the skin on my bare penis inside her. Yet she hated the feel of a condom. She went on the pill, but complained it made her sick. She always had a headache, was too tired, or had her period. My God, Rainey! I was stuck for life! Cindy and I decided to begin a family immediately, so no condom or pill. Maybe having natural sex and planning on a child would warm her up a bit. The sex was still cold, but a little more often. After being married a year, Jason was born. Two years after that, we had Harvey."

CHAPTER 4-4

Jake seemed to take a deep breath, and then continued, "Our sex was always very basic with no participation from her. Many times through the years, I tried speaking to her about foreplay, dirty talk, or changing her position. Books are sometimes helpful with suggestions. I begged her to try something, anything! Several times I attempted to just put my hand between her legs in hope of a reaction. Maybe she would prefer that kind of sex. I wanted her to at least try to find some acceptance and satisfaction with me. She once accused me of being sickening.

"I eventually discussed it with my dad again. He told me that in our family there would be no infidelity. I made a mistake when I chose her, but now I would have to live with it. At that point, we already had Jason and Harvey.

"Except for the occasional sex, she very rarely touched me. Our sons never knew anything was wrong. Sometimes she would let me give her a hug or kiss. As a mom, she was very demonstrative with our sons. We never went on a vacation alone. They were always family vacations. Rainey, I spent many a night, all those years, in the bathroom taking care of myself. After the boys moved out, I slept in the spare room. Several times I went to a bar to get drunk. There were women who approached me. I could have had some flings through the years. Once I came really close, but just couldn't do it. I never heard the voice of God, but I heard the voice of my dad. He was a very wise man, but it was too late. I ignored his advice, and his morality had already rolled over into my soul.

"After our sons were born, Cindy went back on the pill. That meant no more children, and no need for a condom. She still cringed a bit each time I went inside of her. At about the age of 50, she became pre-menopausal and began taking hormones. When she turned 60 years old, she needed a hysterectomy. She blamed me for poisoning her insides with my semen. Of course, that was the end of any sex. She was always off kilter after the surgery. I was going crazy trying to balance my body, my hormones, and morality. I went into a deep depression and knew I needed professional help. I began seeing a therapist. It didn't help much. All he did was give me statistics of how many men lived like me in long marriages. He also told me what I already knew. Through all those years, I did have choices. I could have been discretely unfaithful or divorce her. I used my sons as an excuse for no divorce. They adored their mother. There was no way I could tell them I was leaving her, and give any explanation as to why. Cindy and I were 71 years old when she began slipping into the Alzheimer pattern of behavior. I thought perhaps she always had a type of mental instability. Possibly it was one that manifested itself into issues of touching and sex. We were married fifty-one years when she passed away. I spent my entire marriage almost as a monk. I was totally robbed of feeling like a husband and a man. Her passing gave me freedom to find myself. I did begin dating in hopes of finding a compatible woman at this stage of my life. Well, here I am telling my intimate story to a stranger. A woman who Helen thinks might be the one!"

As he spoke, I couldn't take my eyes off of him. His face was so tan and rugged looking. He had lines as any man his age would have. It was summertime. I could see the tan line around his neck and collar of his shirt. When he stopped, I think he had tears in his eyes. I had them in mine. His hurt was front and center on his face. I did as he asked. I just let him go on and on with no interruptions.

We both sat there quietly for a minute or two. "Helen possibly does talk too much, but I would like to tell you something she shared with me. She repeated things that Cindy told her about you. I think it might help heal you a bit.

"Cindy told her you were a wonderful, incredible man, husband, father, and provider. After telling Helen about the sex issues, she said more. Cindy admitted to hating touching and sex, but not you. She was so sorry that she couldn't be the kind of wife you deserved. There were times when you wanted to talk about what was happening. She always refused and shut you down. It would have been better if you did have an affair. That would have kept you sexually satisfied, and she wouldn't feel guilty. Jake, your marriage was cold, and without any satisfying sex, but Helen and I agreed. There was some love on both sides. Your dad was correct. You and Cindy were totally incompatible. It also became apparent that she had many problems. You're a good man, Dr. Jacob Miller! Hold onto that and go forward."

"I will be brief. There was also love between me and Ian. When we met, I had my first job in a hospital and he was a rotating surgical resident. His time was so limited. We did meet for dinner when he wasn't on call. I was a virgin, but he wasn't. I got through that part easily. We had sex in crazy places, but they were always quickies. We were married when I was 24 and Ian was 27. I'm going to skip through all the aspects of our marriage. All that is important to tell you now is that eventually I too had a missionary marriage. I'm really not sure how or when the change took place. We had sex if and when he felt like it, and always quick. It didn't matter if I was done, as long as he had his jollies. I became his receptacle, like an ashtray. I too spent many years taking care of myself. I did it in a bubble bath. I had the same restrictions you had like no dirty talk. Who had time? It was over so fast. Compared to your years of marriage, I think mine was almost an orgy.

"I just want to tell you one more thing. We belonged to a country club with many of our professional friends. There were always formal functions and we attended them together. The men always told off color dirty jokes, but not Ian. He was the formal prude in the bunch. One time when I had lunch with some of the wives, the topic of oral sex came into the discussion. They had all tried it and told of the results. Most of them loved it after trying it in different ways. One night I told Ian about it. I suggested that we try it. I will never forget his response. He said just the thought of doing that to me made him feel like he could *vomit*, just *vomit*! Additionally, the thought of me taking his dick in my mouth, the dick that he pees from, would make it that he could never kiss me again. His words and tone still ring in my ears and brain.

"Jake, I'm so glad we shared all of this with each other and got it out of the way. Cindy and Ian are both gone, and we're no longer married. We're both legally and morally free. Hopefully, we can go on and find just the right person before we get too old. Possibly, Helen is right. Maybe we are each other's bershert. I'm so tired, and don't want to talk about this anymore. I think we've both had enough emotion for one evening. Helen also told me you like scotch. I don't know how to mix it for you, but I do have a bottle of the good stuff. I know it's good because my son Steven loves it. Or, would you prefer I make some coffee?"

Jake agreed to the coffee and we just talked a bit. He asked me why I chose to be a nurse, especially in ICU/Trauma units. "I always felt the draw towards medicine, but not as a doctor. I read a book, possibly sci-fi when I was in my early teens. It told of the possibility that one who was in the process of passing could hear all of their surroundings. They knew who was in the room and what was being said, especially by loved ones. There was one story about a man in his last moments. His wife was crying and screaming. He could hear her but couldn't comfort her. In the book, it was written as we always say, one should rest in peace. I believe everyone should also pass in peace. They should not be hearing those sounds. They should not know they are leaving a loved one in such horrible pain. There should be nothing but sweet words and thoughts going into the mind of the passing. There were many times I had a patient in the final stage of life. If nobody was there, I always held a hand and whispered sweet words into their mind. That also gave me peace when I lost someone." Jake looked at me with such passion in his face.

I then asked him why he loved and wanted to teach math. "Numbers are fascinating to me. I think in their own way they control everything we do. My preference was to teach high school students, rather than college students. I believed they were more open for learning. You just learned tonight that I love speaking without interruptions. My students always gave me that respect. On complex equations, I always went into the greatest of details. When writing math problems and equations on the board, I used different colors of chalk. I provided them with the same coordinating color markers. They could be used in their workbooks. Colors and shapes were great tools in their learning, and they coordinated with my teachings. I consider myself to be a great orator, and think they would agree. My lessons were never boring. They all knew my passion for what I was teaching, and my hopes to pass it on. I wanted to share all I knew with each and every one of them. It gave me the greatest pleasure when some came to me, shook my hand, and said, thank you, Dr. Miller."

It was now after 9:00. We had been together since 4:00. It was a very long first date. As I opened the door, he leaned over and gave me a nice gentle hug. He then asked if he could give me a goodnight kiss. "Of course!" He gave me a sweet and mostly closed mouth kiss. I was quite receptive. I asked him to call me when he got home. I couldn't walk him to his door, but I wanted to be sure that he got home safely.

CHAPTER 4-5

Jake lived close by, so it didn't take him too long to get home. At 10:15 my telephone rang, and it was him. He invited me for Sunday brunch, and I accepted.

During dinner, we spoke of a restaurant that has a great Sunday brunch. He asked to pick me up this time at 12:00 noon. I had to contain my excitement. At about 11:45, Jake called me from the intercom in the main lobby. I buzzed him in. He took the elevator to the third floor. I opened my door and waited for him. It was summertime. He was wearing khaki slacks, and a very nice preppy looking shirt. I too looked pretty good, so I thought. He stepped in, gave me a hug and kiss, and told me how good I smelled. The hug was a bit closer than when he left on Friday evening. The kiss was much warmer, with a bit more of an open mouth. Again, I was responsive, and opened my mouth a bit more. He gave me a chill! We went downstairs to his car, buckled up, and went for brunch.

The first thing he asked about was my name. I told him my given name is Lorraine Rose, and somehow it got chopped up. While we ate, we told each other about our immediate families. If we continued seeing each other, eventually the other family members would come to light. I told him Ian was a dermatologist. He already knew I was a retired ICU/Trauma nurse. I added that my son Steven is 46, an M.D. with a practice in family medicine. His wife, Hannah, is the receptionist and office manager. She takes care of all the finances and billing for the practice. I have only one grandchild, who is their son. His name is Sam. I call him Sammala, and he calls me Baba. He's 21 years old, in college, and majoring in business. My daughter Steffy is 43, and also an ICU/Trauma nurse. She can't seem to find a place for herself in her personal life. After Ian passed away, she seemed to think I was lost without him. I was really a very strong and independent woman. In retrospect, I don't think I was fair to her. She is a young, beautiful woman, and I took up too much of her life to be with me.

Secrets! I have secrets and lied to him. I held back so much. My secrets are all with Abby and Helen. Additionally, sometimes I still get confused.

Jake already knew about my relationship with Helen. When she spoke to him about meeting me, he was told the history of our friendship. I told him of my other incredible sister. "Her name is Abby, and she's a year older than me. She graduated from high school with honors, and then went onto college and became a teacher. Our mother was a teacher, and our father was an accountant. They're both gone. She married a nice young man, Scott Rubin, also a teacher. They met in the middle school where they both worked. She and Scott have only one child, Emmy. While I was always quite thin, Abby developed more of a womanly figure than me. I had food problems, a story for another time. We have always been so close. As little girls, we danced up and down the street holding hands. Our favorite game was Ring Around the Rosie. We got to dance in a circle holding hands. Neighbors always spoke of how cute we were. As teenagers, we danced to the music on the radio, television or our records, always holding hands. We had quite a collection. Daddy always bought us records. Today, Abby, and Scott are happily married for 51 years. Emmy is also married with seven children. When she married Nick, and converted to Catholicism, our parents weren't very happy. Emmy's children are all married with children. Too many to count! Abby and I are still very close, and best friends. We always hold hands and dance together at family celebrations, or in a time of crisis. Maybe that's why I'm in the habit of reaching out for someone's hand. You seem to have that same habit.

"Jake, I'm going to tell you something about the family which very few people know. It's about our name. Ian had a crazy thing about the name Silver. He seemed to think it was a name to be revered as some type of royalty. When Steven was born, I wanted to name him Steven Todd. His name is Steven Sterling Silver. My crazy husband said if he could, he would name him Silver Silver Silver. When Steffy was born, Stephanie was the closest I let him get to the name Silver. Her middle name is Ruth. My grandson's name is Samuel Sterling Silver. That was Steven's decision."

Now it was Jake's turn to tell me about his family. He began by telling me he had one brother, who passed away at the age of 20. His name was Jason and he had leukemia. There were no treatments then as there are now. Jake was then 16 years old. He helped his mom take care of his brother. Between school and helping with Jason, he had very little time for a social life. A year later, his mom passed away. The doctor said it was her heart. The family always said she passed away of a broken heart. She was never the same after his passing. Until Jake married, he lived with his dad. They both took care of each other. His dad worked in a printing shop. Sometimes he worked double shifts. He had to be sure there was enough money so Jake could go to college.

"I have two sons. Jason is 51, gay, and lives with Craig, his legal husband. In English and Hebrew, he's named after my brother. They live in a small house in Lancaster, and own a gourmet food shop. It's located in an area that draws many visitors. They have become known and liked by many of the Amish residents. While not practicing any formal religion, they occasionally attend some of their prayer meetings. The Amish don't find homosexuality acceptable or God's way, but they really like and respect Jason and Craig. They have come to see them as God's children. Sometimes, one of their Amish friends takes them for rides in the buggy. Out of respect, Jason and Craig keep their shop closed every Sunday.

"My younger son Harvey is 49 and married. He's a computer geek, and makes a very good living creating websites. He sometimes works from home and drives his wife crazy. Her name is Eleanor. She's a waitress at a very large popular restaurant on Street Road. Eleanor is Irish Catholic. My late wife, Cindy, didn't speak to Harvey for several years. Harvey and Eleanor had a private ceremony performed by the priest at her church. I don't believe Harvey converted. It was never mentioned. Eleanor is a wonderful young woman, wife, and mother. My son is happy, so I'm happy for him. The biggest problem Cindy had with this marriage was when the children were born." Of course, Jake and I both know that if the mother is not Jewish then the child is not Jewish. Jake then continued. "Harvey and Eleanor took their time having children. It was several years before they had the boys. Cindy couldn't stand the fact that her only grandchildren would be raised Catholic. Thomas is 14, and Patrick is 15 years old. Cindy really got upset when she saw them wearing neck chains with Catholic medals on them. They were both christened, and attend a private Catholic academy. They are wonderful, handsome, loving boys, and they excel in their classes in school. They call me Pops and I call them Tops!"

Jake exclaimed that his love for family is overwhelming, and the love goes both ways. Jake also added that Harvey was his best friend. He could always go to him when things became too much that last year. Harvey was a warm and touching man, and always knew when to give a great bear hug.

We left the restaurant, went out to the car, and put on our seat belts. Jake turned to me and said, "Hey, Rainey. How about a little bit of blackjack and slots. If you have no other plans, would you like to go to the casino on Street Road for a while?"

"Hey, Jake. How about if we find a Wawa so I can get some money?" We did, and then went to the casino. Jake used valet parking. Apparently, we both loved that world with all the bells, whistles, and flashing lights. We looked at each other, smiled, and almost jumped up and down like two kids. Jake looked for a waitress and got scotch for himself and coffee for me. He pointed to show me which blackjack table he would be sitting at to play. I was going to look around and find new slots to try. We each had a cell phone to keep connected. As Jake walked away, I ran after him. He asked if something was wrong. "Yes, I didn't give you a kiss for luck." Boy did I give him a smoocher!

"Now it's my turn to give you a kiss for luck." We shared an even bigger one.

Someone yelled, "How about if you two old farts get a room." I only knew him two days; it was only our second date, but I could feel myself twitching from head to toe.

We stayed at the casino for about three hours. Jake won a bit and I lost a lot. It was now almost 6:00. We were both hungry but tired. Chinese food sounded good. We stopped at a take-out and brought it back to my apartment. After we ate, I got rid of the trash and we both sat down in the living room. I was tired, and could see he was almost falling asleep. It was now after 10:00. "I hate to say this, but maybe you should leave now while you're still awake enough to drive home." He went into the bathroom, and I could hear the water running. He was really tired. I think he put some cold water on his face. I walked him to the door. He extended his arms out to me for a hug. It wasn't at arm's length. He pulled me towards him; our body parts came pretty close, and then the kiss. It was open mouth from both of us, and we were devouring each other. Eventually we both pulled apart, but not wanting to let go.

"Part of me would like you to stay, but I'm really not ready."

He was so tired, and possibly in a bit of a sexual funk. Again, I asked him to call me when he got home. I wanted to be sure he got home safely. We walked together to the elevator. As the door closed, we threw a kiss.

CHAPTER 4-6

He did call me when he got home. I was slowly learning that he has an adorable, naughty, and playful side, just like me. "I got home safely, and took a cold shower. Now I'm lying in bed naked thinking about you. I like to sleep naked. Perhaps, one night you will take a shower with me, and sleep naked with me. I call it 'skin to skin'." There was that word again. "Perhaps." "Jakey, Jakey, Jakey. You must be high from the MSG in the Chinese food. Go to sleep and call me when you can." We hung up, and I called him right back. I invited him to come for dinner on Tuesday, two days away. He accepted the invitation, but I had to promise to always call him "Jakey". He called Monday morning before we both started our day. We both had full lives with family, friends, appointments, and commitments. The menu for Tuesday's dinner was planned so I could shop and cook for him. He called again Monday night. There was just more talking and sharing of our lives. I asked him to come at 2:00. We would then have time to relax before dinner. He always ate at "early bird special" time, which was 4:00. Relax, hell! All I could think about was the size of his package. Does it still rise to an occasion at the age of 77? Might I be an occasion?

If I feel like I did on Sunday night, this was going to be a Tuesday, 2:00 p.m. to remember. The sexual seduction of Jakey Miller, by Rainey Silver!

It was early Tuesday morning. Jakey said he would like to have sweet and sour meatballs. It had been about eight or nine years since Cindy made them for him. I bought everything on Monday, took out my slow cooker, and got them going. We also agreed on a salad, rice, carrots and challah with butter. "I sometimes like to have a glass of wine with dinner. Should I bring a bottle?" I told him I don't drink, but to bring whatever he would like to have. We can chill it a bit before we eat.

In my fantasy of Jakey early that morning, my body was on fire. Heat burned me everywhere. My breasts ached. What I felt between my legs told me I was more than ready for him. I wanted his hands everywhere seeking, stroking, and rubbing me until I had an orgasm. I felt the sensation all the way down to my clit. I then took him into my hands and began moving from base to tip. In my head, I could hear the sounds he would make. I learned that massaging the tip would bring him the most excitement. How would I even know that of any man? Of course, from my crazy friend Harriet! She knew it all. I shook off the fantasy, got out of bed, and went back to reality.

I have been friends with a few women for many years. They all became divorced or widowed before me. Harriet was a party girl, and always volunteered advice about men and sex. She loved to tell us about her sexual escapades. Every time we got together, Harriet had a new story. Dirty talk and slang words was her thing. She felt like it enhanced her stories. We always laughed until we were choking. Her stories were always that amusing! Harriet was the expert. She said there is only one way a man and woman would know if they wanted to fuck. They had to get into a vertical position standing on the floor. Their bodies would dictate how close they want to get. That means slow dancing. She once said, "Your first sexual encounter with someone new might be ruled by that dance. Trust me. The dance tells a lot. If you have no interest, don't bother. If you are interested, take charge and push your crotch against his. That gives you the chance to discover if you really want to fuck, and if he can." She just loved using that word! In another life, maybe she was a man. Before Jakey arrived, a slow dance with him was the only thing on my mind. What song would I play? Would he agree to the dance? Should I give it a try? Would the results really tell me anything? It's only our third date. I already had so many feelings for him! Hot, cold, and everything in between. There's only thing I know for certain. Harriet is crazy!

He arrived before 2:00. I knew he would. Again, dressed very preppy and summer like. His shirt was open in the front almost like Harry Belafonte. I never even got dressed. I took a shower with some very nice, hopefully enticing body wash. I followed up with the matching lotion. I put on a silky lounging robe, oriental print of course, and nothing else. The robe had a long front zipper in case easy access was needed. Jakey already told me he was lying in bed naked, and thinking of me. What should I believe might happen? He arrived, and I barely got the door closed when he began kissing me. Me? Of course, always receptive! This time, the kisses were almost salacious. His mouth was absolutely delicious! He never mentioned what I was wearing. Nor did he inquire if there was anything underneath. We settled in, and were both so turned on, but I needed a big favor. I had to ask something of him, and would explain later. I took him by the hand and guided him towards the den. Somehow, every time we were together, and moved from place to place, we always reached out for the other one's hand.

We went hand in hand to the den. I asked him to trust me. "Will you slow dance with me?" I held the remote, which was connected to my stereo. I had a slow and romantic song ready to play. Again, I asked him to slow dance with me.

"I'm sure you have a valid reason. Yes, I would love to slow dance with you." We got very close into a dancing position, and I hit the remote. The song began. We were dancing, yet never moved from the spot. It was more like our bodies just pressing against each other, and picking up a sexual rhythm. Until that moment, I didn't know if Jakey could rise. He could and he did!

He slowly pulled back and glanced at my robe. He took the zipper pull and slid it down. I was then totally exposed. He leaned over and began gently massaging and kissing my chest and my breasts. They didn't come into play very often, as they are so very small. Next he held my face in his hands and kissed my forehead, eyelids, each cheek and mouth ever so gently. Then his mouth moved down to my pubic area. I was crazy! There was so much passion, emotion, and warmth in his touch. I knew then that Jakey was not a man who would play me just for the fuck. If that was all he wanted, he could have been fucking his way through the last year since his wife passed away. Maybe he did, but now he was mine. The first night we met, he did tell me he loves sex. I had to hold onto these moments. I leaned forward and motioned for him to lift his arms. I pulled off his shirt. He then leaned over and got himself out of his socks and shoes. My hands were shaking. I was so overwhelmed! I took off his outer Bermuda shorts, and could see Jakey in full bloom! I pulled his briefs down and gently touched his large, hard magnificence. How exciting! We pressed together, rolled to the floor, and he slithered in between my legs on his knees. My body is very thin, and his body is big and muscular. I think that position brought his body up closer to mine. We were a perfect fit. Within minutes, he was inside of me and moans could be heard in China. Dear God, was this really happening? I was a live woman again. It had been too many years since I felt that way. I hope he felt like a live man again.

During our talks, we did establish that neither one of us ever had an STD or any type of lesions. We agreed that the back end of the other was forbidden. Finally, we laughed that we didn't need birth control.

I didn't feel like Jakey and I were just fucking. I felt like we were making love on a third date. We were so crazy hot, yet it was so sweet and gentle with each accommodating the other. The orgasms came at the same time. We still didn't change positions. He stayed inside of me until he had no choice. The passionate kisses continued. Eventually he rolled over and said, "Now I'm ready to hear why the dance, and why as foreplay."

I told him about crazy Harriet. "Foreplay, Jakey? I didn't need any foreplay today. I wanted you from the time we kissed in the casino. I could have stripped down, stripped you down, cleared a blackjack table, and fucked with you right then and there!" How we laughed! "It's a shame we can't tell the world what just happened. A 73 year old woman, and a 77 year old man just had the most incredible fuck ever!

"Sickening, Jakey? You told me Cindy found you to be sickening. She cringed at the sounds you made while having an orgasm. She was your wife! Yes, I believe this was the most incredible fuck ever. Just part of it was because of the sounds you made. It was our first time. I could feel exactly where you were, every step of the way. It went from the time you entered me, until nature caused you to fall out of me. You entered into me smoothly and softly. I was so hot that I was wet, and could allow you to have that smooth entrance. Then you picked up more pushing and thrusting movements. They became harder and harder. Your sounds were like music. While I was enjoying my own passion, I was feeling yours partially from your sounds. They began with passionate moans, and then they changed and intensified. Your breathing was so heavy, and your entire body was almost spastic. I knew the exact moment when you began coming, and when it ended. Your tip was deep in as far as you could go. I could feel the heat of your total experience when you shot inside of me. I could hear the sounds, and feel those final pushes as you were releasing the last drops."

I knew my Jakey commeth! At what point did I come? I'm not sure. I just know it was more than once. This was our first time. Do I dare ask you for more?

CHAPTER 4-7

Jakey got up from the floor, and then helped me get up. I went into my master bathroom, and he went into the hallway bathroom to freshen up. I told him there were baby wipes on the counter. Hence, the name he began calling me was "baby". We then came together again in the hallway. It was after 4:30. "Hey, Rainey. You just worked me to the boner. I mean bone. Now I hope you're going to feed me." Jakey was hungry. I was in a pair of Capri style pajamas. Jakey was back in his briefs, shorts, and shirt. He was still barefooted. Again, we took hands and walked to the kitchen. I had already set the table early in the day. I made sure everything was hot enough. He helped me carry everything from the kitchen to the dining area. He did bring a bottle of wine and drank two glasses. As we sat over dinner, we were both quiet and mellow. Did it mean the sex was over and now nothing? No! Every time I got up from the table, he reached out for me. We were still so emotionally and warmly connected. I made coffee and we took it to the den. Jakey asked me to play the song again used for the dance. He was so deep into me, no pun intended, that he wanted to listen to the words. It would now be our song. It was played the first time we made love. I played it again. We were both familiar with it, and sat quietly and listened. It was about the way we have come to feel about each other when we join hands. "Warm!"

It was now 7:00. We discovered that just one of the genres of music we both liked was reggae. Comcast has music stations and I turned it on. I had the remote and made the music louder. We both got up and danced reggae style, separately at different sides of the room. We did a lot of shaking, gyrating, sensual pelvic moves, and swinging. We continued moving back and forth to different sides of the room. I think Jakey was a bit high from the wine, and I was a lot high from him. His body movements were unbelievably sultry for a man his age! At one point, he took off his shirt and threw it across the room. He came close to me, still dancing. Then he took off my top, and tossed it over to his. The dancing apart continued. We were laughing and having a great time. Next he posed as if he were a male stripper, and took off his shorts. Then I danced over to him and moved my crotch up to his. He took off my Capri bottoms and his briefs. Still with dancing moves, not missing a beat, we lowered ourselves down to the floor again. It had been five hours, and his royal highness appeared again. This time the sex was hot like Caribbean Island hot! We were both so much into passion. He was inside me, and we still held onto the beat of the music. This time we were dancing horizontally. We both reached an orgasm that had us chanting louder than the music.

We were both exhausted! We rolled over separately onto our backs, and Jakey made a request. He asked if next time we could do some dirty talk, possibly as foreplay. I thought "next time!" I said, "Okay." Then came another request. He said our crotches have now formally met, inside and out. Therefore, they should each have a name when making reference to them. How naughty he is! He decided his penis would be called "Mister Cock". I preferred "Rooster", but he won. Then I had to pick a name for myself. I chose "Kitty", but he preferred "Miss Pussy". He won again. I gave my approval for now. It could always be changed and cleaned up.

Several times I heard my cell phone buzz. I checked and there were text messages from Steffy. Each one was almost the same. "Well?" "Did you do it?" "Can he get hard?" "Is he big?" "Was it good?" I asked Jakey to read the messages. We laughed.

I wrote back and said, "Yes to all. Am very tired. Will talk tomorrow. DON'T TELL STEVEN!"

She sent one response: "YEA, MOTHER FINALLY GOT LAID!" I told Jakey there are some things a mother can tell her adult daughter, but not her son.

Jakey then checked his cell phone for messages. There was only one message from Harvey. "Well Dad, did you get laid tonight? You've only been waiting about six years for the right time with the right woman. Is she the right one? Well, come on. You have to tell me." Jakey answered his question in one word: "TWICE! Am still here. Going home soon. It was a magical day and night. Very tired. Will talk in the morning."

"MAZEL TOV DAD. LOVE YOU!"

After all I did with Jakey that day, one might think I would jump at the chance to have him stay all night. I couldn't understand it myself, but I still wasn't ready. Jakey said, "I understand. How about if I come back here again tomorrow evening. I'll bring a pizza. Since not tonight, perhaps tomorrow night you'll take a shower with me, and sleep naked with me. We can be 'skin to skin' in your bed."

This time I said, "Perhaps."

Later we began texting. "I don't like anchovies on pizza. How about if you pack a clean set of underwear, socks, toothbrush, a razor, shaving cream, deodorant, and any other personal toiletries you need for an overnighter. Also, you might want to stop at the men's body spa and find a manly smelling lotion. I can use it to massage your body. If I put mine on you after a shower, you will smell girlie. Although, that might not be so bad. No other woman would want you. I have a lotion to use for my massage. I want to smell girlie for you. I have a king-sized bed. You'll love it."

I waited for a response. "I was taking another cold shower, but not tomorrow. I will now lie in my bed, naked and alone. Miss you already!"

"Miss you too much already! Fuck the pizza and body lotion. How about packing that bag and coming back here right now. I have no plans for tomorrow. If you don't, maybe we could spend the entire day together. I won't shower until you get here. Me and Miss Pussy want and need you so badly! Drive carefully!"

"On the way in about ten minutes."

The intercom rang, and it was Jakey. I buzzed him into the building. He took the elevator. I was waiting naked behind my door. We both pulled his clothes off. He was then "up and in" again on the floor in the den. The floor became so much the immediate fucking place of choice. I needed to have soft throws laid out in the different rooms. It was about midnight. Jakey seemed to be able to rise in five-hour intervals. First, 2:00 Tuesday, then again 7:00 Tuesday, and now midnight. What a man! We took a shower together in my bathroom. Then we went into my bed naked for the first time. It was late and we were very tired. We kissed and fell asleep together as close as any two bodies can be. If anyone peeked in, they would not be able to tell where each of our bodies began and ended. There would only be one way. He's the one with the hairy legs!

Well, everything that has a good side sometimes has a bad side. I'm referring to one of us having to get up to use the bathroom. Our legs and arms are tightly intertwined. Therefore, it's impossible for one of us to freely get out of bed. I was the one who needed to get to the bathroom. I had to nudge him, poke him, and pinch him on his naked adorably shaped tush. He woke up and asked if something was wrong. I got out of bed, went to the bathroom, and returned. He was now wide awake, propped up on the pillows, his legs wide open, and Mister Cock was half-awake. This was the first night we were sleeping together and had to work out something. The only thing we could think of was a smack on the tush. Whoever had to get up would smack the other one, and gently pull out of the hold. Then smack again on return. We'd have to give it a try.

We met only five days ago, and only had three dates. Maybe it was four dates since he left and came back again. Whatever! We would have some adjustments to make, but all good ones. I think Jakey sees me as his hot sexy "Miss Pussy". He'll also learn that I can be a teasing, toying, fun, game playing bitch. He said he loves sex and loves being naked. Have I got surprises for him! He'll love it!

Since he and Mister Cock were awake, I decided to play with them. I told Jakey to lie down and open his legs. I wanted to play with his body. He did lie back down and looked at me almost with fear. After only knowing me five days, he was already crazy wild about me. Also, possibly falling in love with me, but who was I really? What was he thinking? What the fuck is she going to do to me? Should I grab my clothes and run? I got some lotion out of the bathroom, and began a full body massage. I started at his toes and wiggled my fingers up his legs like a spider. Then I zoomed in at his groin and teased him. I decided I wasn't being fair, so I zoomed right in and played with his tip. It was shortly after sex so I knew Mister Cock wouldn't rise so soon. Jakey was still ultra sensitive and did come a bit. Moan? Boy, did he ever!

We both settled back down to sleep. Lying awake or sleeping against Jakey's body is amazing. He smells almost pure and clean. His skin is so soft and almost has a sweet taste.

CHAPTER 4-8

Jakey was already here, and naked in my bed. I think he was still crazy from what I did to him earlier. It was now 6:00, and he has risen with the morning sun. We made love again, and cuddled for a while. Then we showered, dressed, and went into the other room for breakfast. I sent Steffy a text. "Jake is here. We might go to Atlantic City. All is well." Jakey sent a similar message to Harvey.

We did decide to go to Atlantic City for the day. I asked Jakey to drive my car. He took his car, a Lincoln, out on the road when he went to Lancaster to visit his son. My car needed a good run. He asked why I have a bag of peanut butter crackers and hard candies in my car. This gave me the opening to tell him about my condition of hypoglycemia. I also decided to tell him I had a stroke before I met him. I certainly didn't tell him my family called it a nervous breakdown. I thought he should know in the event something happened when he was alone with me. He would know there was a history. He was sorry I had these illnesses, but it didn't change anything between us. When we got to the shore, Jakey parked the car with valet in the casino hotel. I told him I love a hot dog and pistachio ice cream on the boardwalk. We ate sitting on a bench then took a long stroll. Now we were ready to enter the casino and gamble. Again, we separated. Jakey went to a blackjack table, and I went to the slots. We each had a cell phone to keep in touch.

At about 7:00, Jakey sent me a text saying he would like to meet at the casino restaurant and have dinner. It was way past 4:00, his usual dinnertime. He was very hungry. We met at the place he suggested, and had a great dinner. I was sitting directly across from him but sent a text. "We had sex four times in about sixteen hours. Now it's been about another sixteen hours with nothing. Miss Pussy is very horny for you and Mister Cock. How about if you finish your drink, take care of the bill, and relax. I'll go to the hotel desk, and get a room under my name, with my credit card. Will text you with the room number. You can meet me there."

He texted me back saying, "GO ROSEY!"

I wondered why he called me Rosey. I guess it was just a texting error. As I left the table alone, I leaned over and whispered into his ear. "Do you think the salty air enhances a fuck?" His face lit up and I left.

I took care of business and sent him another text. "Dear Mister Cock. Meet me in Tower Room 826. Miss Pussy." It was a night of crazy sex! I asked for a 6:00 wake-up call. We both had commitments for Thursday and had to be home early. We got back to my apartment about 9:00. There was enough time to get ready for the day. He had his breakfast date and golf in the morning. Later in the day, his plan was to pick up Thomas and Patrick from school at 3:00. They were going out to dinner and a movie. I already had my seasonal curly perm, so I just relaxed. My Mah Jong game wasn't until 7:00. I always got home about 10:00. Sam would be coming for breakfast the following morning. We are together every Friday until about noon. I told Jakey I would call him when Sam leaves. He could then plan to come to the apartment. It wasn't the right time yet for them to meet.

I pulled into my parking place at my usual 10:00, and spotted Jakey's car. I went over and saw him sitting behind the wheel sound asleep. He had a book open across his chest. His reading glasses were hanging off of his nose. I tapped lightly on the window and woke him up. "What are you doing here?"

"Your lost little poodle is feeling a bit lost tonight and missed you." I opened the car door. He spun around with his legs apart. I got between them and put my hands on both of his upper thighs. He took a deep breath. He was already hard. I took him by the hand. "Come on you big lug, let's go upstairs." It had again been another sixteen hours since the last sexual encounter. We were naked and he was inside of me in about three minutes. We also loved to take our showers together and do some manual "pleasuring". Let me tell you about that word.

"My grandmother was a great joke teller. Sometimes in her old age, she loved to use the word fuck. Her favorite joke was about an old woman. She lived on the fifth floor in a tenement apartment building in Brooklyn. The kids outside loved to annoy her. They always threw balls at her window. One day she opened the window and yelled out some Yiddish obscenities. One boy yelled, 'Fuck you lady.' She yelled back, 'It would be such a mahiaya (spelling iffy).' Translation is 'It would be a pleasure.'"

Harriet became our Thursday night sex position counselor. She was one of my Mah Jong ladies. She always had a video or pictures of weird positions. We did try two of them. They were successful, but not comfortable. On both, the man has to be long and erect. Jakey was good on that part. Then we had to be in sitting positions on the floor or bed. Woman on top, man inside, legs wrapped around each other, and movements we had never made. They created great internal friction for orgasms, which was amazing. I think these are positions for the younger, more agile couples. We had some of our own great ones! We both loved it when I was on top. His entry took on a different slant.

Jakey came back to the apartment late Friday afternoon. He brought me a beautiful bouquet of long stemmed red roses. I was learning Jakey is a hot and naughty man, but also a sweet and sensitive man. I think in a short period of time he has become "my man". We went out for dinner to the seafood restaurant where we first met. The hostess remembered us and gave Jakey a thumbs-up. She also sent him a complimentary glass of scotch. I just ordered a ginger ale. We still had so much to learn about each other. Jakey had no plans with his family that weekend, but I did. Every Saturday I have brunch with Steffy and Abby. I told Jakey we could meet back at my apartment afterwards. A new request then came from this adorable man. I was not set in my ways, but he was a bit. He told me he didn't like to eat out on Saturday evenings. That was deli night for him. After all, if he had no plans with his family, he could do anything he wanted at any time. He could also eat anything he wanted at any time. I took him downstairs to meet Bob. He's the owner of the deli restaurant in the building lobby. I did the intro, and Jakey picked what he wanted for dinner. Sometimes he liked bagels and fish, and sometimes corned beef with trimmings. That's what he chose this time.

Sunday became brunch out day for us. Helen is so excited that her matchmaking is such a success. She and her husband Leon were now going to join us. The plan was we would meet after they leave church. Perhaps they might also like the casino. The next few days were our normal. We continued with our commitments with family, friends, and activities. But, there was hardly a day that we didn't have a sexual encounter. We managed to make time for it daily. It was either morning, noon, or night. Sometimes, it was all three. On Monday, we both had our activities. Tuesday came and Jakey thought I would cook for him again. I don't know why. Nothing had been mentioned. He believed I would expect him again at 2:00.

Tuesday came and I got a frightening text message from Rainey. "DO NOT COME TO MY APARTMENT AT TWO O'CLOCK!! I REPEAT, DO NOT COME TO MY APARTMENT TODAY." I froze! I called Harvey and told him

I was too afraid to keep reading. Was she tired of me? Had I worn out my welcome with her? Harvey calmed me down and told me I needed to keep reading. He would stay on the line with me. I continued reading. "Come to the Radcliff Hotel, Old Trevose Highway, 4 o'clock. Take the elevator to the third floor. I'll meet you in room 339."

Jakey called me baby, but sometimes he was the baby. I think his past left him insecure about himself as a man. I think I'm falling madly in love with him. I'm going to have a job ahead of me. I will have to help confirm his manhood.

CHAPTER 4-9

I was all tingly. It surely was going to be an evening of extraordinary hot sex. I couldn't wait. On the doorknob was a sign saying "PLEASE ENTER". I expected Rainey to be standing behind the door completely naked. That was how she sometimes greeted me at her apartment. She knew I liked that. I was wrong. She was fully dressed with a red rose in her hair, and make-up that was just perfect. She was wearing the fragrance that always had me nuzzle into her neck. I loved to smell and taste her. She said, "Happy Anniversary." I asked how that was possible. We only knew each other for eleven magical days. She walked over and gave me a very passionate kiss. It's the one week anniversary of the first time we made love.

There was a knock at the door. It was a waiter with a cart carrying a cloth cover and napkins. He took it to a small table in a corner of the room. He went back to the door and wheeled in another cart. It was holding crystal dishes, glasses, and silver flatware. There were also several silver lids covering dishes of various foods. He took a plate with strawberry shortcake, our favorite, and placed it in the small refrigerator. Next he pulled out a chair for both of us, and removed the silver lids. There was an ice bucket chilling a bottle of wine. Rainey slipped something into his hand. I knew it had to be a tip. Under normal circumstances, I would offer to give the tip, but not now. It was clear she had everything planned and in her control.

There was Caesar salad, fresh baked rolls and butter, grilled shrimp, lobster tail, oysters, and steak. On other plates there were baked potatoes, with butter and sour cream. Rainey once told me that with dinner one should always have a vegetable. On the final plate, there were beautifully sliced cooked carrots. I truly believed I was killed in a car accident on the way to the hotel. I had to be in heaven or someplace similar. We began eating and talking quietly. The mood was so warm! That was what we were both needing and looking for. I think we both hoped to find it with each other.

After dinner, we relaxed and just talked on many different subjects. She said we had the room for the night. Check-out time wasn't until noon the next day. Then came the ultimate surprise! Rainey told me to go into the bathroom and close the door. I was not to dare come out until she called my name. "No cheating and no peeking!" When I came out, I was to only be wearing a special pair of briefs she left for me. Oh my God! This is crazy! It was actually a very small G-string. The front pouch was made of a black see-through fabric. I wondered if I could tuck myself into it, even when soft. Again, I thought now I would find her naked. In just those few minutes, I could almost feel Mister Cock rising. Then she called me. I opened the door, walked out, and saw her standing next to the bed. Now I knew for sure that I died. I was speechless and breathless! I was experiencing every man's fantasy, and it was only for me.

Rainey was wearing large pink crystal earrings. On her breasts were matching pasties. As my eyes moved down, there was a large pink crystal in her naval. Lower, I saw she was wearing a black lace garter belt. At the crotch, there was a large pink crystal emblem hanging from the belt. Attached to the belt were black fish net stockings. She was wearing stiletto heels. Yes, I'm dead! She looked at me and in a very sweet, sultry voice said, "Don't you want to touch?" I didn't think I could without having an orgasm inside my G-string. I had some control, but this was asking a lot. I would just have to remember. "Control."

I walked over to her and starting removing the items. I began with the earrings, the pasties, and the crystal in her naval. Then I got to the danger point. How could I keep from just shooting out? Alright, Jakey, keep trying! I decided to stay away from her crotch area as long as possible. I sat down on the floor. One at a time I removed her shoes and stockings. With each stocking, I massaged her from thigh down to her toes. I was still trying to keep it together, but I don't think she was. This was a crazy plan to seduce me. I then removed the emblem from her crotch. Another surprise! Except in magazines, I had never seen a woman wearing a garter belt. I didn't know it was crotchless. She was breathing so heavy and her pelvis was rocking. She was fucking hot and horny for me! I pulled the belt off knowing neither one of us could hold on any longer. We were standing on the floor directly next to the bed. I lifted her, and put her on the bed. Mister Cock was inside of Miss Pussy in a matter of seconds. Wild! Wild! Afterwards, we each reached out both hands to each other. It was four hands together, not two. I think that was the moment it happened. There was no doubt. That was when we both fell madly, wildly, and passionately in love with each other.

We ate the cake from the refrigerator and then went back to the bed. We were so full of food and emotion. All we could do was cuddle up and fall asleep. At 6:00, we woke up, made love again, took a shower, and got dressed. It was about 9:00 when we left the hotel room. We had breakfast in their dining room and were ready to leave for home. Rainey was carrying a small brown paper bag. I saw her throw it into a lobby trash can. She said it was all of the costume pieces from the night before. No reruns. The next times there would be new costumes with new fantasies.

On a serious note, we both came in separate cars. Therefore, I was alone driving to her apartment. I did something out loud I hadn't done in a long time. I talked to God.

"Dear God. Chances are you see what Rainey and I are doing as sinful, but it's not. You know of the cold emptiness we both had in our marriages. Rainey and I needed warm in life and hot in the bed. Both spouses failed us. You know sex, as my father said, is not just for having children. It's also part of the extreme closeness that should be shared between a man and woman in marriage. We didn't have that. Yet Rainey and I honored our vows to them and to you. Now they are gone by your choice. We should be able to find love. Hopefully, you will give us many years together."

It was Wednesday, and we had no plans for the rest of the day. We mutually decided to rest, read, and watch a movie. Of course the day would end with love making, a shower and relaxing. I always make him crazy. Sometimes he looks at me almost with fear in his eyes. They are asking, "What's next?"

His body is so clean and delicious, but I convinced him to go with me for a pedicure. He fought with me all the way to the nail salon. Once he saw other men, he had it done and made an announcement on the way home. "Hey, Rainey, I think I want to have the cute little girl make house calls just for me when I'm home alone." He loved it! One night, I talked him into fucking in the casino parking lot. It was a late summer night. The back lot was totally empty, and all the lights were off in that area. He was wearing Bermuda shorts and me a mini dress with just bikini panties underneath. His Lincoln is very spacious. He moved his driver's side seat back. Next he tilted the steering wheel forward and out of the way. My hands went into his pants and pulled them down. I pulled my panties off as I lifted my dress. By this time, he had a terrific hard on. I was hot and horny and didn't want to wait until we got home. He was hot and horny and petrified! I sat on top of him with Mister Cock inside. He was scared of getting caught, but loving this crazy adventure. This was the first time I heard my Jakey whimper as he was coming instead of moan. He really was scared, but I know he'll do it again.

CHAPTER 4-10

Thursday came and went. All the days and weeks followed with both having the same schedules. We kept our commitments with family and friends, which we both always enjoyed. It was always a given that we would end our day with incredible sex in my apartment. Additionally, we slept together naked in my bed almost every night. We made love when Mister Cock rose with the morning sun.

After six weeks, I approached Jakey and asked for the floor. This time I had a long speech. I needed him to let me go on and on. There was to be no stopping me with any comments, or to ask questions until I finished. He agreed to let me speak.

"Jakey, this is going to be difficult for me. Additionally, I fear your response and reactions. I'm not asking you to marry me. With two separate families, there could be too many complications. What I'm asking is that you very seriously consider us living together. We both hate kissing good night at the door. Then you go back to the house and sleep alone. I too am alone. I'm so lonely on those nights. I love you so much, miss you, and can hardly sleep. All I can think about is you being naked in the bed where you slept with her.

"Do you think I'm selfish because I want you sleeping naked here with me? I want it every night and every morning. Am I selfish for wanting a full life with you as if we were a married couple? After eleven days into our relationship, we held four hands together. There was no doubt. We both had fallen madly, wildly, and passionately in love with each other. I love our sex, but I love our love even more. I want you full time, not just as the man who comes and goes.

"Everybody already knows you spend many nights here with me. We have been honest with Harvey, Steffy, and Abby. I don't care if everybody knows we sleep together and fuck morning, noon, and night. Sam is here early every Friday morning. I shouldn't have to fuck with you, shower with you, and then get rid of you. He's old enough to know you sleep with me all night. He's almost 22 years old, and mature enough to understand. The only approval I need is from you. I love you so much! I don't want you to just hang out with me. I'm asking you to not waste any more of your life. Please come live it with me. Will you think about it?" I was shaking waiting for a response. I was so scared!

"Rainey, my beautiful baby! You know why I call you baby. It's those baby wipes you have in your bathroom. I don't have to think about it. My answer is yes, yes, a thousand times yes! I love you so much! I want you to know that when I go to the house to sleep, it's never in the bed where I slept with Cindy. I sleep in one of the other bedrooms. There are no good memories of ever sharing a bed with her. I only have hopes of permanently sharing a bed with you.

"On our first night, we made love twice. It was only our third date. We only knew each other four days. After all the amazing sex, you sent me back to the house to sleep. I was so confused, hurt, and upset. We shared everything! How could you let me just walk out the door? I thought maybe getting laid was all you needed, and it was over until next time. Then you sent me a text offering me a sleep over for the following night. It still didn't help me much. That made me feel you were unsure of your feelings about us. I considered maybe I was being too premature on everything. Then you sent me the second text. You made my head spin! You wanted me to pack a bag and come back right away. There was to be a sleep over the same night. I threw stuff into a bag and couldn't wait to get back here. Of course, we both know you were already naked waiting for me. All my questions and fears about an 'us' left me the minute I walked in the door. My mind, heart, soul, and Mister Cock told me we were good!

"Again, my answer is that I will come live with you. I don't want to be the man who just comes and goes. Wait a minute. I do want to be the man who comes. I think we need to sit down and discuss business, finances, room space, and rearranging. Let's do it immediately, and tell our kids after we work out everything."

The apartment has two bedrooms, and I want Jakey to feel like it is also his home. Our home! He really loves the way everything is in the apartment, but we need something bigger. Everything could just be moved from one apartment to another within the complex. We need more space for Jakey's clothes and personal belongings. He also has a lot of books. We went to the management office and spoke to Mr. Moore. He informed us that there would be a three-bedroom apartment in the building available in a few weeks. It would be an exact duplicate of mine, but with a third bedroom. We signed the lease together. The third bedroom would be Jakey's man cave. He was so excited! Growing up he always wanted a cowboy room. Now he would create one. We had the size and dimensions of the room and began shopping. I insisted that he pick everything. At age 77, he would now have his cowboy room! He chose the upholstered furniture, tables, lamps, and pictures. He also told me how he loved to see the cowboy shows with their saloons. We got the measurements and ordered a small bar, wide enough for two stools. I didn't tell him, but I'll order a mirror to hang on the wall over the bar. Etched in the mirror, it will say, "JAKE'S SALOON".

When we returned to my apartment, there was a telephone message from Mr. Moore asking me to return the call. He informed me that there would be another apartment available at the same time. There was one difference. This apartment has a spa bathroom. It was too late in the day to see this apartment. We scheduled to see it the following morning.

It was a Wednesday, and we had no plans. Mr. Moore said he would meet us at the apartment at 10:00. It was empty except for workmen revamping the apartment for the next tenant. It was on the second floor in an adjoining building.

There were hallways that follow through from one building to another. Mr. Moore knocked, and one of the workmen opened the door. We knew what the apartment looked like, and just wanted to see the bathroom. Mr. Moore opened the door, and left us in there alone. He said we would need privacy to talk and make a decision. I think he had a vision of us having a quickie in there. He knows we're not married.

It wasn't just a bathroom. It was a "fucking bathroom". I really do mean a "fucking bathroom". The shower was just like in a spa. It had openings in the walls for steam. Around three sides there were wooden benches. Oddly enough, one section was separated from the rest and had bars on both sides. I can only guess that it's for seniors or someone with a physical disability. To me, it looked like a fucking chair. I could see it with the man sitting high up, and the woman on top holding the sidebars.

The bathtub was huge! It had holes on the sides to be used as a whirlpool. Jakey took my hand and pulled me in. "This is more than big enough for us to get into different positions and fuck in here. Can you imagine fucking with bubbles all around us? Maybe we could use oils and slide all around. Oops, I might slide out of you. Mister Cock and Miss Pussy will go wild." We muffled our laughter so the workmen wouldn't hear us. The rent on this unit would be $400 more a month because of the bathroom. We agreed that we could put our money together. It would not be a problem. We went out and told Mr. Moore we would take this apartment. It would be an excellent choice for us due to our ages. Our joint and arthritic issues could really use daily therapy. We tried not to look at each other. We might lose control and laugh.

CHAPTER 4-11

We checked everyone's schedules. Invited for lunch were the Silver family, Miller family, Abby and Scott, along with Helen and Leon Walsh. I reserved the community room in the building. Bob would do the catering. It was a Sunday, and everyone arrived. Our families circled the room and did their own introductions. All was going great. Everyone ate, talked, laughed, and talked across the tables to each other. Sam is a few years older than Thomas and Patrick, but they found things in common to discuss. After everyone had a great amount of food under their belt, Jakey asked for everyone's attention. They all sat down and got quiet. Jakey was a teacher, and loved to stand in front of a group to speak. He was going to tell our families about the life of Jakey and Rainey.

"I would like to begin with an introduction to Helen and Leon Walsh. They have been friends and family to Rainey for over thirty years. There's a reason why they're here today. Helen is a hairdresser, and Leon a barber. They have a joint shop on Old York Road. Cindy, my late wife, was one of Helen's clients for many years. Cindy passed away sixteen months ago from the complications of Alzheimer's disease. There was a period of four years when I couldn't allow Cindy to continue driving. I took her to the salon, and Helen styled her hair. During the last year of Cindy's life, Helen came to the house once a week. Therefore, Helen and I became comfortable with each other. Rainey and Cindy never met. Their appointments at the salon were at different days and times. Rainey has been a widow for several years. Helen attempted her hand at matchmaking, but it never worked. Of course, she would never consider me because I was a married man. After Cindy passed away, I didn't see Helen for a year. We met at the supermarket. That day Helen said a light bulb went off in her head. That's how Rainey and I are now together.

"I know all of you will have a lot of questions and concerns. I hope after hearing me, you will have most of the answers. Rainey and I met through Helen. She believed we would be a perfect match. This time it worked. In a matter of a week, we fell madly in love with each other. We actually knew we were meant to be together on our first date. I reached for her hand and walked her to the table in the restaurant. Later, she reached for my hand. We have been reaching out for the other one's hand ever since. It just took a few more days to be sure. Please don't think it happened too fast. We're not young and don't have time. We are sure!

"I have almost been living in Rainey's apartment all of these weeks. We no longer want to kiss good night at the door. I don't want to leave her alone and go to the house to sleep. We don't want to spend any more nights alone. It's been decided that we want to live together in one place. Please don't sweat it. We're not getting married. In our discussions, we agree that with two separate families, it could get very complicated. Additionally, with the passing of one of us, it could get very ugly. We don't want that to happen. We're hoping for the bonding of families.

"We're now in a two-bedroom apartment. A few days ago we signed a new lease in both names. It's for a three-bedroom apartment in the same building. That third bedroom will be my den. We've already gone shopping. I picked everything for the room. As a kid, I always wanted a room fit for a cowboy. That's what I'm going to have. It will include a bar set up as a saloon. Everything in the apartment now will just be transferred to the new apartment. Rainey has excellent taste, and I love everything. The apartment is elegant, but not frilly and girlie. The new apartment will be available soon. I'll then move my clothes, books, and other personal items out of the house.

"I'm not going to sell the house, but will continue to maintain it one hundred percent. I guess I need to hold onto it because of memories. I watched my sons grow up there, and have special memories of my grandsons being there.

"I know exactly everything about Rainey's finances, and she knows about mine. We have already worked out how we'll divide all expenses. I get a very substantial social security check, a pension from the school board, and interest from a lot of investments. I put money in places many years ago. That was when the interest rate was about 18%. Now it's only about 2%. I would like Steven and Steffy to know I am not a gigolo. I will never be living off of your mother's finances. I love her more than you could ever know! Our wills will stay the same. At the time of passing, my children will inherit from me, and Rainey's children will inherit from her.

"Don't get antsy. I'm almost done. Rainey and I both want you to know our apartment will be home to everyone from all sides. I hope we'll celebrate holidays, birthdays, and special occasions together whenever possible. Rainey and I have also discussed doing a little traveling after we get settled. We hope to have the blessings from all of you. Now, Rainey has a few things to add."

"I want the Miller family to know I love Jake very much. He is very set in his ways on some things, but I'm not. I've already learned he's good and easy on one side. Yet, he can be a little tough on his other side. Therefore, I have already been bending to do some things his way.

"Now, I'm making a request that he hates, but is already honoring. Have you any idea how he has been eating this last year? I'm a nurse and have hypoglycemia. I'm the opposite of a diabetic. My sugar goes too low, not too high if I don't eat properly. My blood levels are good, but not your dad's. His cholesterol and triglycerides are too high. He likes to eat dinner at 4:00. Then he needs a snack at 7:00. His snack was a large piece of cake with a glob of ice cream on top. His evening snack is now something we share. I make a tray with crackers, cheese, fruit, and yogurt. Sometimes we do have ice cream or cake. We always have our snack in the den and that's our relax time. That's also the time when he likes his scotch. Sometimes we read a book together, watch television, a movie, or just fall asleep on the floor. His crazy cholesterol breakfasts are now replaced three times a week with oatmeal. He hates me, and his eyes give me daggers on those mornings. If you call him in the morning and he's grumpy, it's an oatmeal morning. Tons of shrimp is now replaced by alternatives of salmon, flounder, turkey, and chicken. As I said, I love him and don't want to lose him. He can eat the stuff he likes, but not as his regular daily diet.

"In just a short time, we both take care of each other in every way. That's because we are driven by love. I hope you will believe us and bless this union. These are called our 'twilight years'. We have both paid our dues in life. Now we deserve the rewards of being together for as long as God will allow.

"Of course, my family has been in the apartment. I hope Jake will take you upstairs and show it to you. Please just keep in mind that there will be another bedroom at the far end of the hall. After we move, I'm sure Jake will stock up the bar, and we can have a party. No doubt he'll be wearing cowboy boots, jeans, a flannel plaid shirt, and will be the bartender." Everyone seemed happy for us but Harvey.

It's now the end of August, and we had been told the new apartment was ready. The maintenance team from the apartment complex moved all of the furniture from one apartment to the other. When they were available, our children helped with all of the packing and unpacking. Sam, Thomas, and Patrick hung all the pictures for us. The move was quick and easy, but there was one hitch. While packing, Jakey found the metal box in the bottom of my den closet. He asked about its contents. I told him it was nothing. The fact that it was so strategically hidden under blankets told him it was something. He didn't push. I agreed to tell him at another time when we weren't so busy.

We're now living together in our new apartment, and excited about several things. Please keep in mind that we have several places to fuck, make love, or play. Which place would depend on mood, time, and desperation. We have our bed. We consider that the love making place, along with our private shower for pleasuring. Now we have the spa bathroom. This is truly the most exciting sexual place. The shower has the seat with bars on the side. That makes for an incredible position. Jakey sat on the seat with Mister Cock up in the air. I was on top with Mister Cock inside. It was great! I had the bars on the side to hold onto as I went up and down. We called the floor our fun fucks. They were usually when we were desperate, and had no time except to slide onto the floor. The bathtub is a mixture of many things. We have to take the time to fill it up. The warm swishing water enhances the spiking of our arousal. We have to be careful. The first time, we were so active and changed positions. We flooded the bathroom floor.

My self-analysis tells me that every time I left Rainey's apartment, something might happen. She might not want me to come back again. Living together as husband and wife was her idea. Now I'm sure of her love as we live together in "our home". I never have to leave our home or our bed to sleep in another place. I'm happier now than I have ever been in my life.

CHAPTER 4-12

My birthday is August 31st, and I'm now 74 years old. There was a party on Sunday of the Labor Day weekend. It was held at Harvey's house. Everybody was there. I received mostly gift cards for stores and restaurants. Occasionally, Jakey and I went to China Town in Philly for lunch. We also walked around and went in and out of some of the shops. One day, I saw a trinket box. I loved it until I saw the price tag. The cost was $300. No way! Jakey wanted to buy it for me. I wouldn't allow him to spend that much money either. Jakey had a big box for me. My hands were shaking as I opened it. I really had no idea what it might be. The wrapping paper was an oriental print. It was the large wooden trinket box I loved in China Town. It's lined with satin, painted with oriental flowers, and finished with lacquer. There are jewels on the lid to match the colors and motif of the flowers. We have decided to use it for small mementos, which we will place inside and share through our lives. What a joyous surprise!

I grabbed him and gave him a big hug and kiss. Of course I said, "You shouldn't have!" He told me to lift it and read the message on the bottom, but silently. It was personal. He took it somewhere that did inscriptions. They were able to safely put a gold plate on the bottom for the writing. It said, "TO MY BABY. THANK YOU FOR MAKING MY LIFE WARM AND OUR BED HOT. LOVE, YOUR JAKEY."

On the one week anniversary of the first time we made love, Rainey did a surprise set up for me in a hotel room. That was about the middle of June. When we left the following morning, she was carrying a small brown paper bag. I saw her throw it into a lobby trash can. She said the next times there will be new costumes with new fantasies. It's been a while. I have wondered if she's going to surprise me again with something. Maybe for my birthday.

Rainey and I are now living together in our apartment and have been for two months. It's the end of October. One evening she said, "How about if you go to Jake's Saloon for a drink. I'll stay here and get myself ready, but you also have to dress up. I want you to be my cowboy tonight. Take your cowboy boots and hat to the bedroom. In there you'll find some things in a bag, and you have to wear them." I knew this was the night! In the bag was a pair of chaps. I believe the real ones are made of heavy leather that are worn over pants. Not these. They were made of a soft felt. There was a note attached. "TO BE WORN BARE BOTTOMED". It had the ties so I could attach it to my legs. In the front, there was a panel of fabric.

There was another note. "PLEASE REMOVE THIS NOTE AND USE PANEL TO HANG OVER DINGALING". That's another game my baby always plays. When I'm soft, she sometimes gives me a little pinch, and calls me Dingaling. The first night I met her, I knew she was going to be the naughty, playful, frisky woman I always longed to have. She surpasses anyone I ever dreamed of having in my life. The panel wasn't very long, but I am. My tip was hanging out at the bottom. Now I heard her call me to come for a drink. I went in and saw that the bar stools were covered with soft fabric. I picked a stool and sat down. She was behind the bar and began speaking in a western style. She opened up with "Howdy, podner."

She was wearing a bra with the same decorations as my chaps. At the very top, it had two enormous foam breasts protruding out of the bra. We went back and forth with silly talk, and I had some scotch. We both did all we could not to giggle. I came to think it was going to be a fun night, not a sex night. Wrong! Rainey came out from behind the bar. When I saw what she was wearing on the bottom, I was no longer soft. I was no longer Dingaling. The panel pulled up along with me. She was wearing another one of those crotchless garter belts. It had fringe on it which hung down, but not too far down. She walked over to me and said her boss would be angry with her. She forgot to search me when I came into the saloon. He doesn't tolerate any pistols or shooting. "I have to search you now. I think I do see a pistol. Please follow me to the search room so I can confirm that you are really carrying one. Then I can feel if your pistol is real, and if it shoots." Here comes the sex. It was on the floor, and not love making. It was what we called a "fun fuck". Believe it or not, they are both different.

Until the end of the year, there were several holidays and birthdays. Our families were always together. The next big get-together was for Jakey's 78th birthday on November 23rd. That party was at Steven's house and, again, everybody was there. He also got gift cards, a few books and a bottle of his favorite scotch. I bought him a gold watch he saw on a television shopping channel. It's from a designer company that makes mostly men's watches. When he wasn't home, I went on the computer, found it, and bought it. I also had it inscribed. It just says, "TO MY HOT MAN". Also, it was too personal for anybody else to read.

One evening, we had dinner with Eric and Nancy Holmes. They were a couple I knew from the country club. We had an enjoyable time. Nancy called and invited us to join them on New Year's Eve at the country club dinner dance. I knew the other two couples we would sit with, and they hated Ian. Everyone hated Ian. I knew they would welcome Jakey and be happy for me.

The evening was semi-formal. Jakey bought a new black suit, shirt, tie, and shoes. I chose to wear a dress I had in my closet. It was long and covered my spindly legs. Jakey hated it when I used that word for my legs. Before we left, we called our families. Jakey was always more of an outgoing confident person than me. He was happy, but I was a bit nervous. Except for Eric and Nancy, I hadn't seen anybody from the country club since Ian passed away. Jakey looked so handsome. As we were leaving, he stopped me at the door to put on my coat. He almost had a tear in his eye. "I don't want to mess up your hair and make-up, but I must give you a big hug. Last year on this holiday, I was alone and so depressed. I had no idea that a few months later my life would change as it has. I love you so much."

First there was a cocktail hour, followed by a buffet dinner. Liquor was served throughout the evening. Later there was music for dancing. First we did some jitterbug and twist. Then we settled into doing the slow dances. He held me so tight. I was now comfortable, especially being in his arms. Would you believe Jakey was wearing an athletic cup? He was afraid of what could happen when we slow danced. When our crotches come too close, he rises and comes. Without the cup, he would have a terrible mess in his pants. Not a pretty picture! The first time we made love, our crotches met during a slow dance. That ended with us fucking on the floor in the den. Perhaps the other men no longer have that problem, but my hot man does. The men at the table invited Jakey to join them in another open room at the club. Eric told Jakey that at all functions, the men always go to that room to enjoy some fine brandy and a cigar. I remembered they never invited Ian. Of course they didn't. They hated him. The women always go to the ladies room in groups. The four of us went there to talk. They were almost jumping up and down with excitement and joy for me. Nancy told them she and Eric had been out for dinner with us, and what a wonderful time we had. At midnight, everyone hugged, kissed, and slowly parted. All the ladies hugged Jakey, and their husbands hugged me. Jakey had a bit too much to drink, so I drove home. We had an incredible night and were so tired. We peeled off our clothes, threw them on the floor, and got into bed naked as always. Happy New Year 2017! The next holiday was Valentine's Day. We stayed home alone and it was wonderful.

The morning after Valentine's Day, we made love and then Jakey got very serious. "I haven't wanted to push you, but when we moved, you made a promise to me. It was a promise that you would tell me what was in the metal box. I noticed you put it in the bottom of the closet in your den. You also covered it again with blankets. I have never snooped. I would never do that. We have been together now for almost a year. I'm hoping the time has come for you to tell me what you are hiding."

"Yes, I'll tell you. It's a journal. After forty years of marriage, Ian ignored me, was unfaithful, and occasionally physically abusive. I don't know what happened to him. We went into total retirement when I was 67 and he was 70. I had hoped the abuse would stop when he could be more relaxed, but it didn't. It always came unexpectedly, but not on a regular basis. The abuse seemed to follow periods when he was angry or frustrated about something. He got into some heavy gambling and involved with loan sharks. That led to severe financial problems. I did question him about our finances, but he only became annoyed and gave me no answers. He was no longer the Ian I married. The only ones I ever told were Abby and Helen. They wanted to confront Ian, but I wouldn't allow it. I also forbid them to intervene and tell my children. Most times one of them was there to get me through. The journal was when they couldn't be there. I needed a way to vent and explode. Therefore, I did it in writing. At this point in time, it has never been read. Nothing is dated. I only wrote with each incident.

"Ian was unpredictable. Out of nowhere, with no notice, he

would push me out of bed while I was sleeping. It didn't happen too often, but when it did, I was always sore and bruised. The location of my bruises depended on how and where I landed on the floor. Each time it was different because I never slept in the same position. Once I hurt my right knee, and limped for about a week. Another time, I fell on my right wrist. It had to be casted. When asked, I either said I tripped and fell or it was arthritis. I tried to sleep in the other bedroom since the children weren't living there. Ian said I was his wife and could never leave the marriage bed. Being a dermatologist, he had just the right make-up for me. It wasn't anything to make me look pretty. It was the kind used to cover bruises. He made me swear that I would never tell anyone. Once he said, "I'm warning you! Don't you ever tell anyone the Silver family business!" He was always doing such terrible things to me. A warning always followed. I was truly afraid of him. He never knew I told Abby and Helen. Once, my head hit the night table at the corner of my right eye. It was morning and Ian left the house. The pain was so bad, and there was so much blood. I called Abby. She came and took me to the Emergency Room. I needed several stitches and have a scar. I just told the doctor that I fell out of bed. That was the worst injury and the final one. Shortly thereafter, Ian passed away. Jakey, I'm not a black widow. I'm a merry widow! I don't know why, but I can't and won't throw away the journal. Possibly a reminder of how I will never allow myself to be treated that way again."

CHAPTER 4-13

Jakey came over to me, felt the area for the scar, and kissed me right there. We grabbed each other and both cried. My man is a big lug, but never ashamed to privately cry with me. Next he asked me the big question. He asked if I would let him read the journal. I told him I would on one condition. He had to take it into his den, close the door, and read. Afterwards, he had to go into my den and place it back in the metal box in the bottom of the closet, under the blankets. Additionally, we would never speak of it, not ever. He had to agree to those terms. I went into our bedroom with a book and some brandy. Jakey took out the journal and went to his den to read. Later, I heard him open the closet door in my den. He apparently returned the journal as I asked. He came into the bedroom with the longest, saddest face. I was not naked. There were no feelings of love making. The few people who knew of our sexual relationship believed that was all we were to each other. More times than not, we hooked into each other by our minds, hearts, and souls. This was one of those moments.

Summer was now upon us. June 2017 came and it was one year that Jakey and I were together. Age changes began to fall upon us. Jakey was losing his hearing in one ear. He wasn't thrilled, but I took him to an audiologist. He was fitted for a hearing aide. After he adjusted to wearing it, he was fine.

Jakey and I once spoke that Mister Cock would not live forever. When the time would come, I would be fine. He would also have to be fine. I reminded him how lucky he has been that Mister Cock worked so hard for him at his age. He was rising every morning and every night. At times, he spontaneously rose in the middle of the afternoon when we were home alone. Now he only rises once a day, in the morning. Perhaps it's because he and Jakey are both rested. Jakey became a bit depressed and distant. A few times he asked me to help Mister Cock rise as always. He was gone!

It was a Wednesday morning, and my softness threw me into a place where I had never been. I rolled over in the bed, with my back to Rainey. "Go away and leave me alone." She was devastated! That was exactly what Ian said and did to her. It was when he had been with other women, and didn't want her. She went crazy! She got out of bed, walked to my side, and with all her might pushed me onto my back. She got on top of me. Starting from my head to my crotch, she sexually seduced me with her hands, mouth, and naked body. My pelvis moved back and forth and I moaned with joy. My softness had a major orgasm.

She stood up, looked at me, and began ranting and screaming without stopping to take a breath. "If you don't think I'm woman enough to sexually please you, and you don't think you are man enough to sexually please me without Mister Cock, then you are in the wrong bed with the wrong woman. You need to pack up and leave. If I wanted a stud, I would have looked for a 65-year-old man. I wanted you from the minute you reached for my hand in the restaurant. Your voice alone made me hot. I could have come in my pants right then and there. I had no idea if you could fuck me at your age, but I didn't care. I wanted a warm and loving man to want me and love me. I wanted a man who would be dictated by his heart not his prick. Yes, I wanted hot sex. I wanted it all with you, and I had it all with you. Your ego has become stronger than your love for me. Now you have the fucking nerve to turn away from me in our bed, and tell me to go away and leave you alone. You have broken my heart. I trusted you with my love and all we shared. Dr. Jacob Irving Miller, you are a fucking, rotten bastard, stupid ass! I hate you!"

She opened up drawers and closets. She began throwing my clothes on the floor. Then I was the one who was devastated! She never called me by my entire name. In a year, I never heard her raise her voice. She grabbed her robe off the chair and ran sobbing. I heard the water running in the shower, and could still hear her sob. I had to do something. It had to be something crazy. I couldn't believe I hurt her so badly.

Yes, I had to do something crazy, stupid and fast. I couldn't stand the hurt I laid on her. I put on a pair of black socks, white Bermuda shorts, a green shirt, and a red baseball cap. I grabbed a bunch of her necklaces and wrapped them around my neck. I went into the bathroom, opened the shower door, and got in with her. She stopped crying and looked at me. "Dr. Jacob Irving Miller, you really are a fucking, rotten bastard, stupid ass. What is this?"

"I'm a fucking, rotten bastard, stupid ass. I'm so sorry that I was so selfish, and hurt you so badly. Can you forgive me? Do you still love me or do you now really hate me? If you do, I deserve it, and don't deserve you."

She stood there quietly for a moment. "Why the outfit?"

"I thought if I looked pathetic, I would have a better chance of you forgiving me."

Rainey then pulled all the stuff off of me and threw it on the shower floor. "Yes, you are a fucking, rotten bastard, stupid ass. Yes, I forgive you, and yes, I still love you. I never imagined you could or would hurt me so badly." The water was still running into our faces. We grabbed each other and held on. We were together, naked in the shower. Yet there were no thoughts or movements towards anything sexual.

Normally, Rainey would bring juice and coffee into the bedroom for us. On this morning, I sat her down in the bedroom, and I brought her the juice and coffee. We put away all of my clothes.

"I've been dealing with a lot since the end of last summer. I never put it on you, but now I am. Do you remember we only went to the pool twice? I kept on making up excuses as to why I didn't want to go. Well, now I'll tell you everything. I want you to listen to me. You are not to ask questions, or make comments until I'm finished talking. That's the way you like to tell a story, now it's my turn. Do you understand?" He sat back and just nodded.

"There's nothing uglier than gossip coming from a group of horrid women. One might say to just ignore it all. It's easy if it's about somebody else. Some of the women who live here have a name for me. It's Plainey Rainey. It's said these women don't understand how I hooked such a hunk of a man like you. Oh yes, I dress well, my face and hair are nice, but I have no pizzazz. Additionally, I'm so thin, have no ass, am flat chested, and have such skinny legs.

"The reason I stopped going to the pool is because of Gwen on the sixth floor. She is one who might be called the ringleader. The gossip starts with her and the others keep it going. Both times at the pool, she was talking to me, but staring at your crotch. She made a comment to someone about when you came out of the water. You were adjusting yourself, and she saw how big you are. She wondered if you were that big soft or hard. Her humor is disgusting! It was said that if you can still fuck, when you put your prick in me, does it come out the other end. There's more!

"Gwen has very large breasts. I noticed you looking at her. I was remembering what you told me about Cindy. You said she had large breasts and you were a breast man. It is said that I don't have nipples on my breasts. I'm so small that I must have only little nippies. Gwen probably has nipples the size of my entire chest. Word out there is Gwen would like to take you in bed with her. She would like to put your head between her two giant tits like ear muffs. You would probably love to suck on one of her giant nipples. Even if you can't fuck her, the two of you could have a great time in bed. It would have to be much better than being in bed with me. Sometimes I have to keep from closing my eyes. In my mind's eye, I can see what she is describing you doing with her on the sixth floor.

"I have thought about the security guard knocking on our door. He might be there to tell me you were with Gwen and died in her bed. My mind has been crazy with all of this. When we are in the lobby area and we see her, I panic. This is a large complex, not a school or place of employment. Nothing can stop this talking. Probably the only solution is one day another couple will take our place. They'll find reasons to tell ugly stories about them. Please, please don't get any ideas of approaching anyone!

"We're talking about body parts that are out of our control. I accept the fact that Mister Cock will no longer rise. Now you must accept it as well. I have to live with the ugly gossip about my body parts and deal with it for now. Please let's agree that we love each other and nothing is going to change our lives together.

"We both can't be having anxiety attacks, and feeling insecure. No coddling, no insecurities any more. I'm 74 and you're 78 years old. How lucky we are for all that we share! Now, I'm done and you may speak."

CHAPTER 4-14

"Wow! I'm so sorry! We did talk about Mister Cock. He was slowly retiring and one day would just die. We both agreed to be good when it happened. I guess I'm not. For these last months, every time Mister Cock was slow, I thought about our beginnings. My fucking you was what I thought you loved the best. We both loved it. I would always insist that you were naked when I came to the apartment. We both made jokes and said if I was up, I could go right in. We had throws all around the apartment. We could always grab one to throw onto the floor. They were the times when we couldn't even make it to the bedroom. We just slid down to the floor. I was inside in about a minute. Mister Cock and I were like two sex hungry teenagers, and you wanted us both. Perhaps it's because of our age that we didn't want to waste any time. This morning you climbed on top of me. You showed me what our new sex life would be. Instead of foreplay, you called it after play. I did love it, and my body went crazy. Maybe I was feeling insecure. Were you really alright with it when I wasn't? I'm sorry if I doubted your love for me.

"Now, let me go onto the next subject. *Plainey Rainey?* You know I only let go and really curse when I'm pissed off, like now. Those fucking crazy bitches! How dare they give you that name! I'll tell you how and why. There is only one word. That word is *jealousy!* We both know the saying that a woman should be a lady in the parlor, but a whore in her man's bedroom.

Gwen found it necessary to watch me as I adjusted myself. She was curious about my size and status. That bitch is so jealous of you. She is thinking about how I fuck you not her. She would probably like to be my whore in her bedroom. Yes, jealousy is the right word!

"Rainey, you are a beautiful, classy, elegant woman. I mention her because I don't know who the other women are in that group. Again, jealousy! I'm also sorry if you doubted my love for you. There are no tits or nipples big enough to ever take me to the sixth floor, or any other place. You are my whore in the bedroom, the den, and sometimes the living room. You're the best! You are all I want and need in every way in every room! Most of all, you're the love of my life! You are my gift from God. I promise that I will try really hard to not be a stupid ass ever again.

"You're right. These are all insecurities about body parts. I don't ever want to hear you say the word plain along with your name. Also, I don't ever want to hear you say your legs are spindly. They are just the right size for me to slide in between them. The night we declared that we had fallen in love, we said love would be first, and sex would take second place. We both need to grow up and hold onto each other. There should be no doubts that we are still madly, wildly, and passionately in love with each other."

I told him I would still call him my big lug, and my stupid ass.

It was now late Thursday afternoon. Jakey left to pick up Thomas and Patrick for dinner and the evening. I had cancelled my Mah Jong game and decided to just stay home, read, and relax. The last two days had so much upheaval that I needed to just crash alone. I had an apple, peanut butter sandwich, and some brandy. I very rarely drink, but tonight I needed something. Jakey came home about 9:00 and we were both mellow and happy to be on the right track again.

As I sometimes do, I say something stupid. I made Jakey hysterical with laughter, but he went along with me. I decided that since Mister Cock was dead then Miss Pussy was also gone. We now had to pick a new name for his penis and one for my vagina. I had already picked them. I explained that since we are both Jewish, we had to lean towards being more Yiddishkite. His penis would now be called "Schlong", and my vagina would be called "Knish". He grabbed me and we just laughed. The evening was still a bit tense. We didn't make love that night or in the morning. I left at 9:00 to meet Sam for our Friday breakfast. This time we were meeting in a restaurant. Jakey said he would just be home and wait for me. We would then do some shopping and go out for an early dinner.

At 11:00 I sent Jakey a text. "I will be home in about 20 minutes. How about accepting my invitation to a late morning sex orgy for four? Jakey, Schlong, Rainey, and Knish. I need you to get ready. Please go into the bathroom. Put our big play sponges and non-toxic bubble gum soap into the shower. Then get our big towels ready. Next, go into your underwear drawer. I put my favorite bikini briefs for you on top of the pile. Please put them on. I made sure you didn't notice, but I'm wearing your favorite panties with the ruffles and fringes. I'll buzz you as I come into the building. Please respond to this text immediately. I hope you say yes to my invitation." If he were speaking, I would say he was stuttering. The response was "yes" so many times that I lost count.

I buzzed Jakey and I went right upstairs. He was standing there in the bedroom waiting for me. He was wearing the bikini briefs. He had a smile on his face like a Cheshire cat. I took my clothes off. He gave an even bigger smile. That was because he saw me in his favorite panties. "Now you take mine off, I'll take yours off, and I'll be in the shower before you." We couldn't move fast enough. He got there first, turned on the water, and reached his hand out for me. We played, hugged, kissed, tasted, and manually pleasured each other into orgasms. Our sexual pleasure moaning was so loud. I'm surprised they didn't hear us next door and bang on the walls.

Time passed again, and I had another birthday in August 2017. I turned 75 years old. Then November 2017 came and it was Jakey's 79th birthday. We always had a party for all birthdays with both of our families.

January 2018 came, and Jakey and I were together for about 20 months. He developed what seemed to be just a bad head cold. I don't know why, but we always seemed to have a crisis on Wednesdays. It was 5:00 in the morning, and Jakey touched my arm to wake me up. His hand was on fire. I jumped up. His body was so hot, and he was shaking. He had such a bad sore throat that he could hardly speak. I knew he had a high fever, as his eyes were so glassy. We always slept naked, but with top sheets and quilts on the bed. I wrapped him up in the sheet, got the thermometer, and took his temperature. It was 103°. I gave him two Tylenol and called his doctor's answering service. They reached him, and he called the 24-hour pharmacist in our building. He ordered antibiotics, Pedialite, and a swab kit. He wanted me to test if he had just a wicked sore throat or strep. I called downstairs and asked if he would bring everything up to the apartment. Jakey couldn't be left alone. He came up and asked me to do the swab quickly. His courier from the lab comes very early. If Jakey had strep, his antibiotic would have to be changed. I gave him the antibiotic and made him drink the cold Pedialite. I couldn't let him dehydrate from the high fever.

Have you ever heard of a woman lifting up a car when someone she loved was underneath? It would make her adrenalin run. That was me. I'm a certified ICU/Trauma nurse. Now I had to step up and go into my frantic nursing mode.

We have a king-sized bed. Jakey was sweating profusely. The bed under him was wet. I went to his side and pushed him over to my side where it was dry. I know how to roll a patient and change the sheets at the same time. Only this time it was harder because the bed is so wide. I was climbing up and down, on and off the bed, and pushing Jakey back and forth. I was no longer naked. I put on a sweat suit that allowed me to move freely.

I knew the next step had to be cold compresses. Jakey was coherent. Therefore, as I went along, I told him everything I was going to do. I couldn't frighten him. I put him naked on his back. I knew that I had a time frame of no more than about 60 minutes to get that temperature to drop. If not, I would have to call the paramedics. I pulled out about a dozen washcloths and dipped them all in cool water. I put them on his head, neck, chest, stomach, groin on both sides, and his thighs. I kept on touching his body all over and checking the compresses. As they became warm from his body, I ran back and forth to the bathroom to put them in cool water again. I had him drinking so much that he had to urinate. There was no way he could get up, even with my help. I had to empty a jar and use it as a urine bottle. He was so weak and sick, and didn't want to wet himself or the bed. I held the jar in one hand, and his penis in my other hand for him to go. I think he was a bit embarrassed, but we had no choice. I gave him a big kiss on his belly, and he smiled at me. His temperature was now down to 101°. For the third time, I rolled him over and changed the sheets. I put a towel under him, gave him a sponge bath, and washed his face. I put him in a T-shirt and a pair of boxer shorts. Now he needed to sleep, and I needed to collapse.

CHAPTER 4-15

I asked Jakey if I should call Harvey. He said yes, but needed me to know he would be very angry. He will feel I should have called him sooner. I also called Jason. "I'm on my way and Craig will take care of the shop."

"When I wake up, please allow me to have some privacy to explain everything to Harvey," Jakey always said Harvey is his best friend, but not when it comes to me. Jason, on the other hand, is thrilled that his dad is with someone who loves him and makes him happy.

Harvey came to the apartment. Jakey was right. He was furious! There was a reminder that Jakey is his dad. He more or less insinuated that I am nobody. He accused me of keeping him away from his dad when he was so sick. There was a lot of yelling and insulting as I cried. I was so hurt. Harvey was happy that his dad got laid after being lonely all those years. He thought I would just be his dad's booty call. I once told him that his dad and I make most decisions together. The decision to not call him earlier was made by his dad. We never interfere in family decisions.

"Harvey, your dad insisted that I not call you immediately because of what was happening here. I agreed with him. When he wakes up he will explain. I left a pillow and sheet on the sofa near the bed. I don't want him left alone. Now that you're here, I'd appreciate it if you would sit there with him. I got his temperature down from 103° to 101°. If my care didn't take, he would have to be taken to the hospital into ICU. I created my own unit for him right here. I'm a trained ICU/Trauma nurse, and knew what to do. Make no mistake, I did it because I love him.

"My legs and body hurt so badly from all the physical things I had to do. I need to eat, take a shower, and rest. But for now, I'll be in the den making some calls. Your dad wants to talk to you privately when he wakes up, but please call me. I have to take his temperature again, and get him to drink something. His body was dry, so he shouldn't have to be washed or changed again. My sister Abby is on her way to take care of me. I didn't call my sister Helen because she and her husband Leon are on their first cruise. There's nothing they can do."

It was now 1:00 and Jakey was awake. Harvey did call me. I went into the room. He smiled when he saw me. The first thing I did was kiss him on his forehead, not the belly in front of Harvey. I took his temperature and it was 100.6°. It had come down some more. I gave him his next dose of medication and some very cold iced tea. He had to drink. I then excused myself and left Jakey alone with his son as he requested. A few hours had passed, but I was still so tired. Abby would be coming soon. I went back into the den to wait for her. I could hear through the wall. I had no idea that Jakey woke up briefly when Harvey came in, and heard everything.

"Hey, Harvey. I asked Rainey not to call you until she saw if my temperature came down. If it didn't, I would be in the hospital. I told her to expect you to be angry. You are angry! You were so loud that I heard every horrible, ugly word you said to her. I also heard her cry."

"Yes. In so many words I let her know you are my dad. I belittled her, and know I hurt her with my attitude and words. She knows I don't approve of you living with her. Because you're sick, this might not be the right time, but you know what's bothering me. It's about the house. You told everybody you're keeping the house because of memories of your sons and grandsons. You said nothing about mom. She was your wife for over fifty years." Jason arrived and walked into the room. He stood silently and just listened.

"I have spoken to you and Jason at great length about your mom. I have made it clear that she was a wonderful and loving mom to you guys. Apparently, she had mental problems that went way back before the Alzheimer's. My throat hurts so I'm going to talk, but not as much as I would like. I'm just too fucking sick. You had a mom, but I never had a wife, lover, and companion. She couldn't stand to touch my arm or let me touch hers. She emasculated me!

"Now, I'll tell you why I didn't want you here this morning. In order for Rainey to get my temperature down, she had to do a series of cool water compresses. I was naked on my back. She had to put them on my head, neck, chest, stomach, in my groin, and both thighs. It was not your place to watch while she put her hands all over my naked body. All I could do was lay helpless and vulnerable. Additionally, she had to force me to drink and I had to pee. I didn't want to pee on myself or the bed. She had to get a jar, hold it with one hand, and hold my penis into the jar with her other hand. Harvey, do you really think I wanted anybody here except my wife? *Yes,* she is my wife! She did what a wife would do. Your mother would have let me die because she couldn't stand to touch my body. We don't have a piece of paper, but Rainey is my wife and I am her husband. This morning, my wife saved my life."

I think Harvey was shocked and a bit embarrassed. I heard him say, "Dad I love you and I'm sorry. I had no way of knowing what she had to do this morning. Now I understand why both of you decided that I shouldn't be here. Even if it had been mom, it wouldn't be appropriate for me to watch. I'm going out and talk to Rainey."

"No you're not! I'm ashamed of your behavior to my wife in our home. You should have gotten details and reasons before you attacked her. Do you hear me? My wife! My throat hurts so badly and I can't say this any louder. I want you to leave here now. I don't think Rainey can take any more from you. I want you to go home and examine your actions and feelings about her. If and when you can say the words that you're sorry, really sorry, then come back. Your apology must be from your heart, not just words. I love you, Harvey, but this has got to stop. I know you were closer to your mom than Jason, but he understands that I need and deserve a life. Rainey gives me that life with her love and devotion. Therefore, she is my wife!"

While I was in the den, I had called Abby, Steffy, and Steven. I told them everything. Steffy said she would come over at about 5:00. Steven's plan would be to leave his office, go home, eat dinner, change, and come here about 8:00. He will be bringing his medical bag, some fresh clothes, and stay the night. I knew why.

Steffy was going to bring sandwiches for dinner. Jason stayed and ate with us. I never saw him so quiet. He was upset seeing his dad so sick, and also disturbed by his brother's behavior. I checked on Jakey a few times. He was sleeping again. Abby left and said she would come back the following day. Jason went into the bedroom, lounged on the sofa, and watched his dad sleep. When Jakey woke up, I took his temperature again. It was about the same as last time. I also gave him whatever medication was next on the schedule, and made him drink more liquids. Steven arrived and asked for Steffy, Jason, and me to come into the bedroom. He needed to speak to us.

Steven said, "Jake buddy, I know everything Mother did for you this morning. Additionally, she spoke and explained so as not to frighten you. I'm now going to do the same thing. I feel you're family. Tonight I'm going to sleep here in this room with you. But tonight, I'm your doctor first and only. Mother is exhausted, and her sugar has dropped. Now she also needs care. Steffy and Abby are stepping in for that. Just as Mother took care of you, we have to take care of her. We all have to pitch in and get everybody well again. Steffy is going to stay here with Mother for a day or two. She has to get her diet back on track and get her to rest. We all know about you. Just don't get naked in front of my sister." Everybody laughed. "Abby is coming back tomorrow. Steffy will sleep with Mother. Now I'll tell you why I'm going to be sleeping with Jake. I ask that nobody come into the room during the night except Mother.

Jake, your temperature was seriously high for a man your age. That's why Mother worked so frantically to get it down as far as she could. You're in a great place now, but it's not unusual for the temperature to spike again at night. I think with the medication you're on, sleep should come easy. But, I'm going to wake you up every two hours. I need to rotate your medications, get you to drink some fluids, and take your temperature. Don't get nervous or upset, but I also need to listen to your lungs with a stethoscope. I must be sure they are clear of fluid. Jake, you're damn lucky that you met Mother, and she fell so madly in love with you. She comes with an entire medical team. I have to go to my office tomorrow morning to take care of my patients. Then I'll be back for a second night. If all is well, you will go back into the hands of Mother. I do mean hands! By Friday morning, you should be able to swallow some soft foods. Mother can give you applesauce and scramble some eggs. No scotch!"

Jason went to sleep at Harvey's house. He wanted to stay and be sure his dad was improving. He also believed that he and Harvey should do some serious talking. Steven let him know that he would not hear anything during the night if all was well. Mother would call him early in the morning with a report.

CHAPTER 4-16

Jakey asked Steven, "I have noticed you and Steffy never call Rainey Mom, Mommy, or anything similar. You always refer to her as Mother not even my mother. May I ask if there is a reason for this?"

Steven replied, "Our Grandpa Dave, Rainey's dad, always referred to Grandma Jill as Mother. When Steffy and I were old enough to realize it, we questioned him. He said it was somewhat of an old fashioned European way that he liked. If a man's wife gave him children, she was honored by being called Mother. That title put her in a higher category than wife or her given name. Any woman can be a wife, or be called Jill, but not all women can give a man children. It didn't go in reverse. Therefore, Grandma Jill always called him Dave. She had American born parents, a reform Jewish life, and was an only child. Grandpa Dave was born to parents who came from Russia. They settled in a small town in Long Island, NY, and he was raised Orthodox. He had two sisters and was the youngest of the three. As little children, we always called Rainey Mommy. After that explanation, to us she became Mother. We felt she should also be honored by using that as her title. We called our father Daddy. When you and Mother have some quiet time, ask her to tell you of the background of her parents."

Friday came, and Jakey's temperature was normal. Everybody went home except Steffy. She and Steven felt I still needed a bit more care. Now that Jakey didn't have to be naked, she would stay the day and help both of us. She went home Saturday morning. I now had Jakey out of the bed and bedroom. I got him settled into the recliner in his cowboy room. He loved to sit in there. Jakey felt he was up for company, just no huggy kissy. The visitors began arriving. Jakey normally had dinner with Thomas and Patrick on Thursdays. I always had breakfast with Sam on Fridays. The three of them came together late Saturday afternoon. Abby and Scott came early Saturday evening.

Jason went home Friday night and came back with Craig on Sunday. They brought a beautiful brunch tray. There were several items that Jakey and I liked from their shop. Unfortunately, he couldn't eat any of them. My big lug cried when he saw them. I think my poor sweet man was so sick that it made him scared and a bit emotional. Additionally, he was having to deal with his feelings about Harvey. Jason and Craig are the greatest. They took me into their lives and hearts. They believe I am the greatest person to come into the life of their dad. They didn't feel the same as Harvey. There was so much food that Jason called Steffy to join us.

It was Monday morning and Jakey and I were finally alone. I was back on track, but he was still a bit weak. I had been standing him up in the bathroom and helping him with a sponge bath. My hot man was weak, but hot again. He asked me to take him into the shower and join him. Since I could push that big lug across the bed, I knew he would be alright in the shower with me. He explained that his body was used to having an orgasm every day. Now it was almost a week. It was almost like his body was revved up and had nowhere to go. He needed release and asked me to pleasure him in the shower. Instead, I got us both out quickly, dried him and wrapped him in two big towels. I put on my robe and sat him down in the reclining sofa in his cowboy room. I explained that I wanted to give him more than a quickie. I wanted him to put his head back and close his eyes. He said he preferred watching me give him a Schlong massage. Sometimes watching my hands on him and seeing his release made his orgasm greater. His sounds certainly were greater. He changed his position, watched, and had a joyful coming. Me? Normally, I was so hot for my man that I could have an orgasm just watching him walk into a room. Now, my body was still too tired.

The last game night I gave to Jakey was in October. It was now going to be Valentine's Day 2018 and Jakey was fully recovered. I had to do something for him. When I was alone, I went shopping and bought a small bistro table and chairs in a used furniture store. I had it hidden in the trunk of my car.

I cooked and we planned on having dinner home alone. What he didn't know was that I would be serving him dessert. After dinner, I asked him to stay out of my den. He went into the living room. The table and chair was now in my closet, along with the costumes. The hardest thing for me was how to set up everything. I called out and asked him to go to the bedroom. He was to wear what was on our bed. This time it wasn't too much. There was a pair of black bikini briefs, a black paste-on mustache to put on over his, and a black men's French beret. I told him to wait for me to call him into the den. In the meantime, I set up the table and chairs. That morning, I went to the bakery and bought French pastries and chocolate bonbons. He did see the packages, but just assumed they were some things for dinner. I put on my costume and called for him to come to the den.

Dead! I have got to be dead! My woman is trying to kill me. There she was wearing a French maid uniform. The top was black with white ruffles. There were red hearts and roses at the breast area. On her head was a maid's cap also with red hearts and roses hanging from it on the sides. I had become her Schlong Dingaling, but I still needed control to not arrive when not convenient. Control, Jakey, control! All she was wearing on the bottom was a pair of red bikini panties, and a maid's apron. It was short, very, very short! It had layers of ruffles and more red hearts and roses hanging all around. She escorted me to the chair. Her French accent was really lousy. She sat down on my lap sideways, and began feeding me the goodies. Each piece was long. While one end was in my mouth, the other end was in hers. Our mouths met in the middle. I asked her if I could inspect her apron. Was she wearing proper attire underneath? I put my hand under her apron and gave a good feel. She was not wearing the proper panties. The French Maid's Union would discipline her. We joked about her lousy French accent. I then removed the panties and replaced them with my hand. Now she was wearing proper attire. We then left for the bedroom.

It was Valentine's Day. I went into the closet in my den and brought out a few things I had for her. Of course, a dozen red roses. My floral arrangement skills were better than hers. She took out a vase and allowed me to take over. I also bought her a bottle of the fragrance she loves. It's the one I love even more. Finally, I gave her a gold necklace I had made. It was two hands joined together, with small diamonds forming a heart in the middle. She gasped and cried. If this is death, I am so glad to be here with my baby!

In March, we went to Cancun for a week. June was another anniversary for us, two years together. We went to Las Vegas. We were so lucky! Everything was so good.

I didn't tell Jakey, but I was having problems with my right knee. I tried to hide it, but one day I fell in the lobby. Bob saw me on the floor. He picked me up, put me on a chair in his deli, and called Jakey. He didn't even use the elevator. I saw him come out of the exit stairway door. He held onto me and got me up to our apartment. Then it was true confession time. I let him know I had been to see the orthopedic doctor a few times.

Steffy went with me. It was strongly suggested that I get a knee replacement. An appointment was made to see the doctor, and he and Steffy went with me. Yes, it was time. Arrangements were made. I would have the surgery on a Friday and stay in the hospital until Monday. At that time, I would be moved to a rehab for about ten days. My medical insurance would cover everything. One afternoon, we met with a representative from the company. We discussed the after care plan for when I came home. I would definitely need a physical therapist. Steffy told her she is a nurse and would take care of the incision. Jake said he was my husband and would take care of my personal needs.

Sometimes I still get confused. I call him Jakey but forget he is really not my husband. To everybody else he is Jake. I must whisper! He's really my Tommy. SHHHHHHHHHHH!!

I took Mother, Abby, and Jake to the hospital. Mother had to check in that morning at 6:00. The doctor came out to greet us and explained that the surgery would take about three hours. He told us not to worry. Except for her hypoglycemia, she was in excellent health. The IVs would adjust her sugar levels. A nurse came out to get Mother. She hugged and kissed us. I thought Jake wasn't going to let go of her. Off she went, and Abby and I talked Jake into going to the cafeteria with us for breakfast. We ate and then came back to the waiting room.

At about 9:00, the doctor came out to speak to us. He said the surgery went very well, but Mother was in ICU/Trauma. I thought Jake was going to jump out of his skin. He explained that she lost a lot of blood, which lowered her blood pressure. She would now be given three units of blood. Jake asked if he could see her. I explained to the doctor the relationship between Jake and Mother. He said to Jake, "Follow me." He wasn't in there too long, and was much better when he came out. He told us she was drowsy, but alert and gave him a giant smile. He said the nurse was so nice and let him kiss her. That evening, she was moved to a room. We saw her for a few minutes and then went home. Jake was ready to go back early the next morning. I asked him not to go until later in the day. I explained to him about all the activities that would take place early in the day. He waited and went at 4:00. He did the same thing on Sunday, and on Monday she was moved to the rehab. They both really missed each other. I knew that in rehab Mother would have to be dressed every day. She could only sleep in a nightgown or pajamas. The days are full with physical therapy and rest. I packed a bag for her and Jake took it to her. Abby, Steven, Hannah and Sam only went twice during that time. They knew how she would need to work that knee, and rest. Jake went every day in time for her dinner.

Since I had some extra time on my own, I went shopping to buy a surprise for Rainey. She told me she never learned how to ride a bike. I bought her a red two-wheeler bike. After she comes home and completes working with her therapist, I'll teach her how to ride. I believe that in many of the rehab facilities, bike riding is actually part of the therapy. It helps increase the mobility of the joint. I have a bike and I'll take it to the apartment. Going out riding together will extend her therapy and it will be fun!

CHAPTER 4-17

I called Rainey every morning before her therapy sessions began. I let her have the day and didn't go until about 4:00. Rainey told the staff I was her husband. She went into the rehab on a Monday, and by Thursday, I was going crazy again. It had again been a week since my baby and I had a sexual encounter. It also meant I had not had any release in a week. It was as if she could read me. Well, I think she could. That night, she told the aide her husband would take her into the bathroom. He would help her get ready for bed. It would make one less patient for her.

I guess after the anesthesia and therapy I'm over tired. I sometimes get confused. My husband is Tommy, not Jake. This is when I really need my husband Tommy.

Rainey gave me some funny looks, and told me what she needed in the bathroom. We went in and she locked the door. I helped her change, and then she put her finger over her mouth as if to shush me. She opened my pants, took me in hand, and began to massage. I watched. She knew how much I liked to see her hands on my Schlong. I especially liked to watch as I was coming. She held me over the toilet so my release would go directly in. There would be no evidence of what took place. She pleasured me in the bathroom every evening before I went home. I just couldn't moan. After being there for a week, she decided to come home. Steffy and I took her home, and she was great!

The activities now began. While Rainey was in rehab, I had some changes made in our private bathroom, which we would now use. The spa bathroom would be great at a later time. I had a high rise toilet installed, and bars put on the walls of the stall shower for support. The physical therapist came three days a week, and worked with Rainey for an hour. She allowed me to watch her do the exercises. Rainey had to do them twice a day, every day. I helped her and worked with her. She was determined to heal and go back to our life as it had been. Steffy came a few days later and removed the surgical staples from her knee. She said the incision was healing well and looked great.

Family, Rainey's card players and Mah Jong ladies all came to visit. Even crazy Harriet came one evening. When the physical therapist thought she was ready, I took Rainey outside with a walker. Next would be bike riding after I teach her. I took care of her meals and did the laundry. Many evenings, we played 500 Rummy. Most nights we played 10,000 Rummy. She never let me win. From the first time I went to the apartment, I knew there was a cleaning woman who came from a service. We always worked our schedule to when she was coming. We didn't want to have an embarrassing moment. She was still cleaning for us. Bob delivered things from his deli, and somebody always did the grocery shopping. Sam, Thomas, and Patrick did a lot of our errands. It's so great to see how the three of them have bonded.

Steffy suggested that I help her mother into the shower every day, especially after doing the exercises. She said the warm water was a good healing tool. I didn't have to be told twice. I guess Steffy thought I was going to put her in and just stand by to be sure she was safe. Hell no! Steffy had no idea that we showered together almost every day since we met. For the first few weeks, Rainey pleasured me in the shower every night. Again, I watched. I love it! She said her body just didn't require anything yet. She was happy to take care of me again. By the fifth week, my baby was ready. One night she got into bed naked again and said, "I'm crotchless." I knew exactly what she wanted, and possibly in multiples.

All went well and time was passing. The days, nights, weeks, and months seem to go by slowly, but the years seem to fly. There were holidays and birthdays that our families spent together. August came and it was my 76th. Always a party, cake and gifts. Life was so special. Could it get any better?

Jakey and I still went for our Sunday brunches at our favorite place. As we were getting dressed, he did something he had never done. He took a long white dress out of my closet and asked me to wear it. Occasionally, he liked to choose my underwear. There was already a set of lace underwear on the bed. I put on a pair of my favorite white sandals which were encrusted with jewels. I told him it was really a bit too dressy for where we were going. He almost insisted. I did put everything on and finished dressing. We went downstairs; Jakey took me by the hand and led me to the community room. Both of our families were sitting in there. Of course Helen and Leon were invited. After all, Helen was the matchmaker. They are also family! I asked, "What is this?" He pulled out a chair and had me sit down. He stood up at the head of the table. I knew one of his long-winded speeches was about to begin.

"Everybody but Rainey knows why we are all here together today. This week is Rosh Hashanah, the Jewish New Year. I want to begin in a special way. When I was so sick, I made it very clear that Rainey is my wife. We have been together now for over two years, and it's about time that I gave my wife a wedding. I'm going to perform the ceremony. Steffy, will you please get your mother ready?"

Steffy moved me to a corner of the room. There was a screen, and off to the side was a chupah decorated with satin and red roses. She placed a white veil of flowers on my head. Also prepared was a bouquet of the same red roses. They were supposedly rare. Only grown in special nurseries in Montauk, NY. I was in total shock.

Jake walked over to Rainey, walked her under the chupah, and then began. "There will be no official paper from the State of Pennsylvania, but this wedding is just as real as we are together. I, Jacob Irving Miller, am now asking you, Lorraine Rose Silver, to officially be my wife. I can't breathe or live without you, and need for you to know how much I love you. Do you accept my proposal of marriage?"

Mother was crying so hard that she could hardly speak. "Yes. I, Lorraine Rose Silver, accept the proposal of marriage from Jacob Irving Miller. I will officially be your wife. I can't breathe or live without you either. In turn, I ask you to officially be my husband."

"Yes, I also accept your proposal of marriage to officially be your husband. I never snoop into any of my wife's belongings, but I must tell you that I did go in to her jewelry box. I borrowed a ring and took it to the jeweler to find out what size she wears. Of course, I did return the ring. Here in this box are two wedding bands. They are both plain gold bands. Rainey, I would like to place one on your finger and ask if you will place one on mine."

Mother gave him her left hand, and he placed the ring on her finger. He then handed her the other ring and his left hand. She then placed the ring on his finger. He took out a small white napkin, put it on the floor, and stepped on it. You could hear the broken glass. This ceremony ended as any other Jewish marriage ceremony would end, with the breaking of the glass. Jake said, "Now I want to kiss my bride."

There was no Jewish marriage ceremony with Tommy. We didn't have a faux wedding. We had a real one. We were married by a judge. I think when the judge told him to kiss his bride, Tommy thought he told him to fuck his bride. Jake is naughty, but he's not a dirty-mouthed Irishman like my Tommy.

"Hey Rosey darlin', I heard that. I wish I could fuck Jake's bride. You are so right! I am a dirty-mouthed Irishman."

Mother surprised all of us. "Now that I'm officially your wife, I'm going to make you pay for this. How could you let me cry so much that I have blue eyeliner and black mascara running down my face. Not to mention the snot running out of my nose on my wedding day. Does anybody have a tissue? Come here you big lug."

Of course they kissed. Jake grabbed some napkins and took Mother into a small attached room with a door. Apparently they needed to have a private moment. Everybody heard Steven say, "Knowing those two, Schlong and Knish are probably having a wedding fuck. Oops, sorry kids."

CHAPTER 4-18

The next big event was Jakey's 80th birthday. I knew Jason and Harvey would plan something big. I checked with them to see if they had chosen a date. I planned on taking my man to the Poconos for his birthday. I needed to know dates, so I could plan around them. Harvey gave me the date, which was one week before Thanksgiving. I planned our trip two weeks before Thanksgiving.

Jakey's mind was perfect, but his voice was softer and his walking a bit slower. It was difficult to bring it to his attention. I did tell him I believed his leg reflexes were also slowing down. I asked him not to drive any more. He agreed. He no longer needed his car and offered it to one of his grandsons. It was given to Patrick. His Monday night card men and Thursday morning golf club men became his drivers. I offered to drive him and pick him up those times. That he refused! He said that would make him look like I was his soccer mom. He had been close friends with these men for over thirty years. I met them several times, and they were thrilled for Jake that he had such a good life. Since Patrick now had his car, he would pick him up for whatever evening they had plans. Sometimes it changed because the boys were older, and schedules changed. What never changed was their weekly bonding. I too had the same with Sam.

I made the reservations at The Cove, in the Pocono Mountains. We would be there from Friday late afternoon until Sunday after breakfast. The reservation was made for their most deluxe room. The Cove is actually for adults only. I didn't give Jakey any details. I wanted him to be surprised about everything there. All I knew about this resort was from the website on the computer. In mid-November, it can be pretty cold in the mountains, so we packed warm clothes. I was now going to be the only driver. Check-in time was 3:00, so we left late morning. Jakey wanted to be sure I could make several stops on the turnpike. He wanted me to rest my legs and have a snack. He was not used to this type of arrangement, but it was fine because he was so looking forward to this trip.

The scenery on the way up was beautiful. November is the most beautiful time of year to go up there. We arrived before 3:00 and weren't permitted to go to our room. They did take our luggage to hold. The chill in the air was so refreshing. Instead of sitting in the lobby, we decided to take a walk. Management gave out pamphlets showing the walking trails. Arm in arm we walked for close to an hour. It was then 3:00 and we could check in and go to our room. I had already paid for everything and would only have to leave tips at the end of our stay. Jakey walked around and saw the theatre for the night shows, the dining room, game room, and other small areas. They only served breakfast and dinner in the dining room. There was a large snack shop for anyone who needed to eat in the afternoon. With my hypoglycemia, that would probably be me. Jakey had no idea of what he would see when we went to our room. Remember, this was a resort for adults only, and I had only seen some pictures on the computer.

Rainey went in first and just stood there. She had seen the room in a picture on the computer, but this was shocking. I walked around her and yelled, "Holy crap!" The bed was huge and shaped like a heart. The bedding was all white with red roses. It looked like a Valentine's Day card. The room area where the bed sat was slightly enclosed. It had mirrors on the three walls and on the ceiling. That was nothing. We went into the bathroom and we were speechless.

The room was huge and in one area there was a very large stall shower. You could have a gang bang shower in there. There was no normal looking bathtub. It was a small heart shaped swimming pool. You could also have a gang bang bath in there. There was a sign next to the tub telling of the pleasure it would provide. They didn't know we are familiar with the word "pleasure". At the end of the pool, there was a shelf with fancy bottles, and each of them was marked. There were bubble bath salts, oils, fragrant pedals, and a bottle of something for cleansing after each use. The bottle's label said after each personal use to put in a tablet and run the filter for fifteen minutes. I guess they knew how much love juices would be dropped in there with each use.

We got the weekend schedule and decided we were not going to stay in that room all weekend. We signed up for 5:00 dinners for both nights. At 8:00, there was a show in the theatre. We went there and then back to the room. Were we too old for this kind of place? *Not!* We undressed and soaked in the tub. The water was warm and our bodies loved it and each other. Pleasuring each other under water was quite different with the fragrant pedals. We both smelled flowery, but we weren't sure which flower. It was truly a new experience. Schlong Dingaling just bobbed up and down in the water. Jakey took good care of Knish under the water a few times. It was loved by all.

It was amazing doing all kinds of sex acts and positions in the water. It was just as amazing in the bed watching ourselves in the mirrors. At a certain point that first night, sex lost something. It became fun and we did a lot of laughing. Unfortunately, we could no longer have a real fun fuck rolling around on the floor.

We had been to Cancun and Las Vegas, but this place was different. Really different! They had activities and sign-up sheets. I never went to camp, but this is probably similar, except for the sex chamber. We had our meals with three other couples. Two were very young, and the other couple was about our age. We just did the introductions with first names. We were Jake and Rainey and they were Thomas and Patricia. I guess they assumed we were married, as we did with them. It was never said. They did ask if we were there for a special occasion. Rainey jumped in and said we were there to celebrate my 80th birthday.

Rainey and I are not really group activity people, so after breakfast on Saturday we went out for another walk. We then checked the activity sheet and signed up for a 7:00 hayride. We had never been on one and decided it might be fun. During the afternoon, we went into their game room and played cards for a while. This was not the most exciting place, but it was relaxing, except our time in the bedroom. We kept on returning to the room to try new things in the bed and in the pool. We did become a bit obsessed. I bet a good fuck would be incredible in that water. I had to tell myself not to dwell on what could never be again. Rainey made our sex life a new and hot experience each time. That reminds me, it might be time for another one of her play games when we get home.

CHAPTER 4-19

Apparently Thomas and Patricia told the head waiter about my birthday. At dinner, an announcement was made and a giant cake was brought out. Everyone sang to me. The four of us got dressed in our warm clothes and went outside for the hayride. They had large wooden wagons full of hay, and seats along the edges inside. We climbed in and sat across from our new friends. We were given warm blankets. There were cups and large vats of different types of hot ciders. The horses were beautiful and the driver was very friendly. Only the ride was quite a clippity clop. They had designated areas where they drove. Everything was so bright. Lights, pumpkins, and corn stalks were hanging from the almost bare trees. At this time of year, the leaves were already on the ground. All the lights were brown, red, orange, and yellow. It looked like a Fall Christmas. When we got back, Patricia and Rainey went to sit and relax in the lounge with a bit of brandy. Thomas and I went into the game room to shoot pool and have a few beers. They were such nice people. We exchanged contact information. Rainey and I were so tired that we fell asleep with no activity. Morning came quickly. It was time for our final mirrored indoor roll in the hay, and a warm hot sexual bath. We packed to go home and then had breakfast. As we walked to the car, I grabbed my baby and hugged and kissed her for such a fantastic birthday gift. I felt badly that she now had to do all of the driving again to go home. She didn't mind.

It was now the time for Jakey's big birthday party. I helped with the guest list and worked on getting names and addresses. I put Helen and Leon on the list. Jason and Harvey knew some of their dad's old friends from his past. He would want them included. Between family, old friends, and new friends like the ones from my country club, about 40 invitations had to go out. I gave Eleanor the list. She and her sons addressed the envelopes and mailed them. I couldn't do that with Jakey always there.

One might say Jakey was surprised and yet not surprised. He knew that between our families and me there would be something really terrific for him. It really was! It was held in the banquet room at the restaurant where we ate brunch. It was a 1:00 sit-down served meal, open bar, and a small band. Harvey, Eleanor, Jason, and Craig paid for everything. I offered, but they refused to take any money from me. They did all of the planning and coordinating with the banquet manager at the restaurant. It was almost like a wedding or Bar Mitzvah reception. Of course, my man had to give one of his long-winded speeches as he thanked everyone. It was nice. He went back into his past and memories. I saw Harvey cry. I think he might have been thinking about his mother being there instead of me.

When he was opening his gifts, someone asked what I gave him. He very carefully told about our trip leaving out the description of the accommodations. He got all excited telling them about the hayride. He repeated that the scenery looked like a Fall Christmas. There were so many things that sometimes excited him as they would a child. I believe there were a few possible explanations. As a young boy, he had a terminally ill brother. He helped his parents care for him until he passed away. A year later, his mother passed away. He had to be a grown man at a very early age. Fortunately, he and his dad were very close. He then spent over fifty years in a cold empty marriage. For him, everything now was so good and warm. I was happy when he reacted as a child with excitement. That showed me how happy he had become.

One day Jakey opened the mail and there was a beautiful formal envelope with just his name. It was printed in gold letters. It was an invitation to a Christmas Men's Winter Night at the school where Thomas and Patrick attended. They were now 17 and 18, and it was Patrick's last year in that school. It was for brothers, fathers, grandfathers, and uncles. How kind these young men are to my family. Steven, Sam, Scott, and Leon were also invited. There was going to be a Mass in the church on the grounds of the school at 4:00. It would be followed by dinner, and of course, speeches by some of the teachers and clergy. Jakey said the school was probably looking for donations. This was an especially wonderful event for Leon. He is the only male member of my family who is Catholic.

Jason and Craig came to pick up their dad. My Jakey looked so very, very handsome. He was wearing a suit and tie, and his new overcoat. I went shopping with him. He wanted something new for the occasion. The coat was camel hair, and he let me pick out a scarf to coordinate with the coat. He looked so good and smelled so good. I just wanted to eat him up. I didn't have a great dinner, but that night, he was going to be my dessert.

He came home hours later. Steven and Sam brought him home. They all had such a great time. Sam drove because Steven had a bit too much of their favorite libation. Scotch! In time, Harvey did accept his dad's choice and accepted me as his dad's wife. He might not have felt it on the inside, as Jason and Craig, but he showed it on the outside. I didn't care for myself, but Jakey needed to be back in a good and loving relationship with Harvey.

Time was just rolling by. We got through the holidays of Thanksgiving, Hanukkah, Christmas 2018, and New Year's 2019. Jakey and I were spending more time at home. I was doing more cooking. The weather was very cold and it was a very snowy and icy winter. Whoever wanted to see us, knew they were always welcome.

I knew Jakey would be waiting for another one of my games. We were both always good for that. I had to go through my catalogues that I hid from him. I had to find something new and different. As I told him, there would be no reruns. A-ha, I had it. I always ordered everything on the computer. It was always delivered in plain brown packages. He knew to never open them. Wednesdays always seemed to be a bad day for things, so I'm going to turn it around. I'm going to make this Wednesday a good day.

After dinner I had to put on my costume and direct Jakey what to wear. I was going to wear a safari loincloth dress. It had a bustier top and a short crotchless skirt. I got dressed in the bedroom. I told Jakey I left him something he had to wear. It was a pair of Bermuda shorts, but quite different than he had ever seen. The shorts would come down to his knees. Painted on them was a picture of the head of an elephant, including big floppy ears. Where the trunk would be had an opening. Jakey had to put on the shorts, with nothing underneath. Schlong Dingaling had to be hanging out of the opening. It would be the elephant trunk. I would be the one to feed the elephant.

I went into the living room with a large bag of peanuts. I asked Jakey to come out and meet me. One look at him and I lost it. It was the funniest thing I had ever seen. The look on his face was even funnier. Normally, we would roll on the floor and have some form of sex. This time we both fell to the floor laughing until we were almost crying. I told him we had to pull ourselves together and play the game. I planned on doing it in a chair, but the plan changed. I think we had to do it on the floor. The game was that he would have his hand between my legs while I would feed the elephant the peanuts into his trunk. Of course, there would be no mouth under the trunk. I would have to play with the trunk to find a place for the peanuts. Well, something like that. The game as planned didn't work out as I thought it would. It sure did make for a lot of laughs. Of course, he kept his hand between my legs and I played with the elephant trunk. The game lost out, but the sex won the night.

Valentine's Day 2019 came along. Every year, we made it our private time. We spent the day and evening home alone. I decorated our bedroom with hearts and red rose pedals on the bed. This time, no funny games, just love! We had dinner that I cooked, and fed each other cake with white icing and big red rose decorations. We were like a couple feeding each other at their wedding. We both got ready for bed. I put on a short, sheer red negligee, and his favorite fragrance. He loved to nuzzle into my neck and smell and taste me. Of course he gave me red roses. I put one in my hair. Jakey put on a pair of white bikini briefs with red roses painted on them. We took each other by the hand and walked into my den. We put on some quiet romantic music and took our places for a dance. It was like the first night we made love. My man can't rise, but he is big enough that I can press my crotch up against his and feel so much. We just rocked back and forth in time to the music. I think it was the most romantic, loving evening ever. Eventually, we went to the bedroom, took off everything, and made sweet passionate love. We kissed and tasted each other all over. I climbed on top of my mountain and our lower bodies merged into the most incredible orgasms we ever experienced. Well, maybe so. Each time we think it is the most incredible ever. At our age, they all are!

CHAPTER 4-20

One season ran into another. The summer arrived and in August we celebrated my 77th birthday. We loved walking on the boards in Atlantic City. My Jakey always got me my hot dog and pistachio ice cream. We made a reservation and spent two nights at our favorite casino hotel. It was then Labor Day weekend. We were home and spent the holiday with both families at Steven's house. My Jakey had another birthday late November and he's now 81 years old.

Again, the cold weather arrived. I was worried about my sweet man. He seemed to be slowing down a bit more. He agreed to let me take him to a geriatric clinic where they would take an entire battery of tests and scans. I wanted to be sure that there was no underlying cause. Jason left Craig alone in the store for a day and came to Philly to go with us. He's an angel! We sat almost an entire day. The only test that didn't have an immediate result was his blood work. The three of us then met with the doctor. He said all the tests were great, and he didn't expect to find anything bad in his blood. He explained that everyone ages differently. Of course, we knew that. On television, we had just seen a 97-year-old woman bowling. On the way back to the apartment, Jason said, "Hey, perhaps too much sex." I only told Steffy some of my sex life with Jakey, but all of it to Abby. Jakey told Jason he had asked our primary doctor about his amount of sexual activities. I was afraid he might have to slow down on that too. The doctor said it was good for his heart. He named a moving picture star who was pumping out babies with young girls when he was past 90. Jakey told a lot to Jason and lately, none of it to Harvey.

It was now early December with New Year's 2020 in a matter of just weeks away. No matter how warm Jakey's outerwear was, he was still cold when we went outside. We had been doing the grocery shopping together, and then I started going alone. He was upset and didn't want me to carry packages. We then sat together on the computer every two weeks and placed an order for delivery from the local supermarket. Of course, we still got a lot of food from Bob.

Jakey seemed to need little things to do. I made suggestions, but he made his own decisions. He suddenly became interested in the kitchen. One day I went to the mall with Harriet. When I came home, I couldn't find the coffee. He had rearranged everything in all of the cabinets. I just gave him a hug and kiss and told him his organizational skills were better than mine. We both already knew his floral arrangements were better than mine. I was so glad that he took more of an interest in items and rooms in our home. One night he cooked dinner. He made great steaks and baked potatoes. He let me make the salad.

Steven suggested that I go to a hobby shop and see if there was anything I thought might interest Jakey. Nothing caught my attention there. I continued walking and looking in the shops trying to get an idea. Well I did. Since he became so interested in being in the kitchen, I went into a kitchen appliance store. I bought a bread maker and a pasta maker. The salesman put the boxes in the car for me. On the way home, I read the pamphlets in the boxes and stopped at the supermarket. I bought several of the ingredients. The doorman paged the building handy man and he carried the boxes to my door.

I opened the door and yelled, "Yoohoo! It's me. Come see what I bought for you." At first he looked annoyed at my choices. Then he opened the boxes and became interested. We now had our first Shabbat dinner. We cooked together and he made the best fresh challah. He also used the pasta maker to prepare noodles for my chicken soup. I lit the Shabbat candles. He said it reminded him of being home with his parents. He thanked me for giving him such a special memory. Additionally, he drank the wine that makes him dance and become more amorous. That was my favorite part of the evening. While slowing down, my hot man Jakey is still able to have some hot and heavy sex. He does it with his Schlong Dingaling once a day. He is now more than accepting that we can no longer have the kind of sex we had the first year. I have made revisions that he loves and we both have "come" to terms with it all.

It worries me now that Jakey prefers staying home every day and night. He was beginning to slowly cut out his card games at the club. I've talked him into having the Monday night poker game at our apartment. We set up a card table and chairs in the living room. The men love his cowboy den, especially his little saloon. They are all about 80-ish and still driving so Jakey won't let them drink. He still sees Thomas and Patrick one evening a week. Most nights they eat and watch a movie here. Both of these nights, I give him privacy and stay in the bedroom or my den. I've offered to leave the apartment, but he doesn't want me out driving alone at night.

We're making it through. He's still not doing well, but I've been getting him out to walk with me on the grounds of the apartment building. I'm also getting him back to Sunday brunch and a short time in the casino. He refuses to go back to Atlantic City. He doesn't want me to do so much driving. We are both so protective of each other. I guess that's how it is when a couple like us love each other so much and are living as husband and wife.

It was now Saturday, January 18, 2020. Normally Thomas and Patrick picked up Jakey to go out for dinner on Thursdays. This week their schedule changed. He told them the following week they should have dinner at our apartment because he now makes his own pasta. They left at about 3:00. At 4:00, the buzzer at my door rang. It was Harvey on the intercom. He shouted, "Rainey, grab your coat and pocketbook, lock the door, and come right down." Harvey had his car parked right in front of the door. He almost pushed to get me into his car. I knew something had happened to Jakey and I began to cry. He started driving and told me that Patrick called him and said Pops fell on the floor at the restaurant. He was taken to the hospital on the Pike. He called Harvey because he didn't have my telephone number handy. Harvey said he had no idea of what happened. He just knew we had to get to the hospital. God willing, it's nothing serious. Harvey used valet parking. Steffy was on the 3:00 to 11:00 shift and was waiting for us at the door. I knew that meant it was bad. She told us my Jakey was in ICU/Trauma and was calling for me. Harvey and Steffy each grabbed an arm and almost carried me through the air. I was familiar with the ICU/Trauma because I worked there before I retired. It was on the second floor.

Thomas and Patrick were sitting in the waiting room outside of Jakey's room and crying. Steffy said she called Eleanor. Harvey had already called Jason and Craig. They closed the store and left for Philly. Steffy didn't tell me yet, but she had also called Steven, Hannah, and Sam; Abby and Scott; and Helen and Leon. I knew what that meant. When everybody has been called, it's bad.

I ran into the room, and Jakey was calling for me. He was already hooked up to IVs and monitors. Everything was beeping. I thought I was going to drop and die right then and there. I knew I had to hold myself together for him. The nurse quietly said he had a massive coronary and needed help to breathe. He wouldn't let her touch him until I got there. I said, "I love you and you must let the nurse do her job. I won't leave you, but will just step aside so she can put you on something to help you breathe." He nodded. Steffy was in the room with me, and we both were able to read the monitors. Yes, it was very bad! My husband was dying! His eyes were closed. First, I sat down in a chair right up against the bed and his body. I held his hand and spoke to him. In the meantime, the doctor came in and Steffy told of my relationship with Jake. She also told him I was a retired ICU/Trauma nurse. Therefore, I knew everything that was happening.

CHAPTER 4-21

"Jakey, my love, it's me Rainey. I'm in bed with you now. My body is up against yours the way you like it to be. If you can feel me, will you just flutter your eye lids a bit?" He opened his eyes and looked directly into mine. I'm sure he could see my love for him. Then they quickly closed. He knew I was there and could feel me.

All of the Millers, Silvers, Abby, Scott, Helen and Leon were there in the waiting area outside of Jakey's room. I could see them standing in a circle around the doctor. He was telling them Jakey had very little time. I was alone with him and felt like I could scream and yell. I had to follow what I believed. *My husband Tommy* should only hear sweet things and have sweet thoughts as he was passing. My *Tommy* was dying by the minute. *Tommy, I'm so confused!* My children told the Millers our beliefs in trauma situations. They explained the theory of allowing him to pass without hearing screaming, yelling, and crying. It was good to say "I love you." It was preferred not to say, "I will miss you." Loving someone is good for him to know. Missing someone is like putting a painful burden on the living. They came in a few at a time, spoke to him, and then gathered together quietly in the corner of the room. Steven and Steffy asked them to listen to my words to him.

I spoke softly, but everyone in the room could hear me. "My beloved Jakey. This room is full of love for you. Everybody who loves you is here. I want to ask you to try to think of sweet thoughts. One was when you and Cindy became parents of Jason and Harvey. There is nothing sweeter than two new baby boys. Then years later, you and Cindy became grandparents of Thomas and Patrick, two more sweet baby boys. Think of all the sweet family birthday cakes through all of the years. Can you taste them, my darling? They were always so sweet. We were sweet, weren't we? So sweet, so very, very sweet. I love you, I love you, I love you!"

Mother changed her position a bit. She got into bed and held Jake against her chest. I'm sure he could hear her heart beating with love for him. I made her swallow a mild sedative. I don't know if the Miller family knows that Mother had a stroke before she met Jake. The nurse had been there for many years and knew the Silver family. Therefore, she knew we could read the monitors. She gave us privacy. There was nothing we could do for Jake, but we had to stay with Mother.

"Hey Rainey. They say that when one is about to die, there are pictures of people, places, and things that flash before their eyes. I'm starting to see and hear things from my past. I guess I'm really dying. I'm so sorry, my baby. The powers I believe in are fate, destiny, karma, and God. I guess all four of them are ganging up on me and saying, 'Hey Jake, it's your time you big lug!' I can still hear you, but know you can't hear me. Thanks for the sweet thoughts. You are my sweet and absolutely delicious wife from top to bottom. I would only expect sweet words from you, especially at this time. I know how you must be feeling. This might be one of the most difficult and painful behaviors that you have ever had to display. I know about your theory of not allowing me to leave upset. I am upset for you, my baby. I love you so much!

"You know me and how I love to stand up and give speeches. I also ask for no interruptions until I'm finished. This time, I have to do it lying down attached to all of this crap. Nobody can hear me, so of course, no interruptions. I have some great stories and will be the narrator as things pass by me, but nobody can hear me. I guess I thought there was more time to tell you these things.

"You know my brother Jason passed away when he was 20 years old from leukemia. I was 16 years old. Daddy was always working and I helped mommy take care of him. I spent many days, weeks, and months sitting on the bathroom floor with him playing cards. He threw up from the illness and medication. I rubbed his back. I can now see him sitting on the floor.

I know I told you my mommy passed away about a year after Jason. I just didn't tell you how it happened. She was always so tired and became weak and frail. One day I came home from school and saw her sleeping on the sofa. Rainey, my mommy wasn't sleeping. She passed away while napping. Me and my daddy became so close. There was family, but we just became wrapped up in each other. That's why I was able to go to him and discuss my situation with Cindy. Now the powers that be are showing me my mommy on the sofa.

I had no social life. At about the age of 12 or 13, I discovered how good it felt to play with my dick. Hey, there was the ultimate called an orgasm. I actually shot something out of my dick. Who could I ask about this? I didn't have friends to ask. The only one I played with was myself. I was home all the time after school and on the weekends. I looked it up in the library.

"I'm now 17 years old, in eleventh grade. I was a good student, but still didn't have much of a social life. I just went to a few teen dances, and some make-out parties. The most I got from the girls who 'give' was when a few let me touch their tits. One girl always let the boys put their hands inside her panties. We could play with her pussy so she could come. Dick and pussy were the words used back in the day. Some things change, and some never do. My friend Howard always seemed to look out for me. Hey, Rainey. Howard just walked by and waved. Perhaps he has already gone where I'm going. You know me better than anybody else. I love dirty talk. Do you think I'm going to stop now? Just glad not even you can hear me.

"What's next? Oh, here comes little Dottie. What a cutie! She was my style with broad hips, big tits, and a pouty little mouth wearing bright red lipstick. She had a rep of being one who really did 'give'. It *was said she was also 17 years old and had been fucking for quite a while. She loved it and never said no. Howard told her the boys measured their dicks in the boy's gym locker room. He also told her I had the biggest. She asked me if I ever fucked a girl. Would a 17-year-old boy say he hadn't? Of course, I told her I had. She took out a rubber from her purse and handed it to me. Remember when we called them rubbers? She was getting fucked twice a week, but her boyfriend moved. She was looking for a replacement, and she chose me. I followed her home and knew she would guide me since she was so experienced. She said her parents worked late two nights a week. Therefore, she could do it right in the living room.*

"The sofa had a plastic cover on it. She ran upstairs and got a blanket. I was so nervous. She pulled my pants down and helped me put on the rubber. She said, "I don't want to get prego!" What is prego? That was her word for pregnant. She took off her skirt and panties, laid down on the sofa with her legs apart, pulled me down on top of her, took me by my dick, and placed it inside of her. By that time, I was so hot that I couldn't really fuck her. Twice, slightly in and out, I exploded, softened, and fell out of her. She was so kind but said, 'Hey what about me?' After that, I only saw her a few times at the house for $5 blowjobs. Once I had her red lipstick on my pants. There was no charge for a fuck because she loved it. She had to charge for a blowjob because she got nothing out of it. She just floated past me, but didn't wave. She's probably still pissed off at me.

"Now I see the college dorm building. I didn't live there. I lived at home with my daddy. We couldn't afford the dorm. I had gotten a part time job in a drugstore stocking up the shelves. My boss knew I was a mathematics education major. Sometimes he paid me extra money to help with his financial books. I worked after some of my early classes and on weekends. We really needed the money. Howard came back into my life again. I saw him in one of my classes. He invited me to a college orgy. He said $25 for all the beer you can drink and pussy you can eat. Geez! It's no wonder the powers that be are taking me away from life. I wonder where they will put me. I have such a dirty, filthy mouth. I

went once and it was disgusting. Everybody was doing everything to everybody, and nobody cared who watched. This was not for me. I came to love sex, but privately.

"Rainey, I did tell you I fucked my way through college. Then I met Cindy. I'm trying to see her face, but for some reason I'm not allowed. I'm just seeing faces of friends and teachers float through my mind. You know the story of me and Cindy. With her permission, I had sex with others right up until our wedding day. I thought I loved her enough to wait. What a shock! I think those four powers stepped in at that time too. They were telling me I had enough sex, and were now cutting me off. Roll with it, buddy! I rolled with it for fifty-one years while married, and then another year until I met you.

"My life began and now ends with you holding me, loving me. You have truly been my beloved wife. Please always remember how much I loved you. Perhaps there is a spirit world where we will meet again. If there is, I will look to find you and reach for your hand. I know if you are anywhere near, you will reach back to me. It will again be like the first night we met.

"I have to go now. Everything is fading. All I can see is Jason, my daddy, and my mommy. It looks like they are in a train station waiting room. Daddy and Jason are wearing what they wore at their funeral. A suit, shirt, and tie along with the tallies and yarmulke they each wore at their Bar Mitzvah. Mommy is wearing the pink lace dress she wore at her funeral. She is so beautiful. I don't want to insult you, Rainey, but nobody gives better hugs than my mommy. She is looking at her watch. I know she's waiting for me. She sees me, and reaches out for me. Her face lights up with a big smile. Yes, my mommy sees me. Yes, mommy, it's me. Jacob Irving, Yaakov Israel."

CHAPTER 4-22

Mother is still in the bed holding Jake in her arms. His head is against her chest. Steffy and I knew she heard the alarm. She jumped up and looked at Jake. "I know he's gone." The nurse asked us to leave for a while. Then she would call the entire family back in for final goodbyes. I asked if Mother could be the last one back in the room. She needs a few minutes alone with him. She nodded. As we were walking out of the room, the nurse began closing the door. Mother pushed the door open and asked her to come out. Mother was always soft spoken, even when she wanted to make a point. Not now. She raised her voice and shook her finger at the nurse. Everyone heard her as she said, "You may wash his face, but do not touch his hair! His family knows and I know he never combs or brushes his hair. He likes it tussled. What you see is not an accident. He towel dries his hair after a shower and leaves it wherever it lands. He thinks that look gives him character. I've told him it makes him look like a stupid ass character. He only lets me touch to fix it a bit with my fingers. So, I repeat, do not touch his hair." Everyone, including the nurse had to laugh through all the tears. Steffy, Abby, and I put Mother into a chair.

Abby sat down next to me and we held hands. She then took me for a short walk down the hall. We came back, and I asked to speak to Jason and Harvey. I told them their dad gave me strict orders for them if he passed before me. He said they must come directly to the apartment immediately after his passing. He left three things that they must take. The nurse then opened the door. Everybody went in and said their goodbyes. Abby took me into the room and left me there alone on a chair next to the bed.

I weakly stood up, kissed his hand, and tried to walk. Abby came back and brought me out.

"I had to keep myself together for my Jakey, but now I need somebody to take me outside to let loose. I need to scream, yell, shriek, and cry." Sam took her by the arm and walked her down the exit steps to the outside. We all looked out the window. She had her arms reached out to the sky, and we could hear her screaming. She then fell to the ground. Steven ran down the steps. He sat on the ground and pulled her onto his lap. Mother always called Jake a big lug, but we all know that Steven is a bigger lug. She began to rock, and he held on and rocked with her. He took out his cell phone, and then Hannah's phone buzzed. Steven asked her to go get the car and bring it to where they were sitting. She got the car, and she and Sam got in front. Steven lifted Mother and took her in the back of the car with him. Hannah drove and they went to the apartment.

Steffy and Abby also came directly to the apartment. A short time later, Jason and Harvey arrived, and I took them into Jakey's cowboy room. I asked for privacy and closed the door. I had been sedated and asked them to listen closely because my voice wasn't too strong.

"After your dad recuperated from that very serious flu, he became very philosophical. He told me that each of you had a copy of his will, which took care of business. I was also told that both of you had shared Power of Attorney for medical issues. He left me three things to give you immediately after his passing." I began by opening their dad's closet. I showed and gave them the suit and shirt he wanted to wear at his funeral. He got it ready a while ago. He said a tie is only for formal wear and don't let anyone put a tie on him. His funeral would not be a formal event. I also gave them a blue velvet bag. In that bag was the tallis and yarmulke he wore on his Bar Mitzvah day. It's the Miller family tradition for him to wear it at his funeral. "Now, here's a letter. It took him a long time to write. First he sat alone at the computer so he could cut, paste, and delete. He had to be sure it was exactly as he wanted it to read. Then he wrote it by hand. After he completed the letter in his own handwriting, he sealed it in this envelope. I have never seen it, and I know nothing of its contents. He asked for you to read it out loud in front of me."

CHAPTER 4-23

2018
Dear Jason and Harvey,

On the top is the year I wrote this letter, but I have no way of knowing if or when you will read it. If Rainey goes first, all will be different.

I guess you know I have just passed away. I instructed Rainey to give you this letter immediately. There are things I need you to know. They are things one doesn't put in a will. That's too formal, and takes too long.

I'm sure Rainey just gave you the suit and shirt with orders that there is to be no tie. Also, she has probably given you the blue velvet bag. You will need to have these things to prepare me for my funeral. I will also need my burial cover. *Let me tell you about my hair. If I know Rainey, as quiet as she can be, I'm sure she told somebody about my hair. Towel dry only! No combing and brushing. The tussled look is what I prefer. I always said that look gives me character. Rainey says it makes me look like a stupid ass character. That's OK. She loves me.*

There are four things that you must give to Rainey. They are my watch, my gold chain with a Star of David attached, and the wedding band I've worn since the day I made her my bride. Additionally, she loves to wear my sweatshirts over her clothes. Let her pick which ones she likes the best.

Rainey and I met with Rabbi Daniel. He is the resident rabbi in our apartment building. We have discussed with him what we want to do when one of us passes. It was agreed that Rainey would not come to my funeral. She would have to be sedated because of her medical issues. Additionally, she feels there is no need for her to sit and listen to me being eulogized. She already knows I was great. The subject came up that I would have a traditional Jewish funeral, followed by cremation. My ashes are to be mixed with those of your mother's. Rainey agrees that your parents should be together. She will request that her family attend the funeral since they had such a great loving relationship with me.

Rabbi Daniel told us that in the Bible days, there was no city hall. Therefore, no papers were filed making a marriage official. He believes God would accept that Rainey and I are married. Therefore, the day of my funeral, he will place a black mourning ribbon on her, cut it, and say the appropriate prayers as he would for my widow. She will wear the ribbon as she goes through thirty days of mourning. He will set up for three days of Shiva at our apartment beginning the day of the funeral. Traditionally, Shiva should be held in the home of the deceased. The apartment was my home. Bob, who owns the deli in the building lobby, will be notified. He will take care of the set-ups for food trays and beverages. Rabbi Daniel will make all the arrangements. Steffy will know which one of Rainey's friends and relatives to contact.

NOTHING of mine is to be removed from the apartment until after the thirty-day mourning period. After that, please feel free and take everything that is considered to be mine with one exception. You are NOT to ever take the bar and mirror that hangs over it on the wall. Rainey will need to sit there with me while I sip my scotch.

You know your dad. I love to stand up and give my long-winded speeches with no interruptions. This time I'm not standing up, and I didn't even have to consider that there might be interruptions.

It has been my greatest pleasure in life to have you as my sons. I love you both so much. I'm very proud of the men you have become. I don't know if you ever caught on, but I'm a spiritual guy. I believe there are four powers that be who control our lives. They are fate, destiny, karma, and God. Please know that I will be watching both of you and your families. Jason, tell Craig I love him as he were my own son. Harvey, I love Eleanor as if she were my daughter. She is special! My

Tops, Thomas and Patrick. What can I say about them? What I can say is that I love them and have also been very proud to be their Pops. One more thing. I hate to say anything at a time like this that could be a downer, but I'm dead. There can't be much more of a downer than that. We have spoken at great length that you had an incredible loving mother, but I never had a wife. Rosey was the true definition of what a wife is supposed to be to a man. You need to understand how quickly and deeply we fell in love with each other. There was no infidelity. When we met, your mom was gone a little over one year. Her husband was gone for about four years.

Rosey has an incredible loving, devoted family. I'm sure they will stand by her and help her get through my loss. I hope you will check in with her periodically, and always treat her with respect.

Rosey darlin', my beloved wife. I have asked for you to be present at the time Jason and Harvey read this letter out loud for a reason. I never hide my feelings about you. At our wedding, we pledged our love and each said, "I can't breathe or live without you." Just know by our spirituality that one day we will join hands and be together again. You will recognize me because I will be carrying the biggest bouquet of red roses you have ever seen. In the meantime, you must remain healthy and strong. I will come for you, my baby. Then we can do some of the things we loved doing together. There were the hotel rooms, and sex games. Don't forget the small flowered satchel with fresh underwear for when we stayed overnight. You were always a stickler for fresh underwear. Hey, Rainey, remember what you made me do in the car on that deserted area behind the casino? I was so afraid of getting caught.

My baby, one day you will join me, and I will take you on the best sex ride of all times.

SORRY, GUYS!

Be good to yourselves and to your loved ones. I'm so sorry that I had to leave you so soon.

Love, Dad
Love, Your Jakey

CHAPTER 4-24

An obituary was placed in the Philadelphia newspaper.

Jacob Irving Miller, Ph.D. (Jake)

It is with the deepest sorrow that we announce the passing of Jacob Irving Miller, Ph.D. (Jake) on Saturday, January 18, 2020. Jake was 81 years old. He lived in Cheltenham, Pennsylvania for almost all of his life.

Jake was a teacher of Mathematics in the local high school from 1961 until his retirement in 2006. He was well known, liked, respected, and known as Dr. Miller.

Jake was the husband of the late Cindy Miller for fifty-one years. He is survived by his sons, Jason (Craig) and Harvey (Eleanor), and his grandsons Thomas and Patrick.

He will be missed by his live-in beloved companion Lorraine Rose Silver, her children Steven, Hannah, Stephanie, and her grandson Samuel Silver. He will also be missed by Abigail and Scott Rubin and Helen and Leon Walsh.

Funeral and Shiva Arrangements are Pending.

I sat Shiva for three days. I wore a black dress, black stockings, and no shoes. Each day I wore one of Jakey's sweatshirts over my clothes. I pinned the black ribbon on them. I sat in different places in the apartment where Jakey liked to sit. When there were no visitors, I put myself in the bed on the side where he slept. I would be naked as he liked me to be. I can still feel and smell him. When visitors came, I had chairs put into Jakey's cowboy room. I would have them sit in the chairs while I sat in his sofa recliner. That was where he sometimes sat when he wanted to watch me pleasure him. A few times I sat at the bar and could see him sitting there sipping his scotch. He knows I can see him and touch him. I hope he feels my kisses on his belly. He loved that!

Steven and Steffy kept me on an antidepressant. Steven and Hannah had to return to their office. Sam, Steffy, and Abby were with me from morning to night. I demanded that they leave at bedtime. I needed my nights alone naked in bed with my Jakey. Steffy was in charge of my food choices. I didn't want to eat, but Jakey told me in his letter that he wanted me to be healthy and strong for when we'll be together again. I had a lot of visitors, but I'm not sure who they were. Jason and Harvey only sat one day for their dad. Jason and Craig stayed over one night after the funeral. They spent several hours with me before they went home. Eleanor, Thomas, and Patrick came once for a short visit. I never saw Harvey. I guess he still didn't want to accept me as his dad's wife or widow.

I always wear the fragrance Jakey loved. He would always nuzzle into my neck to smell and taste me. I can already feel a spark and tickle in my neck. He's already looking for me. He'll be here very soon. I'm so excited!

PART FIVE

CHAPTER 5-1

It's now Wednesday, November 23, 2016 and been a really horrible year. Tommy passed away on Monday, January 18, 2016. At first Mother was up and down. Nobody knew where her mind was at any time. She was able to tell Helen some of the requests made by Tommy. He and Mother did discuss his wishes if he was the first to pass away. Helen made all of the funeral arrangements because Tommy was Catholic. Mother wouldn't know how to plan a proper funeral service or Mass. She did request to meet with a Rabbi in order to be guided as a widow in her Jewish faith. A Rabbi was found in Sag Harbor and he attended Tommy's funeral with both families. Beforehand, he placed a black ribbon on her, cut it, and said the proper prayers. We all stood with her and watched. The ribbon was put on a sweatshirt of Tommy's that she would not remove. She wore it over her clothes.

Steven sedated her before the funeral. Nobody knew what her reaction would be when she saw Tommy in the casket. Steven asked that she please not touch him. He and Steffy held her. She spoke to Tommy until we had to take her to another room. That would be when the casket would be closed. She never cried, but instead smiled. Anybody who heard what she was saying was in shock. It was believed that it was either the medication or the beginning of insanity. I think I remember some of what she told him.

"I'm so sorry that you heard me scream as you were passing. It just happened so fast that I was in shock. It's alright now. Steven explained everything to me. He said the last thing you saw was the love I have for you in my eyes. You were also in my arms with your head on my chest. I'm now sure the last thing you heard was my heart beating with love for you. Since we became spiritual as one, I have no doubt that you will come for me very soon. You'll find me because I'll be wearing the fragrance you like. You can nuzzle into my neck to smell and taste me like you always did. Reach out your hand to me and I'll reach mine out to you. Then we'll be together and go to hotels again. We can stay overnight and have more great sex. I'll bring my small flowered satchel with fresh underwear for both of us. You can have dinner at 4:00 every day. Perhaps in our new world together there will be strawberry shortcake. You doubted me when I said you are handsome. Everyone here agrees. I'm so excited my husband. Tommy, I love you and can't wait for you to come and take me. You know I can't breathe or live without you. I was told not to touch you. I'll just wait and then touch and taste you all over. I know how much you love it when I kiss your belly. You know it means I'm working my way down to you know where. In the meantime, I'll try to take my mind elsewhere and not dwell on missing you so much."

After the funeral and burial, everybody left Montauk and took Mother to her house in Philly. Hours later she had a nervous breakdown. She lost all touch with reality, and had no memory of ever being with Tommy. He renamed her Rosey, but she had always been Rainey. That's the only name she responds to. Admission to the psychiatric unit at the hospital on the Pike became necessary the beginning of February. She refused to believe it was mental, and told everyone she had a stroke. On May 27, 2016, she came home still in her own world. She had no memory of Tommy other than briefly meeting him in 1984. Her confusion and memory loss was with her, but she was doing fairly well. She was on a lot of medication and could no longer drive. If going out with the

278

family or one of her lady friends, someone always picked her up at the house.

We hired a transportation service (TS) for her. Their phone number was programmed into her cell phone. The service was used when she went out alone. All she had to do was push the numbered key. She would be connected to a dispatcher to reserve a ride and give a desired pick-up time. She didn't know that every move she made was monitored by the system. We always knew what time she went out, what time she came home, and where she had been. She had to continue seeing her psychiatrist, Dr. John Gillespie, once a week as an outpatient.

Mother had brunch with me and Abby every Saturday for many years. We knew that Wednesday November 23, 2016 was Tommy's birthday. We had to stop trying to get her to remember him. She only became agitated and had to be medicated. Dr. Gillespie told us to never mention him. It only made her mental status worse. We hoped if she knew the date it would give her a spark of memory. We were so wrong! After realizing what we were trying to do made it worse, we stopped. Dr. Gillespie explained that remembering him is too painful. That's why she's in this mental state. We gave her a stupid explanation of why we were changing our brunch day from the usual Saturday to a Wednesday. Abby was going to pick her up at 11:00. Mother sent her a text saying it was a lovely day for November and she would wait outside.

As Abby was driving, she received a text from Gloria, Mother's next-door neighbor. She was a lonely widow with no family. We told her everything about Mother's condition and why. She loved Mother. We knew she would never break confidentiality. The highlight of her days was to look out the window. She hoped somebody would stop to talk a bit. She and Mother spent a lot of time together. Gloria never questioned her or probed. She was a very kind woman. The text said, "I was looking out of my window. I always look out on Saturdays because I know you or Steffy will be coming to pick up Rainey. Today is Wednesday, but just another day to look out my window. I'm very upset and you need to get here as soon as possible. I looked out and saw your sister sitting on the ground in her driveway. I have no idea how long she was out there. She sometimes sits outside, but in a chair. I called to her but she didn't answer. Maybe she just didn't hear me. I went outside, and it was almost like she didn't see me. I helped her up and brought her into my house. Hopefully it wasn't a mistake, but I couldn't just leave her there. She is sitting in my living room. Please come quickly!"

Hey Tommy. Gloria is such an interfering nosey bitch. I was on the ground for a reason. I was in the middle of dying from a stroke. It's Wednesday, November 23, 2016, your birthday. We planned on being together and she fucked it up!

Abby responded telling her she was running late and would be there in about twenty minutes. When she got there, Gloria was waiting for her at the door. Mother was unresponsive, and Abby called the paramedics. She was taken to our not-so-favorite place, the hospital on the Pike. Abby sent a text to everyone including Helen and Leon. Of course Mother was not aware, but Helen and Leon were already in Philly. There was a plan for everybody, except Mother, to have dinner together. We could not forget that today is Tommy's birthday.

Abby was with Mother at the hospital. The family all arrived within an hour.

Steven and I are well known all over that hospital because we are on staff there. We were told that Mother already had a CT scan and this time she did have a stroke. It was not another nervous breakdown. We had to wait in the hallway outside her room. She was in Intensive Care Unit #12. The neurologist assigned to her case was Dr. Edward Chudy. He was in the room doing a total evaluation. Dr. Chudy wanted to speak to the entire family together. We were briefly told she was in satisfactory condition, not critical or grave. Mother's records showed that she had been in the psychiatric unit earlier in the year. He asked if one of the immediate family members would contact Dr. Gillespie. It would be appropriate for him to see her. Steven and I both have Medical Power of Attorney, but I allowed him to take charge.

We did go in and out of the room. Slowly we began to understand why he needed us to be together. He didn't want to tell his story more than once. There was something else going on that we needed to be aware of now.

At about 3:00, Steven, Hannah, and Sam went into her room. They came out with half smiles. She recognized them, knew their names, and said, "I guess I had this second stroke because I'm still mourning the loss of my Jake. Certainly you remember he passed away earlier this year on Saturday, January 18, 2020. We bonded in June 2016 until he passed away. It was exactly three years and seven months that we were together." There was the clue! Stroke patients get confused, but who is Jake and why 2020? Abby, Scott, and I went in next. She repeated the same thing to us. I asked her about Jake. She said, "Steffy, which one of us had the stroke? You and our family and Jake's family did everything together. It continued for three years and seven months until he passed away." Helen and Leon went in briefly before conferencing with Dr. Chudy. She also recognized them, but didn't mention Jake.

Dr. Chudy introduced himself to everyone again and asked of our relationship with Lorraine. He asked why her chart says Lorraine Rose Monahan, but she told him her last name is Silver. The reason was far too long and complicated. We gave a very brief explanation. He again repeated that physically her condition is satisfactory, but possibly not her mental status.

"Most stroke patients are usually quiet, but she doesn't want to stop talking. She kept on telling me how Jake passed away earlier this year in 2020, and how much she misses him. She repeated the same things over and over again. I asked her about Jake. She said his name was Dr. Jacob Miller. He had a Ph.D. in Mathematics and was a high school math teacher. She added that they were never legally married. Therefore, her last name is still Silver. They were very much in love, and lived together in her apartment for three years and seven months until he passed away. She believes that today is Wednesday, November 23, 2020, his 82nd birthday.

"The only physical problems I can see are some loss of feelings on her right side. I would like to keep her here for possibly three or four days. Then I'll send her to our rehab facility. She will need physical therapy. As I'm speaking about Jake, you all look so puzzled. My guess is that Lorraine and your entire family needs to meet with Dr. Gillespie."

In closing, Dr. Chudy asked us to go in and see her briefly. She was too excited about Jake and needed to sleep. "After you leave, I'm going back in and speak to her. First, I will explain that I'm not putting her into a drug-induced coma. I just want her to sleep for several hours in order for her brain to rest. With her background as an ICU/Trauma nurse, she will understand. I already have the cell phone number for Steven. If anything changes, I'll call. Otherwise, please feel free to call the hospital and they will page me. Now, go have some dinner and relax a bit."

We all stood up to leave when Steven said, "I have an incredible idea of where to have dinner. Today is Tommy's birthday. We don't know anything about Jake, but we all knew and loved Tommy. I have a friend since high school and college. I went on and became a doctor. My friend always wanted to be a chef. He worked in his dad's restaurant and eventually bought his own. Would you believe his name is Michael James Connelly? To me he's Mikey. He has a restaurant and bar up here on the Pike. The family and I have eaten there many times. Another one for you to believe is that it's called Mike's Irish Rose. That was his mother's name." Helen and Leon went with Steffy, and we all left to have a late supper together.

As we were leaving the hospital, I heard my brother call Mikey. He asked him to set up a table for drinks and dinner for ten people. Mikey already knew the long story of Mother and Tommy. We got there and saw he put up a screen to give us a bit of privacy. Steven introduced him to Helen and Leon and told him of their relationship to Tommy. He gave Helen a big hug and offered condolences. The table was set for ten people. Steven said the two extra seats were for Mother and Tommy. They were spiritual. His real hope was that Tommy was in bed with Mother. If he holds her in his arms, she will feel his presence.

"Hey Rosey darlin. Something went wrong! I wanted you with me for my birthday. I know you had a stroke. I thought it would be the day you die and would come to me."

"Hey Tommy. I could feel the stroke coming on. Why the fuck do you think I just sat on the ground? I too can curse! I was waiting to die right then and there and go with you. I knew it was your birthday. I was so excited. That nosey bitch next door ruined everything. As a nurse, I knew if I just sat there with no medical help the stroke would take hold and kill me. She took me into her house and contacted Abby.

"Tommy, it's been so long since I've heard from you. Please don't be angry with me, but in my fantasy I killed Jake. He had to die. You and I were together for three years and seven months. We went from June 2012 until January 2016. In my fantasy, I was with Jake the same amount of time. I was with him from June 2016 until Saturday, January 18, 2020. I came to hate him. He's not you! Now that I had the stroke, I'm making this the right time for Jake to come out of the confines of my mind. Now I'll make the family go crazy. I'm sane and know exactly how to play them. I've been doing it since they believe I forgot you. I will pretend to mourn Jake, but I will be mourning you.

Too many dates! Real ones for us, and fantasy ones for Jake. I'm sorry, Husband Tommy. I'm confused without you.

"There must be a way to make it the right time. Are you permitted to schedule a meeting with all three powers? Can you make a request? We need to find a way to be together! I do know the only way is if I die. No suicide! I tried to make your birthday the time that is right. I'm so sorry! I guess it's not my call or yours. Lady Karma has to make that decision. Somehow, everything we have always had to do, or wait for, was dictated by 'when the time is right'. It wasn't right for us until Ian died.

"In my fantasy, it is Wednesday, November 23, 2020. I know it is really 2016. Please do what you can at your end. I will work my end. I know it's a long way off, but I have a date in mind. I want to be sure we are together for August 30th and 31st, 2017. Those dates are our fifth wedding anniversary and my 75th birthday. I will do anything and everything possible to make something happen.

"Would you believe our family went out for dinner together? They're going to celebrate your birthday at Mike's Irish Rose without us. I heard Steven order a large strawberry short cake."

CHAPTER 5-2

We were seated and ordered Irish whiskey all around except for Sam. He had a beer. Mikey brought out plates full of every appetizer available. We all ordered steaks with all of the trimmings. Before dessert, Helen stood up and asked to speak. "When my beloved brother passed away, there was too much devastation. Therefore, no eulogies were given at the funeral. I think now on his birthday, we each need to stand up and tell a story. It should be of something you shared with him. Tonight, we should memorialize and celebrate him."

Everyone voted thumbs-up on that one. Mikey stepped up to the table and joined us. Two of his waiters walked out carrying a giant strawberry shortcake. Steven had asked Mikey if he could get one. That was the kind Tommy liked best. We always had one for him. There was one large candle in the middle. Helen was asked to say a prayer and blow out the candle in memory of her brother. The tears began! Mikey then asked Helen to stand with him. He knew an Irish song he wanted to sing. As he began, she noted being familiar with that song. She tried to sing, but it was too much for her. We all sang "Happy Birthday" to Tommy and had our cake. It was now time to get a bit quiet and begin telling memorial stories each of us had about Tommy.

Helen asked if she could be the first since she knew Tommy the longest. At this point, we were all a bit tipsy. Helen stood up and began.

"Tommy and I were born in Ireland. In 1957, when I was 14 and Tommy was 10 years old, we were brought to Montauk. That town was chosen because we had a relative there who financially sponsored our move. I don't remember meeting a man who might have been our father. At one time, something was said that made us think we had two different fathers. Tommy and I were never sure if we were really true brother and sister. We loved each other so much that we never mentioned it again.

"Most times, I took care of Tommy. After high school in 1961, I got a job in a beauty shop. The owner thought I had talent. She helped pay for beauty school for me. That was where I met Leon, who became a barber. We were married in 1964 and opened a shop together. Tommy graduated from high school in 1965. His grades were excellent. He was given a full paid scholarship to Montauk County College. Tommy got a degree in English Literature in 1969. He immediately got a job teaching English in the local high school. Tommy worked there until he retired in 2013. We were always so proud of him.

"Tommy was actually a bit of an introvert. He spent a lot of time in the apartment reading and writing. He had very little interest in sports. Socializing and dating wasn't something he did until after he started working. Tommy could then provide a substantial amount of money towards living expenses. He took a summer job for when school was closed. He began operating the ferry that went from Montauk to Block Island. Tommy had a good head for finances and began making major investments.

"Leon told me he heard Tommy was screwing around Montauk. He was dating, but never had a steady girlfriend. I certainly couldn't question him. Leon was elected.

"Tommy told Leon he was a virgin until he started working. He was already 22 years old, and decided to begin following his manly needs. Once he fucked the first time, he wasn't going to stop. It was the greatest thing he ever felt. Tommy was always discreet. Many times he stayed out all night. We knew what he was doing, but he never missed a day at work. He just hoped one day to fall in love, and wouldn't just be fucking. Then he would make love. Yes, I will have to go to confession for my language!

"Tommy was still single and fucking around until he was 36 years old. One summer on the ferry, a young woman approached him. Her name was Cynthia (Cindy) Matteo. She flirted with him. When they reached Block Island, he had lunch with her. She was a 34-year-old gorgeous blonde, with a great body and large breasts. Cindy was a high priced attorney in New York City. Tommy wouldn't move there. She agreed to move to Montauk and commute on the train. She was Italian, not Irish, but was Catholic. Six weeks later, they were married in the private study of Father Chesney at our church. At first, she moved into the apartment with Tommy. He was very well off financially, but Cindy was very wealthy. They did a search and found a parcel of land on the beach. She designed a house and then hired architects and contractors. The house was built totally to her specifications giving Tommy no say.

"At first Tommy seemed very happy, but Leon and I could see changes taking place. We didn't like her. She treated me and Leon like we were beneath her. She stayed away more and more. We tried talking to Tommy. He rejected the idea of discussing his marriage. Bottom line was his life was lonely for 25 years with her. He loved to fuck so much. We wondered if he was doing it with her. We knew he would never be unfaithful. Leon and I knew she was fucking with men in New York City, and then she left him. He was 62 years old and wasted all those years. The talk was that after Tommy's divorce became final, he was out there fucking again. I do believe Tommy spent a lot of time in the confessional. Tomorrow morning I must go to Mass and confession!

"I've just given you story of Tommy's life. Now I want to tell you a story of his character.

"Tommy lived in that giant house all alone. He wanted someone there when he came home from work. Tommy always loved dogs. On a Saturday morning he went to the pound to rescue one. He wanted a large dog fitting for a man to run with on the beach. Directly inside the door, there was a little cage on the floor. Four eyes looked up at him. In the cage were two toy poodles. One was white and one brown. They were skinny and their fur was matted. He tried not to look at them. He wanted a big dog. How could these two dogs run on the beach with him? Walk away? Not Tommy. He picked them up; they licked his face, and they became his girls. It was instant love. He bought everything he needed and took them home. As he drove, they were both on his lap. Tommy was a spiritual man and believed that fate, destiny, karma, and God sent him there to save those little girls.

"After feeding them, he gave them baths and cut off the pieces of furry curls that were matted. He bought four beds. He didn't want them sleeping in his bedroom. He put two beds in the downstairs living room and two in the upstairs den. They were frightened! They had been in a little cage. Now they were in this huge open space. Tommy stayed up all night with them, and called out of work the next day. Now he had to give them names. He named the white one 'Sugar Cookie' and the brown one 'Coco Chanel'. Would you believe he typed up pedigree papers, printed and framed them for the wall? They became Sugar Cookie and Coco Chanel from the Home on Monahan Drive.

"Tommy went bike riding almost every evening. He went to a fabric store. There was a woman who padded the inside of his basket. She then covered the padding with pink fabric. He put the girls in the basket, took them riding, and was no longer alone. There was talk about the possibility of him being gay. First

288

he didn't marry until he was 36 years old. Next, his wife left him, and then he rode around with little poodles. He didn't care.

"Wait a minute. I have another spiritual story about Tommy. Many times he spoke of those four powers he believed controlled our lives. He and Rosey met briefly the first time in 1984. They didn't see each other again until about 2010. That was when Rosey was with me and Leon when Ian traveled. I don't remember the exact time, but both confided in me. Both told me they had begun to fall in love. I knew it by the way they looked at each other. I did everything possible to keep them apart. At that time Tommy was divorced, but Rosey was married. Tommy also told me he believed God and the spirits would one day bring them together. 'Helen, don't get upset. We won't do anything sinful. It will happen when the time is right. I was meant to save Sugar and Coco. One day I will save Rosey!'

"On day thirty-one after Ian passed away, Rosey went to Tommy's house. They bonded their love for the first time. We had dinner with them that evening. Leon said they were both so happy that they were glowing in the dark. Tommy talked a lot dirty and Leon just some. My husband asked Rosey if Tommy was as good as he always bragged to be. With a big grin, she said, 'Bigger and better.' Tommy said, 'We had a full body, physical geographical tour of each other.' He was always so clever with words.

"The following evening we had dinner together again. That night Tommy said something, but without an explanation. 'You know Rosey and I bonded yesterday. Something special happened between us, which shall be unsaid. All I will say is that we are no longer a couple. Our belief in God and the spirits made us spiritually together forever. We are now *one!*'

"Tommy was a tall, broad-shouldered, handsome man. I don't think I ever told him I thought he was handsome.

"Well, I think I've talked myself out on my brother. I think Leon should go next."

"Tommy was never my brother-in-law. He was my brother and best friend. I was raised with two sisters, and we all settled in different parts of New York State. We hardly see each other. Years after I married Helen, I got a new family. Tommy and then unfortunately, the bitch. I mean Cindy. I really didn't like her from day one. Tommy deserved better. In time he did get better, the best. Tommy's reward in life finally came when he bonded with and married Rosey.

"Now I want to tell a few things about Tommy. Helen told you something of his character. Tommy was a character. He was one of a kind. I should say two of a kind. One side of Tommy was partly the man that Helen told you about. At the right time, he was the dirtiest mouthed Irishman I ever met. He loved to curse. Privately, he loved to tell me about his sex life. He didn't have one until he was 22 years old. Tommy loved the word *fuck!* He also told me over and over again how much he loved to do it, as often as possible. He bragged about his size. Since I'm stinking drunk, I'll tell you he called it his Cock. I think if he could, he would have hung it on the outside of his pants for everyone to see.

"Tommy had such weird beliefs. He thought that masturbating was sinful, but fucking girls in and around Montauk was not. He told me he always provided protection. He would never want a girl knocking on his door with a baby. Even though his sex life with Cindy was only very basic, he was never unfaithful. Helen and I hoped one day he would see what we were seeing. When Cindy stayed away all week, Tommy said she was working on a large lawsuit. Helen said she was working on a man wearing a large law suit."

CHAPTER 5-3

"Steven, you're next."

"Alright, I'll go next. I want to say everybody here knows about Ian Silver. Please note that we never refer to him as Father or Grandfather. Only Ian!

"I think a lot of what will be said tonight is already known about Tommy. He became the most loving and special man in all of our lives. When he married Mother in 2012, he got an entire family, but it went both ways. Steffy, Hannah, and I got a loving dad, and Sam got a Pops. Since 1984, we already had a loving Aunt Helen and Uncle Leon.

"There are too many qualities to tell about Tommy, but there is one that stands out in my mind and heart. We were never just his family. He wanted to know each of us individually. He made each one feel special. When at the house in Montauk, I noticed he and one family member were always missing. That person was alone someplace with Tommy. I think I might have been the first.

"'Hey, Steven. Let's take a walk.' He guided me to the cement path across the driveway. It led to part of his private beach. There was a large bench. He invited me to sit down with him. First there was small talk. Then he began asking me a lot of questions. He really wanted to learn as much about me as he could. One of the subjects he zoomed in on was my becoming a doctor. I told him what it took to get where I am. He shuttered and asked me how I felt the first time I saw a dead person, and when I was given a cadaver. I was shocked at such questions.

"Tommy and I spoke about Mother, and all she tolerated to protect me and the family. He made sure I knew how he and Mother fell in love. It was during the time she spent in Montauk. He also strongly emphasized that there had never been an affair. It was exactly as it was said at the wedding. Mother lived in a dark hole until God came along and showed her light. He took Ian, and left Tommy in his place. He and fate, destiny, and karma gave love and life to her through Tommy. Now I call on Hannah, my wife."

"I too was singled out by Tommy. He took me out to the hot tub. I had never seen one. It was much bigger than I imagined. On the outside, there were wide benches and a ladder to get in easily. It was in the warm weather. He asked if I would like to take my shoes off and put my feet into the tub. Oh, yes! We both took our shoes off, dangled our feet, and talked. He also asked me a lot of questions. He told me how much Mother loves me. Yes, I also call her Mother. We talked about how lucky I was to have her as a mother-in-law. He never spoke of himself. He just wanted to know about me and my life. He was so sweet and kind. He made me feel so special. That was his way. I think I've said enough because I'm trying not to cry. Now I call on my son Sam."

"I think my story is going to be the best. Because you are all family, you know how I came to call my grandmother Baba. I'll tell it again for Mikey. When I was a baby, Baba gave me a red stuffed puppy. I took it every place. I peed on it, threw up on it, and only called it Red Puppy. Just as I was learning how to speak everyone's name, I got a bit confused. I was told to call my grandmother Bubby. Then I couldn't remember who was Puppy and who was Bubby? One day, Bubby sat down with me and took away my confusion. She told me to call her Baba.

"Now there's another side of this. My name is Samuel. She called me Sammala. As I got older, she called me Sammy.

Sammala became only a name she whispered in my ear. But there was another name she whispered in my ear. It was the Yiddish word for little boy. The word is Boychik. On my Bar Mitzvah day, I announced to everyone that I was now to be called Sam. Baba kept her word and never embarrassed me. Sammala and Boychik were only whispered in my ear when she gave me a hug.

"Apparently, Baba told Tommy the entire story. One day he invited me out for a drive. We went down to one of the piers. He gave me a walking tour of some of the fishing boat areas. As we walked, he asked me a lot of questions. He asked me about school, if I was dating and had a girlfriend. I clammed up a bit about a girlfriend, and he didn't push. We drove back to the house. When we got out of the car, he stopped me. He reached out to give me a hug. He got up close. In one ear he said, 'Hey, Sammala.' In the other ear he said, 'Hey, Boychik.' All I could do was laugh. I'm sorry I never thought to ask if I could call him Zayda, the Yiddish word for grandfather.

"He did the hugs and whispering those names in my ears several times at the house. One day we both put on bathing trunks and prepared to get into the hot tub. 'Hey, Pops. On the day you married Baba, I noticed you had a nice flat stomach. Why do you now have this old man pot belly?' 'Sam, you and I are very lucky. You have a grandmother who is a blessing from God. I have a wife who is a blessing from God. She fills my belly with good food and my entire body with good love.' This time, I grabbed him and gave him a big hug. I didn't whisper. I just said out loud, 'Pops, you too are a blessing from God.' He splashed the hell out of my face in the water. Now I call on Steffy."

"Perhaps, my story is going to be a bit different. As I speak, you might wonder how it connects to honoring my dad Tommy, but it will. He also singled me out more than once. He and I both love ice cream. He took me to a drive-up ice cream shop. We got large sundaes, ate in the car, and talked. His questions to me were about why I chose nursing and about my life. I found him easy to talk with on personal aspects of my love life. He was a great listener. He never judged!

"Mother's parents, Grandpa Dave and Grandma Jill, were fairly religious. She and Abby were raised to have certain Jewish values. They were told that marrying within one's own faith was important. It was easier on the marriage and especially on any children they would have.

"Many years ago, I had some fun with Helen. I went to Montauk alone for a visit. I taught her some Yiddish slang words like putts, schmuck, knish, and korva. I also taught her the word shiksa. It's not a derogatory word, but a descriptive word. I told Helen that she is a shiksa. It only means that she is a Gentile woman.

"Since my grandparents had two daughters, they were taught the word shegetz. It's also not a derogatory word, but a descriptive word. Tommy would have been called a shegetz. It meant he was a Gentile man.

"Abby and Scott met per chance at their first job after college. Scott is Jewish, and things worked out well. As you can see they are here together and still in love. Their daughter, Emmy, married Nick. He is Catholic and she converted to Catholicism. At first it wasn't easy, but love won out. They have seven children and many grandchildren. Fortunately, Nick has a wonderful white-collar government job. Unfortunately, he and Emmy travel a lot. Abby and Scott don't see her very often. Their bottom line is that their daughter is happy, healthy, and safe with Nick. Remember the word 'safe'.

"Now I'll slowly get to Tommy. When Mother was engaged to Ian, the family was so excited. Oh my God, Rainey is marrying a Jewish man. Not only is he Jewish, but he's a doctor. That was the biggest dream of any Jewish girl and her parents. Mother and Abby were always told to run away from a shegetz. The stereotype description said he would be a blue-collar worker, not a good provider, would be a beer guzzler, have tattoos, and not be kind to his wife. We all know what happened to Mother. Her Jewish doctor became a nightmare. We only know of the last few years of her life with Ian. Chances are bad things happened to her way before those years.

"Well, Mother married a shegetz named Thomas Patrick Monahan. She told me it was a shame that she couldn't clone a younger version of Tommy for me. There aren't enough words to tell of the bright light and love that Tommy brought to all of us. He was the most loving, caring man. Ian loved the name SILVER. His behavior tarnished the name. Mother has a saying which is, '**IT MAY ALL BE A MISCONCEPTION OR AN ILLUSION**.'

"Tommy was neither one. He was for real! Sometimes I can still hear his low, almost gruff, raspy voice in my head. I loved the sound of his slight brogue. I'm glad Helen and Leon opened the door for me to use the word fuck. No confession for me! Tommy had a two-line song he liked to quietly sing. The words were:

Tommy and Rosey sitting on a swing KISSING.
Tommy and Rosey laying in a bed FUCKING.

"The first time I heard him sing those words, he saw me blush. He knew I was embarrassed. 'Hey, Steffy. Your mother is 70 years old, and I'm 65 years old. We are two consenting married adults. I hope you don't think we're too old to fuck.' Maybe it's best that Mother has lost him in her head. His loss is so painful for me. I can't imagine what it would be for her if she were aware."

CHAPTER 5-4

"Hey, Scott. You go next. I want to save Abby for last. I have a feeling that she will be the one with the best stories."

"In the short amount of time I spent with Tommy, I also came to see him as my brother. Tommy was real. We all know about Tommy's drinking problem after Cindy left him. He went into rehab and never drank again. His life and profession as a teacher was too important for him to ever have a slip. He loved the English language, poetry, and the students. He once told me he saw them as the children he would never have.

"One day he took me and Abby for a ride. He drove around Montauk and acted as a tour guide. When he parked the car, we were in front of the high school where he taught. He thought Abby and I would want to see it because we were both teachers. Tommy sat in the front and moved himself sideways against his driver's side door. We were in the back where we could look at each other to talk. Almost face-to-face. He liked that. He asked us to tell a story of the most awful or rewarding experience we had while teaching. We each told him a story. Then it was his turn. Please understand that while we are honoring Tommy, Rainey was always part of a good story about Tommy. They were one!

"The school had approved poetry reading in Tommy's classes once a month. He would choose different poetry for each class. He was in high school and the age range went from about 15 to 18. Their interest and comprehension was different at each age. He would make copies of a poem he chose. They were given to each class and then readings were scheduled. The students were asked to read them and then a discussion would follow in class. Some of the students participated, and some just sat quietly and listened. There were students who came to school drunk and some high. The teachers were happy if they just came to class. Perhaps they might still hear and grasp something. They could stay as long as they were not disruptive.

"One day, a young man stood up and began shouting ugly things. 'Hey, Mr. Monahan. I heard in your young days you were a male whore, hiding in the closet. You didn't get married until you were in your thirties. I guess it took a lot of years until she found out you were a fag poet and left you. Then there you were riding around with little pink doggies. Now I hear you married a beautiful cougar. Maybe she can teach you how to be a man.'

"Tommy was just taking deep breaths, and let him go on until he mentioned his wife. Then some of the boys held onto Tommy as he lunged forward. Some of the other boys grabbed the kid and pulled him out of the room. Tommy just sat at his desk with total support from all the students. They loved him! The principal came into the room. The kid was high and the police were going to remove him from the school. He asked Tommy to go home. Another teacher would take his classes for the day. Tommy agreed and left.

"The principal called Rainey. He thought she should know there was an incident at school. She was told Tommy was on his way home. They both knew what a fine and peaceful man he was. Tommy once told us he never thinks about a drink because his life is so wonderful with Rosey. All she did was send him a text. 'I just got a call from Chuck that there was an incident at school. He said you were on your way home. It's January and a very cold, windy, blustery morning. I'm standing in the middle of the driveway waiting for you. I will not go back into the house without you.' Even with his peace disrupted, he would not go to a bar. He would never let her stand outside on a cold, windy, blustery morning. He knew she wasn't bluffing. She would rather stay outside and freeze to death than know he went to a bar. She was *his* everything and he was hers. Okay, Abby. We've saved you for last."

"First, please let me go back to referring to my sister as Rainey. As children, she was frail and sickly until she was about 10 years old. She was diagnosed with hypoglycemia and always had to be watched. Thank God she grew up to be a strong and healthy young woman. I'm a year older than Rainey, but many thought we were twins. It wasn't because we looked alike. It was more of the closeness we shared. I was the big sister, and at every age *Rainey told me everything!*

"I remember when she was dating Ian. After six months she told me they were ready to be intimate. She took the pill and couldn't wait to know the feeling of an orgasm. It finally happened. I'm sure it happened many times through the years, but that was all that happened. Ian was a very cold man. She lived in a very structured sexual missionary marriage with him. When she bonded with Tommy, she was 70 years old. She had only been with one man, and certainly was not a cougar. Tommy was the one who knew it all, did it all, felt it all, and was going to teach it all. He was referring to teaching her what sex should be when mixed with passionate love. Tommy and my sister had that kind of love. It quickly led to the commitment of marriage.

Earlier I wasn't sure how much to say tonight, but decided to tell all. I also wasn't sure if I should use the word fuck! I think Helen and Leon opened that door. The difference is I also don't have to go to confession. Since I'm telling you about Tommy, I'm going to use the word fuck a lot. Why shouldn't I? If he were here, he would use that word. Additionally, Scott and I have now been doing some quiet talking. He has given me permission to tell you *everything!*

"Tommy and Rainey fell in love from afar. She was a married woman! When that changed, they were both free to declare their love for each other. She went to his house one morning. Within minutes they were fucking. Of course it was sex, but it was driven by love. It was the kind that exploded after loving and wanting each other for at least a year or more. They both fantasized of the moment, and it finally became reality. Rainey knew they both had a massive orgasm, but thought it was over until the next fuck. Tommy wanted more and was ready to teach her. He would have to first verbally spell it out for her.

"He asked if she ever did after play. No, she hadn't. She told Tommy that Ian was a fuck, come, and go man. When it was over, it was over. Tommy said it was the same with Cindy. He explained what it entailed. Tommy told her after play is to follow a great fuck. Both would still be totally aroused. They would need and want more. It was a great benefit for a woman who could have multiple orgasms. One at a time, one to the other had to create and perform a seduction. Tommy would lie on his back in the bed. Rainey could do anything she wanted to him. Then he could do the same to her. Of course, in general conversation, they had already established that the back end was forbidden. Also, there was always the option to say 'STOP'.

"It was decided that she would begin first on Tommy. She climbed up on his muscular chest to begin. His chest would then be referred to as her mountain. He agreed. She had loved him for so long and wanted him for so long. Now was her chance to act. She began kissing at his neck. With her hands, mouth, and open legs, she began moving slowly down. When she told me the story, there was one thing she emphasized. She said his body was clean, sweet, and delicious. Need I explain what she did to him? Need I continue? I think not!

"Next it was Tommy's turn to seduce her. There are only so many things that one can do to a human body to create a

300

seduction. He did it all! Nobody said 'STOP'. The only difference was that Tommy would definitely have to go to confession.

"There is a reason why I'm being so explicit. Tommy was a fairly religious man, but also very spiritual. He believed that there were four powers that controlled our lives. They are fate, destiny, karma, and God. Tommy also believed that a fuck could be without love, minds, hearts, and souls. He had sex with so many women until he was 36 years old. To him it was all sex with no love, minds, hearts, and souls. It was nothing more than just a pure fuck. It was two people satisfying a need with no strings attached. Then he married Cindy and thought it would be different. He also had a very structured sexual missionary marriage. After Cindy, he went out fucking again until he and my sister bonded.

"As I said, Rainey told me everything. She explained the act they performed on each other that made them spiritual. Once they became spiritual, they were no longer a couple. They had become one! Even death could not part them. I was standing next to Tommy's casket and heard everything my sister told him. She seemed almost happy and excited as she spoke to him. I know she never cried and she smiled a few times. Does she really believe one day he will come for her? Is she really waiting for him? Is her memory loss intentional? My sister rocks in her seat when in crisis. She didn't rock, but has she blocked him out of her mind to survive his loss? I'm sorry for crying. She's my sister!

"I have another story to tell you about Tommy and the wonderful thing he did for me and Scott. Rainey gave me details of what she and Tommy did to make them spiritual. It was something Tommy learned when he was 22 years old. He was with a woman who was almost like a gypsy fortune teller, among other things. The first time Tommy and Rainey bonded in sex, they both did it on instinct alone. He had been with that woman 43 years prior. Suddenly, he remembered what she told him. His sharing it with Rainey is what convinced her that even death could never part them.

"I tried talking to Scott about it and he wouldn't listen. One day Tommy called Scott. He asked if we would take the train to New York City, and he and Rainey would do the same. He wanted to meet for lunch and talk. We met with Tommy and Rainey three times. Tommy did all of the talking, explaining, and asking each time to accept his suggestions. A few times Scott was annoyed and just wanted to have lunch and get back on the train. Eventually, Scott gave in. Please keep in mind that Scott and I are in our seventies, and have been married 51 years. Scott takes a lot of medication. Our sex life had become hugs, cuddling, touching, kissing and then falling asleep. We are very much in love and happy to still be together. We didn't know there could be more.

"Tommy's beliefs and persistence with Scott has given us more than we could ever imagine. We have followed Tommy's recipe for a new life within our 51-year marriage. We do everything Tommy suggested, and love it all. If not for Tommy and what he shared, we would have remained two veggies. We now feel like two hot and sexy newlyweds. We do everything but fuck. It's incredible! Scott and I have also come to believe we are no longer a couple. We are now *one*. This has allowed us to have peace. We never think about the time one of us will pass away. We believe we will be joined together again.

"Now one final story! Helen, Leon, Scott, and I are aware of something my sister was experiencing. We all thought when Ian died she was free of his night horrors. Not so. Rainey didn't want her Silver family to know because they already worried about her. They didn't need to know any more. Tommy didn't want them to know either. He felt that she was his wife, and he loved her so much. He would take care of her.

Occasionally, she would have a nightmare of Ian pushing her out of the bed. She would wake up with such a jolt that the bed shook. It would awaken Tommy. He would find her standing on the floor facing the bed. The first time, she told him she had to get out of bed before he had a chance to push her. Tommy put her back into the bed. She was shaking and became very quiet. He covered her with blankets. They both loved to drink hot tea when they were relaxing. Tommy told her not to get up, and just wait for him to return. He went downstairs to make her some tea. They had beautiful teapots with a small strand of pearls that wrapped from the lid to the spout. Rainey only likes spearmint tea.

He brought the tea up to the spa bathroom. Next he filled the tub with warm water and bubbles. Rainey loved to relax in bubbles. Tommy went to the bedroom, gently carried her, and placed her into the tub. She was still very quiet. He held the cup up to her mouth to drink. When telling the story in one of our New York City visits, Tommy threw in some humor. 'Hey, Scott. I sat on the edge of the tub with my feet in the water. I had to put on a pair of tight jockey shorts to hold my package together. Can you imagine a big cock and balls just hanging over the edge onto a ceramic tub?'

"When Tommy thought she was better, he carried her back to the bedroom. She was rocking and shaking. Once as a joke, he bought her a pair of flannel pajamas. This was no joke! He put them on her, gave her half a Xanax, and got into bed with her. He rocked with her until she fell asleep. The first time was the hardest for Tommy. He was so frightened by her behavior. Then he knew what to do each time. He always called out of work the following day and called Helen. After that first time, she knew not to call, text, email, or visit. Rainey was in good and loving hands with her husband Tommy. Who helped her after Tommy passed away? Hopefully, the nightmares stopped.

"I'm so fucking drunk, but my head is spinning in so many directions. Questions, I have questions. Today is Tommy's birthday. Did he want his Rosey to be with him? Did she have a stroke today because he wanted her? Was she supposed to die today? Did the powers that Tommy believes in stop it from happening? Did they tell him he couldn't have her today? If not today, then when? I believe the day will come when she will join him.

"There is one more thing I would like to do. Steven had two extra chairs and two pieces of strawberry shortcake set up at the table. I want to create a spiritual scene. I'm going to sit on one of those chairs, and be a spiritual version of my sister. I will be Rosey, as Tommy called her. I would ask Helen to sit on the other chair, and be a spiritual version of her brother Tommy. I ask that we hold hands. Hey, Sister Helen! Who the fuck would ever waste two beautiful pieces of strawberry shortcake? Certainly not Tommy and Rosey! Let's eat!"

CHAPTER 5-5

It's Thursday, November 24, 2016. Only a day after Mother had a stroke. She's in the hospital and the family celebrated Tommy's birthday last night. We were all so drunk that Mikey sent us home in cabs. This morning we all had to go back to the Pike and get our cars. Now it's back to reality.

Helen, Abby and I went to brunch and then to the hospital. Mother is great!

Her spirits are high and she was eating lunch. We all hugged and kissed. She showed us how she doesn't have full movement on her right side. As we were reassuring her that physical therapy would help, Dr. Chudy walked into the room. Mother told him she didn't think hospital care was necessary. She was anxious to have therapy to recover. He told us her vitals are perfect and agreed to have her moved by the following day. She would be going to the rehab attached to the hospital. We left and promised we would return later in the day. She asked me to pack a bag for her. In rehab, one must be dressed every day.

Helen and Abby had errands. I went home and made some calls. I work for an agency who has been assigning me to ICU/Trauma units in area hospitals. They also have a home care department. I just set up to be Mother's nurse when she goes home. I have taken the 6:00 a.m. to 6:00 p.m. shift. I want to be sure that Mother eats properly. This would not be a good time for her hypoglycemia to get out of whack. I can also be the one to get her bathed and dressed every morning. There will be a night nurse assigned. I don't believe Mother is going to be an invalid. I won't allow her to become one, but she will need care.

While I was home, I researched medical supply companies on my computer.

When she had a knee replacement, Tommy had the bathroom set up for her. He got a high rise toilet, and had safety bars installed in the shower. I knew she would need a new bed, a walker, and possibly a wheel chair.

Helen and Abby met me back at the hospital late in the afternoon. We told Mother of our plans to redecorate her bedroom. I told her there is a great bed I found on line. It's a three-quarter-sized bed. It actually measures between a twin and full-sized bed. It has a velvet tufted headboard. There's a remote that moves the entire bed up and down, and just the feet and head up and down. There are safety sidebars also operated with a remote device. We asked for her input on decorator schemes. She asked for white bedding with red rose pedals, and a white headboard. If possible, she asked for a white walker. It should have red roses painted on it, and a red basket and cup holder. Helen asked her if she ever saw a walker like that. She said there was one, but didn't remember where. All she remembered was that it had three wheels like a tricycle and hand brakes.

They brought her dinner. We helped her and left. Out in the hospital lobby, we sat down to talk. Helen asked, "Could it be? Is she beginning to remember sparks of Tommy? Where is her head? It's almost spooky!" What we remembered was Dr. Gillespie instructing us not to push any memories of him onto her. We really didn't. It all came from her. In the morning, I called Dr. Gillespie. He said we were not to suggest, but it was alright if she made requests. That's what happened.

The following day, Helen and Abby met me at the neighborhood deli again for brunch. I don't think we should get on a scale. We've been eating out a lot. Next, we went to the medical supply company to shop. The bed was lovely. It had everything needed as a hospital bed, but with a complete designer look. They did have white bedding with red rose pedals. We bought several sets along with new pillows and quilts. There is a chair in the bedroom, which will have to be replaced. We found a red velour recliner. The night nurse would need a comfortable place to sleep in Mother's room. We did look at walkers. There was a three wheel white walker with hand brakes. They are a safety feature when one is walking alone. None of them had red roses painted on them. We bought one, along with the red basket and cup holder she requested.

The entire family spent time with Mother while in rehab. Dr. Gillespie was also seeing her in therapy sessions. She worked hard at therapy, but she never stopped babbling about Jake. The strange thing was she never spoke of him in front of Helen and Leon.

It was now Thursday, December 1, 2016. Mother was doing very well and felt she was ready to go home. It was agreed by all of the medical and physical therapy (PT) staff that she could go on Wednesday, December 7th. There would be follow up with PT staff at home three times a week. Dr. Gillespie would continue with her outpatient sessions at home. There was so much going on with her that we all needed therapy. Dr. Gillespie did ask for the entire family to meet with him on Monday, December 5th, 6:00 p.m. in his office.

We all arrived and went into his conference room. He told us that he had a lot to say. He asked for our patience to listen. Afterwards, we could comment or question anything. Funny how some professional men like to just talk with no interruptions. Just a joke, but with interruptions do they lose their train of thought?

"I believe you all know and understand HIPPA. Therefore, I want you to know I have recorded every session with Lorraine since February of 2016. That was when she entered the psychiatric unit under my care. I also recorded all of the family meetings I had with you. They are not covered under HIPPA. None of you were my patients, and you were not in therapy sessions with me. You were her family telling me about her life, especially with her late husband Thomas Monahan (Tommy). I needed that information in hopes of understanding her frame of mind. I'm not permitted to tell you anything that was said by her. I can only tell you what she did not say. At that time, there was no mention of Tommy and no mention of Jake. Apparently, he is a new character in her life or her mind.

"I would again like to ask for your cooperation. I have an idea of what's happening in Lorraine's mind. In order to get confirmation, I need to know more about Jake. Lorraine is bursting to tell me about him, but then I can't tell you. Please turn it around. Whatever she tells you as a family member is again not covered under HIPPA. Therefore, I'm asking you to share information with me. I think I can then come up with a diagnosis, which I can share with you. I'm sorry if you think I'm taking you in circles. I just want to help Lorraine."

In the next few days, Leon and Scott cleared out Mother's bedroom and we waited for the new furniture. Helen, Abby, and I got everything set up. Steven, Hannah, and Sam were going to spend many hours on the weekends with Mother. She would only have night nurses. My days with Mother would be tough. I needed the weekend and nights for myself.

Mother continued talking about Jake. She expected me to remember what she was referencing. She said talking about him kept him alive in her memory. She had to do that.

CHAPTER 5-6

It was now Wednesday, December 7th. Mother didn't need an ambulance. Steven and Sam brought her home. Helen and Leon had been at the house since the day Mother had the stroke. They wouldn't leave and have to drive back and forth to and from Montauk. We were all thrilled that they stayed. Tommy's girls were always at the house. Mother believed they belonged to Helen and Leon. Now that Mother was home, they were going back to Montauk for a few weeks. They didn't want to be in the way with all the nursing care Mother would need. She regained a lot of feeling and movement, but would never be able to live alone without help. The vision in her right eye was still blurry. She could stumble and fall. We would never place her in assisted living with strangers. A nursing home was totally out of the question. Mother would stay in her own home, and we would give her the best care. Helen reminded us that when she sold Tommy's house, an account to take care of Mother's medical needs was set up.

Helen asked if she could have some time alone with Mother and Abby. Of course! She had a surprise announcement. The three of them had been sisters since 1984. Now that they were getting older, she wanted to be with her family. The condo she and Leon had in Montauk was for sale. They were looking to buy another one in the Philly area. Mother was thrilled, but asked, "What about your brother Tommy? Isn't he still living there?" Helen told her that Tommy passed away several years prior. Mother hugged her and offered condolences. That's where it ended.

We were all so happy to hear the news. Scott offered to help them with the move. Mother was incredible! She loved the bed. She had full bodily functions, and only needed help to walk to the bathroom. I took her into the kitchen for meals. When possible, we took her to restaurants. I said I would never allow her to become an invalid. She didn't want that either.

Mother still continued speaking of Jake. As time passed, stories she was telling became familiar. I decided to buy a small tape recorder and suggested others in the family do the same. She didn't have to know what we were doing. I began taping some of her stories about Jake. I heard most of it because I was alone with her five days a week on a twelve-hour shift. She didn't see me as her nurse. I was her daughter. She could share her memories of Jake with me because I knew him. I wasn't permitted to mention Tommy, but I wasn't told not to question Mother about Jake. To the contrary! Dr. Gillespie wanted information on Jake. I asked Mother to describe him. She became a bit annoyed believing I knew what he looked like. I supposedly also spent three years and seven months with him. "Jake was about six feet. His body was broad, rugged, and muscular. He had a great tan on his arms and legs. His face was dark, tan, and ruddy. I guess that was because he played a lot of golf. He was out in the sun quite often. Steffy, his naked body was so beautiful. I loved it inside and outside of me. His hair was salt and pepper, tussled, and he had a matching mustache. He always had to pull out his reading glasses. You must remember he always needed them in a restaurant when he had to look at the menu. His big blue eyes actually danced when he laughed. Steffy, the time came when he could no longer perform sexually. He was more upset than me. He thought because he had such a big Cock that it would always function. I reminded him that we bonded when he was 77 years old. He was still going strong for another year. I also told him if I wanted a stud, I would have looked for a 65 year old man."

Oh my God! What's going on here? The description of Jake is exactly the same description of Tommy. He was 65 years old when he and Mother bonded and got married. Mother loved to brag that Tommy was a stud. She also told me and Abby that his penis was very big. He called it a Cock. Mother asked for a white, three-wheeled walker with red roses painted on it. Tommy gave her a white tricycle with red roses painted on it as a joke wedding present. I know because I was there. I think I'm getting nauseous!

I hated to be the only family spy. After that session, I asked Steven and Abby to begin using a small tape recorder when sitting with Mother. She really was bursting to talk about Jake to keep him alive in her memory. They did, and by December 28th, we handed over the tapes to Dr. Gillespie for his review. He asked for a few more weeks and he would then schedule another family meeting. Steven and I already believed we had the answer. Since he was a medical doctor and me a registered nurse, we did have rotations in psychiatric medicine.

In the meantime, Helen, Abby and I got Mother out of the house several hours a week. It was wintertime and she loved going to the mall. It would be too much walking for her so we used a wheelchair. She also requested a white one with red roses painted on it. There was no such thing. We just got a plain red one. I got a gourmet coffee and transferred her to a bench to drink. She was a people watcher. She did that with Tommy! While in the mall, she spotted a home store. There were decorative changes she wanted to make in her bedroom. She picked out pictures with red rose gardens and beaches.

We celebrated Hanukkah, Christmas, and the New Year of 2017 together. We took Mother to Steven's house for each holiday. She was in her glory being surrounded by family. Her confusion now had her believing it was the year of 2021. She also believed January 18, 2021 would be a year since Jake passed away. We had to allow her to mourn, but not dwell on the day.

Dr. Gillespie called and asked the family to come to his office on Monday, January 23rd at 6:00 p.m. Again, he asked for us to listen and be patient with him. He repeated all of the rules of HIPPA. He also explained that what he was about to tell us came from the family meetings. They were from last February, and the tapes we gave him a few weeks ago.

"I have a feeling that Steven and Steffy know what I'm about to tell you. To put it bluntly, there never was a Jake. He is actually Tommy! We think she forgot him. She thinks she forgot him, but he is actively in her mind. He has just taken on another persona as Jake.

"Hours after Tommy passed away, Lorraine's family arrived in Montauk. She sat alone with Steven and asked him to bring Tommy back to life for just five minutes. He went too quickly. There was no chance to say sweet things into his ear as he passed. Steven knew how important that was to her. The last thing Tommy heard was her screaming. She let him pass knowing the pain he caused. She needed him for just five minutes for a do-over. I believe Steven pacified her telling how Tommy saw love in her eyes before passing. He also felt the love in her heartbeat as she held him. Of course, Steven couldn't give her a do-over. I believe her mind took her to a fantasy where she did the do-over on her own. She invented Jake and took him into a three year and seven month relationship. It ended with the passing of Jake, but she did whisper sweet things into his ear as he passed. Therefore, while upset with his loss, she could be at peace. Tommy's passing as he did left her with a form of insanity. She lost total memory, sense of timing, and all of reality. She began the fantasy on or about June of 2016 after she was released from the hospital. In her mind, it went from then until January 18, 2020, which was exactly three years and seven months later. A fantasy can go on and off with the blink of an eye. There is no true timing in a fantasy.

CHAPTER 5-7

We asked Dr. Gillespie to give us all the details of his diagnosis. He agreed since it was vital for us to know where Mother's head is now.

"I have composed two lists, which I will share with you. Each of you having a copy will possibly give you a chance to review at a later time. Hopefully, it will answer some of your questions. One is the total similarities between Tommy and Jake. The other is the differences created in Lorraine's fantasy. Some of these descriptions come from my family meetings with you regarding Tommy. The others are from stories told to you about Jake. Nobody was my patient."

Similarities

- *Physical description and voice tones of Tommy and Jake are almost exactly the same. One exception is that Jake was not Irish and didn't have a brogue.*

- *They were both high school teachers.*

- *They both needed to eat dinner at 4:00 p.m. according to lifestyle of each.*

- *She met Tommy through his sister Helen, a hairdresser in Montauk. She met Jake through Helen, a hairdresser in Elkins Park.*

- *They both gave her the same gold necklace. It was two hands joined together, with small diamonds forming a heart in the middle. She had a trinket box with each for mementos.*

- *Tommy's reality wedding and Jake's faux wedding both had a chupah decorated with satin and red roses. Both wore gold wedding bands. They ate a white iced wedding cake with red rose decorations. She wore a white dress, lace panties, and jeweled sandals for both weddings.*

- *Needing occasional changes from everyday life, she went to hotels for overnighters with each. They had dinner brought to the room, including strawberry shortcake. She always carried a small flowered satchel with fresh underwear for the next morning. Sometimes at home and sometimes in a hotel, she surprised both with costumes to play sexual games.*

- *They always showered together, and both had a spa bathroom. There was a spa shower and a whirlpool bathtub in Tommy's house. She and Jake had them in her apartment, where she believed they lived together.*

- *She had a knee replacement while with Tommy and Jake. They were her caregivers when she went home. Both men needed sexual release. She manually pleasured them when needed. It was when she wasn't able to have intercourse or any other sexual activity.*

- *They both had a frightening episode of the flu with a very high fever. She became the ICU/Trauma nurse who took care of them while at home.*

- *Both men chose to sleep naked. They called it being skin to skin.*

- *Both men used the same slang words for sexual body parts.*

314

Differences

• *The frequency and intensity of her sex lives with Tommy and Jake were almost identical with one exception. Tommy was 65 and Lorraine was 70 years old when they bonded. Jake was 77 and Lorraine was 73 years old when they bonded. Eventually, there were issues with Jake and not with Tommy. It was because of the age difference as they went forward in time. Lorraine made a point of telling how they had to have very active sex lives because of their ages. She told a family member that they had no time to waste.*

• *Tommy knew of the abuse to Lorraine because of the time she spent in Montauk. She never told Jake. In her fantasy she kept a journal, which he found and she allowed him to read. That was where she made entries of each abusive event. That journal was never found.*

• *Tommy knew the story of Ian's gambling and loss of the big family house. When he and Lorraine were in Philadelphia, they stayed at the small replacement house. Lorraine tells her story of Jake after becoming a very rich widow. She lived in a very expensive exclusive apartment with Jake.*

• *Tommy was a recovering alcoholic. Jake loved fine scotch and Lorraine had a bar set up for him.*

• *Tommy was Irish Catholic and Jake was Jewish.*

"There is one final and very important story I would like to share with everyone, specifically Helen and Leon. Tommy's first wife was Cindy. It is believed that he wanted children with her, but it just didn't happen. In Lorraine's story about Jake, his late wife was Cindy. In her fantasy, Jake and Cindy had two sons. One son married an Irish Catholic girl named Eleanor. They gave Jake two grandsons. Lorraine named one Thomas and one

Patrick. They attended a private Catholic Academy, and wore a Miraculous Medal around their necks. The name they had for Jake was Pops. I believe that Lorraine loved Tommy so much more than anyone might know. In her fantasy, she gave him something not possible in reality. She was too old. Through Jake, she gave him sons and grandsons.

"Again, I would like to repeat that all of my evaluations have come from you as Lorraine's family. While in sessions with me, Lorraine never spoke of Tommy because she has no memory of him. She never spoke of Jake because he didn't come out from her mind until last November 23, 2016. That was the date she believed was his birthday, but in the year 2020. That was also the day she had a stroke. I have been a psychiatrist for over twenty years. Most of my patients are labeled textbook cases, but not Lorraine.

"I think I've talked enough. I would like to continue seeing Lorraine once a month. Please bring her to my office for the appointments. She no longer needs to see me at her home. I would like to suggest that you give her more of an active social life. She loves live entertainment. It would be nice to occasionally take her to the theatre. There was a time when she played the card game called canasta. Perhaps you could find three women who would play once a week. She has enough feeling and mobility in her right hand now to enable her to hold the cards."

Steffy continues to be with Mother five days a week from 6:00 a.m. to 6:00 p.m. Mother really doesn't need a nurse. I believe we need to get her an aide. All she needs is help showering and getting dressed in the morning, and getting her ready for bed at night. It has been over two months since she had the stroke. She is quite capable of staying home alone. Her manual capabilities have somewhat improved. Her biggest problem is her eyesight. She doesn't use the range or oven, but can use small appliances. Helen and Abby cook and pack meals for her.

She only has to place them into the microwave oven. We must keep her safe. Mother is determined to be an independent woman. We have purchased a help alarm system. She wears a lovely necklace that is attached to the system. If she is feeling anything out of the ordinary, she knows to push the button on the necklace. She is never to remove it. The system is extremely technically sophisticated. If she falls, they can detect that she is on the floor. If she is not responsive, the system can pick up on her breathing pattern. There is a box attached to her telephone line. She and a dispatcher can speak to each other via the box. If and when necessary, the paramedics will be sent to the house. I will also be called. It is amazing!

Another suggestion I will offer to the family is to find her a female companion. Helen and Abby spend a lot of social time with her, but they each have a husband. Steffy needs to go back to her own life. Maybe she can find the time to possibly fall in love and have a husband. I have noticed changes in Steffy that I don't like. Sometimes I think Mother is pulling her into believing the fantasy world of Jake. Mother never stops talking about Jake, and Steffy discusses him with her. While Mother is talking about Jake, I think Steffy is relating to Tommy. It's really gotten weird. My sister is getting weird!

My nephew Steven has asked me to help find a companion for my sister. I suggested finding a group of ladies for her to bond with for social time. I made inquiries and found a senior social center in the neighborhood. She can go anywhere because she still has the TS. I think she has come to know of being monitored when traveling alone. She doesn't mind. Helen and I called and made arrangements for the three of us to join. We went and they gave us paper work listing their activities. They invited us to stay for lunch. There were about 90% women. Very few men! There was also a bulletin board. Mother noticed the names of three women. They were in search of a fourth woman to play in a weekly canasta game. They would play at the center and then have lunch. Rainey played in a group before moving to Montauk. She called the telephone number on the list when she got home. My incredible sister is now going to be the fourth in the weekly game. She will be playing with Ruth, Sandy, and Rhoda. I found a card holder at a medical supply store. She can use it for her right hand. They are three fine women, and are planning other trips outside of the center. They are discussing museums, art galleries, and live theatre. Sandy is the youngest and still drives. There will also be occasional trips to the area casinos.

I'm really thrilled to be getting back to normal after two strokes. Of course, there will always be time with family. We are always together on birthdays, anniversaries, and holidays. I must try to stop talking about Jake. My time with him was incredible, but it's over. He's gone. His family never bothered to call me after his passing. I'm starting to worry about Steffy's mental health. I keep on trying to not talk about him, but now she won't stop. It's almost as if now she can't let go of him. I guess it's because he became like a dad to her. She also became very close to Jason and Craig. She never heard from them either. We all have to let go and move ahead. I have somewhere specific where I must go. Somebody's waiting to hear from me.

"Hey, Tommy. I don't know if you can hear me, but I'm still playing the Jake game, especially with Steffy. Just part of my plan. I think I already told you I killed him. He supposedly died on Saturday, January 18, 2020. I had my stroke on Wednesday, November 23, 2016, but played with the dates. I said it was 2020. Jake had been a fantasy in the confines of my mind. I know I've needed him to keep me from missing you, but no more. Sometimes I shuttered when just imaging him inside of me. I need you inside of me.

"I think it's time to put my plan into works. I must die! I hope you won't hate me for what I'm about to do."

"Rosie darlin', I could never hate you. I don't care what you do. I need to be inside of you no matter what it takes."

CHAPTER 5-8

"Steffy, we need to talk. Before we do, I want to ask that you take your clothes off except your undergarments. I also want you to empty your pocketbook. I know about the tape recorders." Steffy did what I asked. No tape recorders anywhere.

"When your father did terrible things, he always said the same words to me. 'I'm warning you! Nobody, especially our children, can ever know what I've done!' I never asked him what he would do if I betrayed him. I guess I really didn't want to know. Well, I've been doing something since Tommy passed away on Monday, January 18, 2016. Yes, I remember Tommy. I never forgot him. I know today is Wednesday, August 9, 2017 not 2021. Now, I'm issuing you a warning. You spent a lot of time alone with me listening to Jake stories. This has put up some flags. Steven seems to think you are buying into my stories. Your brother thinks you are possibly bordering on a bit of mental illness. Additionally, I have been helping it along by planting seeds in his head. I'm now going to tell you *everything*! Just between Mother and her only daughter.

"There are several different Jewish laws pertaining to a widow. One asks her to mourn for thirty days after the loss of her husband. One also says she is permitted to remarry on day thirty-one. Details of how it happened are not important. Tommy and I became spiritual the first time we made love. It was on June 2, 2012, day thirty-one. That was the day it was declared we were not going to be a couple. We had become *one.* Not even death could part us. Losing my husband Tommy so quickly devastated me at first. It was such a shock! I was able to compose myself for his funeral. You and Steven were with me as I spoke to Tommy in the casket. I know you heard what I told him. He heard me too. Try and remember my final words to him. *'In the meantime, I'll try to take my mind elsewhere and not dwell on missing you so much.'* With Tommy's help, that's exactly what I did. I created Jake."

"Mother, you really are insane! The family knows there was never a man named Jake. Your mind mixed up memories of Tommy with the fantasy of Jake. You spent months in a mental hospital! Your fantasy of Jake began in June 2016 after your release. You insisted you had been with him for three years and seven months. That was the amount of time you were with Tommy. You claimed to believe it was the year 2020. You told everyone you had a stroke, not a mental breakdown. On November 23, 2016, which was Tommy's birthday, you really did have a stroke. That was when you began the obsession of telling us stories of your life with Jake. Mother, what's going on? I'm not sure who you are or what's happened to your mind."

"Steffy, let me start from the beginning. I was willing to be in the hospital because Tommy was with me. He spoke to me the entire time. Please keep in mind that his degree was in English Literature. He knew stories going back hundreds of years. We played different parts of the stories. I even fooled Dr. Gillespie. As an R.N., I knew just how far to fake my behavior. I allowed myself to have therapy, but after Tommy's funeral, no medication. I needed to be awake and alert for my husband. After Tommy's birthday and my stroke, it was the one year anniversary of his passing. You believed I was mourning Jake, but it was Tommy. As I told you my stories, I could see the looks on your face. I made certain that you would recognize some things in regards to Tommy. The best part of my incredible fantasy was I could change things around. Who would know? Tommy's first wife was Cindy. There were no children. I gave Jake a wife named Cindy. They had two sons and two grandsons. I don't know where Tommy was, but he was hysterically laughing. Why? I named the grandsons Thomas and Patrick. I gave them an Irish Catholic mother even though Jake was Jewish.

"I did have a science fiction book that I read while in high school. That was when I came to believe in the spiritual world. You and Steven know that's why I believe one should pass hearing only sweet words. I don't remember if I told Tommy about the book. I think I did tell one of the stories from the book to Jake. I think the book was in my bedroom closet in the house in Montauk. It was in a metal box underneath some blankets. I guess I forgot about it after I moved into the house with Tommy.

"There were two other stores I remember from that book. Please keep in mind that it was possibly science fiction. One story told of a woman who was in ICU at the final stages of her life. She had cancer and was just being kept comfortable. She, her late husband, and their son believed in reincarnation. They were cat lovers. It was noticed that a cat continuously looked in their window. Finally, the son put it into a cat box and took it to the vet. It was a male. He was healthy and taken back to the house as their pet. The cat loved to sit on the woman almost every time she sat or reclined in her bed. They made jokes that he had to be a reincarnation of her husband, and his father. It was also believed that when the cat would pass away, he would again be a person. The son went to the hospital every day for weeks. His mother's condition went back and forth. One morning he asked to see the doctor. He told him his mother was going to pass away before the end of the day. It was because he found the cat dead on the floor that morning. The story of reincarnation was told to the doctor. The son told him the cat had to die first. Then his father would be ready to take his wife to the other side. The young man's mother passed away that night at 11:30 p.m.

"The other story was about the husband and wife who were spiritually connected. He passed away first. They couldn't touch each other, but they did speak to each other. There was only one way they could be together again physically. She had to die!

"In our world, a man or woman can go out and find another partner. In the spiritual world, a man or woman must wait for the spouse with whom they were *one*. I don't want another partner. I want to die and be with my husband Tommy. Steffy, I need you to kill me! It will be out of love and mercy.

"There are always rules. My daddy always believed in following rules. He said they were meant to be followed, not broken. Tommy is in a world called 'spirit', and there are rules. One of them is suicide is not acceptable. I must die by nature or at the hands of another. If I take my own life, we will not be joined. He's not sure where we will be. He just knows we will not be together. Another rule is he can't take me. As I spoke to him in the casket, I told him I would wait for him. It's the other way. I have to be sent to him by death. I was sick and did know I was stroking. That's why I went outside and sat down on the ground with no medical care. I was waiting to die and be with Tommy, especially on is birthday. If that meddling Gloria didn't take me inside, call Abby and 911, I would have died. I should have died on November 23, 2016, Tommy's birthday."

"Mother, you are insane! On the other hand, you are quite cunning, manipulating, and maneuvering. You really have fooled everyone. I hope you don't think I'm going to buy this bullshit and kill you. I'm your daughter. You always called me Princess Steffy. I too read a book about the spiritual world. It was about a young girl who passed away at the age of thirteen. She was able to appear as a quick twinkling star to members of her family. It happened at different times. I didn't believe it then and don't believe it now. Mother, I'll get caught and go to prison. Is that what you want for me?"

"Here is a set of papers. I want you to take them home and read thoroughly. Tommy and I had them written after we were married. It spells out wishes for when each of us would pass away. They were written by us. You will see they are legal documents. They were signed by us, two witnesses and notarized. Tommy and I bought a grave and monument in a nonsectarian cemetery in Montauk. He had the full Catholic funeral and Mass by his written request given to Helen. I just reminded her of the paper the day he passed away. He is buried in that grave. You will also see the cemetery is part of a US Corporation. There is one in Philly and one in Montauk. I don't want a viewing and funeral. They always make a woman look like a clown. Whether I pass in Philly or Montauk, I will be immediately taken and cremated. Nobody will ever examine my body. Both cities have an urn we chose for my ashes. Helen will arrange for Tommy's grave to be opened. The urn will be placed in with him. It will be a family decision as to whether or not to have any service.

"Tommy and I came from two different worlds. I grew up in a Jewish home with my parents and sister Abby. I had a great childhood. Abby and I sang, danced, and played girlie games. We had outside friends, but were always there for the other. There were family vacations like the ones in Montauk. Tommy was raised by a devout Catholic mom and sister. Helen once told me he was actually a bit of an introvert. Tommy spent a lot of time in the apartment where he lived with only his mom. Reading and writing was how he spent his time outside of school. He had very little interest in sports, and never had a boy's childhood. Socializing and dating weren't something he did until after he started working. He was a virgin until he was 22 years old. Tommy himself told the stories of how he loved to fuck. He did it almost constantly before and after Cindy. Then

I came along. Our worlds, bodies, minds, souls and spirits merged into *one*.

"I gave Tommy a childhood. We did the craziest things together. Many of them were girlie, but he didn't care. The house had a long, black asphalt driveway. He brought some colored chalk from school. I had him draw a hopscotch. We used keychains and I taught him how to play. My knee was bad and hopping wasn't too easy for me. One day I fell. Tommy lifted me, and we both fell on the ground. We were wearing shorts. Tommy scraped his knee. I had to wash it and put a Band-Aid on it. Of course, I had to kiss his boo-boo. Then I kept on kissing and moving up.

"Another thing we did was chew big globs of pink bubble gum. We would put our mouths together and pass the gum back and forth. It went from my mouth to his then the other way around. Once I convinced him to play Ring Around the Rosie with me like I did with Abby. He agreed. But it had to be inside the house. It couldn't be outside like the hopscotch.

"Tommy had a cock like a flag pole when he was erect. It stood straight out and was so hard. When he went inside me, his movements were like a jack hammer. We sometimes called him Rosey's Riveter. He loved sex but always private. It would always be somewhere in the house or in our hot tub. I was the daring one. He refused me nothing. One night I talked him into getting naked on the bottom and fucking me in the car. He was scared, but he did it.

"Tommy had a passion for poetry and me. We both loved sitting together in the recliner. His body was so broad and muscular. I'm so thin and almost bony. Helen said I needed some meat and potatoes on my bones. Tommy said he was the meat and potatoes on my bones. We would sit together with pots of tea and he would read to me. Out of everything we did together, I think that was the most special. It wasn't hot sex. It was warm love!

"You must understand what life was for us together and what it's like for us apart. He is in limbo and lonely. I have very little vision in my right eye. My right hand is so weak that I need a special holder for my cards. I need help to shower and dress every morning, can only warm up food cooked for me by Helen and Abby, and can't hold a sandwich. Someone has to cut it up for me to eat with a fork. I can't drive, need a hospital bed to move me around, and need a walker to go from room to room. *Dignity!* That's the right word! I no longer have dignity. I was an ICU/Trauma nurse. Now I need care from an ICU/Trauma nurse. You, Steffy.

"We once took a course in suicide. We told people not to take their own life. One day things can get better, and they will miss out. For me, it will never get better. As I age, my muscles will atrophy and my bones will become brittle. I will become an invalid! I will just be 'poor Mother, poor Rainey, and poor Baba'."

"You really thought of everything. Well almost. How am I supposed to carry out this act of mercy?"

"I want you to digest everything. You will not be taking my life. You will be doing a blessing. You will be giving me life with my husband Tommy. Take a week to think about everything. Join me back here next week on Wednesday, August 16th. Bring lunch and gourmet coffee. A salad for me would be good. I will then give you the plan. You are my beautiful Princess Steffy. I would not ask you to do this if it meant getting caught and going to prison. Trust Mother!"

"How can there be trust? You are not thinking clearly or rationally. Let's say I believe you and Tommy talk to each other. I know how much you both loved each other. I'm beginning to think you are possibly suicidal, but just can't do it yourself.

"What if there is no spirit world? What if Tommy is not somewhere waiting for you? What if your ashes are going to be put into the grave with Tommy and that's it. He's dead and you are dead. There is no after life. Do you want to do this to the family? Losing Tommy has been too much for everyone. Then you?"

"Steffy, we all suffer with the passing of loved ones, but we adjust. We go on. So the family will do the same with my loss. I love all of you, but I'd rather be just plain dead than live my life as it is now. Tommy does talk to me! It's not my imagination, and I am not insane! I need to be with my husband. You are the only one who can make it happen."

"*Tommy. As you can possibly hear, I am desperate. I had to get rid of Jake, and now I want to leave my family in pain. I'm not a whole person or woman anymore. Sometimes I really can't breathe without you. Can you understand that my love for you is greater than life for me or anybody else? Why did Fate, Destiny, and Lady Karma feel the time was right when they took you from me?*

"*Steffy won't get caught or go to prison. My memory isn't so great, but I do remember the cremation papers. Keep on singing and hopefully she will hear you.*

Tommy and Rosey sitting on a swing KISSING.
Tommy and Rosey laying in a bed FUCKING.
Steffy Silver have a heart, please don't keep us apart."

CHAPTER 5-9

"Steffy, I hope you remembered to keep our last meeting a secret. If word got out, one of us might end up in a padded cell. Chances are it won't be me. Again, I need you to take your clothes off except your undergarments. I also want you to empty your pocketbook.

"I need to be sent to Tommy no later than Monday, August 21st. Tommy said after I pass, it will take three to five days before I will reach him. This will give us just enough time to find each other. We need to be together before Wednesday, August 30th, our fifth wedding anniversary. Also, we want to celebrate my 75th birthday together on Thursday, August 31st. Of course now, the year of 2017!

"I play canasta every Monday morning at 10:00. We can find a reason to have dinner with the family that Sunday. Early Monday morning you and I will have breakfast alone together in this house. We will hug, kiss, and say our last goodbyes. I won't call the TS. You may drive me to the center. Throughout the game, I will complain of a headache getting unbearably worse. I will call the TS to take me home. The ladies will only know that I'm going home to take medication and go to sleep. On my way home, I will send you a text saying I'm going home and in pain. You will then send me a text telling me you will come to the house ASAP. Of course, Gloria is always at the window. I will excuse myself to go to bed."

"Mother, I can't believe you really have a total A to Z plan. I feel like I'm sitting with a scriptwriter for a movie. I can hardly wait to hear the whacky way you have planned for me to kill you. I think I shall write a movie or a book."

"You know I do get bad headaches. I hate to take pain pills. I always take Xanax. It puts me into a deep sleep. I will make sure I'm looking pretty. I'll be dressed nicely. I'll do my own makeup in the morning. Nobody will be able to make me look like a clown. I'll take some Xanax and go into a deep sleep. Now, enters Steffy. You will have the instrument of mercy to send Mother to her husband Tommy. We are nurses. You know what happens if a needle with air is injected into the carotid. A quick massive stroke! It will be my final one. Nobody will be suspicious. All you have to do is see me take my final breath, call Steven, and call the paramedics. Of course, you must hide the needle in the very bottom of your pocketbook. I have faith in you. I believe you can and will do this, and be crying when the family arrives. They will all want to see me looking so pretty before the crematory staff comes for me. Now do you have it clear as to how I want to die? As your Mother I denied you nothing. Do you recall I never asked anything from you except your love and respect? Now I need you to do this one thing for me. I always chose to live with dignity. The stroke took it away from me. Now I choose to die with dignity and go be with my beloved Tommy."

"Only an insane woman could come up with such a plan. I can't believe my ears. I think you're playing me! You toyed with the entire family and fooled Dr. Gillespie with your Jake games. What is the reason for this?"

"You know the reason. How much more do I have to say? Keep in mind that you can never tell anyone. If you kill me you won't go to prison. If you betray me, you don't want to know what will happen to you, not me. I love you, but this mercy killing must be done."

It's now Monday, August 21ˢᵗ. I had breakfast with Mother. She looked so pretty. Not like a clown. I had the needle in my pocketbook. We said our final goodbyes. She went to play cards and I went home. Just as planned, she sent me a text and I sent one to her. She took the Xanax. I waited two hours and went to the house. Gloria was at the window. I waved and walked away quickly. Mother was in bed, still looking pretty. I took out the needle and put it into Mother's artery. She gasped once, and it was over. I put the needle into the very bottom of my pocketbook under tons of tissues. I called Steven and the paramedics. Steven arrived first and declared that Mother had passed. No doubt from a massive stroke. Her medical history and headache made it a positive cause of natural death.

The entire family arrived to see her. Everyone was sobbing. Mother would not like to have heard that. Nobody was there to whisper sweet things to her. I certainly didn't. I killed her! It was almost like the day of Tommy's funeral. Everybody drove from Montauk back to Philly. Mother went into the bedroom, and the family was in the kitchen. This time, Mother was already in the bedroom. The paramedics came and left after speaking to Steven.

As we sat, the funeral home gentlemen arrived to take Mother. "Steven, they can't take her. The papers said she was to be taken for immediate cremation."

"Steffy, those papers were modified after the first set. Everything for Tommy remained the same. Mother decided she would have a traditional Jewish funeral service and a viewing. She would then be taken for cremation. Abby, Helen, and I have the new set of papers."

I was shaking so badly. Everyone assumed it was a reaction to losing Mother. I was also the one who found her. It was decided that Steven, Hannah, and Sam would go later in the day to make the funeral arrangements.

Everyone left by late afternoon. Steffy and I were the only two left in the house. The door bell rang. I opened the door and saw an unmarked black car. At the door were two men dressed in black suits, white shirts, and black ties. I assumed they were from the funeral home. One handed me a card. I asked them to come into the house. The card said he was a detective. His name was James Fontana. His partner introduced himself as Detective Martin Bailey. They invited us to come to the police station with them.

We were each taken to different rooms. Steffy with Fontana and me with Bailey. Separately, we were told that when Mother's body was examined at the funeral home; there was a question. Why was there a fresh puncture mark at her carotid artery? Her body was immediately taken to the medical examiner. It was determined that Mother's death was a homicide.

The guilt and horror was excruciating. They suspected me and Steven. He has a family and is innocent. I had to confess. I told Steven and the detectives all the stories Mother told me. She was very convincing. That last week, I was hearing Tommy's voice. It was low, deep, raspy with a slight Irish brogue. I told them Mother's stories made me believe I would be sending her to Tommy.

"Steffy, she was insane, tormented, and demented! Do you remember the supposed letter Jake wrote to her and his sons? She couldn't create it with her right hand. She was clumsy with her left. After seeing the letter, I checked her computer. She found just the right font size and style of font. She apparently typed it with her left hand and was able to turn on the printer. If you paid attention, you would have read something about a burial cover. Tommy had one on him in the casket. In the letter, he also referred to Mother as Rosey darlin'. Didn't you ever notice her behavior when she moved into a corner of a room? She would smile and softly giggle. Sometimes her lips were moving. I think she was having a conversation with Tommy or Jake. Who the fuck knew which one?

"Dr. Gillespie told us she was not a textbook psychiatric case. How could you have believed what she told you? How could you have killed Mother believing you sent her to Tommy? He is dead, in a casket in the grave in Montauk. She will be cremated and her ashes will be placed in the urn she chose. That will be placed in the grave with Tommy.

"Steffy, they will be together but not in a spiritual world! There is no such place! They are now both dead. After we take her ashes to Montauk, they will only be together in the same hole in the ground!"

I didn't need bail money. She would not be released. I called an attorney to get her through the arraignment. I stayed with her while she was being processed. She had to take off all of her jewelry and they gave it to me. She was photographed, fingerprinted, and taken away. The last thing I heard was her singing a song. She said Tommy sang the first two lines to her. Then he added a third. It was his voice that convinced her to let him have Mother.

Tommy and Rosey sitting on a swing KISSING.
Tommy and Rosey laying in a bed FUCKING.
Steffy Silver have a heart, please don't keep us apart.
"Steven, I did the right thing. Their spirits just appeared to me as sparkling red hearts. They were thanking me for not keeping them apart."

The family went to Montauk to place Mother's urn into the grave with Tommy. Helen had the monument inscribed.

THOMAS PATRICK MONAHAN
LORRAINE ROSE MONAHAN

(TOMMY)	(ROSEY)
1947 – 2016	1942 – 2017

TOGETHER ALWAYS AS ONE

Helen got permission to plant a red rose garden around the monument.

CHAPTER 5-10

Almost all family decisions were made together. It may seem strange, but that's who we were. The family was once ten. We are now seven. My wife, son, and I made major decisions on our own. It was now time to give the family the details. We invited everyone to our house for a Sunday dinner. It would be the last one.

After dinner, I began telling the changes we had made. None of it was open for discussion. It was all a done deal.

"The name Silver seems to have carried a curse. Ian didn't have a funeral because he was a monster. Mother didn't have a funeral because of how she passed. The newspapers and TV stations were full of the name Silver. They called Steffy one who committed matricide. One who murdered her own mother! First, we decided to get rid of our last name. We went to a law firm who made all of the changes. All paperwork, going back to school, has been changed. We are now legally Steven Goldberg, Samuel Goldberg and Hannah Joy Goldberg. The middle name of Sterling is gone. Sam and I insisted that Hannah keep her middle name. She certainly is a Joy!

"We have been traveling back and forth to Las Vegas for the last three months. There is a new casino hotel just opening. Sam is going to be business associate. He is considered to be an executive, so he will be given an efficiency apartment within the hotel.

"I am going to be the day shift house physician. Hannah has gotten an office job for a real estate company. This house and my medical practice have already been sold. The buyer of the house will be keeping all of the furniture. We have discovered that it's cheaper to buy all new furniture. What we have would cost a fortune to hire a mover to take it across country.

"Hannah and I had enough money, and have already bought a house. It's located in Henderson, suburban Las Vegas. It's a three-bedroom, two-bathroom ranch house. One bedroom is for us and the other two are for family. I am referring to Abby and Scott, and Helen and Leon. We have already furnished the entire house. A small truck drove our personal things to the house last week. You must have noticed the house looks different. We are flying to Vegas tomorrow.

I have given each of you a large envelope. There are front view pictures of the casino hotel where Sam and I will be working. There are also pictures of the new house. Tommy had the most beautiful flower garden outside the house in Montauk. I asked him to name each flower for me. I wrote it down planning to make a garden at the house here. I never did. There is now a duplicate of Tommy's garden at my new house. Additionally, Sam has put up two white trellises on the sides of the house. Red rose gardens have been planted. One has red paint on it saying Rosey, and the other one says Tommy. There has been so much trauma and pain for this family. Hannah, Sam, and I feel we have created the beauty of Tommy and Mother around our new house. I'm sorry to break down crying like this!

"Additionally, you will find round trip plan tickets to Vegas. Please use them as soon as you can come for a short or long visit. We also hope you will spend a few months a year with us during the winter. I think you will love being there. The food buffets and prices are incredible. Hey, Leon and Scott. Every night there are shows with topless, bikini-clad dancers."

Mother passed away on Monday, August 21, 2017. Mother and Tommy's 5th wedding anniversary would have been on the 30th. Mother's 75th birthday is on the 31st. In the insanity of

Mother and my sister Steffy, was there a reason for the date mother needed to pass? Am I now insane wondering if they were together on those two days?

Hannah and I moved into our new home in Henderson on Monday, December 4th. Our two aunts and uncles came to Vegas on Tuesday, December 19th. It was decided that they would stay through until the end of March. They came only partially prepared with clothing and personal items. Big time shopping was on their agenda. We had a very quiet holiday season together. They promised to do a lot of thinking when they got back to Philly. There's a chance they might also move to Vegas. The only family we have is each other. Nobody will ever know the loss and pain we have shared.

It is now April 2018 and all is well with our jobs. As a family, we have had three great losses of our loved ones. Each of us mourns in our own way, in our own time.

Sam and I received a memo from top management of the casino hotel where we were working. It was a request to attend the first major corporate meeting since the opening. Sam is considered to be at the executive level. While I'm not, I have been included due to my professional position. It was scheduled to be a very early breakfast meeting from 7:30 to 9:00 a.m., before official business hours for the team.

The meeting began with introductions. The Chief Executive Officer, Anthony Lewis, welcomed everyone. Then business was conducted. Reports were given from all top level executives, mostly on finances. Each of us was then asked if we had any comments or suggestions. There were a few. Before ending, Harry Bartlett, the 3:00 to 11:00 p.m. desk clerk asked to speak.

"About three weeks after we opened, a very strange couple came to the desk. They were approximately in their late seventies. Their clothing was almost identical. Both were wearing white sneakers, white Bermuda shorts, and white polo shirts. The only difference was that her shirt had a ruffled sleeve.

I assumed they were married. They were both wearing the same gold wedding band. The only other jewelry was shiny studs in her ears. They looked like diamonds. She spoke first and asked for a deluxe room for the night. Additionally, she wanted to see the room service menu for dinner. He then spoke and told me he likes to eat his dinner at about 4:00. I asked for identification and how they were going to pay. She spoke again. I was told they have no identification or credit cards, just cash.

"He then said, 'As you can see we are senior citizens. We both receive social security checks. They are deposited into one of the main bank branches here on the strip. Once a month, we take out cash. We live in a very small apartment. Occasionally we treat ourselves to a night in a hotel. We have been to all of the others. This is our first time here because you have just opened.'

"She was carrying a small flowered satchel. I asked if I could see what she had in there. I reached across the desk and took it from her. She smelled like roses. I opened it and there were only two sets of underwear. Certainly, nothing threatening! He opened a wallet and asked me to calculate the exact amount for the room, dinner, and all appropriate tips. They just went back and forth. While he pulled out a wad of cash, she ordered the dinner. Of course, I asked their names. They would have to sign the register.

"They did stay the night, had dinner, and left early the next morning. The room was left quite orderly. They have been back twice since then. Once a month!"

Mr. Lewis asked for a physical description. "She is about 5'8", extremely thin, a beautiful fresh looking face, long brown hair in a pony tail, and is very well spoken. Perhaps she was once in a professional line of work. He is about six feet, broad and muscular, has salt and pepper wiry hair, a mustache, giant blue eyes, and dark ruddy skin. His voice was deep and raspy, and I detect a slight Irish brogue."

My dad and I looked at each other in amazement. I should say in total shock. Mr. Lewis noticed we were possibly turning colors. He asked if we knew this couple. Dad said the only family we have is two aunts and uncles. They don't look anything like the description just given. Dad also added that they live in his house.

Mr. Bartlett closed in saying he signs the registry as simply "Mr. & Mrs. M".

We all began leaving the room. Everybody went in a different direction. I walked with dad. We looked at each other and said ,"Uh huh"!

"Hey, Dad, did you just see that? Two sparkling red hearts. Do you remember something Baba always said? You should never believe anything or anyone from what you see and hear."

IT MAY ALL BE A MISCONCEPTION OR AN ILLUSION.